THE
DAUGHTER
SHE USED
TO BE

Books by Rosalind Noonan

ONE SEPTEMBER MORNING

IN A HEARTBEAT

THE DAUGHTER SHE USED TO BE

Published by Kensington Publishing Corporation

THE
DAUGHTER
SHE USED
TO BE

ROSALIND NOONAN

KENSINGTON BOOKS
www.kensingtonbooks.com

KENSINGTON BOOKS are published by

Kensington Publishing Corp.
119 West 40th Street
New York, NY 10018

All Kensington titles, imprints, and distributed lines are available at special quantity discounts for bulk purchases for sales promotion, premiums, fund-raising, educational, or institutional use.

Special book excerpts or customized printings can also be created to fit specific needs. For details, write or phone the office of the Kensington Special Sales Manager: Kensington Publishing Corp., 119 West 40th Street, New York, NY 10018. Attn. Special Sales Department. Phone: 1-800-221-2647.

Kensington and the K logo Reg. U.S. Pat. & TM Off.

ISBN-13: 978-0-7582-4168-9
ISBN-10: 0-7582-4168-2

First Kensington Trade Paperback Printing: November 2011
10 9 8 7 6 5 4 3 2 1

Printed in the United States of America

For Sergeant Seidel—
Still the Finest

PART I

Chapter 1

On a gray Sunday in the end of February Bernie Sullivan leaned into the steam of a large pot in her parents' kitchen and jabbed at a field of potatoes with the masher. Once upon a time Bernie had loved mashed potatoes. The earthy smell, the smooth texture, the heavy burden of butter that was mandatory in the Sullivan household. But love was lost as, over the years, mashing the spuds had become her job; back in the day when her mother had five kids to feed, everyone in the family had become responsible for contributing a dish to dinner. Well, every female. The role of the males was to eat so they'd have the strength to get out and make New York City a safer place.

Tonight Bernie's side dish was behind schedule. The roast was carved and sitting in its own juice on the platter. Buttered carrots and string beans sat under plates to keep them warm, and now the rolls were done, too.

"You shoulda started mashing earlier," her mother said. Peg didn't look up as she moved rolls from the baking tray to a bowl lined with a napkin. "Didn't you hear me calling you?"

"I know, Ma." Bernie had been engrossed in her brother's story of how he'd come upon two children who had suffered abuse. Told over chips and dip, while the little ones were playing in the back room and the respectable women were in the kitchen preparing the meal, the story was unusual because it had transpired over a few weeks, and patrol cops like Brendan rarely dealt with situations that lasted longer than their eight-hour tour.

"I met them back in November," Brendan had said. "I remember telling Sarah about it. Two little girls alone in an apartment in the projects by the seven train. Both of them had those enormous waif eyes." He made two circles with his fingers and peered through them. "They looked up at me like I was God or something. The older one, she must have been schooled by someone because she trusted me and she was very polite. Called me officer. 'You got to help us, officer.'" Brendan stared down at his can of beer as if he could read the future there. "That's the kind of thing that breaks your heart."

Staring into the pot as she mashed, Bernie could see the two little girls peering up at Brendan in his dark blue uniform, twenty pounds of gun and flashlight and equipment hanging from his belt. The Superman Suit, Dad used to call it. It was a wonder the little girls weren't intimidated. God bless them.

"The job came in as a noise complaint, and we found these two kids alone. We called family services, but while we were waiting for the social worker the older girl started opening up to us. Destiny, that's her name. Nine years old and she starts dropping her pants. I started to leave, but Indigo takes a look and she sees burn marks on the girl's butt. Turns out the father burned her. Scars, too. She said she'd been putting up with it, but that night was the first time he went after the younger sister. That's when Destiny put up a fight, and the screaming got one of the neighbors to call nine-one-one."

"Oh, man." Bernie pressed a hand to her chest, indignant on the little girls' behalf. The dead air in the rest of the room wasn't unusual; cops did not shock easily.

On the other side of the chip bowl, her father and oldest brother, James, barely seemed fazed. They'd both been street cops for years, seen it all. James was now a sergeant at the Police Academy, and Sully had retired six years ago.

"Said she could have put up with the father hitting her, but was worried he'd kill her little sister. Destiny is already deaf in one ear, they think from the old man beating on her. A nine-year-old."

"That's a crying shame." James shook his head. "A lot of sick bastards out there."

"And the mother's into the wind?" Sully asked.

"They say she's an addict. The girls haven't seen her for more than two years." Brendan explained that he and his partner, Indigo, had testified in a hearing that week at Family Court on Jamaica Avenue. "And we won, but it's frustrating. Makes you wonder."

"You did good, son," Sully said with a heavy nod.

"Yeah, but it's a bittersweet victory, Dad. The judge removed the kids from their father's custody, but it's no picnic. What are they going to get in foster care? A bed and a couple of meals at somebody else's house. I'm not sure we're doing these kids any favors."

Sully nodded, a glimmer of regret in the blue eyes Bernie always wished she had inherited. "That's a tough one."

"Still . . . it's better than what they had." James rose from the easy chair and craned his neck to the side, trying to address the chronic back pain that always made him seem distant to Bernie.

"It is better," Bernie agreed, catching Brendan's eye. "You may have saved their lives, Bren."

He shook his head. "It's a sad alternative. Sad-ass, sorry foster care."

"Dinner!" Peg called through the house. "Let's go."

"You can't let it get to you, son." Sully stood up. His six-foot-plus frame was softer now, as if the muscles and taut strength had been passed on to his sons, along with the hair. Her father's gray hair grew mostly around the sides now, and he kept it clipped so short that his bald head now shone on the top. "It'll eat you away if you let it."

"Everything's done but the potatoes." Peg's voice prickled with irritation. "Bernadette..."

Bernie had snapped to attention at the firm tone. Twenty-seven years old, and her mother's voice still had that power over her.

"Are you mashing these potatoes, or are we having them boiled?"

"Coming..."

Chapter 2

On a bus rocketing through the night, Peyton Curtis sank into the darkness that had closed in hours ago. He was really lost now.

Going nowhere. That was what his prison counselor had said. Jeff, the new Angel. "You need a plan for when you get out of prison, Peyton. A place to live. A job. That's the only way you'll stay off drugs and out of trouble."

But Peyton never did any drugs. Didn't drink, either. And that just proved to him that Jeff didn't even look at that fat file they had on Peyton. Jeff was in it for a paycheck. Jeff didn't give a rat's ass about Peyton or any of the other inmates he logged time with.

Jeff had just laughed when Peyton said he didn't want to leave Lakeview Shock, that he wanted to stay and keep working in the library there. Steady meals and a warm, dry place to sleep and nobody beating up on him. Five years of Lakeview Shock, and he knew how to do it now. No reason to give that up for the darkness ahead.

"You're getting your freedom back, man." Jeff had puffed up real big, the way Curtis saw the rats grow bigger when their body hair stood on end. Trying to look big and bad, laughing at him. Peyton was used to that. The snickers and laughs. It didn't bother him. "You'll be on parole, but you're free to get a job," Jeff said. "See your family. Hang with your friends—as long as they're not using."

Jeff had one of those patches of hair on his chin, shaped like a triangle. Made him look like the devil.

Or maybe he thought of that because Jeff was the opposite of Angel. If she was still his counselor, she would have listened. Angel would have helped him stay.

But the devil man, he wanted Peyton gone. One less prisoner to talk to, write all his doctor's notes about. One less case to handle. And not long after Jeff took over, Lakeview, the home Curtis had come to know over the best five years of his life, turned cold on him. They gave him a suit of clothes, told him to get a job and see his parole officer once a week.

And now he was on that bus, trying to ignore his stomach growling over the smell of pizza some woman got at a rest stop and the other inmate, a rangy white man in the back of the bus, who kept mouthing off about how canned peaches were the secret to his good health.

Strange people in a stranger world. Peyton gripped the handle of his walking stick, letting his thumb stroke the dark grooves cut into the carving. "Faux scrimshaw," Angel had called it. Scrimshaw was the carvings sailors made in whale bones and teeth, but faux meant it wasn't real. Probably just plastic, but that was even better. What was the sense of killing a whale to get a walking stick? Peyton was fine with faux.

The animal carved on the handle had the face of a mouse, the elongated body of a rat, and the back end of a horse. "The man at the thrift shop said it was a running horse," Angel had told him, but they'd spent a few minutes talking about how the sculptor had screwed up. In his own head, Peyton decided it was a deformed rat, and it gave him comfort to stroke the worn surface.

He kept his face turned toward the window so people didn't see him twitching, but with the lights on inside, the dark glass was like a mirror. Mirrors everywhere on this bus showing a whole lot of ugly nobody wanted to see.

What was the sense of it when they lock you up for five years and you doing time and when they finally let you out you get dumped in the armpit of New York City in the middle of the night. What was the sense in that?

No parole officer going to see you at night, and your family, if they goin' to let you in, don't want you to come knocking at two in the morning. What was the sense in that?

But Lakeview Shock Incarceration Correctional Facility didn't care where you going and what time you got there. Just as long as you got on the bus and got the hell out of their facility, they happy.

At least the bus had headlights. He could see out there when he stood up, lights burning air, turning part of the highway to day. Good thing the driver had lights to see by, 'cause Peyton himself couldn't see ahead. He pulled the lid on his numb eye shut, hunched toward the window on his right, and gnawed on his worries, like a rat working a dry bone. How was he going to see the parole man when he was getting to the city at two or three in the morning? And where would he go? His mama wouldn't be quick to unlock her door in the middle of the night, even for her own son.

He could see his mother, peering through the crack of the triple-chained door. "What kind of person comes knocking at a door at three in the morning when he ain't been around for more than five years? Go on back to prison, Peyton. Get on out of here, before you wake up half the neighborhood."

But Mama, it's me. It's your son, Peyton, he would call out.

And the door would slam in his face.

And then he'd be stuck out in Queens. He'd be a black man moving through Asian Invasion Flushing, a place where black men weren't so invisible as they were in other parts of the city.

He rocked in his seat, thinking about the skells that'd be messing with him in the city this time of night. They'd be pulling into the Port Authority any minute, and some smelly lump would scurry up to him, try to steal his walking stick, or beg some change. He would have to get out of there. Get to someplace warm. Maybe the subway, if he could hop a turnstile.

"What you want to go and do that for?" Darnell would say. "You just a few hours out of prison and you gonna throw the dice on something that easy? You're just as stupid as I remember."

He could see the flame of hatred in his brother's eyes, the flare of his nostrils. Darnell was always spitting mad about something.

Peyton had once seen a male rat come along to a pack of newborn rats. Pups. And damned if that full-grown rat didn't kill the weakest baby, drag it off, and eat it. Wasn't even his baby to kill, but he took it.

That rat was Darnell.

I just might bust through the subway gate, Peyton thought. *And bust up Darnell's face.*

Chapter 3

As she spooned the creamy potatoes into a deep casserole dish, Bernie wondered what would become of the two little girls Brendan and his partner had come upon . . . Destiny and her little sister. In cases like that, other family members were usually called on to take the children in, but Brendan had mentioned foster care.

Bernie appreciated her brother's desire to help them. She and Brendan were the soft hearts of the family. Brendan was a helper, and she had the curse of seeing injustice all around her and feeling personally obliged to right it.

In second grade she reported the teacher for picking on Juan Arechiga every blessed day until he cried. At Cardoza High School she founded the Multicultural Club to encourage tolerance and celebrate diversity. She once got in the grill of an irate vendor at a subway newspaper kiosk when the guy yelled at two veiled women that he didn't do business with "Ay-rabs." When she graduated from law school nearly three years ago, Bernie joined the Manhattan District Attorney's office to do her part in maintaining justice. Bernie wanted to "get the bad guys," just as her father and brothers had done for decades. She'd once toyed with the notion of joining the NYPD herself, but in her heart she knew that would have been a bad move. Bernie lacked muscle, and she knew she was a wimp. Some nights she was afraid to peek behind the closed shower curtain before bed.

But wimp or not, she couldn't resist a good cop story, and on Sunday nights in the Sullivan house, the air was thick with it.

Heavy dish in hand, she tromped into the dining room, the space hot and noisy and crowded with extra chairs squeezed in to accommodate eleven people. Well, ten plus the empty spot for Mary Kate's husband, Tony, who showed up late when he bothered to show up at all. Food was being dished out, but no one would dare begin eating before grace was said.

"Potatoes!" Brendan growled heartily. "Send them down my way." He tucked the bowl in the crook of his elbow, pretending they were all for him, which made his daughters, Grace and Maisey, giggle.

"Share, Daddy," Grace said, wise for her nine years.

As Bernie headed to the empty seat at the back of the dining room, she caught her own image in the china cabinet mirror. The tawny hair that she tied back for work was wild from the humidity in the kitchen, the ends curled, the top frizzy. The reflection was cloudy, but there was no missing her smaller version of the Sullivan pug nose and her mucky brown eyes. Her eyeglasses were smart, but glasses nonetheless. They masked the big, soulful eyes that made her look like a teenaged runaway. "Jailbait" her friend Keesh called her back in law school.

She took a seat next to her father, who always sat at the head of the table in the patriarch's seat. The opposite end was up for grabs, as Mom always sat near the kitchen so she could hop up and heat the gravy, get more bread, or spoon out more potatoes from the pot.

Across from Bernie, James Jr. passed the roast to his wife, Deb. Now that their two kids were older—Keaton studying at Cornell, Kelly a forensics expert in San Francisco—the two of them never missed a Sunday dinner in Bayside. James and Deb were empty-nesters, while Bernie didn't even have a nest of her own yet. She'd even noticed a little gray in the front of James's hair, but Deb didn't seem to mind. Late forties and they still seemed to like each other. That was sweet.

"Who wants to say grace?" Sully asked. He smiled with pride, lording over the family table. "Grace?" He nodded at his nine-year-old granddaughter.

"Grace will say grace. That has a nice ring to it." Brendan grinned at his daughter, who giggled as if she hadn't heard the joke a million times.

The smiles and laughter gave way to bowed heads as Grace began. "Bless us, O Lord, and these thy gifts . . ."

After a chorus of amens, conversation tapered off as everyone dug in. Sully asked how Keaton and Kelly were doing, and Deb responded with anecdotes about the price of a college education and the dearth of affordable housing in San Francisco. Peg inquired about Mary Kate's middle boy, Conner, who dropped out of SUNY Buffalo and was back at home, attending community college.

"Why doesn't he come to Sunday dinner?" Peg's cajoling didn't cover her disappointment. "Did he forget where we live?"

"He's got friends, Ma." Mary Kate chewed rapidly, reminding Bernie of a rabbit. "There's school papers and he works at the cinema now. Conner has a lot of things to do."

"We've all got friends and plenty of things to do." Peg put a dollop of potatoes into her mouth, then paused. "Mmm. There's lumps in the potatoes. Did you heat the milk?"

"Some people like a little texture," Bernie said. Was it too much to hope that her mother would take the task away from her because she'd failed?

"That's why you heat the milk," Peg said. "It smooths things out. I like creamy potatoes. And I'd like to see my grandson, too."

"I'll tell him you guys missed him." Mary Kate leaned onto the empty chair beside her, as if she could extract herself from family scrutiny. "You know how college kids are. They eat dinner at midnight instead of two in the afternoon."

"Dinner at midnight!" Maisey rolled her eyes, holding her fork of impaled carrots upright like a flag. "That's crazy."

"It sure is." Peg grinned with satisfaction as she cut a piece of beef.

"Eat your carrots," Sarah said. "You've got a busy week ahead. The school show on Tuesday, and then your birthday Friday."

"That's right," Peg said. "I've got the show on my calendar. You're coming here for dessert afterward."

"We are?" Grace's eyes went wide. "Thank you, Nana."

"You're welcome." Peg nodded approvingly at Brendan and Sarah. "Such good girls."

"And you're all invited." Sarah grinned as her blue eyes scanned the faces at the table. "The show starts at six-thirty. 'Songs of Winter.' I know you can't resist."

"I have to work," James said, "but I'm sorry to miss it."

Bernie smiled at Grace, who seemed to soak up the conversation like a sponge. "I'll be there," Bernie said. "I love to see you guys perform."

Maisey looked around the table. "Is the 'nother aunt going to come to the show?"

Everyone looked at Mary Kate, who blinked. "Oh, I could probably make the end."

"Not you; the 'nother aunt."

Sarah's mouth opened in a wide O. "Lucy?"

Maisey nodded.

"Aunt Lucy lives in Delaware," Sarah explained. "And that's a long way to drive in the middle of the week, with traffic and everything."

A lame excuse, but no one seemed to hold the true explanation for Lucy's departure from the family. She had pursued a scholarly profession, converted to Judaism, married a doctor, and emerged from her Queens cocoon "a very cultured lady," as Ma would say. None of those things alone were a problem, but they all added up to detachment.

Lucy had left, and she didn't seem to care if she ever saw her family again.

"I'm surprised you remember her, pumpkin. When was the last time she visited?"

"She came for my First Communion last year," Grace said.

"That's right; she did." Brendan rubbed his jaw. "Now if you're done, you can take your plates into the kitchen and help Nana clean up."

As if on cue, Sarah and Deb rose and began to clear away dishes.

"Excellent meal, Peg." Dad lifted his squat juice glass of red wine in salute. "Roast was good as ever. Nice and tender."

"Yeah, well, I hope you saved room for dessert. Sarah baked those mini cherry tarts, and Bernie brought cookies from Marietta."

Since Bernie refused to bake, she chiseled away at her guilt by contributing sweets from the local businesses her parents had frequented for the last forty years, most of them merchants on nearby Bell Boulevard.

"Can I have a cookie?" Maisey asked.

"Go have a cookie," Peg said, shooing the girl toward the kitchen, "but we don't set dessert out until after the dishes are done."

Eyes on her plate, Bernie lingered, poking her fork at the round disks of carrots on her plate so that she could stay at the table with the men and engage in more of the conversation she loved.

Cop stories.

The good stories, uncensored and full of color, didn't come out until after the women and children left the table. Bernie was raised on war stories, just as the Horak twins next door were raised on frozen dinners with little compartments to separate peas and mashed potatoes—the envy of Bernie and her sibs back in the day.

With three bottles of salad dressing in one hand, Ma reached for the beef platter with the other.

"I was going to leave that for Tony." Mary Kate nodded to the empty chair where the unused china and silverware still sparkled. "He should be here any minute."

Nothing registered on the faces of the men at the table; from their bland expressions one would never know that this scene was replayed nearly every Sunday evening.

"We'll make him a plate in the kitchen." Ma's grip on the platter was strong, unrelenting, and Bernie felt grateful for her mother's backbone. Thank God Peggy Sullivan was not one to sit around and let good food spoil or delusions grow.

"He can't help it if he's got to work miserable midnights," Mary Kate muttered as a fork thunked to the wood floor.

"We all know how that is, darlin'." Sully's blue eyes sparkled for his oldest daughter.

Mary Kate's face was expressionless as she hugged her load of plates and escaped to the kitchen.

Sully sat back in his chair at the head of the table and linked his hands in the prayer position on the edge of the gold table-cloth. Just like Father Tillman in the confessional booth, Bernie thought. "I used to hate midnights."

Brendan and Jimmy agreed. Although Bernie was tempted to point out that she was stuck working night shifts right now, and yet she managed to get here for dinner, she restrained herself. She didn't want to be the one who pushed Mary Kate over the edge.

Bernie used to feel sorry for her frazzled sister, who was clearly in denial over whatever was or was not going on in her marriage. She had trusted her sister to figure things out. But now that she dealt with Tony Marino professionally—he was always trying to shove some arrest down the DA's throat—she had lost patience. Why her sister kept covering for Tony, who was "quite a swordsman" according to the office rumor mill, she had no idea. But she was done feeding the delusion.

"Peggy, where do you keep the decaf?" Sarah called from the kitchen. Long before she married Brendan, Sarah was a part of the kitchen klatch, coordinating meals, tidying up afterward.

"We're outta decaf." Peggy's lips pursed in that grin-and-bear-it frown as she headed into the kitchen. "Your father forgot to bring it home from the shop."

The shop was a small coffee shop across the street from the 109th Precinct, Sully's home precinct for years. After retirement he'd bought the shop, a favorite hangout spot for cops, and renamed it "Sully's Cup."

"The memory is shot," Sully said. "Looks like you guys are stuck with leaded tonight."

"Fine with me." Bernie pushed her glasses onto her head to rub her eyes. "When I work Lobster Shift, I always hit that wall around four in the morning." For some reason lawyers called the shift from one to nine in the morning the Lobster Shift, and Bernie was still a green enough prosecutor to rotate into the weird hours from time to time. Secretly, she didn't mind because she and Keesh worked the same schedule, but she didn't talk about her relationship with Keesh at the family table. Sully didn't approve of his daughter having a relationship with "some potential terrorist from the Middle East." Keesh was Rashid Kerobyan, son of an Armenian brain surgeon who hailed from Ohio. In Bernie's opinion, you couldn't get much more American than Ohio, but there was no arguing with her father.

Brendan bumped her playfully on the shoulder. "You need to get off those night shifts, Peanut."

"One of these days. But I don't have the Lobster Shift all the time," she said, softened by the endearment. When was the last time Brendan called her Peanut? Of all her siblings, she was most simpatico with Bren, who was closest in age. That was no surprise, considering that Jimmy Jr. was nearly twenty and out of the house when Bernie was born. "She was my 'oops' baby," Peggy liked to say of Bernadette, "but she kept Sully and me on our toes."

"And Dad . . ." James's brows arched over his eyes in an earnest expression as he turned to their father at the head of the table. "How can a man like yourself, who serves coffee to hundreds of people a week, have no decaf in the house?"

The guys chuckled, and Sully pointed a finger at his oldest son. "Watch it, Jimbo, or we'll cut you off without a drop of French Roast."

James clutched his chest. "You're breaking my heart."

Over the laughter and cawing no one heard the side door open, but from the kitchen came Gracie's animated voice. "Uncle Tony! Where were you?"

After the hellos Tony appeared at the kitchen door. "Hey, sports fans." He extended a hand to Bernie's father, the only man in the room afforded the courtesy. Tony knew how to work a room. "How's it going, Sully?"

"I can't complain. You want a beer?"

"I'd love one, but I'm working tonight."

Brendan pointed a thumb toward Bernie. "She is, too. Sarah's making coffee."

"And here's your dinner." Mary Kate's voice was thick with pride as she placed a steaming plate of food in front of her husband. "I nuked it for you."

"Thanks, sweetheart," he said.

Bernie turned away from the spectacle: fawning wife, philandering husband. Did Mary Kate know that he called every female in the DA's office "sweetheart"?

"Let me know if you want seconds." Mary Kate backed toward the kitchen. "There's plenty more."

"I'm good." Tony unfolded Ma's cloth napkin and tucked it into the top of his button-down shirt. A shirt no doubt pressed with love by Mary Kate.

"Do you two ever cross paths at work?" Sully asked from the head of the table.

"I wish," Tony said. "Somehow I always get stuck with those ADAs who think they know it all." Tony gestured with a fork. He was one of those guys who could pull off eating in front of a group. It wasn't just his high self-esteem; he never seemed to end up with seeds stuck between his teeth or grease shining on his lips. Bernie saw it as part of his natural charm, an ornate façade for an architecturally unsound building.

"Sometimes we run into each other in the office." Bernie didn't mention that she tried to dodge any cases that came into the Complaint Room with "Marino" listed as the arresting officer.

Sully leaned back in his chair, palms on the table. "I'll tell you, I sleep well at night knowing that this city is in good hands. My sons out there on the streets. My daughter prosecuting the scum of the earth. I'm proud of you all." James Sullivan Sr. had joined the New York City Police Department in the early sixties at the age of eighteen. Sometimes Bernie had trouble wrapping her brain around the image of her father, a teenager in the sixties, getting a buzz cut and saluting the establishment while, all around him, the hip generation was espousing free love. Sully stayed on the job until he reached the limit—his sixty-third birthday—and loved every minute in between.

Pride flickered in Bernie's chest. "You set us all on the path, Dad."

Sully swatted off her comment. "You guys are the new heroes. The new generation."

"Yeah, and sometimes I wonder about the next generation," James said. He explained how half a dozen recruits had to be cut from the academy because they couldn't pass the physical exam. "These guys, and a girl, they couldn't run at all. Fat pales, all of them." Now that Jimmy taught at the Police Academy, his stories tended more toward comedy than heartbreak, but at times his eyes were shaded by pain. Sully said a cop never forgot the street. "You can take a cop off the streets, but you'll never take the street out of a cop."

Talk turned to James's new hours at the Police Academy. He had a shot at steady days, but didn't want to lose the night differential.

"But days are sweet," Brendan said. "It's good to work when the sun is up."

"You day shift guys are lucky," Tony said. "Nights are hard on a family. You never see your kids, at least not 'til they're in college like my kids. Then they act like *they're* working nights."

At least Tony had that part right. Bernie pressed a napkin to her mouth to hide her smile.

"Yeah, steady days are good. I love having the afternoon to pick up the girls from school and day care. Best part of my day." The shadows under Brendan's eyes deepened as he glanced toward the kitchen. "I want my kids to know who their father is. Grace and Maisey are going to grow up right."

"Yeah, it's getting harder and harder to take care of a family these days." Tony buttered a roll as he spoke. "I still can't get over that horror show in Connecticut. What those monsters did to the Stevens family. Fuckin' animals."

Bernie looked toward the door to see if the kids were out of earshot. As a rule, her father wanted the street language kept on the street.

"They should be fried," Tony added.

"Heinous crimes," Sully agreed, and though they had discussed the home-invasion-turned-murder before, Sully and James recounted the story, repeating certain details that they all knew by heart. Two ex-cons. A ladder at the back window. A blood-soaked scarf.

"I'd pull the switch on them," James said.

"We need some good lawyers like Bernie up there to make sure they get what they deserve," Sully said. "What do you say, honey? One day maybe you'll be the one facing down these monsters in court, getting the big fish."

"Dad . . ." Bernie raked a hand through one side of her hair. "I'm an ADA. The prosecutors on those cases have years of experience behind them."

"But you're good, sweetheart," Sully said. "You could do it."

Brendan leaned back and tucked his hands behind his neck so that his arms folded out to the sides like two huge gray wings. There was turmoil in his eyes, but Bernie couldn't quite read it.

"You could fry them," Tony said. "Wouldn't that be the bomb if little Bernie sent some piece of shit off to fry."

"If it happened in New York, they'd probably use lethal injection," Bernie said, trying to ground the conversation. "And the chances of execution here are slim. New York hasn't used capital punishment since 1963."

"And I hope we never do." Brendan's words seemed to suck the air from the room.

All eyes were on him.

Brendan dropped his arms, but he held his ground. "How does that make things right—killing a killer? In my book, that makes us animals, too."

"True." Sully stared off in the distance, surprising Bernie. If anyone else had said that, her father would have been all over them. "But sometimes you've got to do the hard thing, son. Sometimes you got to stop the bleeding."

"Amen to dat." Tony could be such a jerk, but at times it provided comic relief. "Hey, Bernie, what's the word on the subway rapist down by City Hall?"

"You tell me," she said. "You guys going fishing downtown?" Tony worked in Street Crime, a plainclothes unit that worked in all five boroughs.

"As a matter of fact, we're setting up operations in some of the subways tonight. I'd love to snag this guy."

"I read in the paper that they almost caught him the last

time he attacked," Sully said as his wife brought a Corning-Ware pot of coffee to the table. "Wednesday, right?"

"That's what I read," Bernie agreed, accepting a clean mug from Grace. "Victims report that he walks with a limp, or else he's intox. He lurks at the end of the platform."

"You're not riding the subway at night, are you?" Peg stared down at her daughter.

Bernie felt like a butterfly pinned to a board. "I don't ride in the middle of the night."

Peg let her head roll back, her eyes to the ceiling. "Lord in heaven above, watch over the foolish."

"We got extra patrols and undercovers in the subways." Tony clapped a comforting hand on Peggy's shoulder, as if he had it all under control. "We'll get this guy, Peg."

"But till then, it's not safe." Peg's mouth was set tight. "I don't want you down there, Bernadette."

There was that name, inspired by the saint, or more accurately the movie *The Song of Bernadette,* which had won her mother's heart when she was a girl. The name meant serious business. "Okay, Ma. I'll spring for a taxi and deal with the perverts on the street."

"Very funny." Peg frowned as she put out the platter from the bakery. "Now listen to your mother. And have a cookie."

Tony reached for a petit four. "I love these things. You know what else? I'd love to catch that rapist. That would pave my path with gold. The guy who snags him will be a hero. There's a gold shield there."

James nodded, but Brendan shook his head.

"What?" Tony spread his hands.

Brendan folded his arms across his chest. "You are such a one-way . . ." He looked to his daughters, climbing back onto their chairs at the table. "You're a one-way fudgesicle."

"The real heroes are the guys who come through in small moments, day after day," Bernie said, stirring milk into her coffee. She thought of Brendan and the little girls who had to be removed from their abusive father. "Small moments that have big results. Aiding a victim. Resolving an argument. Even giving directions. It's really about service more than enforcement."

"That's my daughter," Sully said proudly.

"You tell him, sister girl." Brendan held up his hand and Bernie slapped him five.

"Still . . ." Tony poured himself a cup. "I'd love to nail that guy."

Chapter 4

The burning at the back of her throat was probably indigestion from the seasonings on Ma's roast, but Mary Kate equated it with sickness of heart. Like those pictures of Christ that revealed his heart, a red, glowing heart shape sometimes on fire with faith or burdened with his crown of thorns. One look at a picture of the Sacred Heart of Jesus and your eyes bugged out. That heart was the only thing you noticed.

And right now, Mary Kate's heart radiated pain through the rest of her body.

I'm suffering from a broken heart, she thought as she rinsed the large carrot bowl clean. At forty-two, she seemed far too old to be suffering romance problems. Forty-two and three kids in college; she was over the hill. The thought made her eyes sting, a tear forming as she recalled those black and white "over the hill" banners the kids had hung for her fortieth two years ago. She was over the hill, and losing her husband, and once it was all over, drained like the dirty dishwater in the sink at her hands, she'd be an old matron. Like Mrs. Harmon across the street who lived and died alone after her husband left her. "They'll carry Mrs. Harmon out of that place someday," Sully used to say when people asked if he worried that their neighbor might sell the house. And her father had been right. They'd all been here for dinner the day the coroner's station wagon came to get her. "Ah, the meat wagon," Tony had said, with barely a hint of sadness.

The bastard. Sadness wasn't in his repertoire, probably because he was too busy tap dancing into someone else's limelight.

She wondered if anyone sensed the trouble.

Was that why Ma had argued with her about clearing away Tony's place at the table? And the pressure to bring Conner along . . . one more push and she'd be over the edge. Of course Conner didn't really want to come to his grandparents' house, and right now she couldn't risk him spilling their secrets. Not now, when the slamming doors and muted sobs still hadn't given way to any sort of resolution.

As Mary Kate rinsed the roast pan and gave it a moment to drip into the stainless steel sink, she sensed her sister-in-law Sarah moving behind her. Lingering close.

"Oh, look at you, finished scrubbing all the pots and pans single-handedly." She touched MK's shoulder, and Mary Kate felt her composure crumbling. Sarah was kind and smart, a big help in the kitchen, unlike Bernie. Mary Kate and Sarah had a lot in common with their kids, their husbands on the job.

Only Sarah's husband wasn't about to move in with his twentysomething girlfriend.

"Why don't you take a break and let me load the dishwasher?" Sarah stepped up beside her, rolling up the sleeves of her sweater. "Give me the gloves." In a low voice, mimicking a cop, she added: "Surrender the gloves and step away from the sink, ma'am."

"Okay." Mary Kate forced a trembling smile as she stripped off the rubber gloves. "I'll dry and put away."

"Get outta here. You're not an indentured slave. Go out there and sit with your husband. I'll be done with this stuff in two minutes."

"I'm good." Mary Kate took a clean towel from the drawer

and began to dry the towering mound of pans on the counter. She had a love-hate relationship with this kitchen she'd grown up in. She resented the splatter and grit of kitchen chores, but when her insides twisted with worry, this was the room that brought her comfort. The vinyl floor, worn but still shiny, held a million footprints of their family history. The wallpaper over the table had been wiped clean so many times its flowers had faded from periwinkle to a soft baby blue, and yet no one wanted to change it. Her mother's kitchen was hallowed ground.

She hoisted a squat casserole dish into the towel. "This dish is a relic," she told Sarah. She'd dried the piece with tiny blue flowers on the side all her life. When she'd been a kid, dreaming about her devout life in the convent. She wanted to be the Flying Nun! As a stupid teen, when she gave up the nun plan for Brian Finnegan. Then, even more stupid, when she got pregnant with Erin and had to drop out of college at twenty. Not that she regretted any of her kids, God bless them, but what if she'd taken a different track?

What if she was sitting out there with the men, tossing around her own stories like Bernie?

Bitterness stung the back of her tongue as she wondered how things had unraveled in the patterns they all lived. You'd think Mary Kate would be endeared to her father because she'd married a cop. But then along comes Bernie, going to law school and working in the DA's office. Already she'd trumped MK, and she didn't have a husband and kids yet.

Cradling the roasting pan in her arms, Mary Kate paced toward the dining room door and peeked out. Her Tony seemed to glow from the center of the table, probably because he sat under the hanging light. That and the tan, which he'd gotten from the salon upon his doctor's recommendation for "light therapy." A lot of hooey. He might have a little less hair, and it was graying, salt and pepper, her mother called it, but he was still a handsome man. His hair was longish now for anticrime, and that made him look kind of roguish. Or maybe he kept it longer to cover up the bare spot on top. She had noticed, oh, yes, she had, but she had kept it to herself, knowing how sensitive Tony was about his looks.

And that beard . . . When he first grew it for undercover work, she'd liked it. But now, now it was one of the things that turned him into another person, a man she didn't know or trust.

She watched the back of Bernie's head bob, the chandelier bouncing gold and red lights on her hair. Mary Kate reached up to her own A-line cut, curled demurely at her chin. She got the Kenny hair, thin and wispy. Bernie was telling a story, and her brothers watched her, riveted.

Dad looked on with that distant look, reserving judgment, while Tony had his finger in the air, waiting for an opportunity to interject something.

All these years, Bernie had her place at the table with the men. Even as a girl, she'd seemed welcome there. MK rubbed the towel vigorously over a small spot on the pan, shining it to a gloss as she contemplated the dining room dynamic.

"Did you ever notice how Bernie always lingers at the table?" Mary Kate worked to keep jealousy from leaching into her voice. "She does that every week. Ignores all the cleanup while she talks locker-room scuttlebutt with the men."

"She enjoys it," Sarah said as she scraped a plate into the garbage. "Bernie's the smart one, avoiding the kitchen."

Peg entered with an armful of dessert plates, just in time to pick up the gist of their conversation. "Bernie will find her way to the kitchen," Peg said. "The right motivation will turn her around. She just needs to find the right guy, is all."

Mary Kate felt her lips harden. That had always been Ma's goal for her daughters. Find the right man.

"Sarah, your cherry tarts are a big hit, as usual," Peg said. "I don't know how you find the time."

"They're not hard to make, as long as I can keep Brendan away from the batter. Your son has a sweet tooth."

Peg smiled. "Oh, you just have to cut him off. You know, when he was a boy he used to pay Bernie to bake cupcakes for him."

"That wasn't Bernie, Ma, it was me." Mary Kate felt stung. Was Bernie now going to get credit for Mary Kate's part in the family history?

"Oh, was it?" Peg's brown eyes opened wide for a second. "Well, of course. Bernie doesn't like the kitchen."

"We were just saying." Sarah nodded toward the dining room. "She likes to play with the big boys."

Peg nodded, as she bent over the table to transfer more desserts to the platter. "Yeah, God broke the mold with Bernie."

"I don't know about blaming God," Mary Kate said. "But she definitely got cheated on domestic skills. Have you ever seen her apartment?"

"I try to avoid it," Peg said. "I keep my nose out."

"It's a train wreck." Mary Kate didn't know where this venom was coming from, but now that it was flowing she couldn't put a cork in it. "And look at her—almost thirty and no kids. I don't know how she can keep choosing the career track over the mommy track when her ovaries are drying up by the minute."

There. She'd said it, and it felt good to hit a bull's-eye.

Until Bernie stepped into the kitchen. "What's that about my ovaries?"

With a jab of guilt, Mary Kate stared down at the roasting pan. "I was just saying, you manage to avoid the kitchen. Like you're allergic to dishes or something."

"You know that kitchens make my glasses steam up." Bernie leaned over the open dishwasher to stow her mug. "So, yeah, I guess I'm allergic. Besides, I have to get to work."

Always racing off to work, Mary Kate thought. *Or are you just trying to remind us that you're a big-shot lawyer now?*

"It's ungodly hours like that that are keeping you from getting a husband," Peg said.

Thank you for jumping in, Ma, Mary Kate thought. Finally, someone had her back.

Sarah laughed, covering her mouth. "Really? Is that the secret to landing a man?"

"I'll tell you all the tricks," Tony announced from the kitchen door. "I'm off to work, sweetheart." He bussed Mary Kate on the cheek, bits of his facial hair brushing against her. It had the feel of a small animal.

It was sick how her heart jumped when he called her sweetheart, but the perfunctory kiss reminded her that there was no passion, no strong attraction. He could have been kissing the winner of a PBA scholarship or his great-aunt Mary.

"So what do you want to know about landing a man?" Tony asked.

"Nothing from you." Bernie held one hand up like a crossing guard. "No, thanks."

"Seriously, what do you want to know? Advice is free."

"And talk is cheap," Bernie said, grabbing her coat from the hook in the hall.

"We're just wondering why Bernie can't seem to hold on to a guy," Mary Kate said as she shoved the roasting pan into the cabinet with a thud.

Tony glanced at Bernie and shrugged. "Guys don't make passes at girls who wear glasses."

"I'll wear my contacts next time I go hunting," Bernie said. " 'Nuff said."

"And you'll never find a man if you keep working that ridiculous shift," Mary Kate added before she could stop herself.

"Whose business is it what hours I work?" Bernie paused, her brown eyes squinting at Mary Kate as if an intruder were lurking in her sister's body. "It's part of my job, and I don't even do it all the time, okay? All the junior prosecutors in the trial bureau work the Complaint Room on a rotating basis. Besides, Tony works the night shift, and he found a spouse."

Mary Kate whipped the towel over one shoulder. "A good wife learns to work around the breadwinner's schedule."

"Right." Bernie bit her bottom lip, retreating from the attack. "Maybe I need a wife then."

Chapter 5

The dingy concrete was cold under his butt, the white tiles that supported his head grimy from soot, but he had to lean. With his hands cuffed behind his back, he kept falling toward his right side, the bad side, and he needed the wall to hold him up. From time to time a draft sneaked down the stairs, flooding them with more cold.

But the chill of the subway did nothing to cool the fury burning in his gut over getting slammed by the cops. It burned from his toes on up to the cap on his head. Injustice didn't sting. It burned like a spitting furnace.

Busted for walking in the subway.

What was the sense in that?

Five years might be a long time, but the city had changed while he was gone. A man could get arrested just for being in the subway at night. No sense in that at all.

And how long had they made him sit here, hot and cold?

Hot and cold.

He was going to blow up inside, Fourth of July, while his body froze to the cement.

Besides the two guys in plainclothes, three other uniforms lingered.

Now one of the cops' radios crackled, and a female voice said something about transporting a prisoner.

They were talking about him . . . a prisoner again. Hot and cold . . .

Blue jean legs in leather boots stepped into his line of vision. The Italian cop who seemed to think he was some movie star nudged him with the toe of his boot. He wore his silver badge on a ribbon around his neck, like an Olympic medalist.

"Get up, you piece of shit." Of the two cops, the one who thought he was Al Pacino was playing badass cop. "You ready to take a walk?"

"I told you, I didn't do nothing."

Pacino got down low, stuck his pretty face in Peyton's grill. A Hollywood tan with very straight teeth. A pretty face, but the leather coat and boots? The guy could have stepped out of an old movie. "Because we caught you before you had a chance to attack tonight. But don't think I didn't see you eyeballing that woman. Closing in. You thought you were going to take her down, like all the others. Friggin' animal."

The cop's words fanned the fire in Peyton's belly. He was not an animal. Just because he didn't walk straight, just because his skin was the color of black coffee, that didn't make him a beast.

"You have a good heart," Angel used to say. "The heart makes the man."

But Al Badass Pacino didn't want to hear about his heart.

"Come on, get up," the cop growled. "Get up, get up."

Peyton bent his good leg and pushed, but with his hands cuffed behind his back he couldn't get real leverage. He sank back down to the ground.

"Are you kidding me?" The cop was screaming like a drill sergeant. "You think this is a big joke?" When Peyton didn't answer, the cop sputtered, "Do you?"

"No, sir." Peyton felt himself slipping into the closet, a place of shadows where he'd hidden from people like Big Pa and Darnell. Only it wasn't a real closet anymore, but a pretend one where he could be safe.

"Get up!" Pacino growled again.

Peyton scrambled again, but this time it didn't amount to much more than his shoe scratching the ground.

"He needs a hand," the other cop said. "He's got a bum leg. Right? Is that it?" he asked, looking down at Peyton. This guy was older, with a gut, a banana nose, and a shiny pink head.

When Peyton nodded, the old cop bent down, grabbed him by the shoulder, and pulled. Peyton pushed with his good leg, wobbled for balance, and finally stood on his own.

Pacino's beady eyes watched suspiciously. "All right. Let's go."

"Wait." Peyton knew Pacino had no use for him, but maybe the other cop would listen. "I can't walk on my own. I need my walking stick."

The cop supporting him paused long enough for Peyton to glance over at the bench, where the white-handled stick had clattered to the ground when the two undercovers had sprung out at him.

That stick was the only good thing he owned, a gift from Angel. She told him she wouldn't have been able to get it through most prisons, but since the inmates at Lakeview Shock were nonviolent offenders, they let him have it. Peyton didn't want to lose it now. He knew Pacino wouldn't give him any play, but this other cop, the old guy, he seemed okay.

"Officers . . ." Peyton swallowed. He would not beg, but he could make a simple request. "I need help walking. Can you please bring along my walking stick?"

Pacino backed away until he could see the wood stick, only half-hidden by the bench. "Is this it? This what you're talking about?" He held up the stick. Its white enamel tip seemed shiny clean in the fluorescent lights.

"Yes, sir, officer. I need it to walk."

The cop stuck his foot under the bench and rolled it out with the toe of his leather boot. "A stick."

"Pick it up already, Marino, and let's get this guy to the Tombs."

Badass Marino picked it up, examined both ends like maybe

there'd be some kind of secret compartment for drugs or a knife. Like Peyton was James Bond or something.

"It's just a stick." Marino waved it around. "Ladies and gentlemen, Justin Timberlake." He hopped, a bad dancer. "Moonwalk!"

He's burning me, fanning the fire. The rage inside him swelled to a fury. Hot and cold. Peyton considered throwing himself at the cop, handcuffs and all. Take him right down. He imagined the two of them rolling, toppling down to the tracks to a quick *thwack* of electrocution on the third rail.

The cop didn't think Peyton had it in him, a cripple with a bad limp, but he could take him down. He could do it, and it would feel good. And it would be the right thing to do.

"For the Lord has a day of vengeance . . ." That was what it said in the Bible, Book of Isaiah.

Adrenaline stung his blood as he stepped toward Marino, and stumbled.

"Whoa . . ." The older cop planted himself under Peyton's shoulder and saved him from falling. A human crutch.

Peyton closed his eyes, reconsidering. He could just hang back. Curl up inside. Go to the closet.

"Hey, what's that show—*So You Think You Can Dance?*" Marino's cackles fired like a nail gun, but at least now he was far away . . . in the distance.

"That thing can be vouchered as a weapon," Duval said from beside Peyton. "Stop monkeying around and let's go."

And though the injustice of it all burned inside him, Peyton thought this cop guiding him along wasn't a terrible person. And if he had really broken the law again, his first night out of prison, maybe it was an easy ticket back.

Back to Lakeview Shock.

He kept thinking on that, his old cell, shared with just one other guy, as the cops stuffed him into the back of a patrol car and rolled into the night. The car smelled of humanity but the seat was soft and the warmth eased his achy muscles as he thought of having his own bed again. His own place to go.

Outside the car, people walked into the street without looking. The old seaport blocks were still buzzing with tourists and drunk brokers, but beyond that were the metal roll gates of closed shops and dark alleyways. This city had grown too cold. Not his city anymore.

In the front of the car, Marino's mouth ran like a faucet. Every story was twisted to make him look good. Now he was telling the uniformed cop driving about a coffee shop owned by his father-in-law.

"Sully's Cup. Roosevelt and Union in Flushing. You know it?"

The uniform had heard of it. "But everybody knows Sully. He's really your in-law?"

"You know it." Then Marino made a joke and cackled like a hyena.

Peyton closed his eyes and wished himself back in the prison near Lake Erie, far from here.

"Last stop, jail!" Marino laughed as the other guy squeezed into a spot. "This is your stop, Doe."

They were calling him John Doe because he wouldn't give his name. What was the sense in giving the cops anything? Peyton knew he didn't have much power, but the name thing was a small token of it. With no ID on him, they'd have to work awhile to figure him out.

By then, he hoped he'd have figured out a way back to Lakeview Shock. This arrest might be a good way back, but Peyton didn't want to lose the little bit of control he had.

They chained him to a chair in the middle of a big room at the place they called Central Booking. At least now he could close his bad eye, which was getting all dried from being awake too long, and that could be bad. Cops all around looked right through him, like he was invisible. They took all his stuff, not that he had a lot, but he was worried about his walking stick. He didn't like the way the cop called Marino had played around with it.

And the way Marino the cop kept bragging and pointing at

him, showing him off like he was a trophy. "I got him!" he kept saying. "He walked right into our stakeout. Imagine dat!"

And then Peyton tuned in and listened to the garbage that was running from Marino's mouth.

"Sarge, we got the serial subway rapist here."

"Rapist?" Peyton's head rose slowly. "You're crazy."

Marino cocked his head smugly. "I know, you're innocent, right?"

Peyton pressed his eye closed and dropped out again, back to the closet to sort this out. They were trying to get him for raping someone? First, he didn't do it.

Second, they didn't allow violent prisoners at Lakeview Shock. He couldn't ride this one out if he wanted to get back there.

"I didn't rape anyone," he said.

No one answered. No one seemed to hear him, but as he retreated, their words began to fit together like puzzle pieces.

Fits the description . . . height and weight, black man, no facial hair . . .

Duval argued that Peyton didn't have the strength to take down those women with his limp and bum leg. "Did you see? I think his whole right side is bad."

"That's an act," Marino argued. "I can tell."

"Better talk to the DA's office. See if they can make it stick."

"Will do." Marino cackled again, that sick noise, and said something about having friends in high places.

And suddenly Peyton was being poked and jostled out of the chair. "Come on, Mr. Doe," Marino said, standing over him. The light behind him made the top of his head shine. It gave a sharpness to his cheeks and a pointed edge to his beard.

Just like the devil.

"You're going down, buddy," Marino said. "Way, way down to the Tombs."

Chapter 6

"Change is good," Keesh said under his breath. Not that any of the other prosecutors in nearby cubicles of the Complaint Room would care that he was talking to himself.

He turned away from the open document—a complaint he'd drafted based on a misdemeanor arrest. The suspect would be arraigned in the morning when the judges were out of bed and back on the bench. Judges no longer had night court, but the district attorney's office needed staff to process intake twenty-four, seven. Such was the business of being a prosecutor. Would it be any better in Queens? He tried to imagine life without Manhattan. If he accepted the job offer, he would live and work in Queens. No more backup at the Midtown Tunnel, no more commutes in on the Long Island Rail Road. No more mosh pit on the seven train.

No more Bernie.

That was the biggest downside.

He'd also miss the Christmas lights in the winter and downing lunch as he walked through the park in the spring, but he figured they'd have lights and parks in Kew Gardens, too.

Cutting out Bernie would be the problem.

Of course, they would vow to stay friends, see each other on weekends, call, e-mail, text, tweet. But none of those synthetic forms of life made up for being with someone.

So, if he took the offer to move to the Queens District Attorney's Office, the hardest part would be slashing through his relationship with Bernie.

They'd met during law school in that horrific class every law student complained about, the one where the professor called on students randomly and expected them to know the fact, issue, holding and rule of any one of a thousand torts. She'd been tight with Amy Silverstein already, friends from high school, and for the first week or so, he'd been content to watch.

Like an art student, he'd studied Bernie from various angles.

From the back, her hair was the main attraction, thick and bouncy and shiny. Like a precious metal, it gleamed with various hues: bronze, gold, and copper. From the side, you couldn't miss the cute Irish pug he called her "ski slope nose." Its cuteness was offset by her strong cheekbones and chin. Seeing her prominent profile, he had imagined her arguing a case before a judge.

But by far, Bernie's outstanding feature, her most unforgettable quality, was her eyes. Her dark brown eyes seemed wise for their age. Those eyes had the ability to see past the physical façade to people's souls. For a person in pain, Bernie's eyes were a window of compassion, and though he always teased her that she was a pushover for a sob story, he cherished her gift for empathy.

Observing her back in that university lecture hall, he could tell she and Amy were tight, and he wasn't about to play fifth wheel.

But one day, Amy didn't show up for class. He waited in the seat behind Bernie and, as the professor went to take the podium, he slid into the empty seat beside her.

Her quick glance was meant to dismiss him.

That was disappointing, but he could deal.

As the lecture began, he flipped open his notebook and wrote the date. Beyond the weird vibe of sitting next to a very pretty girl, it was any other day.

As the professor gave final notes, he felt her beside him and realized her eyes had strayed to his notebook.

She gulped, suppressing a giggle. Then the noise of conversation and scurrying feet took over, and she let out a full-on laugh, bubbly and frenetic, like a bottle of seltzer opened too fast.

"Nice doodles," she said.

He glanced down at the sketches that framed his notes, a landscape of geese flying in front of sunsets, a pirate ship riding a curling wave, a planet covered with Monopoly-style houses. "I like to keep my pen moving," he said. "Especially in classes like this, when we're not allowed to have laptops."

She pointed to one in the corner. "This is my favorite."

It was a sketch of a dragon, a goofy one with a pudgy paunch and only a small flame puffing from its mouth, which was missing two front teeth. He had captioned it in childish scrawl: "I drewd a dragon."

"You can keep the flaming swords," she said, "but my niece would enjoy that dragon."

"Then she should have him." He tore off the corner of the page, handed it to her, then glanced at the flip side. "And if she's interested, she can brush up on Vaughan versus Menlove."

"Thanks." She pressed the scrap of paper to her heart, as if it were a precious thing. "She's four, but you never know when a classic tort will come in handy. I'm Bernie Sullivan, by the way."

"Rashid Kerobyan, but my friends call me Keesh."

"Okay, Keesh. Since you've gifted me with this fine etching, let me get you a latte or something."

"Coffee would be good."

They grabbed coffee, then lunch. He'd gone home to study that day, but he couldn't stop thinking about her, about that unpredictable spark of energy Bernie possessed. She agreed to meet him at the library to study together. The next day they brought Amy and a few others into the study group. By the end of that semester he was sneaking her into his parents' house whenever they went off for conferences or vacations. He'd had girlfriends before, but Bernie was the closest he'd found to a real partner.

They were great together, but it was too good to last, that was how Keesh looked at it. When his parents took them out to dinner after graduation, Dr. Ara Kerobyan did not hide his dislike of Bernie, who was most decidedly not an Armenian girl. Afterward, there'd been a showdown with his father. "That's racism, pure and simple," he told his father. "It's about preserving a culture," his father defended, his dark eyes penetrating and demanding as always. "Isn't it bad enough that you did not go into the medical field?"

I'm not you, Keesh wanted to tell the old man. But his father did not allow him the luxury of a real argument, point for point. Instead, he had simply scowled and turned back to his computer, "the glue pot," Keesh's mother called it.

When Keesh shared the story with Bernie, he'd expected her to rally with him. Damn the torpedoes and your old man, too. But instead, she had admitted to getting flack from her own family. Her father, who in his career had served in Queens, the most ethnically diverse county in the country, could not be comfortable with having Keesh in his home.

"It's because of nine-eleven," Bernie said. "I never thought of my father as a man with biases, but he keeps going back to the Twin Towers. When I tell him that being Middle Eastern doesn't make you a terrorist, he clams up and tells me that I don't understand because I wasn't at Ground Zero."

The small fissure in his gut, the wound begun by his father's words, was torn wider by Bernie's words. She was falling for their fathers' brands of racism. She was willing to let cultural differences screw up the best thing that had ever happened to him.

That realization had hurt almost as much as his father's demands.

He had tried to talk it out with Bernie, tried to make a case for them standing on their own two feet and doing what they thought was right. But in the end, practicality won out. Two law school students living at home, eating Mom and Dad's food—yeah, they had needed to keep their parents' support.

But they had stayed friends, good friends.

Bernie still framed his days, the way a simple frame could bring order and longevity to a picture of your life. But what would happen when Bernie faded from the picture?

Because he was going to take that job in Queens. He'd be a fool not to. They were offering a promotion and a place in their Trial Division, a spot that rarely opened up here in Manhattan.

"Knock, knock."

He turned at the sound of Bernie's voice and found her tapping on the wall of the cubicle. Her hair was pulled back in a scrunchie—she did that to look older and more authoritative—and she was wearing the tortoiseshell-frame glasses that always reminded him of the sexy schoolteacher who had to reprimand her pupil for being naughty.

God help him, he still wanted her.

"Hey. What's up?" he asked.

"My question first. What happened with the interview? Did you ace it, or what?"

He straightened his necktie. "They want me to start April first."

"Keesh! That's great." She came around the half wall and plopped in the visitor's chair. "I knew they'd love you. Who doesn't, right?"

Well, you, for starters.

"But I don't know if I can allow you to go. Our study group is really breaking up, with Amy in private practice and now you going to Queens."

"Well. We are out of law school now. All three of us passed the bar. I'd call the study group a success."

She cocked her head to the side. "Wise guy. But I'm here on a mission." She leaned to her side and crossed her legs, and though her pantsuit and black pinstripe jacket were supremely professional, he could remember a time when she had stretched out on his bed in a similar position, nearly naked. Those were some sweet days, and naughty nights.

He blinked, resolving to rein it in and focus on what she was saying.

"I just got a call from my brother-in-law Tony. He said that you caught a case of his. The complaint report would have just come in an hour ago."

Keesh moved the mouse and clicked open his files. "What was it about?"

"Tony thinks he's found the serial subway rapist."

"That would be the case of a lifetime. How'd I miss that one?"

"Look under Tony Marino?"

He found the file. "Yeah, I asked him to release the suspect. Not really a suspect. No witnesses, but this says the man is disabled. Apparent limp and weakness on the right side. Some facial paralysis. Walks with a cane, and apparently this condition is new. From our forensics, the bruising and injury patterns, we think our rapist is right-handed. This guy isn't taking anyone down with his right hand."

"Mmm." She frowned. "It sounds pretty clear-cut, but Tony wanted me to ask you if you'd reconsider."

Keesh sat back in his chair and winced. "I hate to arraign a suspect when I got nothing on him. A black man walking in the subway at night reeks of racial profiling. That's not great detective work, and it will probably end up being a waste of time and money. Not to mention a miscarriage of justice."

"Maybe Tony knows something that isn't in the complaint report," she said, her mouth twisted to one side in an expression of doubt.

"Maybe." The one time he'd met this Tony, Keesh hadn't liked him much. Still, he was part of Bernie's family, even if by marriage. "Why don't you call him? Have Tony and his partner come up and talk with us."

She smiled. "He's on his way over." And then she let out a laugh, that bubbling, contagious laugh. "I knew you'd do me a favor. Thanks, Keesh."

She started to get up, but he held up a hand. "Sit tight there, missy. If this case is any good, I'll need your legal-eagle mind."

"If this case is legit, Tony will make detective and he'll be even more intolerable than he is now." When he shot her a look of surprise, she covered her mouth. "Did I say that? Bad Bernie. Bad."

Chapter 7

Sitting across from him, shooting the bull, she felt dread begin to seep in, like seawater into a leaky boat. So Keesh was really leaving. Without Keesh, the office would be drab and cold, and when she rotated into duty in the Complaint Room . . . she couldn't imagine this frenzied process without him.

Keesh was her hero, and for a girl surrounded by men in blue, that was significant. Dad was legendary in the precincts he'd worked in; it seemed like everyone in the department knew Sully, the cop who'd worked till they forced him out, then opened a coffee shop right across the street from his beloved precinct. James did the right thing in his quiet way, and Brendan was always a helper, too.

But Keesh, broad-shouldered, beanpole slim in a suit, with eyes as dark as midnight and a thick five o'clock shadow that could give her an abrasive facial when he held her close . . . no, those intimate days were over. But no one said she wasn't allowed to get a jones from watching the smart, quick way he worked a case without diminishing anyone involved in it. Keesh stood his ground, but she'd never seen him yell, a feat in the very vocal playground of the district attorney's office. He was her go-to guy, a touchstone for ideas, a safety net when she fell off the deep end.

"I don't know what I'll do without you hanging around here." She kept it light, knowing he'd only feel guilty if she shared her true dismay.

His dark eyes remained steady, unfazed. "You'll get some real work done for the first time in years."

"Catch up on my files, maybe?" She captured his scratch pad and started doodling on it. "But that's the big joke. You never catch up in the DA's office. It's like products riding on a conveyor belt. The bad guys just keep on coming." As she spoke she drew a sad face with teardrops falling from its eyes. The caption read: We'll miss you, Keesh!

"But you've got a lot going on here," he said. "You've started the advocacy group for Women Against Violence, and you're making yourself a specialist in that area. People are starting to come to you when they land a domestic violence or rape case. One day you'll be giving expert testimony in that area."

She frowned, sliding the paper over to him. "Nice speech, but I'm still going to miss you."

He checked out her doodle. "Nice sentiment, but that's a terrible illustration."

As he spoke she noticed Tony across the Complaint Room. His skin was the color of roasted squash. Unnatural. She waved him over, wondering how MK felt about her husband's new look.

"Hey, sweetheart! How's it going?" Tony reached out to her for a kiss on the cheek.

Bernie didn't mind the kiss, but she didn't like being called sweetheart. Thank God Keesh had caught this complaint instead of her. Generally, the junior prosecutors manning the Complaint Room worked their shift evaluating felony and misdemeanor arrests and drafting complaints for the cases they deemed worthy of taking before a judge for arraignment, when formal charges were read. And once an attorney caught a case in the Complaint Room, they usually handled it until the final disposition.

The one time that Bernie hadn't been able to extract herself from working with Tony, it hadn't gone well. He'd wanted to charge an inebriated stockbroker with assault just because the guy had cursed him out. Much as she appreciated Tony's gusto, his chauvinism and stubbornness infuriated her.

Keesh rose and shook hands with Tony. "Officer Marino."

"Tony. We've met before."

"So you remember I go by Keesh." Keesh pulled over an extra chair. "So tell me about this suspect."

"I got a strong feeling about this guy." Tony combed his beard with his fingertips. "He refuses to give us his name, pissing me off, but we're running his prints now. I'd bet you dollars to donuts he's got a record."

"I didn't know he was a John Doe," Bernie said. It was a booking nightmare, but sometimes suspects without ID withheld their names to jam up a case. Whether through fingerprinting or some other detective work, the police eventually identified these suspects, but the extra investigation was time-consuming, and the suspect might have to log in excessive hours in the jails under Central Booking.

"I'm a little concerned about this guy's profile." Keesh's dark eyes were a sea of calm. "He doesn't really fit our serial rapist, who's a pretty strong guy. He drags or carries these women into remote locations. Your guy is disabled, right? Walks with a cane and has slight paralysis on the right side?"

Tony pointed his index finger into the air. "I think he's faking that."

"Well, you're not in a position to give a diagnosis," Keesh said evenly.

"And the thing is, his walking stick does fit the profile." Tony stretched his arms wide. "It's this long, with hard lacquer on one end. Soon as I saw that stick, I remembered that the victims reported the serial rapist hitting them with a stick, right?"

"Good point." Keesh cradled his jaw in one hand. "So we'll keep him in the Tombs until we can ID him."

"Good." Tony made a fist. "If you saw this perp malingering down on that subway platform, you'd have busted him, too. I got a feeling about this guy, and my instincts are pretty reliable."

"Okay." Keesh turned back to the computer. "If he came in around three this morning, we have all day to arraign him."

As a rule, the district attorney's office tried to get suspects arraigned within twenty-four hours of arrest, as lengthy waits in the holding cells of the Tombs were deemed inhumane.

"I'll change the status, but let me check first . . ." Keesh clicked to a few different screens, his face registering surprise. "Oh. Looks like the computer got a hit on him."

"So he probably does have a record." Maybe Tony's instincts were better than she'd thought. Bernie moved behind Keesh so that she could read over his shoulder.

"His name is Peyton Curtis, thirty-one years old, and he does have a criminal record." Keesh's dark eyes skimmed the monitor. "Five years up in Lakeview Shock for first-degree robbery."

"And he was released . . ." Bernie did a double take to be sure she was right. "Yesterday. Wow. This guy must have just stepped off the bus."

Keesh nodded. "Hasn't even met his parole officer yet. This could jam things up for him."

"But we've got nothing on him," Bernie pointed out. "Prison is an excellent alibi."

"Aw, you're kidding me?" Tony threw up his hands. "I just can't get a break here."

"Yeah, it looks like Mr. Peyton Curtis was just walking in the wrong subway station at the wrong time."

"Are you sure about that?" Tony left the chair to join them at the computer screen. "I mean, maybe you got the dates wrong? Transposed the numbers. People do that all the time."

"Not this time." Keesh pointed to the release date. "Mr. Curtis just received an official NYPD welcome back to the city."

"Damn." Tony squinted, rubbing the back of his neck. "Of all the bad luck . . ."

Bernie wasn't sure if he meant the bad luck belonged to him or to Peyton Curtis. Surely this suspect, fresh from prison, had just been through a harrowing experience, but she didn't think Tony saw it that way. Tony had trouble seeing beyond Tony.

"Ach. I'm outta here." Tony held up a hand. "Thanks for taking another look, Keesh." He winced. "I gotta go cry in my cornflakes."

Bernie smiled. Self-deprecating Tony could be funny. "I think you'll survive. Remind Mary Kate that Grace and Maisey's school show is tomorrow night."

"Will do."

As Tony left, Bernie slumped back into the chair. "Thanks for going the extra step for him," she said.

Keesh turned away from the computer, his dark eyes tugging at her resolve to keep things casual and friendly between them. Why did she feel chemistry only with the one guy she couldn't have?

"You're welcome." His eyes were dark as bittersweet chocolate. "But don't get too comfortable there. You've probably got a dozen complaint reports sitting in your in-box over there," he said, nodding at the desk across the aisle.

She clapped her palms on the surface of the desk. "You're right."

He was already lost in his work, jabbing at the computer keyboard as if nothing had changed.

But it had.

The planet had shifted in its orbit. Keesh wouldn't be hammering away at complaints here for much longer. And Bernie was going to be left to deal with a hole in her life.

Chapter 8

When the train screeched to a halt at Main Street Flushing, Peyton palmed the open doorway and stepped out warily, unsure that his right leg would support him.

Tucked in the deep pocket of his jacket was the stub of his walking stick, the smooth rat-horse carved from faux. The snapped stick was the only possession the property clerk had returned to him from the downtown jail, and Peyton knew who to thank for its destruction.

Marino.

Peyton's teeth ground as he imagined his hand closing over the carved rat, holding tight with his left hand, real tight with his good hand as he plunged the spike of the broken stick into the cop's chest. He could pop it right into one of those big veins, the aorta or something. That'd show him, the cop who broke his stick. What was the sense in that? Destroying a man's belongings for no reason at all.

Peyton's bad arm was tucked into his pocket. His good hand was filthy, palm black with soot from holding on to every handrail and skimming every wall between here and downtown Manhattan, just to keep his balance. Without his stick, he couldn't be sure of anything. Climbing stairs was like climbing a mountain with one hand, and even simple stuff like walking on pavement held hazards. One slip, one hitch in his bad leg, and he'd be down, eating the cement, his head smacking the street.

And he knew who to thank. Yeah, he had to do something real nice for the cop that had him hobbling into the projects like an old man. That Marino would be hearing from him. Sooner or later, it all floated to the top for the world to see. People would learn who Marino really was.

The grounds of the Blair Housing Project were smaller than he remembered. It was a lot like the prison yard; no plants and only a handful of bare trees, their gray bark sad and dry as an old man's tough skin. And here, instead of guards in the watchtower, was the elevated platform for the Long Island Rail Road. Every so often a train glided into the station and all the people looked out over the projects like they were some kind of miniature train set rich people set up at Christmastime.

The playground had been stripped down, the jungle gym gone with only a bare spot of dirt to mark the ancient crime scene. The carousel and the seesaw, he couldn't see any signs of where they used to be. They'd been ripped out so long ago, the earth already rose up and healed over the terrible wound.

He looked down at his withered arm, his leg scraping the pavement. Not all scars healed over.

The elevator in his mother's building was broken, and the climb tore at his tired muscles. His shuffling feet whispered in the hollow corridor until he paused in front of her door.

Did his mother still live here?

He squeezed his eyes shut, so tired. But someone at Lakeview Shock had checked. Said his mama was here.

He made a fist with his grimy hand and knocked.

No one answered, but he'd counted on that. He banged again, this time calling for her.

"Mama? Mama, you in there? It's Peyton. It's your son Peyton come back to you." He waited for a time, then called again. "Mama? Open the door. I'm so tired, I'm gon' fall flat on the floor right here in the hallway."

There was the rattle of metal, then the steel door opened,

just a few inches. The dark face that peered through the crack was too young to be his mama. Her hair was scraped back from a big forehead that creased when she looked at him.

"Who you?" The smoke of suspicion billowed through the crack.

"Hey, girl. I'm looking for my mama, Yvonne. She there?"

She shook her head, staring. "You Darnell?"

"Nah, I'm Peyton. You gon' let me in or make me stand out here all day? 'Cuz I'm tired, and I know my mama'd let me in." He didn't really know that for sure, but he needed a place to rest, and he figured his mama'd have pity on him after he wore her down. But this girl . . . he couldn't tell about her.

"What your name again?" she asked through the sliver of light.

"Peyton."

"Hold on." She closed the door and he was left alone in the long shadowy hallway smelling of humanity and cooking odors. It brought him back to the dark bus, a rocket to nowhere, and he fell into the wall, planting his palm against the painted concrete to get a grip.

The door squeaked, cracking open and the girl peeked out. "Yeah, he alone," she said.

Talking on a phone, he realized.

A second later the door slammed, opened wide, and the girl, maybe twelve or thirteen, stood there in a tight white T-shirt and jeans. "Your mama said you can come in, but said you behave and don't make a mess. You hear?"

He nodded, stepping into the apartment. Watery sunlight warmed the living room, where a TV was on, some show about girls who wanted to be models. A baby boy in tiny overalls dragged himself across the rug, all the while chewing on a plastic cup. Plastic containers and lids were scattered around him, but otherwise the place was neat.

"There's peanut butter and bread in there." The girl pointed to the refrigerator, but Peyton wasn't hungry. He looked down at his dirty hand, then looked toward the kitchen sink.

"Don't be thinking about washing in the kitchen sink. Bathroom's down the hall." She bent over to pick up the plastic tubs. "Come on and help me, William. We goin' out." She tidied up fast, picking up and stacking.

"Isn't it too cold out there for your baby?" he asked.

"Nah, and he's not my baby. He's my brother."

He squinted. "Who are you? You know my mama?"

She laughed, a trickling sound like rain dancing on the roof. "She's my grandma."

"What's your name?"

"I'm Kiki. Gwen's daughter. Gwen's your sister, right?"

He scratched his head, remembering two girls who pulled each other's hair and loved to help Mama cook. "That's right." He went into the bathroom and washed his hands, lathering up real good with sweet-smelling soap. When he came out, Kiki and the baby had their coats on. She showed Peyton a room he could use to rest, then carried the boy out of the apartment on her hip.

The sound of the locks clicking behind her gave him peace. He went into the bedroom and sat down on the bed with his coat still on. He didn't know who might come in, but it was hot in here, the heat billowing in the air. Peyton slipped off his jacket and shoes, dropped down on the bed, and fell into a deep sleep.

"Peyton!"

It was hard to pull himself from sleep, but the voice was persistent, repeating his name over and over.

"Peyton, wake up."

He rolled onto his back, the old mattress folding under his weight. His body was still sore and it felt like he'd barely slept at all, but he could see from the window that the sun was gone.

"Peyton, come on or I'm gon' smack you upside the head."

The sting of a slap on his face made him snap back and curl into a fetal position. What the—

"Yeah, that got your attention. Now sit up and tell me what the hell you doin' back here to suck our mother dry."

He knew that voice now.

The voice of evil.

"Darnell." Still wincing in pain, Peyton rubbed his cheek, then used his good hand to push back, away from Darnell. He didn't stop till he was at the top of the bed, propped against the wall. "What the hell you got to do that for? What's the sense in waking a person when he's in a deep sleep?"

"No sense at all." Darnell laughed, that rich, dark sound that made people smile unless he was laughing at them. Some people liked to laugh with Darnell, and some laughed because they didn't want to get on the bad side of a big, bad mo-fo like Darnell.

Peyton didn't think there'd been peace around here since the day Darnell was born. His younger brother seemed to enjoy hurting people, and because of his size—he was a foot taller than Peyton by seventh grade—it was easy for Darnell to inflict pain.

"What you want, Darnell?" Peyton kept his body curled back, suspicious. He didn't have any money for Darnell to steal. The only thing he had left was the carved faux head of his walking stick, but Darnell wouldn't see the value in that with the shaft broken.

Or would he? Peyton let his eyes move to his jacket at the foot of the bed. Had Darnell searched through it already? From the lump at the pocket, Peyton knew the carved rat's stump was still there, and he wished he had it in his hand now. He could use it to defend himself, or else it would just be a calming thing to hold on to.

"You know what this is about." Darnell's smile faded. "We been over it a hundred times. The way you pull Mama down. Keep mooching off her like a leech."

"I been away for five years," Peyton said.

"Yeah, and now you back with nowhere to go, right? No

job and nowhere to sleep, and sooner or later you're gon' be one more lazy-ass empty belly to feed around here."

Peyton felt himself heating up at Darnell's lies. "I'll get a job, Darnell. You'll see. I'll get a job with pay, and then Mama won't have to work so hard."

Darnell just laughed. "We know that's not gon' happen. Nobody's gonna hire a cripple like you, Peyton. And you can't blame them, with that lame leg and half your face all shriveled up." He hunkered to the side and let his jaw drop in a mean imitation of Peyton.

From that spark a fire roared to life inside Peyton. "Let me ask you this, Darnell," he said, his voice strong and clear. "Did you ever tell Mama the story of how I got this way? That the fall on the playground wasn't a fall after all?"

Darnell rolled his eyes. "Not that again. Nobody wants to hear it, Peyton."

"Did you tell her how you and your friends held me down and dropped a stone on my head to see what would happen? Because you thought it be funny?" Anger raced ahead of his thoughts, but Peyton tried to hold it all back, wanting this moment with his brother. After all this time, he deserved the truth.

And Darnell needed to hear it.

"All this time and you're still on that?" Darnell's smile was cold, his teeth bright white against the sheen of his dark skin. "You didn't learn then and you didn't learn now."

"What's that supposed to mean?" Peyton wished he had that walking stick spear in his hand now. One quick jab at his boy Darnell and he wouldn't be taunting anyone anymore.

"I'm talking about this cop, Marino. The one that threw you in jail, then showed everyone what a fool you are."

Peyton reached for his right hand and twisted his fingers open. "How'd you know about that?"

"I heard. Everybody heard. So what you gon' do about it?" He nodded at the bed. "Gon' to sleep on it?"

"I'm taking care of the cop," Peyton said slowly. That had

been his plan all along, right? You couldn't let evil like that walk away. Cruelty had to be punished, like it said in the Good Book. " 'If you do wrong, be afraid,' " he said aloud, quoting a passage from the Bible. Somewhere in the Bible. How did it end? Something about an angel of wrath, that would be him. "An angel of wrath will punish the wrong-doer." He looked Darnell in the eyes and felt his back straighten with his mission. "I'm the dark angel."

"You gon' foul this up, like you screwed up everything else."

"Not this time." The thought of punishing Marino cleared his mind. That was his purpose. An angel of wrath.

He knew what he needed to do.

Chapter 9

Yvonne Curtis tried not to limp like an old lady as she crossed the common space in front of the Blair Houses, but the bottom of her feet throbbed and the pain in the knots on top of her big toes stabbed through her feet like someone had hammered nails in there.

Arthritis, he'd told her. An hour and a half waiting for that specialist doctor to bring her into the office and tell her she had arthritis in the toes. That was a big waste of time. No, thank you.

She wanted to tell him it was from working long shifts on her feet. She wanted to say, "Doctor, you try standing on your feet all night in a laundry and tell me how your toes feel." Hotel laundry, giant vats of sheets and towels, a million germs and stains and sins all burned away with bleach. Yes, doctor, your dirty sheets, too!

It would have been worth the look on his face, but she minded her manners and listened as he wrote down the things she should do. Doctor told her to watch her weight, too, and she told him one more comment like that and she'd have to start charging *him.*

Yvonne snorted as she reached the elevator and pressed the button. Hopefully, they'd fixed it. She couldn't wait to get home and put her feet up. Got her dinner in this bag, enough to share with whoever was around, Gwen and Kiki, and lil' William, if he was still awake.

She thought of the call from Kiki, and remembered that her son Peyton was up there, fresh out of prison. Five long years she'd been worrying over him, praying for him at night. It was wrong that he got sent away for a robbery that she knew was Darnell's doing. Everyone knew it was Darnell who put the gun in Peyton's hand and pushed him into the lead, but when the two of them got hauled in by the police, Darnell claimed he was innocent and Peyton admitted to everything. Sentenced to five years. Her oldest son turned thirty in jail.

She cried that day of the trial, when they sentenced him and took her baby away for five years. Five years and he didn't even hurt anybody. That was justice for you.

She keyed her way in, calling, "Peyton? Where's my boy, after all these years?"

At first she thought no one was home; then she saw him sitting on the sofa, bent over and staring like he was thinking real serious.

"Baby, what you doin' sitting all alone in the dark?" She flicked the light on, saw that he had his sneakers on her coffee table. "Get your shoes off my table and come give your mama a hug."

Peyton rose, and she saw he was wearing a jacket with a bulge in his pocket. She hoped that wasn't a gun. Eyes on the ground, he shuffled over to her. "Hey, Mama."

"Oh, baby..." She folded him into her arms. "All these years, I been worried about you up there all alone in that prison."

"I know, Mama. I'm sorry."

"It's not your fault, Peyton. I know how it is. But you're back now and I brought you fried chicken." She patted his shoulder. "You want some chicken, baby? Biscuits, too."

"No, Mama, I can't eat. I . . . I can't take your food."

She squinted at him. "What? You been taking it since the day you were born."

He shook his head, staring at the floor. "I can't eat, Mama. Don't be mad."

"Who's mad? It's more for me, and it's my last bucket for a while, after doctor killjoy. Where's your sister and the others?"

"They went to eat with Gwen's boyfriend."

"Okay. You just relax now, honey. Now that you're out of prison, the worst is over, okay? Baby, you look so down. What they do to you in that prison?"

"It wasn't so bad." He shrugged, standing in the same spot as she went to the kitchen and took the chicken from the bag. "I had a friend there. My counselor, Angel."

"So you had an angel of mercy?" she called from the kitchen area. "That's good. You sure you don't want a plate? There's wings in here."

"No. No, thank you."

She felt a surge of pride. Five years in prison and her boy still said thank you. She had done something right.

"Well, I hope you don't mind if I eat, because I've been working in the laundry all day and I am tired and hungry." She emerged from the kitchen area with a plate and lowered herself to a chair opposite the couch.

"From what the man from Lakeview Shock said on the phone, I thought you'd be here yesterday. You make some stops?"

"I . . . I got arrested last night."

She stopped chewing. "Oh, Peyton. What did you do?"

"Nothing. I was just in the subway, minding my business when this cop, this . . . Marino is his name . . ." He shook his head as his face crumpled in pain.

"But they let you go?"

He nodded. "It was a mistake. They were looking at me for some rapes that happened while I was locked up."

She rolled her eyes. "When are those cops going to leave you alone?"

He just shook his head. "I don't know, Mama, but this time I didn't do anything wrong, I swear."

"Don't swear, but I believe you, sure I do. You've been having a string of bad luck, baby, and I don't believe it's your fault
at all."

Here she was, talking to her grown son of thirty-one years
old like he was a twelve-year-old boy, but that was always the
way she'd had to handle Peyton. He was around twelve when
he had that accident down on the playground. Hurt his head
bad, and never really recovered from it. After that he had the
limp and the bad hand. Half his face sagging. One doctor said
it was a palsy he would grow out of, but he never got better.
Just stayed the same, and she believed he was somehow locked
into the world of a ten-year-old, whatever that was.

Her eyes grew wide as he reached into the bulging pocket of
his jacket. The object he took out wasn't familiar. A white
statue on a stick, sort of.

"What's that?"

"A cane. This is just the handle that's left. Angel gave it to
me." He held it toward her. "See the animal? Angel said it was
a horse, but I think it looks like a rat. I call it a rat-horse. It's
made of faux."

"Okay." She nodded at the sculpture that more than filled
his hand. Its beady black rat eyes gave her the creeps. "So
what you planning? Of course, you can stay here. Gwen will
sleep with me so you can have a room."

"I don't want to be a bother, Mama."

"No bother." At least, not for now. Down the road it would
be great if he met a nice girl and got the hell out of here. Men
his age shouldn't be living with their mothers. But right now
he was just a worry, with that haunted look in his eyes.

"I won't be another lazy-ass empty belly to feed."

"Watch your language, and sure you won't be a problem.
You'll find some work this time. There's jobs in the city and
you got a brain, Peyton." And a handicap. He could make that
work for him.

He stood up, cradling the handle of the stick in the crook of
his arm like a baby. "G'night, Mama."

"You get some rest, now. You'll feel better in the morning."

She watched him head down the hall, then grabbed another drumstick and sank onto the couch and into a funk of regrets.

What was wrong with him? He used to be such a fine son. Had a good mind. That boy was going places. Might have gotten a scholarship but something went wrong after he got hurt. He just seemed to give up, didn't listen when she told him you got to keep on keeping on.

Peyton was her firstborn, her baby when she was a baby, too. She'd thought his daddy would stick around, but no. That man stuck her with little man Peyton and another one on the way, stuck her living with her own crazy mama. It was too much back then, with Peyton and Gwen. And then she met Darnell's daddy and whoo. Another mistake.

But God bless Peyton. Your first baby is the one you never forget, no matter how much you screw up with them. She did much better with the girls. Boys were near impossible to raise.

Like Darnell. Well, he was another story, not blood kin but she took him in and tried to set him right. That Darnell had a mind of his own and got him into a mess of trouble.

But the girls turned out better.

She crunched on a piece of crispy skin, thinking if she'd had all girls like Rhonda Shakes on the third floor, her life would have been so much easier.

Chapter 10

"Just call me back, okay?" Sarah tried not to sound whiny as she ended the message to her husband, but she was tired and on a roll here at work, and it seemed grossly unfair that she would be called upon, once again, to leave work and go home and deal with child-care issues when Brendan had been off for an hour already.

She took the packs of disheveled paper from her in-box and stacked them neatly on the desk. *If I could just have two more hours here, I could get this stuff done.*

Not that it was interesting. God, no. As an architect with the New York City Department of Buildings, Sarah was charged with reviewing blueprints, permits, building and demolition applications.

Of course, when she'd signed on she was convinced that she'd eventually be promoted into a dynamic, worthwhile position in which she would be hobnobbing with developers like the Donald and architects like Gluckman or Kondylis. She had thought she would be fundamental in revitalizing the tired structures and replacing the dead with buildings that reflected the pizzazz, elegance, and strength of New York City.

Ha.

She had thought she'd have a hand in preserving the great structures—the Flatiron Building, the Brooklyn Bridge, the

Chrysler Building—and addressing the "problem areas," like . . . well, most of Queens; the Mets' new stadium, where too many seats had a restricted view; the boxy Cineplexes; the Unisphere—please! She could go on complaining for an hour.

But no one was consulting Sarah on the façades of New York City. Instead, she was approving plans for bumped-out kitchens, family room extensions, mother-daughter additions, and apartments over garages.

I'm just here to rubber-stamp things, she thought as she literally pounded a rubber stamp on the blueprints for a boxy family room to be added to a residential dwelling in Rockaway Beach. With windows for ventilation and an outside door for escape, the room was up to code, but Sarah would be the first to agree that the design was hideous.

Back in architecture school, she had been told that a strong architect possessed the eye of an artist along with the pragmatism of an engineer. The idea seemed charming and yet grounded, but she was still waiting for a chance to reveal her creativity here in this dusty, airless city office.

And this application for a variance so that the homeowner could build a shed near the property line . . . really? Was this what she attended architecture school for?

Sarah had begun to dread the tedium of her job, but secretly she enjoyed the cut-and-dried approval process that appealed to her organizational skills. Besides, getting out of the house, taking a break from the bickering and cleaning, even wearing heels and a nice sweater were perks she couldn't bear to give up right now.

"But what if we have another?" Brendan kept asking her. "Let's have a third, hon. A little boy, or a mini-you. Another little Sarah."

She had been dragging her feet on a decision, knowing that, if they had a third kid, this job would become the indulgence that would have to be sacrificed.

But she was getting older . . . Brendan, too. He'd just turned thirty-four, and she was staring at the big three-oh next month. If they were going to make a move, the time was now.

Yeah, the time really was now, because she was overdue on refilling her birth control prescription. By the time she got out of here this evening, their local pharmacy would be closed. Damn. She wanted to switch to one of those twenty-four-hour places, but Brendan was fiercely loyal to the neighborhood they'd grown up in. In Bayside Hills you got your prescriptions filled by Joe, you bought rock salt and hardware from Posners and bagels from Oasis. Loyal to a fault and defender of the meek, that was Brendan.

It was the quality that had first drawn her to him in high school. They'd had coed gym together, and when athletic, popular Brendan had captained a dodge ball team, he'd picked Steven Yi, a kid with some kind of physical handicap, first. Sarah had expected the other guys in the class to groan, but when Brendan stood tall with his hand on Steven's shoulder, no one made a peep. Later in the process Sarah had been picked for Brendan's team, and she was still by his side.

She was rubber-stamping a plan for a breezeway when the phone rang. It was Brendan, with a bad connection.

"Got your message," he said. Then there was something about being in the truck, and she heard him say "Puchinko." Kevin Puchinko was one of the cops he worked with in the 109th Precinct, and over the last year the guys had put together a landscaping business.

"You're breaking up," she told him. "What are you and Kevin doing?"

"Estimates. Remember I told you about it? We've got appointments with people. One lady wants a fountain in her backyard."

"Oh. At least I can hear you now." She had forgotten about the landscaping appointments. "So that's why Peg picked the girls up from school today. Okay, I get it. The problem is, they want Gracie to wear a red T-shirt in one scene of the show, and

I'm not sure there's one in the house that fits her. Can you stop by the house and see?"

"A red T-shirt?" He made it sound ludicrous. "You can't check?"

"I can't leave work now. And if she doesn't have one, one of us is going to have to get her out shopping. Tonight. Before the stores close." That would screw up dinner and bedtime. She stared at the picture of a sun-drenched pyramid that was part of her screen saver. Oh, to be there, standing on the hot sands of Egypt . . .

"I guess we can swing by," he said reluctantly.

"Thank you, honey." Sarah hated throwing the task on her husband, but it was impossible to manage everything from her desk at the office. When she'd gotten the call from Peg, who'd been told about the costume change at school, she'd railed against the school for being so disorganized. But she was over it now. It didn't help to point blame. As Brendan liked to say, "Either lead, follow, or get out of the way." She would get out of the way on this one, now that Brendan was in control.

She slipped her shoes off under her desk and rubbed her feet together. "How are the estimates going?"

"Good. I really don't want to stop to do costuming for the pain-in-the-ass school show."

In the background Kevin mentioned something about a costume malfunction and laughed.

"It's so important to Gracie," she said. "She's so nervous about her solo."

"I know, I know. It's just . . . one step up and two steps back."

"I hear ya." The plans in front of her proposed to install four toilets in a residential basement. Really. What were they smoking? She pulled that one aside for further review and glanced up at the majestic sun and moon pagodas on her screen saver. The moon was lit by silver lights, the sun gold, and the sight of the two tiered towers rising gracefully to the heavens always made her want to sigh. Two elegant columns of gems sparkling on the water.

China. Someday she and Brendan would go there to visit the Great Wall, ancient pagodas, and gravity-defying skyscrapers. It was one of the places on the list of architectural gems she'd been compiling.

Someday, they would see them all.

But for now, a red T-shirt, girls' size ten, was the priority of the day.

Chapter 11

Gracie shone onstage, with the help of a sparkling snow-flake on her shirt. The lights onstage caught the wispy edges of her hair as she sang "Winter Wonderland" along with the other fourth graders in the auditorium at St. Peter's Catholic School. The auditorium itself hadn't changed much since Bernie and Brendan and their siblings had attended the school, but Bernie was glad to hear that the format of the pageants now included more updated songs. Back in her school days the raciest song they did was "This Land Is Your Land" with a folk guitar accompaniment.

The ethnicity of the student body had changed as well. It was no longer just neighborhood Catholics who sent their kids here, but also families from nearby communities who were willing to pay for the "safety" of a private school. The faces that now smiled out at the audience reflected the beautiful mosaic that was Queens, mixing kids from white, African-American, Asian, and Hispanic families.

"Oh, that's just wonderful," Mary Sullivan said in a loud voice. Nearly ninety, Granny Mary had lost her sense of decorum along with parts of her memory a few years ago. These days, you could count on Granny Mary to be cheerful but out of it.

Bernie turned to her and patted her shoulder. "We need to be quiet now, Granny, so everyone can hear."

Seated in the row in front of them were Sarah and Brendan, along with Brendan's partner Indigo Hilson and her baby girl, Zuli, who enjoyed standing on the chair backward and mouthing the bar at the top. Sarah turned around and smiled at Bernie, as if to say, *good luck with Granny.*

"Okay, okay." Granny patted the back of her hairdo and turned back to the performers.

On the other side of Mary, her son Sully exchanged a whisper with Peg. Bernie gave them a lot of credit. They'd been attending performances in this drab basement for years, and yet they faced every show with enthusiasm.

The song ended, and applause peppered the air.

"This is a good school, you know," Granny said. Her loud voice wasn't a problem with the applause and the shuffling onstage to set up the next song.

"I know," Bernie agreed.

"I've got a young one coming up next year. He's already registered for kindergarten."

Bernie's mouth dropped open in momentary surprise, but she covered quickly and nodded. "Really?"

"He's a sweet little guy. Those big round eyes, but stubborn as a mule." Lines creased her face as Mary Sullivan smiled.

So you had him in your mideighties? Bernie wanted to say. *We have to get you into the* Guinness Book of World Records, *Granny.*

"Really?" Bernie had to fight to keep a straight face.

"Oh, yeah. And where are your wee ones tonight?" Granny's eyes narrowed. "Are they performing later?"

"Me?" Bernie froze as embarrassment washed over her. It was the great failure of her life, not having kids at age twenty-seven. Not even married yet. The old-maid card had not been in her plans.

"I'm still single, Granny. No kids yet."

"Oh." Although she had explained her childlessness to her grandmother before, it took a moment for Granny to digest the facts. "But you're getting on in your years, honey." She put a hand up to cover her comment, but her voice was as loud as ever. "You know, you can get him to marry you if you get pregnant first."

Sully leaned forward for that one. "Ma, the show's starting again," he said. "Let's keep quiet and watch."

"Okay."

As the third and fourth grades took the stage to sing "Frosty the Snowman," Bernie sank into herself to coddle her wound.

Single and pushing thirty. Why did it bother her so much when women were waiting much longer to have a family? You could still get pregnant at forty, God forbid.

Oh, it hurt when she thought about it. Not just because she craved kids more than chocolate. The real crux of the dilemma was that she had fallen in love, but it didn't work out.

And she was still in love.

Much as she tried to deny it, the attraction was there, the scintillating, addictive lure that had her looking across the aisle at Keesh, calling him when the littlest thing happened, meeting him for breakfast or dinner or coffee whenever she could trump up a lame reason for an invite. Keesh was in her head every night as she tried to drop off to sleep. Sweet thoughts, though lately she'd been worrying about his move to the Queens DA and dreading the day he told her he had a new girlfriend.

Had they made a mistake, calling it quits?

They'd been a good couple, best friends and lovers, until their fathers got involved.

Her first mistake had been telling her father his real first name.

"You're dating a guy named Rashid?" Sully asked her one day after Mass, having overheard her sharing the name with Sarah.

"It's just Keesh, Dad," she had said. Her father had already met him more than once and had found Keesh respectful and polite. "But yeah, his real name is Rashid."

"Good Lord, he sounds like a terrorist!" The stained glass windows in the vestibule of St. Peter's reverberated with the thunder of Sully's voice. "And where did the name Keesh come from? Is that an alias?"

"It's just a nickname his friends dreamed up." She avoided explaining that, as kids, when they called him "Sheed," grown-ups got annoyed because it sounded like "shit."

"My parents wanted me to have a good Armenian name," he'd said. It was important to Salat and Ara Kerobyan to pre-serve their Armenian culture, a goal Bernie respected until she realized it struck her from the list of possible wives for their son. Keesh had explained that *Rashid* was from the Arabian for "teacher" or "tutor." It also meant "walking the right road," an apt description for Keesh.

"And Kerobyan," Keesh told her with a smile, "that comes from *Kerovbeh*, which means 'angel.'"

"A teaching angel? Oh, you're just too good to be true." And she'd kissed him then and pressed against him for an ac-tivity that was the antithesis of angelic.

Oh, she missed those days. Twenty-seven and she was on the downward slope.

Life was fickle. Only in Queens could the son of a world-renowned brain surgeon from Armenia fall in love with the daughter of an Irish Catholic cop who had parlayed his retire-ment into a local coffee shop. And though she understood her father's trauma from the World Trade Center attacks and Dr. Kerobyan's desire to preserve his culture, she sometimes wanted to rail against them both and point out that this was the twenty-first century in the great melting pot of America.

Or as her mother would say, "Get over it."

A song ended and Maisey was in the group taking a bow.

Bernie clapped briskly, shouting, "Go, Maisey!"

Granny Mary looked at her bare wrist and frowned. "It's late. I've got to get home and start the pot roast." She stood up and turned to go, spry as ever, though, in truth, she hadn't cooked a roast for at least ten years.

In a flash, Sully was on his feet, guiding her back to her chair. "Sit down, Ma. You're coming to our house for a bite to eat after the pageant."

"I am?" She patted the back of her hair. "Well, I hope my deodorant doesn't let me down."

Bernie linked her fingers through her grandmother's. "You smell good to me, Granny."

"April fresh!" Mary said.

Brendan leaned back from the row in front and touched Granny's knee. "This is where Grace has her solo," he explained. "That's your great-granddaughter up there."

Granny waved him off. "Oh, I know all that." But she quieted as the pianist began the first notes of the song "Some Children See Him."

The piece was familiar to Bernie, who had heard a version sung by James Taylor.

Four children in red T-shirts stood on stage. Bernie held her breath as the intro slowed and Grace stepped forward.

"Some children see him lily white, the infant Jesus born this night . . ." Grace's voice was thin as a reed, and yet her sincerity and warmth held it together.

A girl with lush dark hair and mocha skin stepped forward to sing the second verse about children who see God "bronzed and brown." The next verse, about an "almond-eyed" God, was sung by David Chong, a Chinese boy whom Brendan's kids knew from the neighborhood.

For the fourth verse, Tasha Hilson, Indigo's daughter, stepped forward and sang: "Some children see Him dark as they, Sweet Mary's Son to whom we pray . . ." Of all the children, Tasha had the voice, a belter. Bravo, Tash. Make it work for you.

The four students joined together for the next verse, which described how children of all races see their own image in Baby Jesus's face. The choice of vocalists for the song hit its message hard, and Bernie wondered if it was having its desired effect. She glanced past Granny Mary to her dad and noticed tears shining in Sully's eyes. Okay, he got it. But could he take it home and really embrace it?

Probably not. As soon as the glow wore off, he would be suspicious once again of a man of Middle Eastern descent named Rashid.

Racism and fear ran deep.

Watching Gracie and the other kids onstage, she felt that maternal tug and her throat grew tight at the possibility that she might never have a baby. How would she get there from here when she didn't even have a boyfriend?

Chapter 12

"Can't we leave Zuli in the car?" Eager to get inside to the party at the Sullivans', Tasha hopped at the edge of the open car door.

"You never leave a child alone in a car," Indigo Hilson told her daughter. "I'll carry her. You just close the door after me, and push the lock button on the keypad, okay?"

"Uh-huh."

"I'm sorry, I can't hear you."

"Yes, ma'am."

"That's better." Indigo extracted Zuli from the car, her feet dangling, her maroon lips hanging open in the throes of sleep.

Dutifully, Tasha slammed the big door, pressed the button to make the car screech to alarm, and ran toward the house.

"What's your hurry?" Indigo called after her.

"Grace said there's cake."

"Give me the keys and you can go."

Tasha looked down at the keys in her hand, as if she had forgotten they were there. She hurried back, put them in her mother's hand, then skipped up the sidewalk toward the lights of the house.

"Thank you," Indigo called after her. She was glad that her daughter didn't share her intimidation about entering the Sullivans' house in Bayside Hills. Not that the place was so grand;

the intimidating part was that it belonged to Sully, the famous cop who'd served till they made him retire. Sully was an NYPD Personality. People talked about him as if he'd run the entire department. And now that he'd retired, Indigo figured the man was one miracle away from sainthood.

Indigo Hilson still found it hard to believe that she was partners with Brendan Sullivan. Two years ago, when they first landed in the 109th Precinct in a group of six transferred patrol officers, she'd been determined to work with a woman. In her experience, working with a man—especially a married man—incited jealousies and got people's tongues wagging, even when you were just friends.

She'd been determined to hook up with Connie Strazinski, and had been resigned to a year or so of Connie's idiot questions like: "Do you think he's into me?" or "Does this uniform make my ass look fat?"

But then she got the phone call, not from Brendan, but from his wife, Sarah. "I don't know if you remember me," Sarah said, "but we chaperoned a class trip together at St. Peter's."

Indigo told her she remembered, and she did. Of the three moms, Sarah had been the only one who didn't have a baby clamped onto her breast or a shiny Mercedes waiting in the parking lot.

"So I just want you to know, Brendan and I, we talk about what goes on at the precinct a lot. You know, he likes to unwind, and I like to hear his stories. Anyway, not to sound like the manipulative wife, but I want you to know that it's totally fine with me if you two hook up as partners. Actually, you're really the best choice, because Puchinko is too much of a talker. Nice guy, but a motormouth. Between you and me, it sounds like Walters has a drinking problem, and Thornton, the guy's been divorced three times. The jokes about giving Brendan a Jacoby and Meyers gift certificate just don't fly around here."

"Wow." Indigo had known that she liked Brendan's wife, but she had no idea that she'd click with her like this. "You've got your finger on the pulse of our little hotbed of law enforcement."

"That's what we're trying to avoid, isn't it? Keep the hotbed out of the precinct and in the home?"

The two women had laughed at the same time, and just like that, they became friends. Over the past two years, they had grown closer, and Indigo had gotten to know Brendan pretty well, too. In truth, it was the first white man she'd ever had as a friend, and boy, did she luck out. Brendan loved his wife and kids, cared about people on the street, came to work every day hoping to help at least one person before the end of the day, unlike some of the rookie guys who wished for a car chase or a chance to use their weapons.

Yeah, Brendan and Sarah were special people.

The door opened, casting light onto Tasha's expectant face.

"There she is!" Peg Sullivan, Brendan's mom, bent down to make a fuss over Tasha. "You were fantastic! Where did you learn to sing like that?"

Tasha shrugged. "My mom."

"Not true," Indigo laughed, stepping into the warmth and music.

"Grace is waiting for you. She told us we're not to cut the cake until you arrive." Peg pointed Tasha toward her friend, then greeted Indigo. "Oh, and the little one's asleep. Want me to take her to the back room? I've got a crib set up there."

"I can take her," Indigo offered.

"Let me have her." With tender efficiency, Peg scooped the baby from her arms. "You get settled and find yourself something to drink. There's coffee, tea, and stronger, if you like." Peg cradled Zuli with affection.

Indigo knew that Peg watched Brendan and Sarah's kids a lot; now she could see it was a labor of love.

"Thank you," Indigo said, "and thank you for inviting us."

"Our pleasure. Grace said it wouldn't be a party without her friend Tasha. Now I think Sarah's in the kitchen, and I see Brendan over in the dining room with the guys."

"I see him." Indigo nodded to Brendan as he raised a hand to gesture her over. Could she pretend she didn't see him? She wanted to join Sarah in the kitchen, where they could be themselves over a cup of tea, away from the cop talk and the pressure of having to face Sully, the bigger-than-life Godfather of Cops. But Brendan was calling her name now.

She followed Peg into the house, and peeled off at the dining room.

"Hey, you." Indigo tapped Brendan's shoulder with her fist. "So what did you think of our girls up there?"

"Awesome performance," Brendan said. "I was proud of all of them."

"Very talented kids." Sully beamed, a highball glass of whiskey rocks in his hand. "And the solos they did . . . take out the two boys and we would've had Charlie's Angels up there."

Brendan and his sister Bernie laughed, though Indigo had to push a smile. She could think of a lot of career aspirations for her daughter that would top undercover bimbo.

Puchinko was also there with his wife, Laura. They also had a kid at St. Pete's, a son in fourth grade who seemed content to watch the SpongeBob movie Peg had set up in the back room.

"So Sully, what's your take on the new crime stats?" Puchinko asked. "Did you see the drop in violent crimes citywide? What do you think about that?"

Indigo stirred her tea, thinking that Puchinko sure liked to hear himself talk.

"I say you guys and gals are doing a good job out there." Sully spread his arms wide, reminding her of a huge eagle, and clapped Brendan and Puchinko on the back.

Brendan rocked forward from the contact, pretending to be spilling his drink.

He acted as if he didn't care, but Indigo happened to know that his father's approval was very important to Brendan. It was a guy thing.

That made her think of Elijah, and sorrow tugged at her.

Yeah, her husband needed that approval, too. Unfortunately, Elijah had lost all chance of pleasing his father when he married Indigo, and now it had crumbled into a situation beyond repair.

As the guys talked business she sipped her tea and wondered if there was something she could do to bring Elijah back to his kids. If he was done with her, she would deal with it, but he wasn't allowed to be done with their kids. Tasha and Zuli had a father, and she was going to make damn sure he didn't abandon them.

They talked about the police contract, and the issue of parity with the fire department. They talked about the education requirements for bosses, and Puchinko complained that the required sixty-four college credits had nothing to do with being a good boss. He was taking two community college classes at night, but said his wife complained that he was never home now.

"You're quiet tonight, Indigo Blue," Sully said, using a nickname Brendan had come up with.

"She just can't get a word in with Puchinko foaming at the mouth here," Brendan said.

Amid the chuckles, Puchinko made a fist and bumped Brendan on the shoulder. "You're lucky I got a thick skin, Sullivan."

"Thick skin and a big mouth," Laura said from the kitchen doorway. "Who wants cake?" She held up two slices of a blue and white frosted sheet cake.

Sully passed, but Brendan and Kevin accepted. "Come to Papa," Kevin said, eyeing the cake, then planting a kiss on his wife's cheek.

"So give me the latest from the 109. What's happening in my old stomping grounds?" Sully asked. "I miss the old grind."

"Ah, but you're on to the new grind," Puchinko said. "The coffee grind. And you're right across the street from the house every day. I bet you've got your finger on the pulse more than most of the bosses."

Sully's blue eyes had a misty quality that intrigued Indigo; masked wisdom. This was a man who had seen things, but didn't want to admit to the center of the spectrum, the wide gray area in which right and wrong mixed and bled into each other.

"I like to keep on top of things," Sully said, surveying the faces there. "You three came through the academy in the same class, right? How long have you been in the 109? Upwards of two years, right? Time for some movement?"

Brendan made eye contact with Indigo and shook his head very slightly. She got the message: keep mum. They had been talking about transferring together to a unit where they'd have weekends off. She had been looking into a parking detail in the precinct. It was boring, thankless work writing parkers all day long, but the hours were flexible. She could work when her kids were in school and be off for them on the weekends.

"Put in for it with me," she had told Brendan. "Come on. It'll be tolerable if we do it together."

"My old man would have a cow," he'd told her. "Sarah would love it. I'd love it. But Sully, he'd be mortified that I'd become a meter maid."

"I'm looking at getting into the warrants unit." Puchinko scratched at a spot on his upper arm. He was a broad-shouldered guy who could come off as intimidating, but Indigo had never seen him lose his cool. "I got an application in, but it may be going right into the circular file."

"Warrants . . ." Sully took a sip of his whiskey, considering. "Not a bad place to earn a shield. I could make some calls for you, if you're really interested."

"I'd appreciate it." Kevin clinked his beer against Sully's glass.

When Peg called, Sully excused himself to go snap some photos of the kids.

"Nice move, Puchinko," Indigo said. "But you forgot to drop to your knees and kiss his ring."

Everyone laughed at that.

"But you're missing the point, Indigo," Bernie said. "Dad wasn't a big boss, but he does have a lot of juice still. You need to use that. Everyone knows the plum details are all about the phone call."

Indigo nudged her partner, nodding at Bernie. "How does she know so much about the job?"

Brendan opened his arms wide. "She grew up sitting at this table. A lifetime of cop talk."

"And I always loved it." Cradling her mug, Bernie smiled. "I used to bow out of movies with my friends because I didn't want to miss hanging out here with Dad and his friends."

"God help you, girl." Indigo hadn't realized that everyone in the family had the father-worship issue. Who knew it would be so hard to have a father destined for sainthood?

Thank God her dad was just an ordinary bus driver.

Chapter 13

Someone was banging on his head. He rolled to his side, but the banging didn't stop.

The door. He looked to the window. Still dark.

Banging on the door in the middle of the night is never a good sign in the projects.

He pushed out of bed with his good arm and shuffled to the hall.

"Who the hell is it?" his mother asked, wrapping a robe around her bulk.

"Open up! New York City Police."

The cops. Aw, no. Hadn't they razzed him enough?

"Don't let them in, Mama." He gathered the front of his shirt, pulling it close around his neck. The heat was blazing in this building, but he was suddenly cold. Shivering.

He couldn't let the cops see him shaking like a scared chicken. "Don't open it."

"Open the door, or we'll break it down," the voice boomed.

Yvonne pressed her palms to her face. "You sure you got the right address?"

She threw the bolt and cracked the door as wide as the chain allowed. Peyton could see the sheen of the hall lights on the helmet of one of the cops. These guys weren't playing.

"That's a start, ma'am, but if you don't open it all the way, we'll have to break it."

"Officer, you must have the wrong address. Ain't nobody here that—"

Before she could finish, the door burst open, chains popping, and an armed soldier inched through the opening.

"Get back! Against the wall!"

Uniforms stormed in, along with men in dark clothes with black jackets that had something printed on them. Peyton couldn't see what was written there because he was thrown against the wall, the weak side of his face smashed to the plaster. It pressed through his cheek, boring into his bone.

He moaned, but someone kept pushing him. Hands searched his body. Through the haze of pain he heard his mother talking to them.

"What you doing? Don't hurt him! He's hurt already!"

"We've got a warrant for his arrest."

Was that Marino? Had the cop come to salt his wounds?

"What the—that's a mistake. It has to be."

With one pop eye he saw cops move into the living room, their guns drawn like soldiers in Afghanistan. A dozen feet pounded the floor, the foul stench of sweat soiling the air.

Suddenly the pressure lifted and he was pulled from the wall, someone's hand yanking him by the neck of his shirt. He gasped at the air, stumbling back. The big man swung him round till he was leaning against the wall. He wasn't shaking anymore, just reeling from the pain in his head.

"This our guy?" One of the cops held a wrinkled paper, a mug shot, next to Peyton's face. "I don't think it's him."

"Nope."

"Who you looking for?" Mama asked.

"Jason Miller."

"Jason Miller? He's not here. I'm telling you, he doesn't live here."

"You know where we can find him?" the cop asked.

"What you want him for?"

Peyton slid down the wall, miserable. Jason Miller. He didn't know who that was. Or . . . wait. Was it the guy Gwen hooked up with?

"We have a warrant for his arrest." The main cop, the one in charge, had a cue ball head and dark eyebrows. It wasn't Marino. But that didn't mean Marino didn't put him up to it.

He stayed there on the floor, right there where he'd dropped. What was the sense in messing with the cops, who'd only push him 'round or find some other reason to arrest him?

He sat still and quiet, but he wasn't quiet inside. Hatred was tearing at him, a growl that got louder every time he breathed against the pain that cop gave him at the back of his neck.

Breathing like a wild animal, it was roaring in his head by the time the cops left.

Peyton got his shoes on while Mama went from room to room, worrying over anything the cops might have moved.

"Not too bad," she said, "but I'd sure as hell like to know what they want Jason for. I told Gwen something didn't sit right with that man when I met him, but—"

Peyton rose and pulled on his jacket.

"Where you think you're goin'?"

He didn't answer. He couldn't form words over the roaring in his head.

"Peyton . . ." She stepped in front of him. "You wait a minute before you go chargin' out of here."

He felt bad for disrespecting her, but he had to go. It was the only way to keep the noise from getting louder and crushing him.

"Peyton? Baby, hold on!" She grabbed at his shoulder, but he broke free and was out the door.

He knew what he had to do.

It was clear now.

Riding the elevator down, he didn't care that it smelled like old paint and piss. He wouldn't be coming back to this hellhole, and that was fine by him.

He had something to do.

* * *

He kept to the handrail as he lowered himself down the steps of the Seaport subway station. Almost four o'clock. The digital numbers hurt his eyes—red glare—and he looked down at the turnstile to make sure he ran the card through right. He didn't want to give the cops any reason to pick him up again.

The platform was vacant, not as cold as the other night when Marino had made him sit on the platform, shivering in the draft. He walked right by that spot now, glad the place was empty. Maybe the cops had found their rapist. Maybe they were just working another station tonight.

At the far end of the platform, he had to swing around a lip to reach the steel rods of the ladder. Most people didn't know it was there, but he'd found it years ago. New York subway stations had plenty of hidey-holes, if you knew where to look.

The steel rods of the ladder were clean and the tiles were shiny. Like someone steam-cleaned it recently. That made him nervous. He didn't want subway workers snooping around here.

He hoped they didn't find his hiding place. Four tunnels came together here, like worms trying to squeeze into the same apple. He passed the green signal light and went to the short tunnel in the middle, a short track where they sometimes parked maintenance trains.

This part wasn't so clean. The only sound was the shuffling of his feet and the scratch and squeal of rats galloping out of his way. Yeah, his friends were still here. He hoped they didn't build a nest near his stash. He didn't want to hurt them, but he would.

He needed his gun.

When he got his first job he started saving for a gun. Back then he planned to protect himself and get back at all his tormentors.

Tormentors like Darnell, who kicked you and beat on you for no good reason.

The day came when he had enough money for a .38 revolver, but then he knew it wasn't safe at home. He could only hide it in Mama's flour tin for so long before she smacked him upside the head with it. Besides, it wasn't safe from Darnell in the apartment.

So he came down here, late, when no one was around. Working at night, he chiseled out a brick from a wall.

He remembered thinking he was like the Birdman of Alcatraz. Only he'd be the Ratman of Queens.

He had worked the mortar out with a key and a screwdriver until he could slide the concrete block out. There was a place in the hollow of the block for his revolver. And nobody knew about it except the rats and him.

Twelve steps into the darkness and three to the right, and there it was, his stone. The dark putty that he'd put around it was soft and dry, but he hadn't brought anything to pick it out with. He took the sharp, splintered end of his walking stick and poked at it.

Nice and easy, it loosened up. One section peeled out in a long strip. When it was all out, he used the stick as a lever to jimmy the stone out.

And there it was, wrapped in a plastic bag.

The gun had saved his skin plenty of times. He'd needed protection after the beating, when he limped along like a dying dog. Some kids saw him as easy prey then, and he'd had to let them know what was what. The gun had helped.

The plastic bag whispered to the ground as the cold steel fitted itself to his left hand.

He'd learned to do everything with his left hand after his right side got screwed up. There'd been no money for doctors, so he never knew what really happened. One of the prison docs told him it was a brain injury. Real obvious. Another doctor called it Bell's palsy, but that was supposed to get better on its own and that never happened. Not that you get the best care in prison, but you do get to see a doctor.

The distant high-pitched sound of brakes let him know a train was coming. He waited in the shadows.

Light bounced off the walls in the outer tunnel, but his cave stayed dark as the train screeched into the station. This little spur of track was still not being used.

He broke the gun open and checked the chambers. Six bullets, and no backup. That was okay. He only needed one. He was glad he had a revolver. Sitting here five years, some automatics might jam up. Revolvers were more reliable.

He spread his legs and raised his left hand. The cool steel of the gun fit into his left hand. He stood there, practicing in his mind as the train left the station and rattled through the tunnel, churning down to silence. He aimed the piece in the air, pointed it at Marino's orange face. One steady pull of the trigger, and yeah. Marino would have a bullet right between the eyes.

Chapter 14

The third day of the Lobster Shift had ended for Bernie and Keesh, and just when it was over, Bernie was starting to feel as if her body had made the adjustment.

"I have a love-hate thing going on with the Lobster Shift," she said as she stole one of Keesh's French fries. It was cold, but adequately salty. "The complaint reports that surface after midnight, I don't know. There's definitely an edgier feel to them. Working the night shift is like taking a trip to the underworld of the planet. It's a fascinating voyage, but it consumes you. Zaps your energy. Sucks the air out of life. I'm even too exhausted to sleep."

"Yeah. Working from one to nine in the morning is a real kick in the teeth. Screws up your circadian rhythms."

"But the need is real. Somebody has to help these people through the system." She grabbed another fry.

"Do you want me to get you some fries?" With his dark brows lowered, he could look so stern.

"No, thanks. Too much fat."

"You're not on a diet, are you?" he asked, turning to her. "You look fine just the way you are."

The sincerity in his voice nearly made her swoon. "I love you," she said, and they both laughed.

They sat side by side at the counter of Happy's Deli, a spot frequented by downtown lawyers, mostly because of its convenience to 100 Centre Street. A handful of prosecutors working the night shift had agreed to meet after work, partly because it would be Keesh's last Lobster Shift and partly because they were ravenous after staying up all night. But only two others. Meryl DuBois, the Legal Aid attorney who always made Bernie think of a mom who was late for a PTA meeting, had toasted Keesh with coffee, and Rich Lopez had downed a bagel, but headed home to collapse.

So now it was down to the two of them, drunk with exhaustion and unwilling to separate. Keesh was such a good friend. Fun and easy to be with. But right now, with the way the watery light from the window outlined his dark hair—which was a little wild from the long night but could easily qualify as a sexy disarray—right now she felt very attracted to him. His dark eyes, so dark they sometimes reminded her of shiny, black obsidian, often seemed to challenge her to locate the warm center of his personality that he kept buried under that cold façade.

How had she let him go? If she dismissed the fact that their families had put the kibosh on their Irish-Armenian union, she could imagine a wonderful day spent with Keesh. And really, parents be damned, they were two adults in their twenties. What was to stop them from going back to her place? They would slam the door behind them and fall into each other's arms. They'd peel each other's clothes off on the way to the bedroom, then make love like two crazy people atop her overstuffed white comforter. And then, skin against skin, they'd snuggle under the covers and fall asleep in each other's arms.

It was a delicious vision.

Bernie felt a growing hunger, even though she'd just eaten.

Her sister's rotten comment about her dwindling ovaries popped into her head, and she bit her lower lip at the prospect of letting the passion of the moment overcome the pause for birth control.

And maybe she would get pregnant, and then their families

would have to back down and work through their prejudices. Surely, for a new baby in the family, a grandchild . . .

Oh, sleep deprivation didn't slow the hormones.

Of course, Bernie would have to see if Keesh was on board, but right now she was very turned on by the prospect of getting naked with him, and soon.

"So." She wiped her hands on a paper napkin. "Got plans for the day?"

"Sleep." His eyes were on the counter, his lids lowered as if he could drop off right here in the deli.

"Well, yeah." And since I'm one of the few New Yorkers also dropping into bed at nine a.m., how about we keep each other company? She sent him mental vibes, wanting him to ask her, wanting to be courted.

But he just gathered trash onto the plastic tray.

"So." She decided to go for it. "If you're not—"

"Actually, I do have plans today." He stood up and brought the tray over to the garbage can. "Hanging out with a friend later."

"Oh, yeah?" She wasn't deterred. They could still be together now. "One of your buds from college?"

"Actually, she's an attorney, too."

Bernie's coffee went bitter on her tongue. She? His friend was a she?

Of course, he had every right. They'd been officially broken up for months now. But still . . . the news was a dagger in her chest.

"Been seeing her awhile?" she prodded.

He shook his head. "Just . . . it's still kind of new." He pointed to the half-eaten fruit salad in front of her. "You finished with this?"

"Done." She waved it away, sliding off the stool, amazed to find there was solid ground beneath her feet after all. After the news, it didn't seem to be a given anymore.

Keesh was seeing someone. He'd moved on.

The air around her was suddenly cold, and she wrapped her

scarf around her neck and zipped her jacket to the neck. They would walk to the uptown subway, then take the number seven train out to Queens, just like always.

But today was different, the beginning of the end.

She was losing Keesh, losing him to another woman and another job.

And if she was really honest with herself, she'd have to admit that she'd already lost him.

Chapter 15

Six bullets.

It had been a long time since he'd shot a gun, and as he got off the train at Main Street, Flushing, with the weight of the pistol in his jacket, Peyton worried that six bullets would not be enough to kill a monster like Marino.

Six chances.

But you could kill a man with one.

One bullet was all it would take, if he got it right.

Get it right. Can you get it right this time? Darnell's voice sniped at him, but he shook it off. Not now, Darnell. He had something important to do.

He would make it work.

He had to. He had to end the torture, the brutality he'd suffered at that man's hands.

He could still see the glittering hatred in his eyes, hear his animal cackle as the cop stood over him. His bulk had blocked the sun as Peyton looked up, praying for mercy but knowing it would not come.

For a moment as Marino stretched up toward the sky, light eclipsed over the rock in his hands.

And then a starburst explosion that sent Peyton into darkness.

It was wrong, what Marino did, and Peyton was going to stop him from doing it to anyone else.

The subway steps at the Main Street Station were steep, but he struggled up, not wanting attention from taking the elevator.

From the top step the street rose above him, a clutter of store signs, buses, and humanity.

Each step up the hill caused him pain, but he had to get there. It was up to him to set Marino right.

The precinct was at the end of the street, a rundown box of a building. His gut wrenched at the sight of uniformed cops oozing out of the building. He slowed, keeping his eyes on the ground, but they didn't care about him. Two of them passed him without a second look. He watched them climb into a patrol car that was parked crooked on the street. They didn't even see him at all.

He went straight in through the front doors. More cops, but none of them was Marino. He ignored them and went straight to the cop at the front desk. This guy had a neck as thick as a tree trunk. There were medals and a gold badge on his uniform. Someone special. His nameplate said: Todd.

"Can I help you?"

The roar swelled in his head, then went dead as Peyton formed the words he had practiced. "I'm looking for Officer Marino."

"Marino?" He squinted. "Do you have a first name?"

"No. Just Marino."

Todd scratched his neck. "Nope. No Marinos working right now. Is there something I can help you with?"

The noise rose again, rage swelling inside him. Was this cop covering for Marino, or just being a dumb ass?

Peyton didn't trust him. He wanted to dive across the desk and pummel Officer Todd.

He pressed his eyes shut.

You can't pummel anyone. You can barely stand up straight.

He shoved his left hand into his pocket and bumped into the steel, his hand closing around it for comfort.

I can't stand up straight, but I've got a gun.

A gun with six bullets.

Save them for Marino. He's the one.

Peyton's nostrils flared as he sucked in air. This was going to take more time, and he was losing patience.

"Where can I find Marino?" he asked the desk cop.

"Get me a first name. I'm sure there are a hundred Marinos in the department."

A hundred . . .

No, that was no good.

You'll never find him. You can't do nothing right.

Peyton backed away from the desk slowly as the trembling noise began to shudder around him. He had to do something, and if he couldn't find Marino, this might be a place to start, with Officer Todd and his fat neck.

In his pocket, his fingers closed around the gun, and he thought of the six bullets. And if Todd took one—and all these other cops around here—he'd never get to Marino.

Get it right. Get it right, you retard.

The noise reached a burning pitch, shrill and high like the sting of antiseptic on an open wound. It pushed him back from the desk. Back out the door and out of the police precinct.

Not here, not now.

Not yet.

Chapter 16

A t the bank Sully let another customer go in front of him so that he could wait for his favorite teller, Mrs. Jadoon. Sully did not suffer fools gladly, and the middle-aged woman from Pakistan was efficient and accurate, unlike some of the college kids back there whose thoughts were always racing in a million directions.

Years on patrol had carved some life lessons into Sully. Stay in control. Weigh your options. And don't take anything too seriously, because tomorrow, it might be gone anyway.

As he waited, he kept one eye on the line of tellers, the other on the door. Despite cameras and the bulletproof glass protecting the tellers, banks were still apt targets, and his worst nightmare was getting caught unaware, without his gun, radio, or backup. Of course, he had his piece, a small five-shot strapped to his ankle. He'd never needed it, thank God, and any patrol cop knows that your best line of defense is not your gun, but your partner and the cops at the other end of the radio, ready to back you up in an instant.

That was probably the hardest part of retirement for Sully: working without backup. No safety net, no camaraderie. His employees at the coffee shop, they weren't colleagues; just a staff of college students who called in sick when they had finals and didn't have a clue how to scrub a toilet. Or maybe they knew how, but just didn't care to do it.

Kids today. They wanted the good stuff without getting their hands dirty, his own kids included. Sometimes he wondered if his sons would be gainfully employed if he hadn't gotten them on track to take the police exam years ago.

At last, Mrs. Jadoon was free, and he moved up to the bulletproof glass with a smile. "How are you, Mrs. Jadoon?"

"I'm very fine, thank you." A smile graced her round face. Bahaar Jadoon, who'd told Sully she was from Pakistan, was a round woman with a very round face. She seemed to enjoy sparkly things, was always adorned with some kind of bangle earrings, pin, or scarf. "Just the deposit for you today?"

"I'd also appreciate it if you'd run these coins through your machine."

"No problem, Mr. Sully." She took the coin bag and went over to the machine.

Sully turned away from the tellers' glass and eyed the door again. Nothing unusual, though the yelp of a police siren sounded in the distance. He listened a moment, timing it. They were moving fast, and the lights and sirens blared a few seconds as the patrol unit passed. Odd, but it seemed to be going toward the station house.

Mrs. Jadoon returned to the window and slid the deposit ticket under the glass. "Do you want the coins in cash, or deposited to your account?" she asked as two other police cruisers whipped by, lights blinking in the glass doors for a moment.

"Wow. Sounds like your buddies need you," Mrs. Jadoon said.

"Naw . . . I'm an old retired guy now," Sully said, though he was curious to poke his head out the door and check it out. He asked her to deposit the total from the change, and she made quick work of it.

"Thank you, Mrs. Jadoon. I'll see you tomorrow."

"You have a very good day, sir."

He moved toward the door, fighting the urge to break into a run. Sixty-nine years old, and he could still do it. He could run ten blocks and still hold a conversation. Maybe it was pathetic that he still felt the urge to be in the thick of it, negotiating with people and making split-second decisions.

"Take your time, old man," he muttered to himself as he swung out the door. Nothing worse than an old-timer trying to recapture a hit of adrenaline from the old days.

Out on Roosevelt Avenue, the usual flow of traffic and pedestrians clogged the streets and sidewalks. Sully headed back to the shop, pausing to avoid a collision with a tottering young black man in another world. The guy was mumbling something and hugging himself.

Drunk, and it wasn't even noon yet.

"Better get some help, pal," Sully muttered as the guy hobbled down toward the subway station. It was a shame women and children had to put up with derelicts like that.

An ambulance roared onto the street. Sully glanced over as the ambulance shrieked to a stop, stuck behind cars that had nowhere to go. Immediately he fell into police mode and tapped on the glass to get one of the drivers' attention.

"Pull onto the lip of the curb," Sully shouted, motioning the cars off the street.

The driver cut the wheel and got out of the way, and the cars behind him followed. The ambulance edged ahead, then took off, finding its way down the center line.

All the more intrigued now, Sully continued up the street and rounded the corner at Roosevelt and Union. The action on the west side of the street put his senses on alert with that re-flexive feeling cops had walking into possible danger.

The street between Sully's Cup and the station house was blocked completely with a fire truck, ambulances, and patrol cars swung in at crazy angles. Cops were everywhere; some without jackets had obviously spilled out of the precinct. Had there been an incident in the precinct that prompted an evacuation? From the way everyone swarmed it looked like they were using his coffee shop as a command center.

As he picked up the pace to jog the last block, he noticed that one of his windows was missing. Shit. Someone had hit Sully's. Some amateur idiot. He searched the crowd for Padama, their barista. He'd always trained his employees to give up the cash. "Money can be replaced," he liked to say. "You, you're one of a kind."

With each lunging step the details gained focus and the scene looked worse. Much worse.

Tinted glass from the broken shopwindow littered the sidewalk on one side of the store. It looked to Sully like gunfire had blown it out. Someone was cordoning that off with crime scene tape.

On the other side, cops were gathering, some with customers.

A stretcher was poking out the door. Damn, somebody was hurt . . . a big guy . . . and from the way they were working on him, an EMT chasing along, forcing air in through the mask.

Sully grabbed the first cop he came to, a young guy by the name of VanDyke. "What the hell's going on?" he asked.

VanDyke glared at him, and seemed about to order him away when he recognized Sully. "Some guy went crazy with a gun is all I know. Ah . . . I'm sorry. Here. Talk to the boss." He pointed to a lieutenant who was talking into a radio.

But Sully didn't want to talk to a boss. He'd been violated. He had a right to access.

He stopped at the door, tapped a cop, and pointed to the stretcher that was being lifted into the ambulance. "Did you ID that victim, officer?" Sully asked.

"That's Sean Walters, one of the guys in our squad." The cop's voice was broken, his face pale.

And suddenly Sully got it. "One of us."

The cop nodded as images of Sean Walters flashed through

Sully's head. Big guy, almost as tall as Sully. Liked to laugh. Liked his cocktails. The EMTs had been working on him. Sully set his jaw, hoping that Walters would pull through.

Inside the shop, a multitude of observations hit him in a flash. A body. A conscious victim. Blood. EMTs.

The body to his right was covered. From the beefy hand that stuck out, he noted it was a man. Sully would bet he'd been sitting on a bar stool. A pool of blood crept out from under the blanket near the wrappers and trash from the EMT team who had tried to save him. Nearby was another blood smear. Probably from Walters.

In the center of the shop, medical personnel were talking with one of the victims, who was answering. That was a better sign.

The customers had been cleared out, and there were just two other uniforms in here. Keep traffic down to preserve the crime scene; Sully knew procedure, but it seemed bizarre in his own coffee shop. His second home.

A man lay dead on the floor, here. He wanted to yell at somebody to do something, but he had befriended the harsh reality long ago. No one could help this guy now.

You do what you can. Help the living.

Sully moved toward the EMTs gathered around the victim. A girl. In police uniform.

His heartbeat was now a prevalent noise in his chest as he noted her face, felt the sting of recognition.

"Indigo Blue," he said, keeping calm in his voice.

Her eyes caught him, then snapped with pain. "Sully! Oh, Sully, I'm so sorry."

"Easy, darling." He leaned over her and took her hand. "You just take it easy now."

"I didn't see it coming." Tears rolled from her eyes. "None of us did, until it was too late. And now I can't feel my legs." Her lips quivered from shock. "Can't feel my legs and . . . and I can't stop shaking. Is Brendan okay?"

Brendan . . . Of course, he would have been with Indigo.

Sully straightened and turned back to the body, sure that it wasn't his son. Brendan's hands were thinner, his fingers long.

"Sully!" Ed Conklin hissed. Suddenly, the sergeant was in his face. "You're walking all over the crime scene. Holy shit." He turned to the cop guarding the door. "VanDyke! Didn't I say no one gets in here?"

"Ed, where's my son?" Sully kept his voice steady. Calm and in control. "Where's Brendan?"

The Adam's apple on Ed's throat twitched as he swallowed. From that pause, Sully knew it was over. *Holy Mary, Mother of God, pray for us sinners now and at the hour of our death.* "Where is he? I want to see him."

Conklin shook his head. "You don't. It'd be better to ID him later at the morgue."

"I want to see my son."

"Okay, Sully." The sergeant touched Sully's shoulder. "Let's stand back, give them room to get Indigo to the hospital."

The attendants had strapped her to a backboard. As they wheeled her out, she asked if she was going to the same hospital as Brendan.

"You hang in there, Indigo," Sully called after her. He was tempted to tell her that her partner was gone, but it was too much for her now. Too much until she was out of the woods herself.

Sully turned away from the exiting medical team, his calm fraying from the eerie landscape of his shop. Blood lining the grout of the tiles. An abandoned woman's shoe. Someone's laptop, still open. "How'd it happen, Ed? What happened here?"

"Guy standing in line for coffee opens fire on the cops in the place. Brendan was just coming out of the john. Officer Hilson was here, by the sugar and whatnot. Walters and Puchinko were on stools over by the window there. Shooter got them first, close range from behind. They never had a chance."

"Puchinko?" So that was Kevin over there, bleeding out on the tiles. The poor guy had just stood in his dining room last night. He paused, letting the new brand itself on his brain. Sully realized he had reached his threshold and now any new source of grief or pain encoded itself as hard information, like the caption on a complaint report. *Lead us not into temptation, but deliver us from evil.*

"Look, you want to step outside?" Ed suggested.

"I need to see my son." Sully went around the main counter, a kidney-shaped granite creation that had cost him a small fortune, and braced himself. He dreaded the walk down the short corridor to the restrooms but he didn't need to go that far. The body was on the floor to the right of the counter.

His youngest son.

Ed accompanied him as he kneeled beside Brendan's body and lifted the blanket. His eyes were closed, as if he were asleep.

How many times had he heard that on jobs? He'd have to sit with a body, wait for the coroner to come, and some family member would remark: "He looks like he's sleeping." And he'd always wanted to point out that there was a big difference between death and sleep, and that corpse was dead.

But now he understood. It wasn't so much sleep we desired for our loved ones, but peace. A lasting peace.

The small bullet wound in his neck didn't seem to match the volume of blood on the floor.

"Such a small wound," Sully said. "Honestly, it looks like something a person could survive."

"But the exit wound's always bigger. The bullet must have ricocheted. Went out through his skull."

And took off a chunk on its way out. Sully winced, then reined himself in. He pressed a palm to his son's smooth forehead, just as he did when checking for fever when Brendan was a kid.

The skin was cold, but Sully used his thumb to make the sign of the cross between his son's brows.

"Holy Mary, Mother of God, pray for us, now and at the hour of our death, amen."

Moving carefully so that he wouldn't disturb the scene,

Sully pulled back the blanket. Brendan's gun was holstered, not even unlocked. "He didn't even reach for his gun. He didn't see it coming."

"None of them did."

Sully let the blanket drop just below Brendan's chin and leaned back on his haunches. He didn't want to leave his son here; it felt wrong, but he understood that a body was part of the investigation. The techs would photograph and videotape, map and measure before Brendan was allowed to leave.

Leave, but never go home again. Oh, dear Lord, what would those two little girls do without their father?

Gently, he let the blanket drop over his son's head. There was nothing to be done for Brendan on this earth, God rest his soul.

"I want my priest here. Father Tillman. He'll give Brendan last rites." He glanced over his shoulder. "Kevin, too."

Ed winced, scratching his head. "I don't know, Sully. The bosses won't like that."

"He'll be fast." He rose and pulled out his cell phone. "And Peg..." He cupped the phone and pressed it to his chin, suddenly disoriented. What to do first?

There was no procedure for losing your son this way.

He took a breath as he flipped open the cell and thought of the investigation.

"Ed. You got the shooter?"

Ed frowned. "He walked out of here. Exchanged a few words with Officer Hilson, and she gave us a pedigree. Black male, late twenties or thirties. Limping and holding his arm. Sounds like something got to him, maybe a ricochet on these tiles."

"I might have seen him." Sully squinted. "The guy I saw was hurting. He headed toward the subway entrance on Roosevelt and Main, but didn't go down the stairs. He seemed like a local, but I've never seen him around before."

"We've got cars out looking, and bulletins going out to all the area hospitals."

Sully nodded as he located the priest's name in his contacts. Getting Father Tillman here was his first priority now. After that, his overwrought brain would have to snap out of it.

Calm and in control.

He was playing the role okay, but he'd lost track of the point.

Chapter 17

Bernie yawned as she and Keesh waited for the subway doors to open at Main Street Flushing. They had gotten seats together back at the Grand Central Stop; it was one of the perks of working the night shift. Bernie had fallen asleep dreaming of Keesh, thinking of how comfortable his shoulder was, and of how his new girlfriend would not appreciate this attribute the way she had.

Keesh had probably dozed off, too, as they now climbed the stairs like zombies, dazed and determined to move ahead by forcing one foot in front of another. Bernie had her cell phone in hand, ready to fire. In her mind, Bernie was already on her bus texting Amy.

Did you know Keesh is seeing someone?

But the chaos on Roosevelt Avenue slapped them awake as they emerged from the stairwell to a street where cops were directing people to bus detours and television news teams hurried up the block, as if chasing a celebrity. The traffic light at the intersection of Main and Roosevelt was set to flash red, and cops were in the street moving traffic.

"What the hell?" Keesh scraped his hair back, pausing at the top of the stairs.

Immediately Bernie thought back to 9-11, that beautiful September day when New Yorkers had thought the world was ending. Of course, it could be nothing. Sometimes the city closed streets for a parade or demonstration.

Tucking her phone away, she went straight to a cop at the center of a crosswalk, where he was holding back traffic for pedestrians. "Officer, what's going on?"

He looked her over, as if testing her reliability. "There was a shooting up on Union. All this traffic has been diverted from there."

She looked at Keesh. "That's where the coffee shop is."

"I'll go with you," Keesh said as they both retreated from the crosswalk and hurried up the street.

As soon as they turned the corner, Bernie saw the cluster of police vehicles and ambulances parked haphazardly outside Sully's Cup.

Without thinking Bernie broke into a run. She pressed through the crowd and skirted around a reporter setting up for a live broadcast. She ran until she reached the yellow crime scene tape, saw the gaping hole in the side of the shop where glass had once been.

Her heart pounded at the sight of it, the wound in her father's shop, the shards of tinted glass littering the ground like a trashy sidewalk mosaic. Something terrible had happened. A bomb . . . or a robbery.

She ducked under the tape and pressed forward, looking at the cops to find someone she knew.

"Ma'am." A uniform rushed over to stop her. "You can't be here."

"I have to find my father. Sully, the owner." She spoke quickly, not even taking time to look at his face. She had to find her father.

"We're with the DA's office," Keesh said from behind her. She was vaguely aware of Keesh showing the cop his ID as she moved away.

The door was totally blocked by police personnel, but she went to the gaping windows, her boots crunching over the glass as she crept closer. The tumbled café under siege by crime techs was stained by blood; three massive spots gleamed like crimson paint.

And a body.

She gaped at the lump of human form under a blanket.

"Oh, no!" All the air hissed from her body as the dark reality hit her.

And then a hand clamped on her shoulder and she looked up at her father's dear, pale face.

He was alive.

"Oh, Daddy! Oh, my God!" She fell into his arms, sobbing. "What happened? I couldn't find you, but I saw the blown-out window and all the blood and the body."

He hugged her tight.

"Bernadette . . ." His voice was thin, almost hoarse, and he used her formal name, as if calling on the saint she had been named after to perform a miracle.

She leaned back and looked up at him, frightened by the hollow look in his eyes, the gray mask that contorted his face.

Something had rocked his world.

"Dad, what happened?"

He bit his lips together, then let out a sob, the sort of noise a child would make when he thinks his life is coming to an end.

Thinking back on it later, Bernie understood why parents did not want their children to see them cry. It wasn't so much a matter of holding back true feelings as wanting to save a child from a wider dimension of pain. The burden was too great to bear.

Chapter 18

Sarah rode the brakes as the car approached the intersection of Bell and Forty-eighth, hoping for a parking spot on the same block as the pharmacy. She planned to park close, run in and pick up her prescription, then run out and get to work. She cruised by slowly, but there wasn't a spot to be had.

The blare of a horn startled her, and in her rearview mirror she saw an old white truck riding her bumper.

"Calm down," she yelled at the driver, as if he could hear her. She moved through the intersection but he stayed right on her, pressing for her to go faster, when she was already going the twenty-mile-per-hour speed limit.

She was tempted to gun the engine but she stood her ground, staying at twenty-five until she turned right on Fifty-third Avenue and he zoomed past.

"Grrr." She could feel the stress in her hunched shoulders as she pulled up to a stop sign, and much as she told herself to breathe deeply and relax, she knew the tension wouldn't unwind until she got to work.

It didn't help that she was already late. After dropping the girls at St. Pete's, she'd gotten a call from the office. Gracie had forgotten her history notebook, so she'd had to return home, then double back to school, and now this.

But it's better to be late for work than late on your birth control pills, she thought. In fact, she was already two days late, but she figured she could take those two pills this morning and start catching up. The beginning of the cycle shouldn't be a big deal, right? She'd heard of people who remained infertile for months after being on the Pill.

She circled the pharmacy again, and this time she got stuck behind a car double parked on Bell Boulevard.

"This is ridiculous!" She pounded the steering wheel, but that didn't make it any easier to home in and land the car anywhere near the pharmacy.

"Forget it. Just forget it." She buzzed ahead and turned left on Oceania to head toward the office. Worst-case scenario? She got pregnant, and they'd have their third earlier than planned. Brendan would be happy about that, and she might not be too far behind him. With stress like this, she could use a few years off being a full-time mom. Not that it was an easy job, but it was closer to her heart these days.

And honestly, she could be pregnant already. Since she'd started on the Pill she'd gotten lazy about marking a calendar and keeping up with her cycles.

Maybe this is a blessing in disguise, she thought as she pulled into the right lane of the expressway. She could tell Brendan about it tonight, after the kids were in bed. She would snuggle up to him on the couch. Start with a kiss and then wrap her arms around him. Nibbling on the ear always did him in. The television would remain on *Modern Family* or whatever ball game he was watching, but they would sneak into their room and lock the door and switch to something R-rated. And if she told him they were actually trying to make a baby, he would get off on that.

Of the two of them, Brendan was the one who couldn't live without children. "It's what we're here for," he had told her in the early days of their relationship when they'd argued the point. "Our children are our legacy. We have to make this planet better, then our kids carry that on, and then their kids inherit the job. See how well that works?"

He'd been stubborn about the kid issue. In turn, she'd been stubborn about the career issue. Not only had she insisted on having her work, she refused to start a family until Brendan had a real job, with benefits and longevity. "We are not raising a family on the money you make doing landscaping around the neighborhood," she had told him. "There's no job security in mowing Mrs. Hurley's lawn." He'd remarked that grass keeps growing, but in the end, he got the message and took the police test.

She had told him he didn't have to be a cop. She was fine if he wanted to drive a train or bus, fight fires, or sling trash. She smiled, remembering how Brendan had put a hand to his heart as if wounded. "If you think I'd survive Sunday dinners in any of those professions, you haven't been around my family long enough," he'd said.

And so, around ten years ago, he'd been hired by NYPD. Gracie was born some nine months later, and she'd had to put the brakes on awhile or else they'd have ninety kids like his parents. Maisey was almost five now, and very manageable. If they were going to have a third, it was about time.

She smiled as she got off at her exit. There was fun in their future. Sometimes it was the small things in life that changed your course. She always told Brendan that, but she'd lost sight of her own words of wisdom. One morning you can't make it to the pharmacy, next thing you know you're having your third.

After circling once, Sarah found a parking spot four blocks from the office, but this time she didn't mind walking. And no one would care that she was late for work, as long as her paperwork was done. Her boss, Artie Metcalf, was great that way.

Like most city offices, theirs lacked creativity and planning, which Sarah always had found ironic for the office of Building Permits and Planning. Someone had plunked a desk into the hallway outside the door leading to the architects' offices and called it a reception area. Alma Sanchez, a large-breasted, ma-

ternal woman with a love for bright colors, had the unfortunate job of playing reception in the middle of the corridor.

As soon as Sarah stepped into the hall, she could see the two
dark figures hovering near Alma. Two more steps and she
could tell they were cops.

The late police, she said to herself, biting back a smile. She'd
worked herself out of a funk, and she wanted to stay positive.
She assumed they were here to talk with Artie about some per-
mit problems.

"Sarah?" Alma rose from her desk and worked the hem of
her fuchsia sweater over a sizable belly. "I thought that was
you. These officers are waiting for you. I told them you were
late, and they said they'd wait."

For the first time Sarah looked at their faces and saw that
these two men were sucking the life and energy out of the corridor with its asbestos tiles and greenish fluorescent lights.

"Mrs. Sullivan?" The older man spoke, turning his hat in
his hands, and his words scared her. Mrs. Sullivan was her
mother-in-law, Peg, and these were not familiar faces.

"What's going on?" When she paused and made eye contact, the younger cop had to look away, and the older guy
seemed on the verge of either vomiting or bursting into tears.

That was when she knew.

Even before they asked if there was a private place they
could go and talk.

She knew. Oh, dear God, she knew.

Chapter 19

"Rise and shine!" Mary Kate Marino called, knocking on her son's bedroom door. At twenty, Conner should have been setting his own alarm, and maybe he was, but she could hear him snoring in there and couldn't stand to sit by as he slept through his classes at Queens College.

"Come on, come on." She opened the door and stepped over the surly mass of inside-out shirts and jeans. "Out of bed, you lazy bag of bones."

Somewhere in the tangle of the surfboard print comforter was Conner, who had never surfed. "What time is it?" the lump demanded.

"Almost ten. Don't you have a class at eleven-thirty?"

"Yeah." His head materialized from the folds of sheets. "But that means I can sleep for another hour."

"No can do." She picked up a pillow that had fallen off the bed and tossed it at him. "I know you. You won't go out until you eat and shower, and thirty minutes is not going to cut it. If you get up without whining, I'll make you pancakes and sausage."

"Real men don't whine," he called quietly as she left his room. "And how can you be so cheerful this early in the morning?"

"Early? It's almost noon." She grinned as she headed downstairs. When Conner had flunked out his freshman year at the State U, she had worried that having a kid at home again would cramp her style. She and Tony had spent twenty years talking about the things they would do when they finally had an empty nest. But really, having Conner at home had been a blessing. With Tony drifting away from her, she'd had the time to bond with her son as a young adult. They shared the same taste in movies, and Conner had developed his father's gift for storytelling. At the end of the day, Mary Kate enjoyed listening to Conner's tales about campus life and friends while they watched a movie.

Right now the only catch was that Conner didn't know about Tony, and she wasn't sure what to tell him and when to spring it on him. How do you want your eggs, and, oh, by the way, I think your father is having an affair. Or, would you pick up milk on your way home, and tell your father he can keep his mistress and car as long as I get the house.

Well, it hadn't gotten that bad yet, but at the rate Tony was going, she sensed talk of divorce on the horizon. He would say that he still loved her and all that, but if he didn't spend any time with her, how true could that be?

She cracked an egg into the pancake mix and beat it with a fork, wondering how far Tony would go with his lies. So far he had concocted a million stories about overtime and retirement parties and afterhours clubs where "all the guys from work" were going. And she had believed him, or at least she'd given him leeway.

But now ... this routine he'd pulled over the last two days of not coming home at all ... that was just crazy and she wasn't going to put up with it. She didn't know where he was staying. He told her they had cots at the precinct, and she'd smiled bitterly at the thought of her Tony going anywhere near a bed-bug-ridden cot some criminal had peed on. It was one of his half lies. True, they had cots in the precinct. False, if you think Tony Marino would ever sleep on one.

By the time Conner appeared in wet hair and sweats, there

was a stack of pancakes tucked under a bowl to stay warm, and maple sausage links in the skillet.

"Thanks, Mom." He shuffled four hotcakes onto a plate. "Brain food for my history test."

"You have a test? Good thing I got you out of bed. Did you study?"

"It's on the Constitution." Conner grabbed a spot on a stool at the end of the small kitchen island. "How many times do they have to hit you up with the Constitution in school? I memorized the preamble in fifth grade. We wrote mock amendments in high school. I think I got this one down."

She stabbed a sausage link with a fork. "And ironically, some kids will be clueless on the test."

He swallowed a walloping bite of pancakes. "So where's Dad this morning? Another big arrest?"

Despite all her deliberation, she hadn't concocted a quick answer, and she turned toward the sink and ran hot water into the pan.

"What? Is he out chasing girls or something?"

Mary Kate turned back to glare at her son. "Don't say that about your father." Her son's expression of curiosity was so open and genuine that she couldn't bear to face him with another lie. She turned away quickly.

"Crap, it's true!" Conner said. "Erin told me to watch out for you. She thought Dad was dicking around."

"Watch your language," Mary Kate said, gripping the counter. "And what does your sister have to do with this?"

"She suspected something, and since I was going to be living home again, she gave me a heads-up."

So the kids knew. They knew and they were trying to look out for her. A knot of emotion grew in her throat. That was so sweet, but it seemed inappropriate. She didn't want to turn them against their father, even if he was the one acting like a jerk.

She turned back and faced him, a little disconcerted by the dark eyes that resembled his father's. "Honestly, things aren't going well between your father and me right now. I don't really know what he's up to, so I can't say much more. But when I have it figured out, I'll let you know. And tell Erin she can call me directly if she wants to talk about it. Your brother, Joseph, too."

Wow. She didn't know where that speech had come from, but it was worthy of publication in *Parents* magazine.

He nodded, still chewing. "Okay."

Slightly reassured, she was scrubbing pans when the phone rang. She and Conner both glanced at the caller ID.

"Aunt Bernie," he said.

Mary Kate wiped her hands and picked up. "Hey, Bernie."

"MK, thank God you're there. I tried your cell but there was no answer."

Earlier that morning, after trying to reach Tony unsuccessfully, Mary Kate had tossed the damned cell onto her bed and left it there, threatening to toss it into the toilet next. But she didn't think Bernie needed to hear her long explanation; she sounded upset.

"What's the matter, Bernie?"

"Dad asked me to call you, and MK, it's bad." The sound of Bernie's voice cracking and calling her MK brought Mary Kate back to the time when Bernie was little. Mary Kate was already fifteen when her sister was born, but she'd been the built-in sitter, and one-year-old Bernie had been the one to come up with MK when she struggled to say her sister's name.

"What is it, sweetie?"

"There was a shooting at . . . at Dad's coffee shop."

"Oh, no." Mary Kate tried to visualize the sense of this while Bernie took a breath.

"I know you're not supposed to say things like this over the phone, but I can't string you along. Brendan got shot and . . . and they're saying he's dead." The last words barely squeaked out.

"What about Dad?"

"He was at the bank when it happened. Some psycho came

in and shot four cops. I'll give you the rest of the details when you get to the house."

"Okay. I'll . . . okay."

"I'll let you tell Tony." Emotion swelled in Bernie's voice again, and Mary Kate pressed a fist to her mouth as tears filled her eyes.

"I'm on my way," Mary Kate said, her mind moving to the details as she clicked off. She would have to notify work that she wouldn't be in, and then there was Tony, the bastard. Not answering her calls. Well, how would he like to hear about it through the grapevine instead? Hear it on TV? That'd serve him right.

"What happened?" Conner's voice was tentative.

She faced him, once again reminded that he wasn't a kid anymore, and even if he were, there was no way to sugarcoat news like this. "There was a shooting at Sully's Cup. Uncle Brendan is gone."

"Holy shit." His eyes went wide, and he put his fork across the plate. "I thought it was Nana, when you said, you know, your dad."

She nodded, swallowing back the viscous emotions that threatened to choke her. "Grandpa's okay. I'm going to the house." Her parents' house, the center of the universe . . . it would be like Grand Central Station. "But you need to go to your classes."

"I knew you would say that." He put his dishes in the sink. "Let me drive you, Mom. You're not supposed to drive when you just got news like this. I saw it on *Grey's Anatomy*. Besides, Nana and Grandpa are close to Queens College. I'll swing back when I'm done."

"Okay."

"And I'm sorry about your brother. Uncle Brendan was a good guy."

She nodded. "I'm sorry, too. You'd better go put some real clothes on."

He left the kitchen, then returned. "Right now, I find it really hard to believe. Like, I don't feel like crying or anything because it doesn't seem real. Is that weird?"

"It's normal. Didn't you ever study the five stages of death and dying?"

"Nope."

She pointed to the stairs. "Get dressed. We'll talk about it in the car."

As she cleaned up the kitchen, Mary Kate thanked the Lord that Conner was here right now. She prayed for the repose of Brendan's soul, and asked God to give Sarah strength during this difficult time. Then, as she spilled the coffee grounds into the trash, she thanked God that none of her children seemed interested in working in law enforcement.

Chapter 20

When Yvonne Curtis got off the elevator on the second floor and saw the drops of blood leading down the linoleum tiles of the hallway, she had a funny feeling it was going to lead to her apartment, and damned if she wasn't right. That boy Peyton had gotten himself in another pack of trouble.

"Peyton Curtis, what the hell you been doin'?" she hollered as she pushed open the door.

And there he was, sunk down against the wall with blood soaking through his jacket. He curled his neck so that he could press the folded towel down against his shoulder. His good shoulder.

Her temper drained out just like that. "Oh, Peyton. What happened?" She held her breath as she leaned over him, scared by the sight of her baby bleeding on the floor.

"I got hurt, Mama." His dark eyes flashed open, plaintive and pathetic. "Help me fix it up. Help me, please."

"Oh, baby, you're bleeding like crazy. There's blood all over the floor out there. Come on, get up, and we'll get you downstairs. Get you a ride to the hospital. You're gonna need a doctor to look at that."

"No hospital," he moaned, his eyes closing. "I can't do that."

"You need a doctor."

"No doctors, Mama. You know what they do."

"Peyton, what are you not telling me?" She was not going to take any shit from this boy. She knew when someone was laying it on thick. "You got in trouble with the law again?"

"It wasn't my fault, Mama . . ."

"Oh, Peyton." She held a hand to her mouth, not sure what to believe. "I'm gonna help you. And you are gonna tell me the truth." She put her groceries and purse on the kitchen table. "But first, I gotta go out there and Swiffer that hallway. You left a trail of blood that's like a pirate's map with arrows. X marks the spot."

She peered into the hallway and waited while some kids ran to the stairs. When it was empty, she made quick work of swiping up the drops of blood, which were on their way to drying.

Did that make her an accessory now? She didn't know. Only thing she knew right now was, she didn't want anyone beating on her door any sooner than necessary. Maybe Peyton could get better on his own. Maybe he'd be fine and this would all blow over and be done, like a bad day. Peyton was a good boy. He deserved a break.

Inside the apartment he was passed out again. "Come on now, baby. Let's get you into the bathroom to wash up."

"No." He couldn't even open his eyes. "I just need to lie down."

"And get blood all over my bed?"

"Get some towels or something. I only got the energy for one move. One short move."

Yvonne stood over him with her hands on her hips. She didn't want him bleeding on her bed, but she couldn't leave him here. She grabbed a plastic-top tablecloth, spread it on the bed, then brought in some clean towels starched white from the laundry where she worked. She figured if she had to do the work, she might as well be able to use some at home. In the kitchen she dug out a mixing bowl and filled it with warm soapy water. She was no Nancy Nurse, but a mother did what she had to.

"Okay, let's get you up."

The muscles in his face strained with the effort of trying to rise to his feet. Pain made him miserable, and she worried that she was doing the wrong thing. What if he didn't get better? She'd never forgive herself if she lost her baby boy just because he was afraid of the police finding him.

"Okay...I got you," she said as she guided him down the hall. Truth was, she couldn't support him on her own, but he needed distracting. Tears were running down his face from the pain.

At last, she was easing him down to the bed. "Before you lie down, let me get this jacket off."

The smallest tug on the collar and he was bawling like a baby. "It hurts, it hurts."

"I know it does. I know, but I can't clean it out unless you get this off." Her pulse was thudding fast, and it got faster when she saw all the bright red blood. His shirt and jacket were soaked with it.

"Ooh." She cringed when she saw the bullet hole in his shoulder, but this was no time to sit around squealing like a baby. Peyton was doing plenty of crying as she washed the wound out with soapy water.

"It stings!" he complained.

"That means it's working." Damned if that was true. She didn't know. She was just doing her best.

"Now you're going to lie down, and I'm going to keep pressing this towel down to stop the bleeding," she said.

He glanced down at the wound sheepishly. "Did you get the bullet out?"

"No, I didn't get the bullet out. I'm not a surgeon, and there's no way I can do something like that when it hurts you just to be touched. Just lie back."

Sniffing, he eased back against the pillow. "It wasn't my fault."

"I know, baby. You know, I heard that sometimes the doctors leave the bullet in. It's better to leave it than to, I don't know, dig in there and stir everything up."

"Mmm." He started to relax, but when Yvonne pressed the clean towel to the wound he nearly jumped out of the bed. "That hurts!"

"I'll get you some Tylenol when it stops bleeding. Right now I want you to tell me how this happened."

"It must have been a stray bullet. I was walking by this place near Main Street. Sully's Cup. And damned if a bullet didn't come flying out the window. Somebody was shooting it up inside, but I caught a bullet walking by."

"A stray bullet." She kept her tone even, though she was doubtful. Flushing wasn't East New York. "It smells a little to me, you just walking by at the same time somebody was shooting. And you don't have Darnell around to blame for this one."

"Darnell's always to blame," he said.

"In the past, yes. That boy was bad as the devil himself. Torturing you and making a pest of himself. They gave him twenty-five years, but I'm glad he's gone."

"Everyone's glad he's gone."

"But we can't have you going off to join him 'cause you got a bullet in your shoulder with not even one week out of prison."

He opened his eyes slowly. He was all sloppy and in slow motion like a drunk. "I know. You're thinking, a bullet coming out of nowhere. What's the sense of that? But I got hit, and now I got to get out of here. Get me out of here, Mama. Put me on a bus."

"A bus? You must be crazy from delirium. You can't go traveling when you're dripping blood everywhere, and you said yourself that you couldn't even sit in the bathroom while I cleaned it up for you. No, sir, you're staying put. You're probably weak from losing blood."

He didn't answer. His head just rolled to the side. So hurt.

Yvonne pursed her lips as she kept the pressure on his shoulder. If she stopped the bleeding, she could get him some painkillers. And water, too. Or something to drink. Didn't they give out juice when you gave blood for the blood bank? Yes, he needed some medicine and he needed to drink. Maybe she could find a can of chicken soup in the cupboard. And maybe if he rested and got hydrated, he'd get better. Sleep would make him feel better. A good night's sleep and he'd be moving around again, just like his old self.

She closed her eyes and remembered her proud boy, so neat and polite in the Catholic school uniform she'd ironed for him. He'd been a good boy. So smart he got a scholarship to go to school for free.

"It wasn't my fault, Mama."

"I know, baby. I know."

PART II

Chapter 21

Bernie couldn't stop the images from flashing in her mind. The way the tinted glass puddle had sparkled on the sidewalk when the sun had poked through. Kevin's body under the blanket, his hand casually tossed back as if he were hanging out of a car window, catching the air. Her father's big hands covering his face to hold back the tears.

And then there was Brendan's face smiling at her, the face that appeared on his NYPD ID card and in his St. Peter's yearbook. Chipmunk cheeks, freckles, and a grin that could make you forget what you were mad about.

She couldn't get those images to stop burning her thoughts, no matter how much she forced herself to help in the kitchen.

"Ma, there's nowhere to put these sandwiches," Bernie called to her mother as she looked over the chicken drumsticks, casseroles, and bowls on the dining room table. With a perverse flicker, she considered dumping the entire table out the window.

Grief needed company, not food, Bernie thought as she squeezed the platter onto the table. At a time like this, it was reassuring to have plenty of Sullivans available to share the pain. The terrible news had beckoned family members to drop what they were doing and head home for comfort, and they had come . . . Sarah, James and his wife, Deb. Mary Kate and Conner.

James had left the academy as soon as he got word, and now he kept busy feeding wood to the living room fire. Deb had also left work, and she'd spent the last half hour talking with her kids, promising to keep Kelly and Keaton posted on funeral plans. Mary Kate had come immediately, though Tony was conspicuously absent. Bernie didn't have the energy to ask.

Coincidentally, this was Granny Mary's day to visit Peg and Sully, so everything had to be repeated twice, and louder, and even then Mary Sullivan seemed to comprehend about a third of what was going on.

Sarah, who had wobbled in, dazed and red-eyed, had decided to leave Grace and Maisey in school until the end of the day, thinking that would maintain "normal" for as long as possible. Sarah's parents were driving up from North Carolina. Her brother, Mike, would fly in from Chicago.

Family.

Bernie wanted to draw strength from them, but as she scanned the room she bristled at the sight of her siblings playing their usual roles in their usual seats.

This is not fucking Sunday dinner! she wanted to shout.

But she kept her jaws clamped tight as Peg moved her aside and fussed at rearranging the food on the table.

"Don't make anything else, Ma. Why don't you take a break?"

"People have to eat." Peg blinked, her eyes misting over again. "The food will get eaten. Trust me. I've held wakes before." She ducked into the kitchen.

Trying to escape her emotions, Bernie thought. Bernie understood that food was the dance of life, but at times like these you had to let the casserole go cold. She followed into the kitchen, where Peg stood rinsing things at the sink, her back to Bernie.

"Ma . . ." Bernie put her hands on her mother's shoulders

and gave her a little massage. The bones felt thin and brittle in her hands. Had the mother they'd always relied on for strength and fortitude always been just a wisp of a thing?

"You're shrinking away to nothing, Ma," Brendan would have said. And then he'd land a series of karate chops over their mother's tight shoulders.

"It's not natural." Peg's voice cracked, and though she kept her hands in the dishwater, she paused to wipe her eyes against a rolled-up sleeve.

Bernie's mouth puckered at the show of emotion as her hands slipped awkwardly from her mother's back.

"A mother shouldn't have to bury her babies," Peg went on. "Parents are supposed to go first. That's the natural order of things."

"I know."

"He didn't even want to be a cop. Not really. Of all the men in this house, Brendan didn't want it, with his surfing and such. He wanted to go to California."

"But, Mom, that was years ago." Before he'd married Sarah. Before they'd had two kids.

In high school Brendan had dreamed of heading to the West Coast and finding a job in one of the many parks on the Pacific. *Surf while you work,* he used to say. What could be better? And he'd spent a few weeks checking out the coast with a college friend. Pismo Beach. San Onofre and Big Sur. He'd talked about the beaches and surfing for weeks, but Bernie knew he wouldn't leave New York.

Sullivans did not leave Queens.

Well, there was one exception: Lucy Sullivan Strasberg.

Lucy. How could she forget her own sister? *Another pound of guilt to add to the weight on my back.* Bernie paced into the living room.

"I knew I forgot something," she said to anyone who would listen. "I didn't call Lucy." The meaning of the oversight was obvious; for Bernie, Lucy wasn't a part of their family anymore. By moving to Delaware, marrying into money, and converting to Judaism, Lucy Strasberg had divorced herself from the Sullivans in all the ways that mattered, and though Bernie sometimes thought of Lucy in the context of her childhood as the older sister who wore tie-dyed shirts, took in strays, and had the nerve to talk to old Mrs. Epstein, the adult Lucy had no place in the family.

"Good luck getting her to call you back," Mary Kate said.

Granny Mary perked up, her eyes watery fish behind the lenses of her glasses. "Oh, I knew her in the day. You know, before she was president and all the cameras were popping and whatnot."

James's wife, Deb, put a hand on Mary's arm. "Granny, we're talking about Lucy. Your granddaughter Lucy. She's a college professor, not president."

"And you believe that?" Granny waved her off. "It's just her cover."

"I spoke to her already," Peg said from the kitchen doorway, surprising everyone.

Mary Kate squinted. "You're making that up."

Peg shook her head. "She sends her heartfelt condolences to Sarah and the girls. I'm sure we'll see her in the days to come, for the wake and funeral."

Bernie shivered and scooted closer to the fire. Those words always made her think of old people, and it seemed downright creepy to start thinking about Brendan's funeral.

"Well, she can send all the good wishes she wants. Don't expect to see Lucy around," Mary Kate said.

"Yeah," James agreed. "You can't count on her. Back in the day, you could count on her to be goofy in her pink hair and flowered dress and boots."

"Remember that trench coat she had that was lined with fur?" Mary Kate asked.

"The nineties was not a good era for fashion," Deb said.

"Enough." Peg held up a hand to stop the remarks. "She's not here to defend herself. And I'd think you'd have a little more compassion for your own sister."

Bernie twisted to look up at the clock over the mantel. Almost two. Peg would go to pick up the girls soon.

"When do you think Dad will get home?" Mary Kate asked.

"No telling," Peg said.

James got up and opened the fireplace screen. "There's a lot to be done to process the crime scene," he said. "It'll take a while. Of course, Dad doesn't have to be there, but I'm sure he wants to. He wants to make sure no one screws anything up."

Not true, Bernie thought. Sully trusted the detectives on the scene to do the right thing. "He wants to stay with Brendan." The words were out before Bernie could censor them. She glanced up at Sarah apologetically, but Sarah just nodded, as if it was okay to talk about it.

Of course, they had to talk about it. But that didn't make it easy.

"Your father told me he's sticking around to cooperate in the investigation," Peg said.

"I'm sure that part is true, too. But when I was at the coffee shop, I got the feeling Dad is staying for Brendan. He won't leave Brendan alone until the investigation is finished. Then, I don't know. I guess the coroner will do an autopsy?" She shot the question to her brother.

James nodded. "That's the protocol."

"Such a pity." Peg worried the hem of her apron. "They make things difficult for the funeral director. It's just not the same when you want an open coffin."

"There won't be a viewing," Sarah spoke up, and the room was silent but for a *pop* from the fire. "Brendan wouldn't want that. He hated those things, always stayed to the back of the room or outside. Dead bodies creeped him out."

"But we will have a wake," Peg said, her eyes narrowing in that stern expression that warded off disagreement. "That's the Irish way. It brings people together to talk about their loved one. Gives them time to grieve."

"I haven't thought that far ahead," Sarah said.

Bernie caught her mother's eye and shook her head, signaling her to back off. This was no time to badger Sarah.

"So, Bernie, did you see the crime scene?" James asked. "I mean, we've all heard the news, four cops shot, two killed, but I'm trying to get a picture in my head of how it went down."

"I didn't get inside. One of the big windows—the one by the door—was blown out of the shop, and I could see through the opening." Bernie paused, not wanting to mention the body or the blood.

"Did you see Uncle Brendan?" Conner asked from the end of the couch.

"No, but I saw his friend who was killed, Kevin Puchinko."

Behind her, there was a breathless whimper, like the shocked distress of a small child. She turned to find Sarah sobbing, a crumpled tissue pressed to her nose.

"Did somebody die?" Granny asked.

"Your grandson Brendan," Deb said. "He got shot. He's dead, Mary."

"Oh, dear. That's sad."

"I'm sorry, Sarah." Bernie felt awful. "I'll shut up now."

"No, go on." Sarah's voice quavered. "People need to know. We all need to go there before we can let it go."

Was that true? Bernie looked to their faces, the vacant eyes and pinched lips. Were they also scrolling through the details they knew, trying to piece together a strip of memories that would bring them closer to Brendan and reassure them that he hadn't suffered?

"The scene was still pretty chaotic when I was there. Dad said they were taking Sean Walters out on a stretcher when he got there. It looked serious. Indigo was rushed into surgery. The bullet is pressing on her spine and they're worried about some numbness in her legs. But she was able to give the police a description of the shooter. A black man, twenty or thirty-ish. And there were nine other people in the coffee shop at the time. The police were still getting statements from the witnesses when I was there, but there was a consistent story emerging. Apparently the suspect came in, stood in line, and then, without saying anything to anyone, he began shooting. Kevin and Sean by the window were first. He hit Indigo, who was at the sugar bar. Then Brendan came out of the restroom, and the suspect shot him."

"So there were nine other people in the shop, and this guy managed to hit only uniformed cops." James rubbed his chin. "I guess we know what his plan was."

"But why?" Conner asked. "It doesn't sound personal. I mean, it doesn't sound like he even knew them. Why would he do that?"

"Who knows?" Mary Kate said. "The guy's a psycho. I just hope he doesn't hurt anyone else before he's caught."

"And we'll catch him, all right," James said with a dark star in his eyes. "That perp is a dead man walking."

Chapter 22

The house phone was ringing in the kitchen, and Peg jumped up to answer it. Bernie had to restrain herself from ripping the old phone out of the wall. Back in college she had begged her father to replace it with a portable phone that could go anywhere in the house, but he had resisted. Sully didn't want the phone to overrun his home, and Peg liked having her kitchen be the communication center.

"Yes, dear. Everyone's gathering here," Peg was saying. "I'm going to pick up the girls from school soon. How's it going on your end?"

Bernie listened in as she placed two empty glasses beside the sink. A stain on her mother's countertop took her back to the bloodstained tiles in the center of Dad's coffee shop. A heavy smear. Was that where Indigo had gone down? Had she tried to move away, tried to get her gun? Had Brendan had a chance to reach for his gun? A moment to panic?

She shook her head. If she could just shake out the desire to know the terrible truth, the need to be with her brother in those last moments. To know his pain and selfishly catch one last flicker of his goodness.

The shop must be cold by now. Would they be allowed to board up the broken window? As a junior prosecutor, Bernie had never worked on a case that involved a crime scene, so she wasn't sure how the details were handled. But she imagined that the investigation would go on long into the night. The shop would be a golden box in the twilight, its peach walls warm against the night, belying the terrible thing that had happened there.

"Oh, dear." Peg pressed a hand to her heart. "And we thought he was in the clear. We were hoping and praying..." Peg turned away from Bernie and sank onto a kitchen chair. "Yes, it is God's will, but sometimes I don't understand it at all. Of course. I'll tell them. Okay, sweetie. Bye."

Peg was pensive as she hung up and nodded toward the living room. Cold with dread, Bernie stood behind her mother in the doorway.

"That was Sully on the phone with some sad news. Sean Walters is gone, too. The doctors found no sign of brain activity, and so his family took him off life support. God rest his soul." She made the sign of the cross, and Mary Kate and James repeated the gesture.

Bernie gripped the door frame as if it were the only thing that could hold her up on this spinning carousel. With the level of medical care Sean and Indigo were receiving, the best doctors and nurses and techs, she had been sure that they would both pull through.

But now Sean... she searched for a mental picture of Sean Walters. A big man, gregarious and generous. He'd been at the house one day when Grace was selling Girl Scout cookies, and he'd bought a case. Sean was married, but she'd never met his wife, didn't know about kids.

"Look at the time!" Peg switched gears, galvanized for her grandchildren. "I've got to get going and pick up Maisey and Grace. James, there's more firewood out back beside the garage. And Conner, why don't you come with me? I'm eager to see some of those mad driving skills I've been hearing about."

"Sure, Nana." Conner followed Peg out, and the house, the home of her heart, went cold and silent. Bernie couldn't stop shivering. Maybe it was all setting in—the shock, the grief, the lack of sleep.

Peg had left the front closet open, and now Bernie ducked into the closet and found a lined fleece jacket that belonged to her mother. She slipped it on and headed down the hallway to the back rooms, planning to pile on a few blankets and close her eyes for a few minutes.

The door was cracked open. "Knock, knock." Bernie pushed it open to find Sarah sitting on one of the twin beds, hugging herself. The shades were drawn against the waning afternoon light, and the room was dim, lit by a night-light that glowed in ever-changing colors.

"Hey, that's my bed." Bernie bounced down beside her sister-in-law, who gave her a sidelong look.

"You can have it. It sinks in the middle."

"Yeah, I don't think Mom has replaced the mattresses since Bush was in office. George H." She glanced across at the gray lit window. Bernie still had dreams set in this room, as if she were still a kid and her father appeared beyond that window, her hero, her rescuer. It was as if her subconscious still hadn't grown up and realized that you could only rescue yourself.

She slid an arm around Sarah. "You know, you can lean on me. Use me. I'm happy to take the girls whenever you need a break. Gracie can come for sleepovers, and I can stay at your place if you want. I have no hobbies and no love life, so I've got plenty of time on my hands. I'm yours."

Sarah sniffed; then she put her arms around Bernie. "I don't know what I'm going to do without him." Her voice was level, but her body was quivering. Then, she began to sob.

The ache was thick in her throat as Bernie took Sarah in her arms and squeezed tight against the memories. How she ached to hear him tease Grace about saying grace just one more time. She needed his sanity to help navigate their crazy family, but no, he was gone and she was left to deal with zombies staring at the television as if New York 1 would deliver the meaning of life in their next report.

Don't take them too seriously, he would say. *Ma equates food with love. The others just came for the free beer.*

She would smack his shoulder if he were here.

Sarah pressed a fist to her mouth. "How am I going to tell the girls?"

You tell them the truth. Brendan's voice was calm, billowing in like a summer breeze. *As much as they can take.*

"You'll find a way," Bernie said, swiping a tear from her cheek as she slid into the river of memories, deep and heavy with longing. She could see that giddy grin on Brendan's freckled face after he'd successfully split a Popsicle on the edge of the front stoop. The Popsicle was cherry, sweet and cold and mixed with the dust of the playground as he taught her how to bat a ball. She could smell the sun on new-cut grass as they romped on the front lawn. She heard his voice, comforting as a familiar old robe, telling her, *Calm down, Peanut. It'll be fine.*

And there he was on the majestic steps of the auditorium at Columbia University. He cut through the awkwardness of Sully and Peg and literally danced up the stairs to congratulate her. *You did it! I'm going to have to polish up my lawyer jokes now.* She worried that their father had seemed awkward, and he got it. *You know he's proud of you, Peanut. He just can't say the words. He never could.*

When memories ran so rich and vivid, did they cease being memories and transform into the fiber of your being?

Bernie squeezed her eyes shut, wanting to hold on to him in the past so that she could carry a part of him into the bleak future.

Sometimes you just got to keep on keeping on. His voice was solid and clear, but would it remain that way?

You'll get sick of hearing from me, he said.

She shook her head vigorously, wanting to hold on, wanting to hear his voice forever.

Chapter 23

"What are you having to eat, Miss Maisey?" Mary Kate held a plate aloft over the buffet spread. "Chicken drumstick? Baked ziti? Nana makes delicious baked ziti . . ."

"Or you can have *chicken*!" Conner said, tickling her waist.

"Drumstick, drumstick!" Maisey said, playfully slapping away Conner's hands.

"Come on. I'll sit with you at the table." Conner grabbed a plate. "In fact, I'll have some chicken, too."

"All right." Mary Kate set the plate down and lifted her niece onto the chair. She was so proud of the way her son had engaged his young cousin. Conner wasn't always comfortable here at the house, but he'd really stepped up. "Milk, juice, or water?"

Maisey lifted her chin. "Soda?"

"Juice it is." Mary Kate ducked into the kitchen, where Bernie and Grace were sitting with plates of ziti and an open jar of capers, one of Gracie's favorite things to eat.

"I'm going to pray for a miracle, and you can help me, Aunt Bernie," Grace said, holding her glass with both hands.

Mary Kate moved quietly, not wanting to interrupt the intense conversation.

"You're named after St. Bernadette in Nana's movie, right?" Grace asked.

Oh, not that old pearl, Mary Kate thought as she plunked the juice back into the fridge. Peggy had always been in love with *The Song of Bernadette*, a film from the fifties, and she'd managed to make all her grandchildren sit through it with her.

"I was named after the saint." Bernie chased a few tubes of pasta with a fork. "But it doesn't mean I have any saintly powers like a superhero."

Mary Kate quickly ducked out of the kitchen and served the juice to Maisey, who got up on her knees and stared into it. "I don't like orange juice. It has furry things inside."

Conner laughed. "No fur, squirt. That's pulp."

Maisey's rosebud lips creased with displeasure. "I don't like pope."

"Milk?" Mary Kate asked. When Maisey nodded, she ducked back into the kitchen and picked up on the miracle conversation again.

"I'm going to ask God for a miracle," Grace said. "I'm going to pray, and pray and pray really hard that he brings Daddy back to us."

"Wow." Bernie put her fork down. "We'd all love that."

As she poured the milk, Mary Kate couldn't resist butting in. "It would be wonderful, but that's not how God works, Gracie. Remember, it was a really big deal for God to bring Jesus back from the dead. He didn't create people for us to live forever. I know it's hard to take, but that's just how it is." She grabbed the milk, delivered it, and returned to find Grace revamping her plan.

"I still believe in miracles. Can I try it? Sister Catherine says you can tell God anything. Why can't I ask God to bring Daddy back?"

"You can ask," Bernie said, shrugging up at Mary Kate. Bernie had a special relationship with Grace, but she lacked real experience with kids.

"Here's how I see it." Mary Kate slid into a chair. "God does make miracles happen every day, but he rarely goes against the structure of the world he created. Otherwise, mountains would float into the sky and everyone who died could come back to life, right?"

Gracie licked some capers from the tip of a spoon and nodded. "I guess."

"And that would be kind of a crazy world, if dead people came back to life and mountains floated," Bernie said. "Ice cream could grow on trees, and capers could fall from the sky like rain."

Grace's brows rose, but she didn't smile. This was serious business for the kid. "I'd like the caper part. But are you sure? I mean, God can do anything."

"You can pray," Bernie said. "It never hurts."

"We're all praying for your dad, Gracie." Mary Kate reached over to move a lock of hair from Grace's eyes. She'd always thought of Brendan and Sarah's kids as well behaved, but had never had much personal interaction with them before today.

"Maybe the miracle we can hope for is that God will heal our broken hearts." Tears shone in Bernie's dark eyes.

"Now that's something God can help us with," Mary Kate said, thinking of her own pain. Tony. On desperate nights, she had uttered a prayer to St. Jude, but she'd never really prayed to God about it. She wasn't a believer in bringing every little concern to the Big Guy.

Just then there was a knock on the side door, and Mary Kate felt her jaw drop in surprise. Could it be Tony? Wow. Maybe God *was* listening in on every little detail.

Mary Kate popped out of her seat and went to the door, knowing he'd just push his way in after a minute. The door opened and she smiled in relief...

At a dark-haired man with exotic eyes.

"Oh. You're not . . . the person I expected."

"I'm Keesh, Bernie's friend." He stuck a hand out. "I think we've met before."

"Right. I'm her sister, Mary Kate." She smiled as she shook his hand. "Bernie's right here."

He stepped into the kitchen, looking like a model in his navy coat and crimson scarf. Men from Mary Kate's generation didn't wear scarves, but she'd seen it all with her kids and their friends, from woven hats with braids and tassels on top to loud plaid jackets to slippers and pajama pants for school.

"Hey." Bernie looked up at him, love in her eyes. "You didn't have to come."

He leaned down and kissed her on the forehead. "I was worried about you."

An odd mix of jealousy and admiration swirled in Mary Kate's heart. Bernie had found the real thing. Mary Kate had heard that she'd broken up with this guy, but apparently not.

"Is Amy here yet?" he asked.

"Not yet. Grace and I were just having a discussion about miracles," Bernie said.

"Do you believe in them?" Grace asked him.

He was rubbing his jaw, considering, as Mary Kate backed out. She checked on Maisey, who was having a second drumstick.

"Good job, guys," she said, putting a hand on Conner's shoulder. She was so proud of him. Just a few days ago he had refused to come to dinner at his grandparents' house, and now he was here, taxiing people around and entertaining Maisey, who certainly needed the distraction.

"Why haven't you come here before?" Maisey asked him.

"Because I had to fly on a spaceship all the way from Mars," Conner said. "It took, like, thirty million years. Do you know where Mars is?"

Maisey shook her head. "Where's your spaceship?"

"Right out in the driveway. Want to see it?"

She nodded, and Conner gave her a piggyback ride to the front door.

What a good kid, Mary Kate thought as she dumped dishes in the sink, then swept into the living room. When Conner had failed to make the grade in college, she'd been worried, but seeing him tonight had allayed her fears. He was solid, positive, and kind. He'd find his way.

The seat beside Granny Mary was empty, and Mary Kate sat down and smiled at her grandmother.

"Did you get enough to eat? There's more chicken and pasta."

"Not for me." Granny waved her off. "My boyfriend, Patty, is coming for me soon. He's taking me out for a steak dinner."

Mary Kate was about to set her straight, but then didn't see the point. "That's nice. He must really be into you if he's springing for steak."

"Oh, yeah. I got panache. But maybe you can tell me something, doll." She grabbed the sleeve of Mary Kate's sweater. "Why is everyone so sad here?" She pointed across the room to Sarah. "That one doesn't stop crying."

Mary Kate faced her grandmother and looked into her watery eyes. "She lost her husband, Granny. Brendan. Your grandson Brendan. He was killed today."

"Oh, dear!" Mary pressed a hand to her sagging lips. "Brendan. Oh, dear Lord, and he was one of the good ones. I remember when he was yea tall. He used to do chores for candy money. He mowed my lawn for me."

"That's right. That was Brendan," Mary Kate said, relieved that it registered with her grandmother. Granny Mary had her occasional moments of clarity.

"Why did it have to be one of the good ones?" Granny lamented. "It should have been your guy, Tony, not Brendan. Brendan was always such a good boy, but Tony, I never trusted that one."

Mary Kate felt her jaw drop, but she didn't even try to contain her surprise at her grandmother's burst of memory.

The silence in the rest of the room let her know that everyone was watching.

"Yeah? You think Tony can't be trusted?" said Mary Kate.

"I wouldn't trust him as far as I could throw him. I never liked Tony. The man is all polish and no silver."

"You know, Granny, I have to agree with you. When I married him twenty-two years ago, I thought there was more beneath the surface, but now I'm thinking I was wrong."

Deb laughed out loud. "Mary, you don't know what you're saying."

"Actually, I think she does," Mary Kate said. "I think it's one of the clearest thoughts Granny's had in a long time."

Mary beamed. "That's what I do."

"MK, you're terrible." James shook it off with a grin.

But Mary Kate was serious. "Do you know I haven't been able to reach him all day? There's no accountability." Noting that Conner and the girls were out of the room, she added, "Some nights he doesn't come home at all. Sometimes I get a text message saying he's sleeping at the precinct." She scowled at James. "How many times have you slept at the precinct?"

James gave a nervous laugh, but didn't answer.

Mary Kate swung around to Deb. "Has he ever?"

"No. Never."

"I rest my case. He is so getting kicked out of the house." Mary Kate folded her arms. "If he ever comes home."

"Oh, come on now, Mary Kate," Peg's voice came from the dining room. "You'd really kick your husband out? Where would he go?"

"Wherever he goes at night. His Bat Cave. His lair. I don't know and I don't care anymore. Look, I know my timing sucks, but I can't live this way anymore. I'm sorry." She pressed her hands to her face and found that her cheeks were hot to the touch. "I don't want to take away from Brendan or anything. I just . . ." She let out a breath. "It feels really good to be honest about it."

Feeling as if a burden had been lifted from her shoulders, Mary Kate stood, gathered up two empty mugs, and noticed Sarah watching from the dining room. She put a hand to her heart. "No disrespect intended, Sarah. I just . . . it felt really good to come clean with that."

"I wish people would stop tiptoeing around me," Sarah said. "And I respect you more than ever. Just stand your ground, girl. Stand your ground."

I will, Mary Kate thought as she carried the dishes into the kitchen.

Later, when everyone was getting ready to leave, Mary Kate checked her cell phone from her coat pocket and noticed three missed calls from Tony. Well . . . it served him right. Let him decipher events on his own.

When Conner pulled into their driveway, Tony's car was there.

"Dad's home." He turned to his mother. "Where's he been all day?"

"That's a good question."

Tony greeted Conner with a bear hug. He asked how everyone was holding up, and Conner told him about Sarah and the girls and Sully staying at the crime scene all day.

Mary Kate listened as she hung up her coat, slid out of her shoes, then put the kettle on for chamomile tea. Did Tony notice that she wasn't doting? That she wasn't asking him if he'd eaten?

Never again.

Conner headed upstairs, and Tony paused in the kitchen door, his face a mask of sympathy. "You must be devastated," he said in a voice thick with drama.

She wasn't going to fall for the act. "Where were you all day?"

"I know. Bad day to be out of reach, but it couldn't be helped. There was this undercover operation, weeks in the planning, and—"

"I called the precinct, Tony. They said you took a vacation day."

"I . . ." He shook his head. "Who did you speak to?"

"Why? So you can go abuse him for letting the wife in on the truth?" She dunked her tea bag, then cradled the mug for warmth. "You're so tan. I know you didn't go to the Caribbean in one day. Maybe . . . yes. It's a goggle tan." She nodded toward the driveway. "I bet that if I checked right now, I'd find skis in your car."

His lips curved in a peevish smile. The creases at the outer edges of his eyes seemed permanent now, and his hair was limp and dull. From the way it tilted over his forehead, she wondered if he was trying to cover a patch where it was thinning. "Ah, you're killing me. Okay, you found me out. Yes, I snuck off to Hunter Mountain. With the guys. Not what you're thinking."

"Actually, I was thinking that a terrible thing happened today and you didn't respond when this family needed you most."

"I know, I know, babe, and I feel awful about that."

"Stop lying to me." She placed her tea on the kitchen island and met his eyes. "You were off with some woman. That's why your cell phone was turned off. That's why I couldn't reach you."

"What? You don't trust me?"

She remembered Granny Mary's remark: *I wouldn't trust him as far as I could throw him.* "The truth? I really can't trust you anymore."

"Now, Mary Kate, you're overreacting."

"I don't think so." She steeled herself, her palms pressing on the countertop for strength. "I've always loved you, and I wanted to think you loved me. That's why I fell for the stories. The overtime, the trips with the guys. The excuse that you couldn't get time off for our trip to Disney World. So I took the kids on my own, and when we got home, you know what I found? The house was empty and the shower and sinks were bone-dry. You didn't think I noticed, all those years ago, did you? You didn't realize I was putting two and two together. But I was. I just didn't say anything because I was starting to learn that I couldn't trust you."

"Really." He squinted at her. Such a menacing look, but she wasn't going to take him seriously. She'd seen this posturing for years. "So it's all about you, huh? Four cops down, and we're supposed to talk about your problems?"

She shrugged. "Sorry if that's inconvenient for you, Tony, but it's been a long time coming. I think I've been a good wife, except I probably should have spoken up years ago." She had kept it together for the kids; she realized that now. But seeing Conner today, his initiative and his kindness, she realized that he would do okay even if his parents were living apart. In many ways, he'd been doing without his father for a long time. "I just can't take it anymore."

"Babe. Really? You're pulling the plug when I've just had the worst day of my life?"

"Tell me, how was your day so bad? So . . . so exclusively bad that no one else could feel your pain?"

"I lost two of my brothers today, and there are two in the hospital fighting for their lives."

She could have let him know that it was worse than he thought, that Sean Walters had passed, too, but she didn't think he deserved to have that inside information.

"Oh, please." She lowered her voice, deadly calm now. "I lost my real brother today, Tony. My brother. And when it went down I dropped everything and went over to the house to be with my family, because that's what families do."

"Yeah? Well, some of us have jobs." He jabbed a thumb at his chest, so self-righteous.

"I work, too, you know." A year ago she had started working as a receptionist and bookkeeper for their dentist, Dr. Parsons.

"Sure you do. What do you take in a year? Gross income, honey? Is it enough to pay groceries, let alone the mortgage?" His pursed mouth was petulant.

His pettiness saved her from feeling defensive at all. Instead, she saw him through a new lens . . . and it was not a pretty sight. How had she looked beyond the lies and the attitude for all these years? "Wow, I've really had my head in the sand."

"What the hell are you talking about?" he shouted.

She blinked, then picked up her teacup and added some more hot water. "I'm going to take this upstairs. When I come back down, you're going to be gone."

"Where am I supposed to go?" he asked, his arms flying into the air with rage.

"That's up to you." She headed toward the stairs, her feet sure on the fake oriental runner that she'd searched all over Long Island to find. At the time it seemed so important to find the vivid cornflower blue background she wanted. Now? It really wouldn't have mattered if it were brown or black or navy blue.

And maybe that was liberating.

Yes. It was liberating.

Chapter 24

"I'm Maureen, the night nurse."

Indigo nodded, opening her mouth for the thermometer. As the woman with a confident demeanor and a brightly colored smock took her pulse, Indigo wondered how long she'd been out of surgery. Her throat was sore and her tongue felt fuzzy, but her thoughts were taking shape better now, like crystals forming on the glass of a window in familiar patterns.

The events of the day, which had threatened to overwhelm her just hours ago, now seemed secondary compared to the doctor's words when she'd regained consciousness.

"We removed the bullet, relieved the compression on the spine. We're hopeful that you'll regain feeling in your legs and walk again. Right now, we have to wait and see. Now you get some rest."

Wait and see. Rest and wake up.

Hospitals were strange places.

When you needed your rest more than ever, someone was coming 'round every few hours to wake you up and stick a thermometer in your mouth, take your blood pressure and talk about your pain, even when the thing that put you into the hospital had nothing to do with a fever or blood pressure. Even when you weren't in pain.

"No fever, and your blood pressure is good. I'll let you go

back to sleep, unless there's something else you need. Another blanket?"

"Water?" Indigo touched her neck. "Still sore."

"From the breathing tube." The nurse nodded. "You're allowed to have clear liquids. I'll get you a cup with a straw." She went out to the hall and returned a moment later, talking with someone at the door.

"So, do you know the cop standing guard outside?" Maureen asked. "Is he a friend of yours?"

"I didn't even know I was under arrest."

"More like protection. You're a hero, Indigo." Maureen's green eyes reminded her of a cat, calm but perceptive as she handed Indigo the cup. "Do you remember what happened?"

"I do," Indigo said in her sandpaper voice.

"There'll be time to talk about it tomorrow. For now, rest."

Which was what I was trying to do when you came in the room, she thought as the nurse checked the monitors, then left. The cold water soothed her throat, but Indigo knew there was no way to address the tenderness that burned in her chest. She was in pain, but it was nothing the doctors could treat. Her heart ached something fierce.

It ached for the husband who couldn't find his way back to her. It ached for her little girls, who had come close to losing their mother today. It ached to throw off these crisp white blankets, hop to the ground, and walk the hell out of this hospital.

Oh, how her heart and soul ached to walk again.

Indigo reached down to the blankets and pinched one thigh. Nothing . . . still nothing. *Dear Lord in heaven, there has to be some sensation. Please, please, Almighty Father, bring the gift back to me. Let me walk again.*

What had the doctor said? The first forty-eight hours? Or was it seventy-two?

I can wait, Lord, but please . . . don't leave me in a wheelchair.

She didn't know how she would take care of her girls if she

couldn't walk. How would she stop Zuli from running into the street or play tag with Tasha in the park?

Tears stung her eyes, and she turned toward the wall and swiped at them with the back of one hand. She had to walk again. Damn it, she owed that much to Brendan and Kevin, who would not have another chance to chase their kids or kiss them good night.

Soft footsteps from the hall stopped at her doorway.

That was the other weird thing about hospitals. People just breezed into your room, into your private space, without any warning.

She rubbed her eyes and turned toward the door.

"Hey, Indie." He stood there in his old jeans and battered jacket, the black plastic-framed glasses that he'd worn long before they were in fashion, and the suede, rubber-soled shoes he called Hush Puppies.

She had never seen a more beautiful sight in her life.

"Elijah." She sniffed back tears, staring. "You came to see me."

Or was she imagining him? She hadn't seen her husband for more than a month, and it didn't make sense for him to be here. After all, he'd been living in Philadelphia for the past year, kowtowing to his father, who refused to acknowledge that Elijah had a family of his own here in New York.

"I've been waiting downstairs all day, ever since they took you into surgery." He came closer, slid a hand over the bare part of her arm. That touch . . . yes, he was really here.

She knew it was after midnight. "Isn't it a little late for visiting hours?"

"I'm family," he said. "But I got to say, it's not easy to get to you. Did you know they got a cop outside your door? A big man, with a big gun."

She shook her head. Elijah never had liked much about police work. The guard was posted . . . why? Her thoughts were still clouded.

Because the perp is on the loose.

Because he killed your partner. He killed three cops. Almost four.

She put that knowledge to the back of her mind, tamped it down and locked it in.

Elijah cocked his head to the side, that subtle gesture that hinted of humor. "You don't think it's weird to have a man with a gun hanging out in a hospital where they're trying to heal people who get hurt by guns?"

Indigo gave her husband the pat answer. "It's one of the perks of the job."

"You couldn't go for a job that had a vacation in Europe as a perk? Car service? Educational incentive plan?"

She shook her head.

"So how you feeling? I got here as fast as I could."

"And you've been waiting all this time?"

"They let me see you in recovery, but you were still out of it. I set up my laptop in the cafeteria and the nurse texted me with updates." He shifted back, touching the bar at the side of her bed as if testing its temperature. "Are you in pain?"

"No. But pain might be an improvement. 'Lijah, I can't feel my legs. What if I'm paralyzed?" A sob broke in her throat, along with a new wave of tears. Not at all the way she'd planned to greet her husband, who had been missing for weeks, but control was no longer an option.

"I know. I know, Indie." He frowned, squeezing her arm. "You've got good doctors, though. I checked them out online and they're solid. Besides, they told me you have a chance of beating this thing. If I know you, you'll be up, dancing circles around all of us tomorrow."

She sobbed again. She could picture that. Yeah, she could see herself doing some moves for the hospital staff. That was the way she had to keep thinking. Stay positive. Believe that it could happen.

"You're right." She sniffed and took two tissues from the box he handed her. "I have to focus on the goal. I need to see it right here." She pressed two fingers to the space between her

eyes. "I need to see it happening, and then I need to keep praying on it."

"You keep doing that. And I'll keep leaning on the doctors
to make sure they're doing everything you need to have done.
One of the guys on the team looks like he just got back from
surfing in the Fiji Islands. Doctor Dude."

She smiled. "Elijah. I'm glad you're here, but it's bittersweet, you know that. I've got a disappointment coming. It's
never fun to wake up in the morning and find you gone."

He looked away. "I know, baby. But this will be different. I
can't let you and the girls fall down like this."

"Have you seen them?"

"Not yet, but we talked on the phone. They're at your
mother's and, you know, I was staying here, to be here for
you." He pushed his glasses up on his nose and leaned over
her, so close she could see the curls of hair on the side of his
face, where he hadn't been able to shave that day. "I know we
got issues. I know. But right now, let's just be happy and grateful we're both here. Grateful to be alive. You had a close call,
and it makes a man wonder. Anything could happen, baby."

He leaned close and pressed his lips against hers, and Indigo
closed her eyes and gave herself to the kiss.

"You are such a geek."

"Yeah. But I'm your geek."

She wasn't so sure about that.

When she awoke in the morning feeling like her lower half
was a sack of dead fish, she let out a moan.

Please, Lord, she begged, holding the prayer in her heart
like a mantra.

The session with the detectives was exhausting. They were
kind and sympathetic, but there was no tiptoeing around the
facts, no way to avoid the details of the slaughter. She was glad
when the doctor told them it was time to wrap it up.

For some reason the nurse was on to her to eat her delicious clear liquid diet, and she sipped coffee and sucked on Jell-O, wondering if this would be it for the rest of her life.

At least you have a life, girl.

She still couldn't believe what they'd told her about the guys. Brendan and Kevin and Sean.

There was a knock on the door, and the cop on duty at the door, a female named O'Conner, asked if she was cool with a special visitor. "I'm only supposed to let family in, but I got Bernie Sullivan here." Her eyes softened. "Brendan's sister?"

"Please, let her come in."

A moment later, Bernie appeared, her hair a wild cloud around her head, her shiny glasses masking her eyes. "Indigo." Bernie came right up close, gripped Indigo's unfettered hand, and placed a big fat kiss on it. "Oh, my gosh. It's good to see you."

Indigo swallowed over the knot of emotion growing in her throat. "Bernie, what can I say? I'm crushed."

Bernie nodded, her eyes filling with tears. "I know. It's rough."

They remained like that a moment, huddled close, their hands bound. Indigo felt their thoughts weaving, binding, and meandering as details of the incident swirled around them.

"And how about you?" Bernie asked. "What does the doctor say?"

"There's a chance I'll get the feeling back in my legs. Bernie, I need to walk again. I got my girls to take care of."

"Yes, you do. We're all pulling for you. I'll have Mary Kate put the word out to her friends from church. They get together to do novenas."

"What the hell's that?"

"Lots of prayers. It's a Catholic thing. And anything else we can do for you, just ask. I know Gracie wants to hang out with Tasha as soon as all this blows over. How are your girls? Have you seen them since it happened?"

"Not yet. Tasha is freaked out, but I think she'll feel better when she can see that I'm the same old mean mom."

Bernie leaned back slightly, still perched on the edge of the hospital bed. "Have you talked to a counselor here?"

Indigo squinted. "You think I need a shrink?"

"After something like this, we all do. I just think it would help to talk. I saw the coffee shop just after it happened, and I'm having trouble cycling through the images in my head."

"Yeah, there's that." Indigo sighed. "The shooter's face, it keeps haunting me. His eyes, not the psycho eyes you'd expect, but sad and lost. Like a kid who had his bike stolen from him."

Bernie bit her lower lip, listening intently.

"He talked to me. Came right up to me." Indigo stared off. "He had shot me from behind, and while I was squirming on the ground, trying to get my gun out, he came over and stared right into my face. I think he was going to finish me off with a second shot. He was a little freaked out when he realized I was black. He actually apologized for shooting me, said he never meant to take a sister down. It was the color of my hair that threw him. He said, no black woman has hair like that. And then he walked away. I was bracing to take a bullet, but he walked away."

"Oh, man." Bernie pressed a hand to her mouth.

"Right. The Queens DA's going to have a field day with that. But the creepy part is that it made him human. I mean, I hate him for what he did to us. I want to think that he's a savage beast. An animal. But for that one moment, in his sick way, he seemed . . . tender."

"Wow. So I was right about you talking to someone. This is some difficult stuff to weed through."

"I'm talking to you now."

"I'm not a trained therapist," Bernie said.

"You went to law school . . . close enough." Indigo shivered, wishing she could shake off the image of the shooter. His wide forehead, his mouth drooping on one side, his lost eyes. "I don't feel bad about shooting at him, though. It was the right thing to do. The only thing to do. I just wish I'd gotten a shot in at closer range, but my gun was stuck, holstered under ninety pounds of useless legs."

Bernie tilted her head. "I'm going to forget you said that. Those legs are going to be fine. You're going to be fine. And from what I hear, you hit the gunman."

"I heard him let out a yelp, but he moved out of my line of vision."

"Sounds like you got him," Bernie said. "Some witnesses saw a black male matching his description stumbling down the street. My dad almost ran into him. He was holding his arm, walking unsteadily."

Indigo closed her eyes. "I still can't believe he spared me. Please, God, don't let him hurt anyone else."

"If he got shot, he'll turn up sooner or later. You shot him, Indigo. You're a New York hero."

Indigo shook her head. "I don't want to be a hero. I just want to be alive for my kids. Alive and walking."

Chapter 25

Grief was excruciating and delicate, like a cloth woven of spun sugar. One glimmer of a memory, a certain familiar smell or mannerism, and the fabric was rent and disintegrating into dust.

With the images of exploding gunfire and her brother's face still looping through her mind, Bernie was afraid to be alone. She spent the first two nights at Sarah's house, sleeping on the living room sofa. It was all under the guise of being there to help Sarah with the girls. Bernie's haunted heart was her dirty little secret.

The day after the shooting, an autopsy was performed on Brendan's body, and Sarah was told it would be released to the family the following day.

"It's time to go up to Hannigan's on Bell," Peg told Sarah, gripping her by the hands. "You can have the funeral Mass at American Martyrs or St. Pete's, but everyone goes to Hannigan's for the wake. I'll go with you for moral support."

"Do you want me to come, too?" Bernie asked, and behind Peg's back Sarah nodded like a bobblehead. Bernie knew that Ma could be overwhelming, with her steadfast adherence to tradition, but so far Sarah had negotiated with alacrity. She had insisted on cremation, as Brendan had asked for, but she'd conceded to having the traditional Queens Irish wake: two days in a funeral home, closed casket only. Then a funeral service, a celebration of Brendan's life, but no graveside service or grave. Brendan's cremated remains would eventually be scattered on Rockaway Beach, where he had learned to surf.

"I hope this isn't one of those places that tries to gouge you with extras," Sarah said as Peg drove the four of them to the funeral home on Bell Boulevard. Bernie sat in the back with Grace, who had wanted to be involved in the planning of the ceremony for her dad. A brave kid, Bernie thought. So mature for her age. When Bernie was nine, she'd been obsessed with Dippin' Dots and Goosebumps books.

"Hannigan's has served Bayside for generations," Peg said. "They'll do the right thing for our Brendan."

In its day, Hannigan's had been designed to look like one of the loveliest colonial homes on the block. The front was landscaped with sculpted bushes that Brendan would approve of. Its modest white pillars and redbrick façade were steam-cleaned regularly, giving it the perfect look of a building on a film set.

Only the stars here are fading, Bernie thought as Ma pulled into the parking lot and threw the car into PARK. Peg led the way inside, found her contact man, and got them all wrangled into a well-polished but dark office that reminded Bernie of something from the *Addams Family* movies. Bernie didn't really want to think about her own body turning to dust, but she did know she didn't want it being processed with chemicals in a place like this. It just seemed so unnecessary. Cremation was sounding better and better.

"I'm so sorry for your loss," Richard Huffman said, with just the right balance of sincerity and detachment. He made a point of meeting everyone in their group, pausing over Gracie. "What do you think, Mom? Usually it's best for children to wait outside while we take care of things. It can be very upsetting for them."

Upsetting for all of us, Bernie thought, wondering if the process of the funeral would free her mind of the eerie images of her brother falling from gunfire.

"I don't know." Sarah's spine straightened, as if she suddenly realized she might be doing the wrong thing for her daughter. "Honey, do you want to wait outside?"

"I can stay." Grace crossed her legs, one little cowboy boot bobbing in the air under her skirt. She looked way too together for a nine-year-old.

You don't see the freight train coming, Bernie thought.

"Why don't we wait outside?" Bernie suggested.

Curious eyes turned back to the desk and the wall of drab landscape art. "I'm okay," Grace insisted.

But Bernie was already on her feet. "Come with me. We'll talk about the service. We're going to need to pick some readings, right?"

"For the funeral Mass," Peg said. She turned to Richard Huffman. "That's how we're doing it."

Huffman went to the bookshelf and removed a book bound in black leather. "You can take a look while you're waiting. This one has a cross-reference in the back, so you can search out favorite words. Some people find it helpful."

"Thanks." Bernie tucked the Bible under one arm and escorted her niece out the door.

"We won't be too long." Sarah spoke in a parental tone that her daughter couldn't argue with.

Out in the main lobby, they meandered to a velvet sofa under a painting in an enormous gold frame.

"Wow." Bernie could barely take in the dark details of the landscape for the distraction of the ornate, shiny frame. "It's like a museum."

Grace sighed. "But it's a boring picture."

"That's true." They sat down and Bernie pushed the downy hair of Grace's bangs out of her eyes. "Look! You can see again. I'm a miracle worker!"

Grace hung her head, not so easily amused today. "I gave up on the miracle. I talked to Father Tillman when he came to the house, and he said God is a mystery."

"God works in mysterious ways?"

"He said God makes up his own miracles." Grace's frown rumpled the skin under her pug nose. "It's not fair."

"I'm sure he said you could keep praying, right?"

"But I wanted a miracle." Grace folded her arms. "Nobody would help me with it."

"Ah, Gracie, you're too wise for your years." Bernie rubbed Grace's sleeve. She wished she could spare the girl some of these difficult life lessons. "So . . ." She opened the Bible. "What should we read at the service? Something your dad would have liked. That one about faith, hope, and love is good."

"We need something about heaven," Grace said. "To show people that's where Daddy went."

"Okay. Let's look up heaven." Bernie went to the index in the back, then showed Grace how to use it to find references throughout the Bible. "Wow . . . almost half a page of heaven references. It's going to be a lot to choose from."

"I'll find something good." Grace pulled the book away and started checking back through the Bible.

What a good little student. Bernie let her do it on her own, knowing Brendan would be proud of his daughter's independence. If he was watching from heaven, as Bernie wanted to believe.

"My mom might like this because there's some jewelry in it." Grace held her place with her index finger. "It says that the gates of heaven are made of pearls and emeralds."

"Really? Can I see?" When Grace handed the book over, she found the passage in the Book of Revelation, near the end of the Bible. "So there's an angel taking this person to show him the gates of heaven. And each gate is made of a giant pearl." She read on. "And the walls are covered with jasper and sapphire and other unpronounceable gems. Well, there's emeralds; that I can pronounce. And carnelian. I have no idea what that is, but it's fun to say. Car-*nee*-lian."

Grace giggled. "There's too many hard words in that part. But this part is good. It's about heaven. 'I did not see a temple in the city, because the Lord God Almighty and the Lamb are its temple. The city does not need the sun or the moon to shine on it, for the glory of God gives it light, and the Lamb is its lamp.'" She cocked her head to the side. "How can a lamb be a lamp?"

"It's like Father Tillman said, God works in mysterious ways."

"Aunt Bernie? My stomach hurts."

"So. Let's find the bathroom."

The main entryway forked around a central staircase, and Bernie guided Grace toward the left, having been here for a handful of wakes for elderly relatives or parents of her friends. They passed an open door to the left, where a sign said it was the Grace Parlor.

"Hey. It's like me," Grace said, tiptoeing over to the open door. "Look, Aunt Bernie. The room is filled with flowers."

Bernie stepped up to peer inside. The smell of carnations hit her as she scanned the arrangements. Gladioli standing tall as flags. Mixed assortments, some with gold banners reading, BELOVED FATHER or BROTHER. A heart of roses and two flower-covered crosses.

And at the center of the floral displays was an open coffin, its lid lined in shiny blue satin, its resident propped on a pillow so that they could see his waxy face from across the room.

"Oh, no! A dead man!" Grace's face puckered, tinged with scarlet.

"Oh, honey, it's okay." Bernie's arms flew around her niece's shoulders. Quickly she guided her out of the Grace Parlor and into the safety of the hall.

But the damage was done. Grace's head bobbed with silent sobs.

"He's dead!" Grace howled. "He's dead."

"I know, but it's okay." Bernie leaned down, her hands on Grace's shoulders so that she could look her in the eye. "That man's in heaven, and we didn't even know him. But did you see all those flowers? He must have lots of people who loved him."

"Not that man. My daddy! My daddy is dead!"

Of course. Grace had just moved beyond denial.

Bernie folded her niece into her arms and rocked her back and forth. "I know, honey. I know."

Grace felt delicate in her arms as she sobbed against Bernie. The girl was just a delicate attachment of downy skin and thin bones engineered with frail attachments. Would Grace search out the details of her father's death when she was older? Oh, no. Bernie couldn't bear to think of Grace being saddled with the images of blood and shattered skull in her mind.

We humans are so fragile, Bernie thought. People were held together by a fine string of sinew, a delicate vein, and it was a miracle that life could exist at all.

Down the hall she saw Sarah step out of the office, assess the situation, then withdraw again.

Bernie stopped rocking and knelt down in front of Grace, whose puffy face and runny nose broke her heart all over again. "Oh, honey, in a minute I'm going to start crying, too."

"I . . . can't . . . help it!" Grace sobbed.

"Well, then you just go ahead and let it out." Bernie's eyes stung with tears, and she closed her eyes and let them slide down her face as she held tight to the sobbing girl. "That's right, honey," she said in a rough voice. "It's okay to cry."

Friday morning Bernie made the trip she had been dreading and longing for, a visit to Sully's Cup. The shattered glass had been cleaned up and plywood had been fitted into the hole.

Her footsteps slowed as she noticed some of the yellow crime scene tape waving in the wind. So, was it still a crime scene or not?

She ducked into the open door. The lights were on, and evidence markers, dried blood, and overturned furniture littered the place. A young girl sitting on the counter talked a mile a minute. Not just a fast talker, but she had "big hands," gesturing wildly with each word. Sully stood in his usual spot, leaning against the side counter. Bernie realized the girl was Sully's barista, Padama.

"Bernadette, darlin'!" He motioned her in. "Come on in."

Bernie stepped carefully around a plastic card that marked evidence, feeling as if she should tiptoe. "Dad, is this still a crime scene or what?"

"The detectives are done here. They're on their way over to make it all official." Her father's arms wrapped her in a big hug.

She hadn't seen much of him since that awful day.

"Dad, I feel like we haven't talked in years. How is it that you've been here every day, even though this is a crime scene?"

He shrugged. "You know how it is. I had to be here, and the detectives didn't mind bending the rules."

Bernie unzipped her coat as she started taking in details. She wanted him to walk her through the crime scene, but it felt wrong to ask. "It's dark in here without that glass wall. Are you allowed to replace it? I mean, that's the one thing that would keep you from reopening."

"Custom-made. It'll take a week to get here."

"Expensive?"

"Insurance will pay for it. I've got to do it, but I'm not sure about reopening."

"Of course you will reopen," said the girl sitting on the counter. "This neighborhood needs you. The cops need you. And I need my job."

"You remember Padama?" he asked.

Bernie nodded. "You've been working here for two years now, right?"

"Almost two years, and I was working during that terrible

day. Such a terrible day. I was so scared, I was shaking like the leaves on a windy day."

"Wow. You've been through a very traumatic time." Bernie felt a flash of sympathy.

"I will never forget it for as long as I live." She seemed eager to retell her story, which Bernie had seen before in crime victims. "It was such a normal day. The rush was over and it was quiet. I had just served Officer Hilson her coffee, and suddenly... bang! Bang! Four times, he shot."

"And where were you standing?" Bernie asked.

"Right there, behind the counter." Padama pointed. "I heard the shots and I froze. I should have ducked down, but I couldn't move. I just froze stiff like a statue."

Bernie glanced over to the window counter, where she had seen Kevin's body. That area was taped off, the two toppled stools still on the floor. There were also two bloodstains there, from Kevin and Sean, she suspected.

As Padama continued her story, Bernie imagined a map of the coffee shop; the crime scene map. Maybe it was calloused and cold to reduce it to that, but this was what she needed, the only way she could rid her mind of the images of violent death and three young cops.

Bernie let her eyes comb the shop, trying to take in the details a prosecuting attorney might need to try this case. Not that anyone would let a family member even work on a case in the district attorney's office; she just needed to know. She needed to sort it out in her mind.

"He shot the two officers by the window first," Padama said. "The first shot didn't seem real, but then the glass exploded on the second one and all hell broke loose. The other customers, they went crazy. Ducking and crying. It was like a scene from a Vin Diesel movie."

Bernie noticed that her father was unusually quiet. He stood with his arms folded, staring at the ground. Listening. He had heard the story countless times now, and yet he was still listening. For a new clue?

"Then, quick, quick," Padama continued, "he shot Indigo, who was right there at the sugar bar. And just then your Brendan was coming out of the restroom, and, I'm so sorry to say, he shot him."

Sully looked up at her. "You have to speak the truth."

"I know, but it's hard for everyone. And then, the man turned to me and I put my hands up, thinking he's going to shoot. But he just wanted water. 'That's thirsty work,' he said. And he asked if water is free, and I said yes. I gave him a cup, with a lid and a straw, and he picked it up and drank it."

Sully touched Bernie's shoulder. "File that part away. We'll talk about it later."

Bernie nodded, trying to comprehend a killer who worried about the price of a cup of water.

"That's when he noticed that the woman cop, Indigo Hilson, was moving. He pointed his gun at her to get another shot, and I think he got a better look. He said something to her about being his sister, and then he couldn't shoot her. That scared him, and he left. He was limping. And when he was near the door, there was another bang. But that time it was Indigo shooting the bad guy. He still got away, but the shot knocked him to his knees. She definitely hit him. He fell against a stool, trying to get up."

"She's a hero, that Indigo." Sully pushed away from the counter. "Excuse me. Got some detectives to see here."

While Sully went to meet the man and woman at the door, Bernie ventured to the right of the kidney-shaped service counter to take a look at the hallowed spot she still dreaded, the place where her brother had died. A dark brown stain spread over the tiles, and Bernie felt sure it would never come clean.

Sully could scrub day and night, and it would still be there, an organic reminder of a life. The whisper of a priest on Ash Wednesday filled her head: *Remember, man, that you were dust, and unto dust you shall return.*

Padama had slid off the counter, having said something

about the stockroom. Bernie didn't hear because she could not tear her eyes away from Brendan's floor tiles. These ceramic tiles were a portal to another world, the spiritual place where his yin and yang transported to another energy field.

Get the hell out of here, Brendan yelped. *You know I was never into that touchy-feely stuff. Just clean up the mess and move on, Peanut.*

Yep, that was what he would say.

And though his advice was sound, she wasn't sure she could take it.

She felt someone's presence behind her, and turned to find the female detective, bending down to gather up the plastic markers.

"Do you need help?" Bernie asked.

"No, thanks. I'm on it." She straightened, tossing them into a Ziploc bag. "Jane Braden." Despite her brusque demeanor the woman was stunning, with mocha-colored skin that contrasted with her vivid green eyes. Even her clothes, a puffy navy jacket, black pants, and boots, couldn't mask her startling beauty.

"And this is Lieutenant Keefer." Sully clapped the middle-aged man with a red face and short buzz cut on the shoulder. They had approached the main coffee bar, as if they were all going to have a cup. "Braden and Keefer are from the Homicide Investigation Unit."

"I'm Bernadette Sullivan, Sully's daughter." Braden and Keefer stiffened a bit, as if an outsider had penetrated their world.

"Bernie's with the Manhattan DA's office," Sully added, and the detectives' faces were animated once again. Clearly, Bernie was in the club.

"You guys really keep it in the family, don't you?" Keefer said. "One-stop shopping with the Sully family."

"Not to make light of a serious situation," Braden said, reeling the lieutenant in.

"Keefer was just telling me that they got a partial print off the perp's cup."

"That's good," Bernie said, though she was skeptical. There had been legal precedents with partial prints; they were not reliable evidence.

"That and the blood sample. Just a small amount of blood on a stool that the suspect fell against after he was shot." Lieutenant Keefer spoke confidently. "Our forensic team is the best, and we've got cops looking out for him citywide. There's a description out there, and we've already gotten some leads from concerned citizens. Sometimes it's the little things adding up that give you your break. Either way, we're going to get this guy. It's just a matter of time."

As her father walked them to the door, Bernie wished she could feel better about the case they were building. She wanted something to grasp on to, something hopeful, but finding the killer would not bring the victims back.

Chapter 26

The crushing pain had not left Sully's chest since that day. Still, he got out of bed each morning, showered and even had his coffee. He came here to the shop, his only connection to his son now, his only way to help get the man who had had the audacity to steal human lives on Sully's turf.

Peg didn't ask much. She knew to leave him alone. But the kids, their questions about the shop and the investigation, they drove him nuts. Their voices rang in his ears.

The shop was his only escape, but even here the pain rent him in half like a fat vine of thorns spiraling in his chest.

Technically, he wasn't supposed to be admitted to a crime scene, but no one had said a word to stop him. The cops and detectives and bosses realized that he knew police work inside out. They knew he wouldn't go around emptying the trash or picking up overturned furniture. They wouldn't find him mopping the floor or wiping the print dust from the countertop. Not until he got the go-ahead.

These guys and gals knew Sully would bend over backward to assist in the investigation, and they liked having him around. Good ol' Sully, a cop's cop, a gregarious, stand-up guy. You could count on him for backup and a funny story, too.

Every morning he got himself down to the shop to talk the talk and walk the walk.

But inside, he wasn't the same Sully.

Inside, he was broken, and the spirit that had danced him through more than fifty years on the job had drained from him. Empty.

Maybe he'd change the name of the place to Empty Cup.

From the doorway, he watched the detectives head across the street to the precinct. His precinct, the 109. When he'd come up with the idea to have a coffee shop for cops, he'd thought it was brilliant. He'd considered himself a real Einstein. Now he was wondering if it wasn't the idiot blunder of his life.

The sign over the door caught his eye—SULLY'S CUP in neon. A week ago he'd been so proud of it. Now the sight of the sassy cursive letters turned his stomach.

Time to switch on if he wanted to make some headway before Kevin Puchinko's funeral this afternoon. He wheeled around and burst back into the shop. "Okay." He clapped his hands together, then rubbed them vigorously. "Time to make the donuts. They're done with the crime scene. We can give the place a thorough cleaning."

"Do you want me to do the floors first, or the countertops?" Padama asked as she slid an apron over her head.

"Let's start with the countertops and furniture."

"Got it." She finished tying the apron and ducked into the back room.

"Dad, do you want me to help?" Bernie actually looked frightened. She wasn't the domestic type.

"Nah. I'm expecting your sister any minute now."

"Mary Kate?"

He couldn't tell if she was surprised or insulted. "MK's a good worker. Your mother said she didn't have the heart to step foot in here yet, and you've got your prosecutorial stuff to do."

"I know, but there's so much to do here, and I know you

don't want to miss Puchinko's funeral this afternoon." She bit the cuticle of one thumb as her dark eyes swept over the mess.

"I'll be at all the funerals. I owe those guys at least that much." During his career Sully had attended many funerals for cops killed in the line of duty; cops who gave their lives serving this city deserved a hell of a lot more, but an NYPD send-off was a start.

"One day at a time, darlin'." He stepped behind the counter and turned on the spigot of the service sink. "Don't worry, doll. We'll get it done, and I'll see you at the funeral. You just stick to what you do best, the legalese." He was proud of her accomplishments as a prosecutor. "So what did you think about the case we're building? Can you believe the shooter stopped for a drink and left his plastic cup behind? What an idiot. He actually stopped to get a drink." He frowned. "But that's the thing with criminals. We give them more credit than they deserve. Most of them are not that intelligent."

"That's kind of a generalization, but I agree, this guy isn't the brightest bulb on Broadway."

"We're going to get him, Bernie. It's just a matter of time. I only hope the cop who finds him fills him with lead. It's like killing a sick animal; Old Yeller when he's got rabies. You just got to put him out of his misery."

"Dad . . . wow. What about the criminal justice system? Innocent until proven guilty? Every man is entitled to a trial by jury of his peers. Any of this ringing a bell?"

"This is such a clear-cut case." Usually he didn't mind a good argument with his daughter, but right now he wished she would go. He had work to do, and he was in no mood to hear a diatribe about the criminal justice system. "When they find this guy, he'll have the remnants of the hollow point bullet from Indigo's gun inside him. He left prints on the plastic cup."

"Partial prints," Bernie said. "I don't want to burst your bubble, Dad, but partials are not irrefutable. And how do we know he acted alone? Maybe someone put him up to this, and unless we properly interview and prosecute this perp, we'll never know."

I know, Sully thought. *I know he's the one.*

You couldn't survive a lifetime as a cop on the streets without developing excellent instincts, a sixth sense. There wasn't any grand conspiracy, and there was no good reason to waste countless dollars of taxpayer money on the incarceration and trial of an animal like this.

"Sometimes you've got to go with your instincts," he told his daughter.

"Instincts are a wonderful thing. Yours protected you when you worked on the street, Dad. But that's different from street justice. We can't just tar and feather the next black male who limps down the street."

"No, but those detectives will whittle it down. They'll find the man who was in this shop. They'll find the monster who pulled the trigger."

"And he'll stand trial, thank God."

Not if a stand-up cop can get to him first, Sully thought. *Not if we can help it.*

Chapter 27

Mary Kate made sure her car was locked, clubbed, and alarmed with no valuables in sight before she started out of the triple-decker parking lot on Union Street. Downtown Flushing was not one of her haunts, and with the traffic, congestion, and tight parking, she could certainly see why. When she was a kid, Ma had loaded them all on a city bus to come to the dentist here. Dr. Kane had a second-floor office on Roosevelt, with a drugstore and pharmacy underneath. After a checkup, each kid got a certificate for an ice cream cone from the soda shop in the pharmacy down below.

Those days were gone. The billboards touting products in Chinese or Korean made that very clear. Now Mary Kate could barely decipher what sort of businesses most of these shops conducted. Sure, the precinct was still here, and a fruit stand was a fruit stand, but the offices on the second floors were mysteries, as were some of the contemporary storefronts with dark tinted glass and strings of tiny lights.

Driving here today, she'd been astounded by the neon signs that stretched all the way across the street, suspended in the air between buildings, just like in a Jackie Chan movie set in Hong Kong. Flushing was now mostly Asian, and she'd read that some people shunned Chinatown in Manhattan and rode the train out here for authentic Chinese food. She wouldn't go that far, but she had been willing to drive in today and help her dad out, especially when she considered the gruesome task he had ahead of him. Nobody could go that alone.

The wind blew her hair into her face as she left the parking lot. No purse to guard today, just her license and cash buried in her jeans and her keys laced through her right fingers in the pocket of her jacket. She rounded the corner, passing Asian women toting handcarts, mothers with kids, and commuters. Her heart sank a little when Sully's Cup came into view and she saw the giant plywood patch, like a rotten tooth in a pirate's smile. It was no wonder that the spring had gone out of Dad's step. She was worried about him, and was hopeful that he'd open up a bit while they cleaned up the shop.

As she got close, a young woman with wild hair came out of the door. Her sister. She was walking at a good clip in the opposite direction.

"Bernie!" Mary Kate stuck two fingers in her mouth and whistled.

Her baby sister stopped and turned. "You have got to teach me how to do that."

"I didn't expect to see you here today." Mary Kate felt a surprising warmth toward her sister today; they tended to snipe at each other, but tragedy did have a way of pulling people closer together.

"I wanted to check on Dad." Bernie sank her hands into her hair and raked it back. She had gotten the thick hair from Mom's side of the family, while Mary Kate had been stuck with wispy hair the color of sand. Genetics could be so unfair.

"How's the big guy doing?" Mary Kate asked.

"Feeling good enough to argue with me, though he looks a little gray in the gills."

"It was a hard hit for him." Mary Kate looked up at the unlit SULLY'S sign. "His shop was violated. He lost his son and . . . I don't know. None of us could have imagined anything so horrible. Taking down cops on Dad's turf just cut him to the bone."

"I know." Bernie stared down at the ground.

"You're looking a little gray yourself."

"I'm tired. Not sleeping much."

Mary Kate wanted to tell Bernie that she was also up most nights, despite the fact that she had a whole queen-sized bed to herself. They hadn't discussed Tony yet, and Mary Kate didn't like loose ends, but it seemed a little self-absorbed to bring it up with all the other crises that were gripping their family now.

"I'm still sleeping on the sofa at Sarah's," Bernie added.

"Well, that's your problem." Mary Kate smiled. "You need to get back to your own bed for a good night's sleep."

"God, would you stop with the condescending advice?" Bernie clapped her hands atop her head. "You always do that."

Mary Kate's smile soured.

"It's not all that simple," Bernie went on, scraping her hair back. "You always try to simplify things that aren't that simple."

"I'm sorry." Mary Kate was stung. "It's my nature to try and be positive, but that doesn't mean I'm stupid. Yeah, I see the complexity in things. You don't think I have issues? But does it help to sit around and worry and whine?"

Bernie pulled her coat closer against the wind. "Do you think I'm a whiner?"

"Did I say that?" Mary Kate held her hands out. "Now who's oversimplifying?"

When Bernie squeezed her eyes shut, the gray half moons became apparent. "My bad." She opened her eyes and the spark of annoyance had faded. "I'm on edge. The sleep thing, and I don't think I'm dealing well with Brendan's death." She glanced over her shoulder at the shop. "He's haunting me, MK. I pretend things are normal. I cajole Gracie and help Mom in the kitchen, but that's all an act. I'm a wreck, and, to be honest, I came here for some closure."

Mary Kate pulled a hand from her pocket and put it on her

sister's shoulder. "Did it work? Did you find some peace from seeing where it all happened?"

Bernie let out a breath. "I really don't know."

"I'm afraid it may take awhile." Mary Kate tried to say the right things without pissing Bernie off again. "You and Brendan were close. It's a huge loss for all of us, but you were buds."

"I didn't think you noticed."

"You really do think I'm dense."

Bernie shook her head. "You know, MK, you have a surprising sense of humor." She glanced back at the shop. "Dad is expecting you. I hope you wore your grungies, because it's bad."

"Got my rubber gloves in my pocket."

Bernie squinted. "You know, you don't have to do this. We could hire a crew. They have teams that specialize in cleaning up crime scenes."

"For a small fortune, I'm sure. Don't worry. I'll have it under control in no time." She pulled a Ziploc bag of rubber gloves from one coat pocket. "It's been a little awkward, trying to fill my time these last couple of days. They don't expect me at work, and there's not much to do around the house with Tony gone. Conner's pretty self-sufficient. He knows how to make Ramen noodles and scrambled eggs."

"Conner is a great kid," Bernie said. "I'm glad he's started coming around. Have you noticed how Maisey adores him?"

"I think the feeling is mutual." Mary Kate felt warmed by her sister's compliments. She'd always known he was a good kid; at last the family was getting to know and love him, too. "I'd better go."

"Oh, and MK? About Tony. I just wanted to say, it's probably not an easy situation, but I'm proud of you for standing your ground."

Another shock, coming from Bernie. "Ma thinks I should take him back."

"Ma is old school. What do *you* think?"

"I think . . . it's complicated."

Bernie nodded. "I'm sure it is." She bristled against the wind, then lifted her hands from her pockets and gripped Mary Kate in a hug. "I'll see you at the wake."

Chapter 28

The night before Brendan's funeral Bernie hung her black suit in Grace's closet and let her D&G flats drop to the floor, *thunk, thunk.* The day she'd bought those shoes, she'd been ecstatic, thrilled that she could finally afford something that fit her well and had a designer label.

She had not anticipated wearing them to not one, but three cops' funerals.

"Can we watch a movie?" Grace asked from under her pink and purple comforter. She was writing in a journal with a fuchsia feather pen. "I'm not tired."

"We need to get up early tomorrow," Bernie said. "Do you know what you're wearing?"

Grace nodded and pointed the feather pen at her desk chair, where clothes were laid out.

"Of course, you do. You're a lot more organized than your Aunt Bernie." She leaned over the bed and kissed Grace on the forehead. "Good night, Tigger."

"Good night, Pooh." Grace didn't look up from her writing. "Can you leave the light on for a while?"

Bernie shrugged. "Sure."

In the living room, Sarah was opening up a sheet to cover the couch. "Sarah! You don't have to do that."

"What, don't want me to tuck you in?" Sarah teased.

"I'd love nothing more, but go tuck yourself in. Tomorrow's going to be stressful."

Sarah tossed a pillow to Bernie. "Yah think?"

Bernie sat down, hugging a pillow. "And one of these days I'm going to have to go back to my own apartment." She would have to go home, go back to work, go back to her own solitary life, and maybe it was time. The cradle of family was reassuring, but the routine of life would be a good distraction from grief. "It's been almost a week now. I can't keep mooching off you forever."

"Here I thought you were helping with the girls, but you're actually here for the free food?"

"Listen to us. So funny. You'd never know we were depressed."

"Grieving," Sarah said. "There's a difference." She picked up her teacup. "You know you are always welcome here, Bernie. And now . . ." She yawned. "I gotta get horizontal."

"Good night." Catching the yawn, Bernie dropped onto the sofa, pulled the comforter to her chin, and reached up to turn off the lamp on the end table. She was tired, but not so sick anymore. Something had changed today at the coffee shop. A subtle change, but a shift. Somewhere in her subconscious mind she was preparing to let Brendan go.

She must have slipped easily into sleep, because the next thing she recalled was Grace's voice.

"Aunt Bernie? Are you awake?"

"I am." Bernie opened her eyes to see her niece standing before her, the kitchen night-light turning the wispy edges of her hair to gold, like an angel.

"I can't sleep."

Bernie lifted the edge of the comforter. "Climb aboard."

Grace homed in on her warmth, fitting herself to Bernie's side.

Like a sister, Bernie thought, recalling her run-in with Mary Kate today. *My own sister, but I never felt comfortable snuggling up to her or even hugging her.* Of course, they were some fifteen years apart. But MK had reached out to her today, and that had taken a lot of nerve and poise. Mary Kate had surprised her.

"I can't stop thinking about my dad," Grace said, the statement coming from out of nowhere.

"I know what you mean. I was a little obsessed myself."

"What's obsessed?"

"I couldn't stop thinking about him, either. Right now, everyone's thinking about your dad and praying for him. You'll see that tomorrow. Everyone will want to share their Brendan stories. That's sort of the purpose of funerals, to celebrate a person's life."

"Aunt Bernie, do you think he's in heaven now?"

"Absolutely." Although Bernie had her issues with the Catholic Church, she figured that Brendan had more than paid his dues to get through the Gates of Pearl. "You know that your dad and I went to Catholic school, right? At St. Pete's?"

Grace nodded.

"Well, the nuns made sure we did all the right things for our church. Once a month our whole class went to confession. We attended Mass for every holy day, and for the first Friday of every month. One day your dad and I counted the times we'd been to Mass that year. He used a calculator, and it turned out to be more than sixty times." Would Brendan have remembered that day?

"Sixty? Wow." Grace leaned on her shoulder, and Bernie held her close, stroking her hair back.

"We thought of it as a bank account, and each time to Mass was a deposit or a credit, like on a school paper. If we were getting graded, we would have gotten an A."

"Did Dad like going to Mass?"

"He was okay with it, but I think we both found it kind of boring. But when we added everything up, your dad figured God was going to reward us, big-time. He said, 'God's got to let us into heaven now.' So when I think of it now, and I know your dad has been to church a lot of times since then, I'm thinking that God will be happy to have your dad in heaven. He was a good person, plus he went to Mass a zillion times."

She looked down to see if her story had helped Grace feel better, but found that she was asleep. "God bless you, Grace Sullivan."

There was no way the two of them could sleep on the sofa, and she didn't want to wake the girl, so she eased Grace onto the couch and plodded into the girl's bedroom. "Ten again," she said, as she crawled under the pink and purple comforter. It was like a trip to Disney World, falling asleep in a room that reminded her of a box of candy hearts.

She awoke during the night to a tapping on the window. Squinting in the darkness, she tried to make out the details there. Was that a bush, or . . . a person?

A man, she thought, sitting up in bed. Though the window was across the room, it felt as if he could reach right through and grab her.

She gasped, pulling the covers up to her chin, but the man waved his arms, smiling, and fear drained from her as she recognized her dad. It was only her father.

She tossed the covers aside and began to slide out of the bed, but her father's face hardened, the lines beside his eyes becoming dark grooves, the line of his jaw turning to steel until he was not her father at all.

The sinister gleam in his eyes told her she was in trouble.

No! She tried to get away, run and hide, but she was frozen there, stiff with panic as he lifted a shiny pistol and fired through the window.

The shots jolted her awake.

She was rolling back and forth in the twin bed, clutching her chest, gasping for air.

A dream . . . it was all just a dream.

She was safe in Grace's pink and purple candy heart room with the night-light burning by the door and the shade drawn over the window.

Fear still beat a steady tattoo in her chest. That familiar nightmare that had plagued her since childhood. How many times had she awakened from the horrible vision of a man staring into her room, penetrating her soul? A few times she'd been able to change him back to her father and convince herself that the dream was innocuous, but too often he was a menacing, terrifying figure who sent gunfire ripping into her chest.

She used to wake up wailing, and Lucy, in the next bed, was such a heavy sleeper, she didn't even stir. Sometimes Brendan had come in to console her from the room next door. Other times she had made the steep climb to her parents' room upstairs—anything to get away from the wicked man in the window—and she had crawled into bed between Ma and Dad.

Fear still tugged at her as she pushed the comforter away and hunched on the edge of the bed. Whom did she fear? What was she running from?

Death?

Well, she could run, but no one could hide forever.

She took a deep breath and slid out of bed to go check on Grace.

Chapter 29

The long black limousine sat waiting for them in the funeral home parking lot. From the shiny chrome and the driver in a dark suit, Peg Sullivan suspected it had cost Sarah a pretty penny. Normally she didn't abide luxuries like this, but she wasn't going to complain and hurt Sarah's feelings. "Would you look at this? Plush leather seats, and three of them?" Peg tapped Bernie's arm. "It's pretty grand for transportation."

"Haven't you ridden in a limo before, Mom?" Bernie asked. "What about when you and Dad got married?"

"Oh, there was no money for limos back then. No one had money. You got married in the church, then went down to the church basement for punch and cookies." Peg frowned and hooked an index finger over her lips. She tended to ramble on when she was nervous, and today she was sick with nerves and sorrow, but she was determined not to go on like a chatterbox. She wanted to have some semblance of dignity for her boy's funeral.

"Nana, we're right behind you, in case you're wondering," Grace said from the next seat.

"We right behind you, Nana," Maisey echoed.

Peg turned to see Grace, Sarah, and Maisey buckling in behind her. "There you are. Got your own seat, I see."

In the third row, Sully's mother edged onto the seat. "Oh,

la-dee-dah!" she said as she scooted in. Deb and Mary Kate sat on either side of her. Meanwhile, James and Sully were outside talking with the driver, staying out in the cold till the very last minute.

"You know, Mary Kate," Peg called back, "there's room for Tony."

"Oh, not Tony!" Granny Mary lamented. "He gave me a bloody nose last week."

"I seriously doubt that, Mary." Peg didn't mind Mary's outbursts, but sometimes she worried that she was upsetting the little ones, who still couldn't decipher fact from fiction.

"Do you want to call Tony's cell?" Peg asked. She worried that her daughter was being too rash, cutting off her husband of twenty-some years just because of some petty misbehavior. Granted, Tony liked his beers and she herself had seen him flirting, but it was not the first time a gal's husband had made a mistake. She thought Mary Kate should give him a second chance.

"He'll be fine on his own, Ma."

Doors opened and closed again, and now James was in the backseat and Sully was beside her.

"Brendan got a beautiful day," Sully said. "Sunny but cold." He wore sunglasses, which was uncharacteristic of her Sully, but she understood why a man needed to protect his dignity on a day like today. She still believed that the eyes were the mirror of the soul, and on days like this, the soul needed to have its shades drawn.

The driver said something to Sully, called him sir, and they were off, rolling down Bell Boulevard in their fancy limo.

"Where's Daddy?" Gracie asked from the back, which made Bernie grab Peg's wrist and bite her lip. "I mean, where's the car with his coffin?"

"The hearse," Sarah said. "It's following behind us. That's why the driver is going so slowly."

As they approached the first intersection, there was a flurry of flashing lights, and at first Peg thought it was an accident.

But no . . . it was only cops there, blocking traffic from the intersection so that they could go through. Two motorcycle cops and a patrol car peeled away from the edges and fell into place in front of their limo, and suddenly they were riding along with a police escort—an impressive one, at that.

"Would you look at that," Peg said under her breath.

"That's how we do it, Peg." Sully bit his lips together and turned away toward the window.

She worried about him, now more than ever. Oh, there'd been a bad spell six years ago when he'd had to leave the job. When you do something for upwards of fifty years, it begins to define you, and then, when you become the expert on it, they take it away. That was how Sully felt when it was time to retire, God bless him. But he had moved on. He'd come up with the idea of the coffee shop when he'd walked by the empty store across from the precinct. The rent was reasonable, and the landlord, a fellow who was thrilled to rent to an ex-cop, was willing to give him a break if he put some money into renovating. One step fell into place after another, and quick as you could snap your fingers, Sully's Cup was born.

That coffee shop had saved Sully's life. Too many of his friends on the job had retired to their Barcaloungers and eaten their way to depression and heart attacks. But Sully had carved out a new niche for himself, finding work that made the most of his social gift while keeping him close to the cop business he so loved.

Peg stared out the window at the lines of cars with flashing lights that blocked Northern Boulevard, a major thoroughfare in Queens.

"Why are all the police out there?" Grace asked. "Is something wrong?"

"They're stopping the traffic so that we can get by," Sarah explained. "It's out of respect for Daddy. Because he gave his life for this city."

"Oh."

"Your daddy was a hero, girls," Sully said. "A real hero."

"Daddy was a superhero!" Maisey announced, lightening the mood.

Peg touched Sully's knee, but his attention was focused on the police activity outside. He was still so attached to the cop life, but now, most nights, he talked about closing up the shop. She hoped it was just talk, but she understood how the shooting could ruin his love for the shop he had built. That gunman had taken more than three lives; he'd wounded this city.

There was a big holdup crossing Seventy-third Avenue, and Peg couldn't quite make out what the problem was. As the limo rolled closer, though, she saw the sea of uniforms, of men and women in dark blue lined up maybe ten deep along the left side of the road.

"Good Lord, look at all those cops."

There were hundreds of them . . . maybe thousands.

"New York State Police, Dad," James said.

"I see them," Sully said. "And Nassau County. Jersey. But mostly NYPD. Our guys."

The massiveness of it, the shimmering blue wall of humanity put a knot in Peg's throat. They stood at attention, stern and straight, though when Peg looked closely she read emotion in their faces.

"It's overwhelming," Bernie said quietly.

"Mommy, where did they all come from?" Grace asked.

"They're from all over, honey. Doesn't it make you proud?"

"It makes me feel very safe, looking at all those police officers," Gracie said.

They were still blocks from the church, and yet the deep band of brothers stretched on ahead of them. "I've never seen anything like this," Peg said.

"This is how we do it," Sully said, nodding.

Once at the church, Sarah and the family were guided through the service by Richard from Hannigan's, who moved with calm assurance. The opening processional began in the vestibule with young men from the police parade unit playing

"Amazing Grace" on shrill bagpipes while the family escorted the casket down the aisle.

Bagpipes always made Peg think of Ireland, bringing to mind rolling hills of green and smoke rising from small brown shanties. She'd been five when her parents brought her here, just around Maisey's age. She didn't remember much of Ireland, but she knew her parents had had a hard life there, with not enough food and no money for clothes or a place of their own. Things were better for them in America, but her parents never did get over the hard times and the war. Had they any inkling of what their family might become? A line of cops in the greatest city in the world. And now one of them struck down in the line of duty . . .

In many ways, the ceremony was an ordinary Mass, with a few extra touches. There were the readings, and a lovely eulogy done by Brendan's friend Alex. A boy from the neighborhood, Alex talked about how Brendan was an average kid but for his kindness toward people. He talked about how Brendan used to mow one lady's lawn for free because she couldn't afford to pay. In junior high he was always bringing kids home for snacks, at a time when most of his friends were latchkey kids and didn't have anywhere to go after school. "And I don't think I ever got a chance to properly thank you, Mrs. Sullivan," Alex said.

Peg waved him off, touched by his appreciation, though she had always been happy to have the boys around. Better to have them supervised in her yard or basement than out on the street doing God knew what.

Alex remembered the summer Brendan learned to surf, how his friends had trouble getting him out of the water, he loved it so much.

"Brendan was a man who loved his family, his city, and surfing at Rockaway Beach," Alex said. "He loved his Beach Boys tunes, and the way Sarah Spelding rocked his world. He was proud of his daughters, and said that the highlight of his day was picking up Grace and Maisey after school."

Such a good man her son had grown to be. Peg still hadn't figured out how to describe her loss.

Her eyes strayed to the plaques marking the Stations of the Cross. Such a tedious, backbreaking practice. She used to bring the children on Good Friday, and they would get down on their knees at every station. Up and down, up and down. James hated it, sulking that it was boring and asking why God cared if they said the same prayer fourteen times. But Brendan, he had cheerfully squatted down beside her. He was just a toddler, it was so long ago.

She folded her hands together, trying to remember the prayer. When in doubt, start with the Act of Contrition. *O my God, I am heartily sorry for having offended you . . .*

In the station closest to her, Mary, the Mother of God, stood by as they took Jesus down from the cross. Holy Mary lost her son, too. *Holy Mary, Mother of God, how did you do it?*

Her throat was thick with sorrow, and she took a deep breath to quell the turmoil. Peg wouldn't let the children see her cry. A mother had to be strong. It was her job to hold things together. But when she was alone in the shower, with the noise of the running water to drown out her sobs, that was when she let herself go.

When it was time for the offering, Grace and Conner brought the wafers, water, and wine up to the altar. Peg had suggested that Grace and Maisey do the offering, thinking how lovely that would look to have the two girls together, but Sarah had thought Maisey was too young, and she was probably right. At the moment, Maisey was on her knees rearranging the hymnals in the bracket on the back of the pew. Normal for a child that age, but Sarah tugged her hand and had her sit down. Oh, it was a long day for all of them.

After communion, as everyone sat back, the organist played the Beach Boys' "God Only Knows." That was a sweet surprise. Peg closed her eyes and saw her son taking off for the beach in that old rust-bucket van with his surfboard in the back and his radio blasting from the open windows. Those windows stayed down all summer because the air conditioner never did work in that old clunker.

Although Brendan had claimed the Beach Boys as his kind of music, most of their songs had come out in the sixties, when Peg and Sully were a young couple.

I know this song, Peg thought. *I know it well.*

She hummed along, thinking of the words to the chorus: "God only knows what I'd be without you."

What would she be without her Brendan? Just as Sully had come to identify himself with the cops, Peg's identity stemmed from her brood of children. She had loved them all equally, appreciated their talents and foibles. She could deal with Mary Kate's know-it-all sharpness. She was able to draw James out of his quiet moods. And she didn't feel betrayed by Lucy leaving Queens, as long as her daughter answered her calls, which she did. A mother's love didn't end when her child chose to swim away or swim against the current.

But now, Brendan was gone forever, and this was something Peg was not prepared to deal with. She felt the loss like a hole in her body, a hole that wouldn't heal.

She pressed a hand to her lips, tamping down emotion until the wave of grief passed. The moment would pass, but the feeling that she had lost a part of herself would never go away.

A mother's love did not fade.

It would be her cross to bear. The torch in her heart, burning forever.

Chapter 30

He was still alive.

She hadn't gotten a word out of him all morning, but Yvonne could see the slight rise and fall of his chest, and that meant he was breathing, thank the Lord.

The room was quiet, but for the occasional cry of canned voices and loud commercials from Mrs. Nettle next door, who always had to sit in the afternoon and watch her stories. Soaps. You'd think people in these projects had enough drama in their lives.

Yvonne had handled more than her share of it over the last few days. She had been forced to call in sick at the laundry so that she could take care of Peyton twenty-four-seven. Her boss was mad, threatening to dock her, but there was nothing she could do about that. Her hands were chapped from washing them, and she was going stir-crazy cooped up in this apartment day and night. Besides that, she couldn't let Gwen and Kiki and the baby come over, what with a dying man nearly unconscious in the bedroom. Much as Gwen liked to get her daughter and baby out of her hair, Yvonne just kept saying no, acting like she had the flu or something. And damned if Gwen wasn't ready to send her son and daughter over anyway, flu and all, just to get a break.

She studied him now, his sunken eyes and dry skin. His forehead was hot to the touch with fever, but not a lick of sweat. That was odd. The one time she'd helped him to the bathroom, he'd cried out in such anguish that she gave up and left an old plastic cup from a Big Gulp for him to fill. He never asked to go again.

He was always sleeping, so there was never any time to get any food or drink into his belly. He'd lost weight, for sure, and he was a skinny one to start with.

"Peyton? Peyton, you need to wake up and tell me what to do." She stood over him, thinking maybe he'd open one eye and answer. "You really sick, son. I kept thinking you'd turn a corner and start getting your strength back, but something's wrong with your shoulder that I can't fix. You hear me?"

No answer, not a twitch. In fact, he seemed to stop breathing.

She leaned down close, watching his chest.

"Oh, baby, come on and breathe now."

She stared hard, willing him to live, and damned if his chest didn't rise and fall, a gentle breath, like he was sleeping. At least he wasn't moaning in his sleep anymore. She didn't have any real painkillers in the house and she wasn't about to go out and buy him any street drugs that could make him worse off than he was now.

"I wish you would wake up and answer me." She waited. Nothing but the sound of the theme song to *All My Children* next door. "Peyton, this is getting serious. You wake up now and talk to your mama."

This time the silence scared her.

She strode out of the room and paced the hall, hating herself for what she was considering. She didn't want to be the one who got her baby shipped back to prison, but she didn't want him to die, either.

No . . . she couldn't let her baby die, and he was seriously sick. She was no doctor, but she knew that rotting smell in his shoulder was a very bad thing. Not to mention him sleeping all the time and not eating or drinking a lick in the last two days.

She turned and paced back to the bedroom. "Peyton? Please, wake up."

But he lay there, barely breathing.

Her baby was dying.

Her hands shook as she fished her cell phone from the pocket of her sweater and dialed 911.

"Nine-one-one, is your emergency police, fire, or medical?"

"Medical! It's medical. I think my son is dying! We need an ambulance here." She gave the dispatcher her location and answered a whole list of questions about what was wrong with Peyton. Of course, she didn't say anything about a bullet, just an infection. She figured that was good enough.

"Please stay on the line, while I communicate with the other dispatcher," the woman said.

Holding the cell phone to one ear, Yvonne shimmied out of her old, pilly green stay-at-home sweater and searched her closet for something nicer. The woven jacket in burnt orange? That brought out the amber in her eyes. She pulled it on and fixed her hair in the mirror. Not to be vain, but her mama had told her no matter what, you needed to look your best to win people over, and she figured she'd have a lot of persuading to do to get her baby treated at the hospital without the police hearing about it.

"Ma'am, are you still on the line?"

"Yes, yes, I'm here."

"I've got an ambulance on the way. Can you send someone downstairs to direct the unit to your location?"

"There's no one here but me and my son, and he ain't goin' nowhere right now."

"Okay. Stay there, and the EMTs will find you."

"Okay. Are we saying good-bye now?" Yvonne asked.

"Yes, ma'am."

"Okay, then. Thank you!" Yvonne clicked off the phone and headed back to check on Peyton. She was just passing the bathroom when there was a knock on the door.

"Damn, that was fast." She peeked through the hole and

saw a man in uniform, but that didn't worry her. EMS didn't want to come into the projects without a police escort, and she didn't blame them.

She opened the door and motioned for the cops to follow her in. "Well, that is excellent service, because I just called. But we need the stretcher in here. My son's unconscious."

"Really?"

The question seemed so out of place that she stopped in the hall and turned back to face them.

The lead cop, a black man with lines on his forehead and a shine on his head, had his gun drawn.

That was when she realized all four of the cops had been pointing their guns at her.

"You gonna shoot me?" Yvonne put her hands up, her mouth suddenly dry with fear. "You all aren't with the ambulance, are you?"

"NYPD. We have a warrant for Peyton Curtis."

She nodded. "He's here, but he's sick. You're not going to hurt him, are you?"

"We don't want to. Anyone else here?"

"No. Just me and my son."

The black cop—his nameplate said Russell—put his gun back in his holster. "What's your son sick from?"

"An infection?" she said. "At least, that's what I think."

"Step back against the wall, please." Russell and the woman stayed with her while the other two cops went down the hall to the bedroom. "Is it an infection from a bullet, maybe?" he asked.

"Maybe." Her arms were getting tired, and she let them down, daring Russell to say anything.

"Sarge . . ." one of the other cops called down the hall. "It's him, but he's in bad shape. We need a bus here."

"Okay, Mosley," Russell shouted. "But I think we might have one on the way already. Did you call an ambulance?" he asked Yvonne.

"Yes, officer, I did. I was going to take Peyton to the hospital."

Russell asked the lady cop to check on the ambulance. "How'd he get so sick?" he asked Yvonne.

"He said he was walking down the street, minding his own business, when somebody started shooting up a shop, and a bullet came out the store and hit him."

"And you believed that?"

Yvonne crossed her arms over her ample chest. "That's what he told me."

"Sarge," the woman interrupted, "we've got the ambulance downstairs. EMTs are on their way up."

"Okay." Russell stared at Yvonne, rubbing one of his temples like he had a headache. "So you want your son to see a doctor."

"That's right."

"And your name is . . . ?"

"Yvonne Curtis. Peyton is my son."

"All right, Ms. Curtis. We're going to get your son some medical attention."

"Good." Yvonne felt a touch of relief, but she wasn't singing no hallelujah. "What's the catch?"

"He's under arrest. And you're coming along." Russell turned to the female cop. "Pat her down and cuff her."

"Am I under arrest, too?" Yvonne demanded.

Big, tall Sergeant Russell shrugged. "Right now, it looks that way."

Chapter 31

The church service was ending as the aggravating buzz began in Keesh's suit pocket. Amy gave him a look, but he shrugged.

"At least I put it on vibrate," he whispered.

She rolled her eyes as he checked the message.

It was a text message from his friend Clive in the Queens District Attorney's office.

Coffee shop killer suspect in custody at Queens Hospital.

Keesh frowned. Freaky timing, but Bernie would want to know.

He texted back a thanks and asked Clive for more info. Then it was time to rise for another hymn, the last one it seemed, since the pallbearers were rolling the coffin out the door. The priest and the accompanying boys in puffy white blouses stood at the altar as the family filed out, and then the rest of the crowd broke and scattered to different exits.

Another buzz in his pocket, and he took a quick look at the message.

"We need to find Bernie," he said to Amy.

"No duh." Amy had always been impatient with idle chatter.

"No, really. I just heard from my friend at the Queens DA. They've got a suspect in custody for the coffee shop killings."

Amy blinked. "That'll be a relief for her. For a lot of people, actually."

The overflow crowd dissipated quickly, and the seemingly impossible task of finding Bernie began to seem feasible.

The stone steps wrapping the front entrance of the church were still cluttered with people, but it was easy to make out faces along the staggered platforms. Bernie was near the bottom, talking with a handful of uniform cops. Young, buff men.

He tucked his necktie in and buttoned the jacket of his suit, trying to bite back jealousy. They were probably just friends of Brendan.

He joined the group, listening as one of the cops finished a story about Brendan.

"He had a wicked sense of humor at times," Bernie said. She suddenly noticed that she was flanked by Keesh and Amy. "Hey, guys. I saw you there in church."

Amy gave her a hug. "It was a very nice tribute," she said. "I'm so sorry."

Bernie nodded, then turned her big brown eyes up at Keesh. "What do you have to say?"

"A lot, actually." He reached for her for the perfunctory hug, but she moved up against him and buried her face into his jacket, just under his neck. Her desperation surprised him as she clamped on tight, in front of those young cops and everyone else on the church steps.

His arms pulled her closer, and for a moment he closed his eyes and pretended this was all okay, in the name of reassuring a friend in grief.

When she let go and slipped out of his arms, Keesh felt the other people in the circle watching them. Never one to put his personal life out there, he knew it was time to cut out.

"We need to talk," he said. "Can you ride to the restaurant with me?"

"I'll just tell them in the limo." The group of cops began to break up as Bernie gave the message to her older sister Mary Kate.

"What's the deal with the movie kiss?" Amy asked, wiggling her eyebrows.

He swallowed and straightened his tie. "There was no kiss. Just consoling a friend in a time of grief."

"Mm-hmm." Amy fished out her car keys. "I'll meet you guys at the restaurant."

He wanted to argue with Amy, tell her that it wasn't that way with Bernie anymore, that he had started seeing someone else, but to be honest, he wasn't sure of anything anymore. His relationship with Maro, if you could call it that, had gotten off to a rocky start after he'd had to cancel on her Wednesday. He'd tried to make it up to her with a movie Saturday, but afterward, when they went for dinner, she'd been quiet. He hated making conversation when it was like wading through a marsh.

Bernie, who could talk all night, was rarely at a loss for words.

"It was a good send-off, right?" Bernie asked as he guided her to his car, his hand gently touching the back of her coat.

"Classic and from the heart. Any man would have been proud." He pointed down a side street, where his car was parked. "Bernie, I got a text toward the end of the service."

"Keesh, you gotta turn that thing off. It's your third arm."

"From my friend Clive, with the Queens DA."

She stopped walking in the middle of the street. When she turned to him, the shadows seemed to lift from her face.

"They think they've got the Coffee Shop Killer in custody. I've just gotten a few texts, but I wanted to let you know."

"What are the details? Who is he and why did he do it?"

He pulled her out of the street as the lights of a car approached, then scrolled to the message on his phone. "Peyton Curtis is his name, and he's in Queens Hospital with a bullet wound in his arm. They're not sure he's going to make it."

"Did anyone ask him why? What was his motive?" she asked as they reached his car.

So she wanted answers. He bit his lower lip, restraining

from telling her the world would probably never know the answer to "why?" Dramatic deathbed confessions were only scripted for television shows.

"These are all the messages I have." He handed her his cell phone and fished out his keys. "And I'm getting my info from an ADA. Your cop friends would probably know more."

"That's true and . . ." She stared down at his phone. "Oh, my God, they got him!" She threw her arms around Keesh, bouncing on her feet. "They got the killer."

"The suspected killer," he corrected, taking his phone back before she dropped it on the street.

She put her hands on his shoulders, her dark eyes flashing. "I've got an idea. Let's go straight to the hospital and see if we can talk to him. We both work for the DA's office, and you have friends with the Queens DA. You're going to be on staff there in another week or so."

"No, no, and no." He backed out of her reach, unlocked the car, and put his hands on her shoulders to guide her around the car to the passenger side. "Bad idea, Bernie."

"It may not work, but we could try, Keesh. And there's a good chance the cops guarding him will know my dad." She opened the car door. "We have a good shot at getting to him, Keesh."

"And then what? We interrogate the hell out of him so that the public defender can say that his Miranda rights were violated?"

She pointed both hands to her chest. "Is this the face of an interrogator?"

"Give it up and get in the car. It's a bad idea, and I'm freezing my ass off here." He got into the car, cranked the heat up full blast, and stared through the windshield at the gleam of streetlights on the other cars parked on the block. He didn't want to argue with Bernie now, while she was mourning her brother and feeling vulnerable, but there was no way he'd let her do something so crazy.

"Okay." She dropped into the seat beside him and closed

the door. "Maybe that's a terrible idea that could get us both fired."

"And ruin whatever case they might have against this suspect," he added.

"Yeah, yeah, I lost my head there. But can I call Sully and let him know they got a suspect in custody? I didn't bring my cell to the funeral. Somehow it just didn't go with my little black dress."

"Sure."

As he pulled away from the curb, she made the call, but couldn't get through. "Damn it. He's not picking up."

"Maybe he's on the phone getting the details from his cop buddies."

"But I wanted to be the one to tell him." She sighed and ended the connection.

"Keep trying," he said, thinking that she was truly her father's daughter, wrapped up in law enforcement even minutes after her brother's funeral.

And damned if her obsession wasn't endearing.

Chapter 32

Although there'd been more than enough food served at Monahan and Fitzgerald's, in the tradition of Queens Irish endings the party moved on to the house in the evening. Peg rushed to set chips and desserts and other food donations from the neighborhood out on the dining room table, while James and Sully set up coolers of beer outside the kitchen door. Bernie heard Sarah tell the girls they weren't staying long, but then she tucked herself into a chair in the corner of the kitchen and poured herself a glass of cooking sherry. It seemed to be the first time Sarah had really relaxed in days.

Bernie steered her friends out of the kitchen thronging with "moms" and into the living room, where Conner and his sister, Erin, sat watching television.

"Hey, guys." Bernie looked toward the dining room, thinking she'd bring her friends to the table for that rare experience of cop talk, but the room was packed with cops, some James's age, others retired and gray like Sully, who reigned over all from his spot at the head of the table.

Keesh and Amy flopped on the couch while she lingered near the dining room archway, listening for the chatter that had always fascinated her.

"And can you believe he asked Padama for a drink of

water?" Sully said. "He gunned down four cops, then asked for water."

"The shooter did?" someone asked. Bernie couldn't identify all the players, but she knew when the conversation came back to Sully.

"Unbelievable."

"They didn't report that in the paper."

"Yeah, well, you know how I feel about journalists," Sully said. "They got a job to do, but when I worked on the street, I never gave them anything. Nothing. 'Cause they'd print a photo of their own mother dying if they thought it would sell papers."

"What was his name again?"

"Curtis. Peyton Curtis."

"You guys know Billy Cahill?" her father asked around the table. "Patrol in the 109. He's there, standing guard at the hospital. Says this Curtis has a bullet in the shoulder. Infected. That's the emergency surgery they're doing right now."

"And I wonder how that bullet got there?"

"Exactly," Sully said. "Bet you dimes to donuts, they take that slug out and find that it's the hollow point from Indigo Hilson's nine millimeter."

Her father sounded smug, almost delighted. He'd been revitalized by the news about the suspect in the coffee shop killer case. When Bernie had sought him out at the restaurant, he'd already been in the thick of conversation with his cop friends, his blue eyes glimmering with the possibilities of conviction.

"Dad, did you hear?" she had asked. "I just wanted to make sure you heard the news."

"I did, indeed." There'd been hope in his smile. "I heard, and I'm celebrating, darlin'. We got the killer. We got him, and this monster is going to fry. Ooh, he'll fry, and I'll enjoy it."

Bernie's smile had faded as joy had drained from her. She had thought this was something she would celebrate with her father, but suddenly it seemed ghoulish and sick. Besides, they had come to the restaurant for Brendan, to celebrate the hall-marks of his life, right?

Tired and a little confused, she had backed away from her father's circle of mirth and returned to her friends, who preferred to hang on the fringes and observe the varied factions that included Lucy's Ivy League–looking family, the families with little kids from St. Pete's, the pack of solo male cops, many of whom were half-in-bag, as Sully liked to say, and Sully's older, more seasoned crew.

"Who needs drinks?" Bernie asked the living room crowd. Conner and Erin had sodas, but Amy and Keesh wanted seltzer and coffee. Bernie ducked into the kitchen and nearly ran head-on into her sister Lucy.

"How you holding up, kiddo?" Lucy's face was lined, but in a healthy way that suggested sleeping under the stars and walks on a windy beach. Lucy had always been the outdoorsy one. On summer days when the rest of the kids were happy to hole up with Popsicles in front of the TV, Lucy headed off for a bike ride in the park or a day of swimming at a friend's house.

"I'm okay."

"That's a lie." She took Bernie's hand and massaged her forearm, such a mom gesture. Apparently Lucy had learned a thing or two in the suburbs of Wilmington. "You were close to Brendan, don't think I don't remember that. He always reached out to you, and you idolized him."

"Did I?" That was not exactly Bernie's perception, but it was far more insightful than she had expected of Lucy. Lucy Sullivan Strasberg was the fish that got away. Of Sully and Peg's five kids, only Lucy ventured beyond the confines of the New York Metro area, moving to Wilmington, Delaware, where she and her husband had careers. On a global scale it wasn't that far, but Bernie had learned how distant a family member could become when they were separated by two hours of the Jersey Turnpike.

"It's okay to cry," Lucy said. "We all need to grieve; you

just have to let it out. I've learned that in therapy. So don't let Mom tell you to stop crying. I used to hate it when she did that."

"I think Mom's too busy obsessing on trays of lasagna to bring out the tear police."

"Well, you just hang in there." She squeezed Bernie's hand, and then let it go. "Call me crazy, but I always knew something like this would happen. It's such a dangerous job they do."

"You know the details, right? That they weren't on duty. They were in the coffee shop."

"I know that, but they're still a target. Always a target." Lucy squinted as she sorted through the throng of women in the small kitchen. "At least with Dad retired, we just have Jimmy to worry about now."

"He's been teaching at the Police Academy for years. I'd say his risk is minimized."

Lucy's eyes opened wide as she smacked Bernie with a glare. "He still drinks coffee, doesn't he? He wears a uniform. When you do the math, the risk is there."

The back of Bernie's tongue went sour at the disintegration of Lucy's tender, loving attitude. *How your sister can go from caring to crazy in two short minutes . . .*

A neighbor moved away from the table, and Sarah was revealed, hunkered down in her corner.

"There she is . . ." Lucy reached down to hug Sarah, who seemed petite under Lucy's well-honed arm. "Honey, I am so sorry."

Sarah seemed trapped in Lucy's embrace, and for a moment Bernie wondered if Sarah even remembered who Lucy was. The two had only met a few times, and Sarah was overwhelmed right now.

Then Sarah murmured, "Thanks, Lucy."

"How are you holding up?" Lucy asked, plucking an errant hair from the shoulder of Sarah's black dress.

"Still in shock. You never expect something like this . . . never."

"Of course," Lucy agreed. "Of course you don't. How are the girls dealing with it?"

"I don't think they understand," Sarah said.

"Gracie gets it," Bernie said. "Did you hear the readings she picked out? She's a perceptive kid." Bernie didn't know why she felt compelled to defend her niece, but she did not want people condescending toward Grace. "Grace understands."

"They're babies." Sarah let out a gasp, sort of a hiccup of emotion. She covered her mouth, her eyes shiny and distant. "Babies."

"In the scheme of a lifetime, that is so true," Lucy agreed. "I was just telling Bernadette that I knew something like this would happen. When we were kids I worried every time Dad went to work. I would ask our mom, what if some bad man tries to kill him? Do you remember that, Bernie?"

Bernie shook her head and turned to the counter to pour Keesh's coffee. One of her earliest memories of Lucy was just a beanpole girl astride her red bike, the wind tossing her unkempt hair as she pedaled off down the street. After that she remembered Lucy fighting with MK and Jimmy over who would get to use the car. No recollections of a worried Lucy, and Bernie thought she would have noticed, since Lucy had slept just across the room. But then, to be fair, Lucy was thirteen years older than her—a teenager when Bernie was born.

"My parents always ignored me, but the fear never went away." Lucy's hands were pressed to her heart, her eyes flooded with sincerity. "I think it's one of the reasons I had to move so far away, because thinking about the danger every day made me crazy."

"Really?" This was a new story for Bernie, and though she didn't completely buy it, she did see how Lucy was a terrible match for their family. Thank goodness she had found happiness elsewhere. She grabbed the drinks and edged toward the living room. "Excuse me."

Now the conversation in the dining room was swirling around the Coffee Shop Killer. She delivered the drinks, then paced casually back to the edge of the archway to listen in.

"I hear he may not make it?" someone said.

"Aah, wouldn't that be a pity," Sully said sarcastically. "Save hundreds of thousands in legal fees, not to mention the cost of incarceration."

"If he's guilty."

"Of course he's guilty. Black guy dying of a gun wound?"

"I'm just saying . . ."

"You know, they got partial prints on the water cup. And some blood from the crime scene. A DNA match. Is that enough for you, Drallee?"

"It's him," Sully said. "And we'll all be lucky if he dies in surgery. Save me the trouble of doing it myself."

The guys laughed and giggled at that.

"Yeah, I can see you over at the hospital, Sully, pulling the plug on his life support system. Like a scene from *Two and a Half Men*. Oops! I must have tripped over that cord!"

More laughter.

"We laugh," Sully said, "but it's not far from the truth. A monster like that doesn't deserve to live. Believe me, I'd take him out myself if I had the chance."

A hollow pain sank in her belly as the men laughed.

"Aunt Bernie?" Conner was trying to get her attention.

She blinked. "Sorry. What?"

"Do you want this chair? I can get some folding chairs from the basement."

"No, sweetie. No problem." She rubbed her hands over her arms, feeling chilled to the bone. "I'll just sit on the couch with my peeps."

With a last look at the men in the dining room, she noted that the light of the chandelier was not so flattering on red noses and the burnished silver of beer cans.

"TV programming on Sundays leaves much to be desired," Amy said as she scrolled through the channels.

Bernie sat down between Keesh and Amy, feeling the weight of the day as she sank into the sofa cushion. "It seems like this morning happened ten years ago." She kicked off her shoes.

Amy looked down at the floor. "I love your shoes." She picked one up, her brows raised. "Dolce & Gabbana? Pretty nice."

"They're comfortable."

Amy slipped them on and crossed her legs. "Amy like."

Lucy stepped in from the kitchen, dipping a tea bag into a mug of steaming water. "So what's going on in here?" She had such an air of confidence, the way she could take charge of a conversation.

"We're waiting for the news," Erin said. "There might be something about the Coffee Shop Killer."

"If they have the info, I'll bet it's their top story," Lucy said as she paced through the room, pausing to stare at an old family photo by the bookshelves.

Bernie supposed you'd have to be pretty sure of yourself to pick up and move to another place, take on another religion, live a totally different life. Ironically, the Sullivans seemed to think Lucy was the black sheep of the family, but maybe she had proven them all wrong by succeeding.

It was uncanny how much she looked like Mary Kate, with the same wispy hair, high cheekbones, and blue eyes. They could have been twins but for Lucy's stylish short haircut and lack of laugh lines at the outer edges of her eyes.

Lucy strode across the room, glancing toward the next room with a wry smile. "I see Dad is still holding court at the dining room table. Some things never change."

"Their discussion would set the criminal justice system back fifty years if it ever left the room," Keesh said with a deadpan expression.

So he had heard. Bernie felt torn, wondering if she should try to explain how cops think, or just keep mum.

"They're moving on to capital punishment now," Keesh

added. "In another five minutes, they'll have this suspect, Curtis, getting a lethal injection."

Bernie laughed along with the others, though she felt slightly traitorous. Part of her wanted to be sitting at her father's table.

"Do you hear them?" Lucy put a hand to her mouth. "Are they for real?"

In the dining room, someone kept saying: "He's going to fry."

"Lethal injection."

"He's going to fry."

"They don't fry them in New York anymore. It's lethal injection!" The louder voice shut down ancillary conversations.

"Okay, okay, lethal injection. Either way, he's dead."

Lucy swung into the center of the archway, her tweed jacket making her look every inch the college professor. "Gentlemen. Can I make an argument for tolerance and perhaps mercy? Let's assume that the quote, Coffee Shop Killer suspect is found guilty. Is it really necessary to add any more bloodshed to the savage toll?"

The ensuing silence was uncomfortable for Bernie. Lucy could command the field, but the other guys weren't really interested in playing by her rules.

"I think it is," James said. "This guy killed three cops, Luce. He killed our brother. I say he has to go."

"To prison, yes." Lucy tipped her mug at the men. "Remove him from society so that he doesn't have the opportunity to kill again."

"The thing is, darlin', I'm not sure that's an adequate punishment for the crime," Sully said.

"Is there any replacing the lives he took?" Lucy paused, as if waiting for an answer, clearly an adept lecturer. "No. And as for rehabilitation, I heard mention that he's been in prison already. He may not have ever lived a functional life on the outside. You can't rehabilitate a person who has never learned to live in our habitat."

Everyone was quiet as Lucy stepped up to the table, put her mug down, and made eye contact with each man sitting there.

"My guess is that this man is mentally ill," Lucy said solemnly. "Truly, anyone who could perform such a heinous act is mentally ill. To execute a person with a mental deficiency, that's like executing a child."

"Let me ask you this, Luce." The soft tone of their father's voice didn't mask the impatience embedded in his words. "If you were given the choice to execute Adolf Hitler, wouldn't you have taken him down?"

Lucy straightened, her chin rising for a moment of thought. "That's a tough one, Dad. But digging deep for an honest answer, I'd have to say that I'd spare his life. Let him suffer the loss of his freedom for the rest of his life. But I wouldn't stoop to his level by exterminating another human being."

"That's your right, darlin'." Sully squinted up at her. "I bet they love you at that college."

It was a slap in the face; Bernie knew that.

But Lucy stood tall. "Tolerance," she said, nodding at each man at the table. She smiled then, picked up her empty mug, and breezed back into the kitchen like she owned the place.

When Bernie glanced at her friends, Amy wiggled her eyebrows.

"I want to be her when I grow up," Amy said.

"No, you don't." Keesh shook his head. "Besides, your parents don't care that you're already argumentative and self-absorbed."

Bernie smiled, though she strained to listen to the chatter in the dining room.

"Yeah, tolerate this."

"Drallee. Cut it out."

"What's the latest on the negotiations for the new contract?" Sully asked, wisely changing the subject to a safe topic.

Bernie wondered why she felt as if she'd just been through the wringer, when she hadn't argued with the men at all.

"Hey, it's on!" Erin pointed the remote at the TV, where the banner read: COFFEE SHOP KILLER SUSPECT ARRESTED, and turned the volume up.

The mug shot of a young black man filled the screen, and Bernie was surprised that she felt nothing. Was this really the suspect? The skin around one of his eyes drooped slightly and his mouth was crooked, as if he'd thought to smile but changed his mind. And his eyes . . . she had thought she would find malice embedded there, as easy to read as a list of his criminal intent.

Instead, there was only sadness.

This couldn't be the killer.

There were no answers in his eyes.

The reporter said that neighbors in Curtis's housing development painted a picture of a quiet, sickly boy who, as a child, had been mocked for his disabilities.

"Oh, sure, they're going to say that." James had paused in the archway to watch. "Every killer has a deprived and abused background. It's the standard defense now."

But what if it was true? Bernie turned away from the television, haunted by the man's sad eyes. What if he had been abused and denied opportunity all his life?

And who was this Curtis man to Brendan, her strong, noble brother who was fading from the landscape even though half of the city had spent the day honoring his life?

Already his seat at the dining room table was taken. His room upstairs held so few hints that he'd ever reigned in his "man cave," firing away at Nintendo or falling asleep with a book slumped on his chest. The very air in the house, once filtered by his easy grace and humor, now crackled with raw electricity, snapping and mean.

It was all unbalanced.

Off kilter.

He was gone, and no pursuit of justice could ease the ache in her soul.

Mindless of the din surrounding her, Bernie buried her face in her hands and began to cry.

Chapter 33

"Took you long enough to get here." Indigo cocked one eye at Dr. Dude and his two residents. She was only half-kidding, as excitement and nerves had been high since she'd started feeling tingling sensations in her lower extremities. Dr. Dude, whose real name was Carson something unpronounceable, was a West Coast guy with longish blond hair that looked like it was brightened by the sun. She and Elijah had speculated that he was a surfer dude who went to med school in the Caribbean and made a wrong turn somewhere around Atlanta.

"Sorry about that, Lady Cop, but you're not my only patient." He went to the foot of the bed and rolled the blanket up. "Though you're my only celebrity patient. I heard that the mayor was here twice."

"He was." Elijah folded his arms across his chest. "I let him in, but all those reporters, I turned away at the door."

The shooting had brought out Elijah's protective instincts, a side of him Indigo had never seen. She had decided she liked being taken care of when she needed shelter.

"Okay, Lady Cop." Dr. Dude stood at the foot of the bed, rubbing his hands together like a magician about to perform a magic trick. "Just trying to warm my hands. Sorry, but they're cold."

"Whatever." Indigo just wanted to know the truth, whether or not the sensations meant she was coming back from this injury. "Just tell me if it's all real, Doc."

Dude reached for the foot of the bed.

Indigo gasped. "That tickles."

The doctor and his two residents froze for a second, then looked at each other.

With a challenge in his eyes, Dr. Dude lifted his chin. "Let me know if you feel—"

"Ouch!" She grinned. "That was a trick question, wasn't it? You were poking me when . . . Hey! Stop mauling my foot."

"You've got feeling again." Dr. Dude smiled big and proud, as if he'd just conquered Mount Everest.

"Woohoo!" Indigo's arms shot up in the air. Victory!

Even serious, too-cool-to-emote Elijah cracked a smile. "What does it mean, Doc?"

"It means we can start physical therapy to get your wife walking again." Dude came to the head of the bed and shook Indigo's hand. "You did it, Lady Cop. Your prognosis is good. With your determination and spirit, you'll be walking within the year. Maybe in a few weeks or months. It depends on a lot of factors."

"I'm going to be working hard on it. I'm a fighter." Indigo dashed away the tears that rolled down her face.

"I've seen that." Dr. Dude patted her shoulder. "You just keep fighting."

"She will." Elijah still had half a smile. "She's stubborn as all get-out. Indigo doesn't give up."

It was true. She hadn't given up on Elijah, after half a dozen trips to rehab, months and even years of sobriety, and then back to rehab again. She loved the person he was when drugs and alcohol didn't pull him under, and she was determined to do anything in her power to keep him alive and in her life.

She wished she could warn her daughters about the consequences of falling for a reckless guy who'd been encouraged by his friends and parents to kill the pain with a few beers, a shot of Wild Turkey, a crack pipe passed in the alley behind the bar. Hers would be a cautionary tale: Here's what happens when you fall in love with a bad boy . . .

When she'd met Elijah she wasn't a cop yet. It was one of those crazy road trips she used to do with her girlfriends. Out to the Hamptons. Skiing in the Berkshires. Clubbing in Philly.

Elijah's family was rooted in Philadelphia. His father, Max, once a professional musician, owned three bars in the city. Elijah had worked for his father at the Blue Step, a downtown club where jazz and hip-hop groups performed on weekends. Sometimes Max brought out his old-timers to do a few jazz numbers. Other times, Elijah sat at the piano and played in with different groups.

He was amazing on the piano.

Indigo was not musical, but she recognized genius. The way he'd sit there with his eyes closed, letting the music flow through him. Indigo was convinced that the music came from deep inside him, from that tender, distant place that was so difficult to reach. From his soul.

The first night she met him, she knew she wanted to be a part of him.

Those early days when it was all so new, everything had seemed magical. Elijah's volatile talent and tender kisses. The colored lights and curling smoke, the intoxicating music and pink gin drinks. She remembered his perfect white teeth against the brown of her shoulder and his skin so dark it had a silver sheen in the night.

He was her drug, thrilling and addictive, and once she had her taste there was no way to resist a deeper sip. It was easy to stay in his place. Just as easy to go with him to church when they learned they had a baby coming along.

Then came the morning after, time to pay the bills and face the sun. That was when weaving through the layers of talent and tension, the family ties and family secrets, became more than she could handle.

Eventually, she'd had to leave him in order to save her life and his. When your husband is nodding off while he's supposed to be watching your baby daughter . . . it was time.

But she had never given up. Stubborn, he called her. Yeah, she was stubborn. She'd moved the baby up here, back with her family, and had gotten hired by NYPD.

Three years ago, Elijah had come for a visit, and she'd talked him into rehab. Having him back in her life, starting over here in New York . . . she had let herself indulge in hope for their little family again. Hope had emerged kicking and screaming, and they named her Zuli Hilson.

And then, a few months ago, Max had called to say that Elijah's mother was in the hospital. Elijah had packed for a short trip to Philadelphia.

And he didn't return until his wife was paralyzed by a bullet.

Not three feet from her bed, her husband and doctor were discussing her care, talking about physical therapy and rehabilitation facilities, joking about how she would soon be chasing her daughters through the park and her husband through the house.

But Indigo wasn't sure he would be there when she got home. She couldn't rely on him to be there for her, and that was just a cold, hard fact. No reason to throw a pity party.

"You okay?" Dr. Dude stepped closer and touched her shoulder. "Feeling tired?"

"I'm okay."

She was going to be up on her feet again, taking care of her daughters, living her own life, with or without him.

Everything was going to be okay. She was damn sure going to make it okay.

Chapter 34

The smell of the courtroom, that institutional mix of floor wax and dust, was oddly reassuring as Bernie opened her briefcase and placed her stack of blue and yellow folders next to the podium. It was office protocol to color-code cases—blue for misdemeanors and yellow for felonies, with the idea that the cases in the yellow folders—yellowbacks, the assistant district attorneys called them—would stand out and prosecutors would handle each felony with care, following the recommendations of the attorneys in the office's coveted trial bureau.

She counted the files and stacked them beside her podium. Thirty-nine arraignments for her first day back, not bad. After a week of bereavement leave, she was eager to dig in to work and put aside her personal issues for a few hours. Eight days since the shooting, and this was the best thing for her. She had needed to get back to her own apartment, where she could sit down and not be expected to debate labor contracts and Miranda procedures. She had needed to get back to her own bed, read herself to sleep at night, and punctuate everything with some quiet.

As officers began to escort clients in from the concrete holding cells, she sifted through the folders, skimming data sheets for salient points, planning her strategies.

Not that there was much strategizing necessary for three-minute arraignments on charges that ranged from drinking in public to forging a prescription to assault.

Judge Wendy Lowenstein, a slight woman with a kick-ass haircut, took the bench, and the first case was called.

The defendant, a black man in baggy jeans and white tank top, was arraigned for jumping a turnstile. While his attorney asked for a dismissal, Bernie looked in his eyes and saw only exhaustion and some surprise. What did she expect to find there?

She was picturing Peyton Curtis's eyes when Judge Lowenstein asked her what she was waiting for. Bernie quickly tried to recover. The turnstile jumper was dismissed, and the next case called.

This defendant wore a dress shirt and dark slacks—a businessman—but the charge was more serious. Michael Hernandez was arraigned for forging a prescription. A felony, as she noted by the yellowback folder.

Time to step up, Bernie told herself. She asked for ten thousand dollars bail. The Legal Aid attorney wanted him released on his own recognizance, claiming he worked in the community and was not a flight risk.

"Then he can come up with three thousand dollars bail," Judge Lowenstein ruled.

That went okay, Bernie thought, but her palms were sweating. Why was she falling apart here? These were only three-minute arraignments.

The next four cases were misdemeanors. Two for panhandling. Loitering. Possession of an open container of alcohol.

Bernie whipped through them like a pro, starting to feel back on her game. Though she couldn't help but notice that all four defendants were minorities, three of them black. Was the justice system unfair to minorities? Or was this low-level crime tied to poverty?

The next defendant gave Bernie pause.

The young Asian woman had sunken eyes, with dark half

moons beneath them. Maybe the lack of sleep from being in jail overnight. Or maybe something worse. Abuse? That black smudge on the side of her face . . . was it dirt or a bruise?

Rose Wu was being arraigned for Menacing Two, a misdemeanor. Wu had threatened her landlord with a carving knife, and the ADA who had processed the arrest specified two thousand dollars bail. There were notes in the yellow file referring to a counter-complaint that was to be filed against the landlord, whom Ms. Wu said was sexually harassing her, but Bernie didn't have that complaint in her files. Had it been filed? Was it withdrawn out of fear? Was it unfounded? It was the sort of thing Bernie would have checked out with a call to the Early Case Assessment Room. If she were on her game.

But right now, Bernie had to run with this. After all, this was only the arraignment. The reading of formal charges. Her job was to arraign and get these people moving through the system.

"Ms. Sullivan?" Judge Lowenstein prodded. "Are you asking for bail, or shall we release the defendant on her own recognizance?"

"I . . ." Bernie looked down at her folder, trying to get back on track. "Two thousand, Your Honor. The prosecution requests the court post bail in the amount of two thousand dollars."

The Legal Aid attorney, who looked more tired than Ms. Wu, said that her client had acted in self-defense and did not have the money to post bail. "She was defending herself against her landlord, who has persistently trespassed and threatened sexual assault."

The judge frowned. "Lovely. And where is said landlord?"

"My client is filing a complaint."

"I hope so." The judge addressed the defendant. "Ms. Wu. Look at me, please."

The young woman raised her chin.

"These charges against you are serious, but if what you're

saying is true, you need to voice your complaint and protect yourself. You need to work with your lawyer and make this official. Do you understand me?"

Wu's eyes glistened. She gasped and let out a whimper as a tear slid down her cheek. "Yes, ma'am." And then she tipped her face back toward the floor.

"The defendant is released on her own recognizance," the judge ordered.

Swallowing back a wave of concern for Rose Wu, Bernie turned to her next case. There wasn't time to worry about the young woman, and it certainly wasn't her job to advocate for her, but something had shifted, and Bernie was teetering off balance from the change. Somehow the lines of protocol that had once separated Bernie from the other side had faded. The defendants she was charged with prosecuting had sorrow in their hooded eyes. Rose Wu's spirit was broken. Some of them, like Mr. Hernandez, might lose their jobs if convicted.

These were people, not simply criminals.

And that realization made her very uncomfortable. With those clear limits gone, Bernie felt her passion as a prosecutor fading. How could she maintain her stance to punish wrongful behavior when so many of the criminals coming before her were victims themselves?

The next case was called, and Bernie opened the fat yellow folder. Jeremiah Jamison, a black man in his thirties, was charged with robbery and assault for robbing a pharmacy at gunpoint and making off with the supply of OxyContin.

This time, Bernie kept her eyes on her notes; she didn't want to make the mistake of looking at the defendant. Steeling herself, Bernie asked the court for twenty-five thousand dollars bail.

The defense attorney, a wiry young woman with a bad haircut that reminded Bernie of an ex-nun, objected. "Your Honor, my client needs a rehab program, not a stay at Rikers."

"We're talking about Third Degree Robbery," Bernie argued. "He waved a loaded gun in a pharmacist's face." It was easier when she didn't see the defendant.

"Bail is set at twenty thousand," said Judge Lowenstein.

As Bernie turned to jot down the ruling, the defendant caught her eye. Dressed in an old army jacket and unshaven, he had a broad face and a creased forehead that spoke of a troubled life. His eyes, wide open, were shiny with tears.

Was he a war veteran, or had he just happened upon the worn uniform jacket?

She squinted at him as he turned, and saw the name "Jamison" printed over the breast pocket. A thief. An addict. A former soldier.

Why did it have to be so complicated? How had this gray area of consciousness crept into a job that used to be so black and white, so clear-cut for her. Crystal clear.

The next case was called, which sent Bernie fumbling for the file folder. Why was she finding it so hard to keep up today?

"Take a minute if you need it, Ms. Sullivan," Judge Lowenstein said in an uncharacteristic display of patience.

"I'm okay," Bernie insisted, unnerved by the judge's scrutiny, sure that the woman could see she was becoming unhinged. Her palms were damp and now, despite the fact that the old court building was chill and drafty, she felt sweat trickling down between her breasts.

What was wrong with her?

"Maybe you came back to work too soon," Keesh said as he worked on notes in the cubicle beside her. The regular click of his fingers on the keyboard reminded her of the steady patter of raindrops. Cool, soothing rain.

At an adjacent desk, Bernie put her head down and inhaled the scent of paper and Chinese food from a cubicle in the next aisle. She'd worked in this office for more than three years. It was her first real job, and now, out of the blue, she didn't feel fit to do it anymore.

"It's not grief," she said. "Not that I'm free of that beast, but what happened today was about something else. It was as if someone gave me a new pair of eyes in the courtroom, and I could see inside each defendant."

"Sounds like the plot of a sci-fi thriller," Keesh said. "I think I saw that one. Sigourney Weaver's in it."

"No." Bernie pushed her head up and rested her chin on a fist. "It was some sort of breakdown. I started worrying about the defendants. Did you ever notice that almost all of our defendants are minorities? And most of the ADAs are white. It's not balanced. The scales of justice are tipped."

"I get what you're saying, but we don't choose our cases; they come to us." Keesh was on his feet, standing behind her. She would have loved a shoulder massage right now, but she knew he wouldn't touch her. Not in their workplace. Keesh knew better. "Are you finished with your notes?" he asked. "I'll help you knock them off and we can go somewhere for a drink."

"I'm only about half done." She sat up and took the top folder from her stack. "Here's a young woman who's probably being stalked by her landlord, and I had to push for bail."

"Bernie, you do what you gotta do." He picked up the folder and was reading when the voice of their boss came wending through the desk dividers. He was conversing on his Bluetooth, as usual.

"Yeah, let me call you back. I gotta talk to Bernie here. Yeah, okay. I'll get back to you."

Bernie looked up in time to see Mark Schumer end the call, though she had his full attention. Their boss was a small man, five-foot-two or three and slender, but what he lacked in size he more than made up for in persistence. Mark left you alone if you got the job done, but when he became aware of a problem, he didn't back off.

"Bernie, what's this I heard about you falling apart at arraignment proceedings?" He spread his hands wide with an expression that said "What the hell?"

"I didn't fall apart." She rose, folding her arms across her chest. "Not really."

"Corey from Legal Aid said they had to pause the proceedings for you. Judge Lowenstein is worried. Said you were breaking a sweat in the middle of winter. What's going on?"

"I just . . ." What could she say? That she felt a new empathy for the defendants?

"You just fell apart." Mark shook his head. "And I can't have that here. You've worked arraignments when we had fifty cases to get through. You gotta keep moving."

"I know. I just lost focus for a while."

"No can do." Mark looked from Bernie to Keesh, then threw his head back. "Ah, jeez. I'm sorry to come down so hard on you, Bernie. I know you just went through a lot, but I got a job to do here, too."

"I know, Mark. I respect that."

"Maybe you came back too soon."

She thought of her week off, an interlude filled with tasks and family gatherings in the beginning that had dwindled down to a day of such boredom yesterday that she'd forced herself to run in the park, then taken herself out for a pedicure. She didn't want more time off, time alone in her apartment, or hours of rattling conversation in front of the television at the house.

"I can do this job," she said, though the fluttering in her chest told her it wasn't true anymore.

"Are you sure? Because I'm not so sure. Judge Lowenstein isn't sure, either." Mark was never one to sugarcoat things.

She turned to Keesh, who had judiciously remained quiet during the discussion of her professional life. A more domineering man would have jumped in to defend her, but she appreciated Keesh's silence. He knew she could fight her own battles.

"Look." Mark stared at the ceiling a moment. "Why don't you take some time off to sort things out?"

Bernie shook her head quickly. "No, that's okay. I'll make it work here."

But behind Mark's left shoulder Keesh was nodding yes. Take the time. Go for it.

"I can't pay you, since we only get a week of bereavement leave from the city, but I can get you the time, Bernie, and I think you should take advantage of it. Really. Think about it. A chance to get away from this place for a while and relax. What's not to like about that? I could go for a vacation, myself."

Bernie recognized that Mark was in sales-pitch mode now, and though she dreaded the thought of not having this job to distract her, she could see that there would be no dissuading her intractable supervisor.

"I don't know." Bernie looked down at the yellow and blue case folders scattered on the desktop; the task of logging in the court actions on the computer seemed exhausting, if only because she knew she would be stuck with an image of each defendant in her mind, and she would mull over it and worry the edges until the early hours of the morning.

Right now, she felt no love for this job. No fire or passion.

"I guess I could take some time. Do some quilting."

Mark clapped his hands together. "Bernie, that's the best idea I've heard all day."

Behind him, Keesh touched hands folded for prayer to his forehead.

"Okay, then." Mark touched Bernie's shoulder. "I'm going to call HR and see what we have to do to make this happen."

After he was gone, Keesh stepped close enough that Bernie could smell a hint of his cologne, or maybe it was just aftershave. "You did the right thing, Bernie. You've got a stellar record here. You don't want to screw that up because you're going through all this."

She turned away. He was right, but it hurt to be told that you weren't good enough, even if it was a temporary disability.

"And what was that crap about you quilting?" Keesh asked.

"Just a load of bullshit," she said quietly. She sat down at the desk and handed Keesh a bunch of folders. "Help me get these updated on the computer, okay?"

"Okay."

They got to work. Once again the rhythmic tapping of keys in the adjacent cubicle made her think of rain on the roof. Rain that could wash a wealth of sins away.

At least she had Keesh. His help and the reassuring noise of his keystrokes.

She realized that when she came back from her leave, *if* she came back, Keesh would be gone to his new job.

This office would have a different tone, a new tenor.

Her world was changing quickly, becoming so unrecognizable and alien that soon she would be a stranger walking through her own life.

Chapter 35

When Chris Schiavone came into Dr. Parsons's office with his father, Mary Kate let out a squeal as she peered through the pass-through of the reception desk. "Oh, my goodness, look at you! I saw your name in the appointment calendar, but what are you doing here?"

Chris's broad grin still possessed traces of the boy who had gotten into many a scrape with Mary Kate's son Conner. "Spring break from Auburn."

"I just have to hug you!" She ran around to the door and popped into the reception area to throw her arms around the hulking boy. "What are you, six feet now?"

"Six-two."

"He got a full ride at Auburn to play football," Craig said proudly.

"I heard!" Mary Kate patted Chris's shoulder and turned to shake hands with his father, who was almost as tall, but leaner. "Craig, how are you? It's been years."

"It's all good. I didn't know you worked for Dr. Parsons."

"I started a while back. It's been almost a year." She turned to Chris. "Does Conner know you're back?"

"We're supposed to hook up today or tomorrow. I got in touch as soon as I heard about his uncle on the news. I was floored. He was your brother, right?"

Mary Kate nodded, not wanting to go there. Right now the allure of work was that she could escape the things that still kept her awake at night.

"We're so sorry, Mary Kate," Craig said.

"Thank you." She pressed a hand to her throat. "It's still kind of emotional for me."

Craig nodded. "Understandable."

Mary Kate pointed to the coatrack. "Chris, if you want to hang up your coat, we can get you set up and start your X-rays." She got him seated in the gray room, then returned to her desk. "Your son has grown so much. Conner, too. It's hard to believe they were ever scraggly little Cub Scouts."

"You were a great den mother," Craig said. His hands were huge paws on the armrests of the chair.

As Mary Kate remembered, he had played college football. "Are you still working at the high school?"

"Bayside High. I'm a football coach and PE teacher." He picked up a magazine from the table. "I've got a small apartment in Bay Terrace, and Tracey is still in the house in Fresh Meadows."

She nodded. She had forgotten that Chris's parents had divorced when the boys were in high school.

"Are you and Tony still in the same house?"

"I am." She held her breath, starting to hesitate, then realized she had to start saying the words to make it real. "Tony moved out. We're separated."

He didn't seem fazed at all, which helped Mary Kate breathe easy again.

"And Conner is living back home?"

"Right. He transferred to Queens College. I was worried at first, but he's doing well." She looked at the online profile for the Schiavones. "And whose insurance are we using today?"

"Let me get you my insurance card." As he leaned forward to remove his wallet from his back pocket, she noticed again that he was a big bear of a man. She supposed that worked to his advantage when he was trying to supervise huge classes of teenaged boys in the school gymnasium.

She scanned the card, then explained that they would be filing the claim electronically.

"You've really updated old man Parsons's operation," Craig said.

"I can't take credit for that. I just keep it going, and it's a lot easier without paperwork. We can store everything on the computer now." Mary Kate felt a surge of pride in talking about her work, and she realized that Tony had never asked her about her day, let alone any of the details of what she did in Dr. Parsons's office.

"Are you a hygienist, too?" Craig asked.

"Naw. Just a bookkeeper and receptionist." She didn't have medical training, and though the hygienists made more, Mary Kate didn't aspire to their jobs. It would be kind of gross and depressing to have to stare into people's imperfect mouths at stained and chipped teeth all day. "And you know what? I'm happy with that. I'm a little OCD, so I keep the office organized, and the social aspect of working reception keeps the day moving."

"It's great that you found something that works for you." When he looked over at her, his smile was warm. She noticed his eyes were that mossy shade of green. An unusual color, and it suited him well. Craig Schiavone was actually a handsome man.

And he was smiling at her. Was he flirting?

"You know, while I'm here, can you see if I'm due for a checkup?" He tossed the magazine back onto the coffee table and moved to a chair closer to her desk. "I think I got one of those cards in the mail a while back, but you know how that goes."

She clicked on his profile and smiled. "You're a bit overdue. It's been over two years."

"Really?" He rubbed his jaw. "Oops. We'd better schedule an appointment."

She clicked the mouse to open the calendar, wondering if he was really just trying to come up with a reason to see her again. Or was that just wishful thinking? "What works for you?"

"Let's see." He looked down at his phone, one of those new ones that had a computer screen. "Next week is busy, and so is the one after that. Basketball season is wrapping up. What do you have two weeks out? Late afternoon, early evening, say . . . end of March?"

She felt a stab of disappointment that she'd have to wait two weeks, but then that was silly. He might even be remarried. She would have Conner ask Chris. He chose a Tuesday night, and Mary Kate printed a reminder for him. When she handed it to him, she noticed that he didn't wear a wedding ring. It was hopeful.

As they chatted on about the last few years, getting updates on the other kids, Mary Kate felt a ray of hope. She had always thought Tony was it for her, but now she wondered.

New possibilities would be nice.

Chapter 36

Thursday dawned cold and gray. Bernie's internal clock got her up at six, and one look at the frost on the small square of grass in her backyard sent her right back to bed. A few hours later she had coffee and cereal, went for a run in the park, and showered. She tried to relax, but expectancy hung in the air, as if she were waiting for the phone call or the event that would change her day.

After a failed attempt to concentrate on a novel, Bernie surrendered any thought of real relaxation and decided to head over to her parents' house. "All roads lead to the roost," her mom liked to say.

She locked the door of her place, the ground-floor apartment in a two-family house owned by her parents. Keesh had once accused her of mooching off her parents while pretending to be independent, but she'd pointed out that she paid the same rent as the upstairs tenants, Candy and Chuck Wolf.

The walk to her parents' home took her through a cluster of garden apartments and a few blocks of stores. As she passed the post office, the pharmacy, and three different pizza places, she envied the people who strode by her on a mission. That was New York City; millions of keyed-up people with someplace to be, and they were perpetually ten minutes late. How strange not to have a job to be late for anymore.

She arrived at the house to find only Sarah there with Grace and Indigo's daughter Tasha.

"Hey, how's it going?" Bernie gave Tasha a big hug. "I heard the great news about your mom! How's she doing?" Word that Indigo's paralysis was fading had been the only good news to travel through the family lately.

"She's good." Tasha's fingers squeezed the heart-shaped buttons of her sweater. "She says the doctors torture her every day now, but she's getting better."

"Physical therapy," Sarah said. "It's hard, but your mom is pretty determined, isn't she?"

Tasha nodded. "She wanted to walk by tomorrow because she has to go to court."

"The grand jury hearing?" Bernie asked. The Queens DA was probably relying heavily on Indigo's testimony.

Tasha shrugged. "Some court thing. She told the nurse, and the nurse told her she was crazy. So she still isn't walking yet."

"I guess it takes time," Bernie said as Tasha went back to the floor in front of the television, where she and Grace were working on a school project, coloring a map of New York State.

"Where is everybody?" Bernie asked, hanging her jacket on the hook by the door.

Sarah explained that Peg was on an outing with Maisey, and Sully was at the Cup with the glass installer. "And here I am, leading a life of leisure," Sarah said, sitting with one knee bent on the sofa. The television was on, and half a cup of tea sat on the coffee table.

Bernie was about to tell Sarah that she was joining her club, but she stopped herself. What the hell would she say? She needed some semblance of control or direction before she told her story.

A commercial on TV gave way to the handsome face of Rich Willis, a young African-American on-air personality known for his propensity to date celebrities.

"Next on *News at Noon,* our in-depth report on Peyton

Curtis, the suspected Coffee Shop Killer whose case will go to the Manhattan Grand Jury tomorrow." Energetic Rich mellowed to concerned Rich. "We'll see what family and neighbors have to say about him, and we'll hear reaction in the community to his arrest."

Bernie stared at the TV, riveted, as they cut away to a commercial break. The media had been running something on Curtis every day, but this sounded like a more thorough interview.

But Sarah frowned, concerned. "Girls, why don't you take your project into the back room?"

Tasha sat up and started to gather crayons.

"Why can't I see this?" Grace asked.

"You're too young."

"Other kids at school see news reports about him. They all talk about it, and I feel stupid 'cause I'm the only one who doesn't know. And it's my story, Mom. Not theirs."

"Honey, I'm afraid it'll be too upsetting."

Grace's lower lip curled in indignation. "I'm not a baby."

Sarah sighed. "Tash, you can go into the dining room if you want."

"She already saw a picture of the man," Grace said.

When Sarah turned to Tasha, she nodded. "Yes, ma'am. My gramma told me to look at the bad man who shot my mom. She said he had the devil in him."

"She may be right about that." Sarah looked back at Bernie, who shrugged. "Okay. If you want, I'll let you watch." She sank back onto the sofa beside Bernie. "But it's probably a huge mistake," she muttered.

Juanita Perez, one of those reporters with the ability to sling a smile then burn serious in the next second, posed the question of whether Peyton Curtis was "a boy who fell through the cracks or a monster in our midst."

"Curtis remains hospitalized from a bullet wound," the bright-eyed reporter said. "Homicide charges will go before the Queens Grand Jury tomorrow, but tonight we take a look at the man who police say is behind the March second murder of three New York City police officers in a Flushing coffee shop. Peyton Curtis remains in critical condition in an area hospital, but News Four spoke with friends and family who know him."

A black woman in her twenties wearing a red polo shirt, obviously a store uniform, looked down as she spoke. The banner beneath her read: CURTIS'S SISTER GWEN MAHEWS.

"I don't believe he killed those people," Gwen Mahews said. "Peyton's gentle. He's not the kind of person to hurt anyone."

The reporter's voice-over said that Curtis's sister questioned his ability to commit such a crime because of a disability he'd had since he was a child.

"He got hurt a long time ago," the sister said. "Back when he was little. He never walked right after that, and something was wrong with one of his arms. I don't even know if he could pull a trigger."

The report then featured a teacher who'd claimed to have had Curtis in class when he was in junior high. The man remembered Peyton Curtis as being the victim of bullies who picked on him because of his physical disabilities.

"Really?" Sarah squinted at the television. "That was, like, twenty years ago. Would a teacher really remember the specifics of a student profile twenty years later?"

"It's possible, but improbable," Bernie said.

Next they showed a photo of his mother, Yvonne Curtis, who was holding a paper up, probably to block her face from being photographed.

"Curtis's mother, who declined to be interviewed, says she has been threatened by neighbors in the Blair Houses. Curtis says vandals recently painted the words *Cop Killer* on her door.

The camera lingered on the door, where someone had painted COP KILLHER in bloodred paint. Bernie shuddered at the obvious threat.

Grace was sitting up straight now, her arms crossed in front of her chest. "Who did that to her door?"

"We don't know," Sarah said. "But it was the wrong thing to do."

"How will she get the paint off?" Grace asked.

"She'll probably scrub it with soap," Tasha answered.

"Maybe she'll just paint over it," Bernie said.

"Why don't they leave that woman alone?" Grace asked, her eyes glued to the TV.

Bernie tried to explain that the woman's son was accused of killing Grace's father, along with the other two cops. "I know, but the woman didn't do anything," Grace pointed out. "They should leave her alone."

"You're right," Bernie said. "You're absolutely right."

Juanita Perez went on. "No one is claiming responsibility for the vandalism, but some neighbors say they are upset because tenants like Peyton Curtis and his mother, Yvonne, give a bad name to housing projects."

"Many of us here at the Blair Houses, we're hardworking people," said a woman in a wool coat. She stood in front of a brick building, her breath wisps of white air. "People like us, we have jobs and children to raise. We go to church on Sunday and do the right thing. But it's people like that monster who give all the rest of us a bad reputation."

The report ended with mention of a possible death penalty if Curtis was found guilty.

"Well, I'm glad that's over," Sarah said, turning to the girls. "Any questions?"

Both girls shook their heads and went back to their homework, but Bernie noticed that they were subdued.

And the news report had left her feeling unsettled, too. She felt haunted by the profile of Peyton Curtis, disabled and bullied as a child. *Gentle,* his sister had said.

It was not at all the profile she'd been hoping for. She wanted her brother's killer to be a man she could resoundingly despise.

*   *   *

That evening at the dinner table the mood was different, and for once Bernie felt relieved that there would be no cop talk. All her life she had been a cop's daughter, out to get the bad guys, lock them up, and throw away the key, as Sully always said. Things had seemed so simple. Now, as she shook a bottle of salad dressing, she wished for a return to simplicity even as she knew it could not happen.

Sully took his place at the head of the table, but his blue eyes seemed tired and vacant. Although he didn't stumble or slur his words, Bernie suspected that a bottle had been part of his afternoon activity. He seemed distant as he listened to Tasha's accounts of how her dad made eggs differently. The girls talked about the boy at school who had his own iPad. Maisey bragged about the free cookies she got at the store with Nana. Sarah talked about her meeting scheduled with the payroll and benefits section at One Police Plaza. The police matter was the only thing that caught his attention.

"They'll take care of you," Sully said. "You and the girls, you'll be fine. You'll never have to work another day in your life. Unless you want to, of course."

"I might ask for something part-time at work." Sarah put her fork down, her meat loaf still untouched. "I mean, the girls will be at school. What would I do all day?"

You got that right, Bernie wanted to say. She'd had one day off and already she'd run out of things to do.

"Well, I'm happy to have the girls here anytime." Peg added a spoon of corn to Maisey's plate.

"Hey!" Maisey complained.

"Eat," Peg said. "If you need me, I'm here."

"Thank you." Sarah picked up her fork and broke off a piece of meat. "I don't know what we'd do without you."

"Family takes care of family," Sully said quietly, rotating his beer glass on the place mat.

"What's the death penalty?" Grace asked as she lifted a dill pickle spear.

Sully swallowed, lifting his chin. "Where did that come from?"

"We watched a news report on Peyton Curtis," Bernie said.

"Did you?" Peg looked down at Grace. "And they said he's getting the death penalty?"

"Wouldn't that be nice." Sully's malicious grin made Bernie look away.

"Is it the penalty you get when you make someone die?" Grace asked.

"Not exactly," Bernie said, treading cautiously. "The death penalty is when the government takes a person's life to punish them for their crime."

Grace's eyes opened wide. "You mean the government kills them?"

"They get executed," Tasha said with a chilling sureness.

"Do they shoot them, like Daddy?" Grace asked.

"No, honey," Sarah said without looking up from her plate. "The prison doctor gives the criminal a shot that makes them go to sleep."

"And they never wake up," Sully finished. "It's the only way we can be sure that bad men like the one who killed your daddy won't have a chance to hurt other people."

"But Peyton Curtis is disabled," Grace said. "Did you know he was bullied? It's not right to pick on someone who's hurt."

"But sweetheart, he's a monster, a cold-blooded killer," Sully said gently. "It may seem a little harsh right now, Gracie, but you'll understand it when you get a little older."

Not true, Bernie thought. *The older you get, the less you understand. The lines begin to blur.*

Grace put her pickle down and wiped her fingers on a napkin. "No, Grandpa. I won't ever kill a person, not even a bad man. God put it in the Ten Commandments, and it's wrong."

Sully raised his hands in mock surrender. "Okay, okay. Pipe down, darlin'. Nobody's expecting you to break one of God's commandments. That's why grown-ups take care of these things."

"If he's guilty," Bernie added. "I mean, it's looking that way, but the charges haven't even gone to the grand jury yet."

Sully frowned. "Bernadette, is there any doubt in your mind of that man's guilt?"

"Always. That's the way our court system is structured, Dad. Innocent until proven guilty."

"I got enough proof." Sully waved a hand, gesturing to the distant universe. "You got Indigo and Padama testifying tomorrow. The DA asked me to be there as a backup. They got a handful of eyewitnesses, customers who were in the shop. What more do you want, Miss ADA?"

Wounded, Bernie pressed a hand to her chest. "Dad . . . I'm just saying that we need to let the justice system run its course."

"Not enough time in the world to wait around for the lawyers and the judges and juries. By the time they get around to executing this animal, I'll be dead."

Bernie was aware of the silence. She and Sully held the rapt attention of everyone at the table, Maisey included, but she couldn't back down. "And what's the alternative, Dad? What are you suggesting?"

"I'm just saying, it would save a lot of money and grief if they let this fella die in the hospital. Just let him go."

"Kill him?" Bernie echoed Grace's earlier words.

"Alrighty, then." Peg was on her feet. "It's too much for a dinner conversation, talking of these things." She began clearing dishes away. "Why don't you girls come into the kitchen and help me with dessert?"

After the tense exchange, Grace and Tasha seemed more than willing to leave the table.

"I want dessert, too." Maisey slid down to the floor and carried her plate of uneaten corn to the kitchen like a tribal offering.

Sully sat back, his fingers splayed on the table. "We got the new window glass in at the shop today."

"That's good," Sarah said, tiptoeing through the minefield

between Bernie and her father. "Are you going to reopen soon?"

He rubbed his unshaven jaw. "I don't know. I haven't decided what to do yet."

"You've got to reopen Sully's," Sarah said. "It's a Flushing landmark."

"Hmph. Probably for all the wrong reasons."

The notion of gawkers coming to the coffee shop to eyeball the scene of the tragedy made Bernie shift uncomfortably in her seat. Someone had suggested installing a small memorial there, a plaque or photo of the three fallen cops, but that seemed like crass commercialism, too.

"You're quiet there, Bernadette." Sully's gravelly voice held a tender note. It was the closest he would ever come to an apology. "What's new over in the DA's office? Get any interesting cases recently?"

"Always." Bernie pushed her plate away. "I handled a slew of arraignments yesterday." She thought of the defendants' faces, the gray pallor of men who'd sat up all night in a holding cell, the flame of fear in Rose Wu's eyes. Somehow it seemed wrong to tell a story that exposed the raw edge those people had teetered on.

"Any good ones?" Sully prodded.

Hesitating, Bernie stared down at the tablecloth. She didn't want to spill the truth, but better for them to hear it from her than some friend of Sully's. "According to the judge, the real drama queen was me. I had trouble staying on track. My mind just kept wandering."

"Oh, no." Sarah reached across the table to squeeze Bernie's forearm. "You okay, Bernie?"

"I'll be fine. But I'm taking a break. I guess I need more time than I realized."

"One week is not nearly enough time to get over something like this." Sarah gathered the bottles of salad dressing between her two hands. "Be patient with yourself, Bernie."

When Sarah ducked into the kitchen, Sully pulled his beer

glass to the center of his place mat. "She's right, you know. You can take your time. You got that luxury, darlin'. You don't have a family to support. No kids."

Although she knew he was trying to make her feel better, the reminder that she was nowhere near starting her own family at the age of twenty-seven only made her feel worse.

"You could come home. Move in here with us," he said. "We still got your bed in the back. You could move back without missing a beat. Then, maybe down the road you want to get your own place again, we'll fix you up with something."

Bernie's heart sank low as she worked to keep her face void of emotion. Was this really how her father thought of her . . . as a young maiden who could be returned to the castle tower?

Even without Bernie's dramatic wash, the whole notion was demeaning. Was her only life role being his daughter? And did her father really think she could move backward in time and be content to live under his roof again?

"I'll figure something out, Dad. Even if I have to get a job scooping ice cream," Bernie said, grateful to have an exit line so that she could leave the legendary family table. "Give me some time and I'll figure something out."

Chapter 37

Sarah tiptoed through the quiet house, not wanting to wake the kids. She was waiting on the pregnancy test set up in the bathroom, waiting and worried. She knew what the answer would be, but for now, for ten more minutes, she just wanted to pretend it was a negative, that she could focus on the two angels asleep in their beds and start moving on. Focus on making a healthy adjustment. Focus on learning how to go through a whole day without crying.

She sat on the couch and curled her legs underneath her. On the table was a folder of benefit options from NYPD's pension section at One Police Plaza. Sarah hadn't made a final decision yet, but the payout would be generous. She could afford to quit her job and stay home with the girls. That seemed like the only choice at this point, though she dreaded the thought of losing her last vestige of architectural ties and dissolving into a full-time mom. Despite all its benefits, mommyhood did not offer much intellectual stimulation and the hours, in any other forum, would have been condemned as slavery. Never had she considered being a single parent; she had always known that parenting required two.

This was so unfair.

She clicked the remote, thinking how she used to yell at

Brendan to slow down when he clicked from one station to the next.

She missed him.

This morning when she awoke and felt the emptiness on his side of the bed, she fully expected to find Brendan in the kitchen, filling the coffee carafe with water, measuring grounds into the basket. Somewhere between rolling over and touching the bedroom carpet with her feet, the truth had hit her.

He was gone.

She missed the reassuring weight of his presence beside her on the couch. She missed his laugh and his talent for packing a school lunch in less than two minutes.

She even missed tripping over his big clunker shoes by the door.

He had been the navigator in their relationship, always charting a course, setting goals, and steering toward adventure. Now that he was gone, she was adrift. Lost.

She pulled the afghan from the back of the couch and huddled under it. This time of year, she was always feeling a chill. Brendan had run hot; he'd had no use for sweaters, and down comforters made him break out in a sweat. She tucked her icy hands between her thighs, wishing for his warmth.

It was time to go read the test in the bathroom. She could check the results and warm her icy hands under hot water, but she wanted to sit here and savor the peace and fantasize about all the things she had mentioned at the dinner table tonight. She imagined her life moving ahead from here without a baby, and it was a relief to drive to the office with only one booster seat in the car. She would find satisfaction in reviewing the plans for kitchen extensions and added bathrooms. There would be joy in rubber-stamping when it punctuated her freedom.

Maybe the queasy feeling in her stomach was just the flu? Wouldn't that be a relief? She could stay in bed for a few days, leaning on Nana Peg for help with the girls. And one day she would wake up and it would be over and she could continue patching up their broken lives and trying to learn how to navigate for the girls.

Or Plan B, the unplanned plan that would have her up all night with a sick baby . . . or maybe three sick children. Or if only one was sick, she would need to lug all three to the doctor, then to the pharmacy. She was going to be lugging three children all over town like the old woman in the shoe.

How could Brendan die and leave her alone with all this?

Sarah realized she was curled in a ball, and her nose and cheeks were cold. This wasn't right.

She pushed off the couch and checked the thermostat. Fifty-nine, and it was set on sixty-five. Flipping the switch back and forth didn't elicit the groan of the furnace in the basement.

"This is your fault," she muttered, tossing the afghan onto the sofa as she stomped to the basement door. Late on a winter night and she had to go down to the basement to what? Kick the furnace?

She flicked the light switch by the kitchen door and proceeded down the creaky wood stairs.

"You were supposed to take care of these things. Take care of us . . ."

The fuse box swung open with a whine, and she ran her hand down all the switches. Nothing had popped. She located the switch marked "furnace" and reset it, hoping it would make the cranky old beast grumble to life.

Still, dead silence.

"Oh, no." She pressed a trembling hand to her mouth and began to cry.

He'd left them with a broken furnace. She balled up her fists and went over to the monster squatting in the corner, its belly rough with the asbestos clay that had been lathered on seventy years ago. "No!" She aimed a kick at it, but her socked foot did no harm to the belly of the beast.

Ooh, if she had a gun she'd shoot holes into it. They had talked about replacing it, but there would be the added expense of asbestos removal before they even got to the cost of a new furnace, so it was one of those repairs slated for the distant future.

And now Brendan was gone and she would have to figure it all out herself. Damn him.

She climbed the wood stairs, feeling the grit of the basement on the bottom of her socks. If Brendan were here, he would be downstairs in the basement tomorrow with a vacuum. He would figure out a way to rig the old furnace to work until he could get estimates from three asbestos removal companies. Then he'd have the new furnace installer lined up right behind them.

Who installed furnaces anyway? Plumbers or electricians or . . . maybe she needed to shop for a heating specialist.

It was too much.

She fell back on the couch, balled the afghan into her arms, and sobbed into it.

It was all too much.

In the morning she would start making calls to heating companies. She would also call Dr. Newbury's office and ask about terminating a pregnancy. She couldn't bear to discuss her options with anyone outside the doctor's office, but no one would have to know.

Dr. Newbury could be her salvation.

Chapter 38

Bernie knew there would be nothing to see.

A grand jury hearing was always a closed proceeding, during which only the prosecution presented its case. In New York City, homicide cases were always brought before a grand jury, a group of men and women who decided if the prosecutors had sufficient evidence to substantiate the charges. From what she'd heard and read, Bernie figured the Queens DA's office would have no problem making their case at this stage. The proceeding would be perfunctory and routine.

And yet, she couldn't stay away.

Although the hearings were closed, no one could stop her from getting a look at the prosecution's witnesses as they waited to testify, and knowing the witness list might give her a sense of their case.

Besides, she didn't have anywhere else she needed to be on a balmy Friday in March.

The Queens Criminal Courthouse was built in a period that Sarah with her architect degree would call "unfortunate." The white cement façade was flat and dull; the recessed entrance on the ground floor gave more of a sense of dark alleyway than grand porch. The only feature that lifted the building from totally bald-eagle ugly was the arched windows on the top story, but by the time the eyes went up that far, most people were already sneering.

Although the location of the hearing wasn't publicized, she had gotten the information from Indigo, who would be brought over in a wheelchair-accessible van. Padama, the barista from the coffee shop, had also been called to testify, and Sully had mentioned being called in as a backup. Bernie felt that she had a small edge, having heard personal accounts from those three witnesses.

As if it matters, she thought. She could gather all the evidence in the world and the case wouldn't be hers. She knew that, in a professional capacity, the DA's office would not let her anywhere near a case she was personally involved with.

So what the hell are you doing here? she asked herself as her heels clicked on the old tile floors.

She just needed to know.

People moved through the corridors, attorneys and witnesses, and family members. Most of the criminal cases were open to visitors, but not the grand jury, the one Bernie wanted to see.

The case would be open to the public eventually. For now, she would find out whatever she could about the preliminaries.

Her trip to the courthouse turned out to be a bust. When she finally reached Indigo by phone, she was told to stay away.

"I'd love to visit with you, but I'm not supposed to talk to anyone about the case. They've got us sequestered here so we don't even see the other witnesses. The DA would be pissed if he knew how much I told you already."

"But we're friends," Bernie insisted.

"Yeah, and I'm a sworn police officer. I've got a job to do here."

"I know. I'm sorry if I got you in trouble. I've never had a case that went before the grand jury before."

"And even if you had, you'd be bending the rules anyway," Indigo said. "That's how you Sullivans operate. Ask forgiveness, not permission."

"That would be the Sullivan men. We women just clean up their messes."

"I need to hang up," Indigo said. "But one of the court officers told me the DA usually holds a press conference on the courthouse steps after high-profile cases like these. Elijah is going to wheel me out there when we're done here. I'll see you there if you want to stick around."

"Sure. I'll see you there." After all, Bernie had nowhere else she needed to be.

It wasn't a terrible day to wait outside. The air was damp but warm for spring, and Bernie bought a fat pretzel from a rolling cart across the street and sat on a bench, watching for any sign of a gathering.

A half hour later, two TV news vans with satellite dishes on their roofs pulled up and dispatched their crews. Bernie recognized Juanita Perez outside one van, fixing her hair and pulling a scarlet blazer on.

So Bernie was in the right place.

As the crowd began to assemble, Bernie moved to the courthouse steps and wove toward the center of the group. Two reporters behind her were joking about the weather when Bernie's cell phone buzzed in her pocket. It was from her parents' house, probably her mother.

"Hello?"

"Oh, Bernie, I'm so glad I reached you. I've been worried all morning." Peg's voice was more shrill than usual. "Your father left in a huff and I'm wondering if you've seen him there?"

Bernie scanned the faces lined up in tiers on the stairs. "Not yet, but I heard that the witnesses are in private waiting rooms."

"Dear Lord, I hope he went there. He's in a bad way, Bernie. In fifty years of marriage I've never seen him in such a way." Peg's voice sounded thick.

"Ma, are you okay?"

"I'm worried, is all. It's not like your father to walk out on me on such a foul note. Stormed out and left his cell phone so I can't call him to talk it out. And he's been distracted lately. Not himself."

"That's understandable, with Brendan and everything."

"Of course it is."

"Mom?" Bernie bit her lower lip. "What were you arguing about?"

"This terrible case, of course. He . . . oh, you know what he's going through. I thought it would help to have a suspect in custody, someone to pin the blame on, but it's all he talks about now. This eye-for-an-eye business."

From the security personnel circling the staircase, Bernie could tell that the press conference was about to start. She needed to get off the phone. "Is there something you want me to do?"

"Just ask him to get home safe, would you, dear?"

"Sure, Ma. I gotta go."

"Bye then."

The courthouse doors opened and the Queens District Attorney Marvin Green emerged. He stood to the side of the doors, waiting as Elijah wheeled Indigo to the edge of the landing. Then Green joined her.

Of course, Bernie thought. Indigo is the hero of this case. How foolish for Bernie to think that she could have breezed in and hung out with her.

In his designer suit, Marvin Green cut a smooth, smart appearance as the Queens DA. New Yorkers had been a little taken aback when the Harvard-educated black man had been hired from outside the city to champion the role of lead prosecutor, but Green's crisp, no-nonsense demeanor had soon won approval.

Other people spilled out the doors behind them. There was Padama, looking sophisticated in heels and a black and white print dress with a black jacket. She suspected some of the people were customers who had witnessed the shooting in Sully's Cup, but she couldn't be sure.

And there were at least a dozen cops. Security, or witnesses of some kind? She didn't know.

"The action of the grand jury to file an indictment against Peyton Curtis shows that our system works," Green said, trying to project his voice. There was no PA system, and it was hard to hear unless you were close. As Green began to speak about the wheels of justice moving forward, Bernie thought she saw her father, but she had to do a double take to be sure that hard, menacing face was his. Sully was almost unrecognizable, his eyes glittering, his demeanor cold. He was with a group of cops. First responders to Sully's Cup that day?

Had the cops testified?

She wondered if Sully had been called on to testify. If so she would hear the tale, over and again, until it became part of the family archive.

At the top of the stairs, Marvin Green talked about the excellent work of the officers and detectives of the police department and the diligence of his own attorneys in coming this far with the case of the "so-called Coffee Shop Killer."

As Green introduced Indigo Hilson to the gathered reporters, Bernie glanced up at Padama, then back down to where her father stood with the cops. Ma had wanted her to intervene, talk to him, but she felt confident that he'd be okay hanging with his cop buddies. Sully was a social creature, comfortable until he was alone. There was safety in numbers, she thought.

People applauded Indigo, who rose from her chair with Elijah's help and smiled at the crowd. The DA thanked the media for coming, and turned away.

Immediately, the crowd began to break up.

Bernie dropped down a few steps, closer to her father and the cops. The other men were tall like Sully, and they stood in half a circle with their shoulders back, talking but also observing the human traffic around them, like sideline coaches who might be called upon to catch a ball in midair or dodge a player running out of bounds.

Someone tossed off a comment and they all chuckled, a low rumble, a shared moment, but not enough to distract from the scene before them.

Bernie edged closer, dropping down the stairs behind her father, still vacillating about whether to interrupt him or to just let him be.

"We're out of here." One of the cops shook hands with Sully. "You need a lift somewhere or you got a car here?"

"What idiot would drive a car to the courthouse? I took the bus."

"So you need a ride?"

"You headed back to the precinct?"

"Going in that general direction."

"You can drop me at Queens General then."

They all turned to go then, Sully walking with the group of cops descending the courthouse steps. He passed within five feet of her without noticing. She started to call out to him, but restrained herself. He was in his element, with the guys, and she didn't want to spoil it.

As she turned toward Padama and Indigo at the top of the stairs, she wondered why he'd asked for a ride to the hospital. Why would he be going there?

Her first thought was that he wasn't feeling well . . . a heart attack? That was her inner drama queen acting out. He looked fine.

Then it hit her. Oh, no.

She had to get to the hospital.

She searched the streets beyond the courthouse for a yellow cab. There were none in sight, and she would wait an eternity if she called for one.

She turned and raced up the stairs.

The reporter and other people crowded around Indigo made it impossible to get to her. Bernie saw Padama on the fringes, trying to press into the group.

"I was in the coffee shop," she said, tapping one of the cameramen on the shoulder. "I was there for the whole thing."

The cameraman ignored her, focusing on Indigo.

"Padama, did you drive here?"

"Yes, yes," she said, swatting Bernie away as if she were a pesky fly.

"Can you give me a ride to the hospital?" Bernie grabbed the girl's arm. "I need to go. Now."

"What? Are you having a baby?"

"It's an emergency. We have to go now."

Padama rolled her eyes. "Not now, Bernie, I—" When she faced Bernie, her expression changed. "You're serious."

Bernie nodded. "Where are you parked?"

"On the street, two blocks that way."

Her pulse roaring in her ears, Bernie was already hurrying down the stairs.

Chapter 39

W hat a beautiful day.
It was unseasonably warm for March, and Sully kept thinking he would ditch the jacket, but he needed to keep it on for now. He didn't want to alert anyone at the hospital to the fact that he was packing. For the moment, his old off-duty five-shot revolver was best kept a secret if he was going to get a chance to use it.

He approached the hospital entrance and the electronic door whooshed open for him. Two black security cameras caught his eye, but he walked right past, whistling as he headed toward the elevators. If they caught him . . . not if, but when, well, he hoped no one got in trouble for not stopping him. He wasn't out to hurt a working man trying to make an honest buck for his family.

But who in their right mind would stop an old man from whistling his way down a hospital corridor?

That was the challenge of security on a hospital or college campus. You needed to allow access for the community, but you were mandated to keep members of that community safe from each other. It was quite a pickle, an enigma within a dilemma. Sully was glad he wasn't director of security in a place like this.

He paused in front of the elevator bank, then changed his

mind and headed to the cafeteria. He'd had no stomach for coffee this morning, had left the house without it in the bluster of that argument with Peg. No breakfast or coffee, but now he had a craving, and who knew? This could be his last cup for a long time.

Sully's Cup.

It was the coffee shop that had gotten them all into this mess in the first place. Maybe it was too much of a vanity, to have his own little café to serve cops. Maybe he shouldn't have put his name on it at all. Vanity.

The cafeteria coffee was serviceable, and not a bad price. He ran into a few uniforms down there who knew him. They gave their condolences, and he felt the blade turn in his gut. Did that terrible feeling ever go away? Probably not. In his experience, only the good things like hair and taste buds and sex receded.

He couldn't place these guys, with his mind jam-packed with stress and exhaustion right now. Their name tags said Woods and Ammitrano, but they could have said Rosencrantz and Guildenstern for all he cared. The only cop he cared about right now was the kid guarding Curtis's room on the third floor. According to the schedule, a young rookie named Kelleher was on duty right now. Sully had been counting on it being a rookie, and he hoped these guys weren't some last-minute replacement.

"So what are you guys doing here at the hospital today?" he asked Rosencrantz and Guildenstern.

"Getting a cup of coffee," the short one said, cackling.

Woods explained that they'd responded to a domestic dispute that had turned ugly. They'd come to deliver a cop for an MRI after someone had winged a kitchen pan at his head.

"It's a tough job you guys do." Sully rubbed his chin, freshly shaved that morning. "How's your guy doing?"

"He seems okay," Woods said. "But it's worth checking out."

"Absolutely."

With the bitter sting of coffee on the back of his tongue, Sully left them in the cafeteria and headed up to the third floor where Cahill had told him the prisoner was being lodged. He'd sweated the details of this for days, worried that he'd fall apart, that the schedule would change, or that the young cop would call him out. But he'd awakened this morning with the clearest head he'd had since the shootings. He knew what to do. Every step had led here. And now that he was in the midst of it he felt robotic, like a machine programmed to tap this elevator button, turn left in the corridor, press through the double doors. None of this was difficult, not when you knew you were in the right.

He'd spent the days since Curtis's arrest trying to think of a reasonable distraction, and yesterday, he'd thought he had it. The roster. He had to hit the room when the guard was a rookie. But to do that, he'd had to do some fishing. He'd made a few phone calls, found out the name of one of the cops he knew who'd been assigned guard duty. Officer Billy Cahill, a real stand-up guy. Cahill had sounded pleased when Sully touched base and started asking questions about the guard detail at the hospital.

"Sully, this guy's a cop killer," Cahill had said on the phone. "We're watching him like a hawk. Not that he's given us any problems. Mostly he's been unconscious, but he's cuffed to the bed. Cuffed, and the nurses keep those restraints on him."

The third floor smelled like all the others—antiseptic mixed with paint and that iron smell. Sully's shoes trod lightly on the tile floor, calm, steady footsteps. Curtis's room was down at the end. A private room, lucky bastard.

Halfway down the hall, Sully chucked his coffee cup in a trash bin by the nurses' station. He had to look somewhat professional here.

He opened up his coat so that his gun was exposed, then reached into his pocket for his old badge. It was actually a replica he'd had made, probably thirty years ago. Most cops paid to have a replica pressed in metal, as the penalty for a lost or stolen shield could be a week or two of vacation. The replicas looked so authentic that most cops wore the fakes and kept their real shield in a safe place at home. And an added bonus was that cops like Sully got to keep the fake shield after retirement. He clipped the silver shield onto a lanyard and took his ID card out of his pocket. The card had RETIRED stamped across it, but the rookie probably wouldn't ask to see it if Sully talked the talk.

With his shield and weapon showing, Sully continued down the corridor. He didn't see the officer standing guard until he passed a gurney sitting in the hall, and there was the cop. Definitely a rookie. The kid actually had freckles scattered over his nose. Thick reddish hair, and lots of it. Kelleher; that was what his nameplate said.

"Good morning, Officer." Sully didn't smile; he didn't want to come on too strong. "How's it going?"

"Fine." Kelleher squinted over Sully's shoulder, as if expecting to see others behind him. "How you doing?"

"Very good. I know you're new to the 109. Don't think we've met. I'm John Keenan. Street crime. Sergeant Todd is shorthanded today, had to tap into the plainclothes unit. Looks like I'm your meal replacement."

"Is that right?" Kelleher checked his watch. "That's weird. I'm not really due for a break till sixteen hundred."

"I guess this was the only way the sarge could work it." Sully kept his tone even, though the back of his mind was shrieking what an idiot he was. All the time people told him he didn't look his age, but he was banking on this guy buying that he was around ten years younger. Counting on the kid not to have ever stopped into Sully's Cup, though Cahill had said he'd only been transferred over from the Bronx a few weeks ago.

Kelleher scratched the back of his head. "I wish Todd would have called me. I'd rather go later."

"You know, I can mention that when I get back to the precinct. Maybe he can send someone to relieve you again later." Sully paused a moment, trying to sell it, but not too hard. "But if I were you, I'd take a meal now. You know how this job is. Use it or lose it."

"Yeah."

Sully nodded toward the closed door. "How's the patient doing?"

"Quiet. The nurse said he's still pretty drugged up." Kelleher picked up his duty jacket from a chair and shrugged it on. "You won't have any trouble."

"Good." Sully slid his hands back along his belt, pushing his jacket back to reveal the holster clipped to the side of it. The weight of the gun on his hip reminded him of his days on the job, urban cowboy days.

"I'll be back in forty minutes or so," Kelleher said.

"Take your time." Sully stood at ease, his legs three feet apart, weight evenly distributed, and waited for the kid to disappear. He was dying to peel off his jacket and wipe the sweat from the back of his neck, but he didn't want the kid to see how the back of his shirt was drenched. Probably the pits, too.

Jesus, he'd come close there, but that was what happened when you scrabbled together a half-assed plan.

A nurse came out of the station halfway down the hall and fell into step with Kelleher. Good. Maybe she could keep him distracted awhile.

Once he saw them turn the corner to the elevator, Sully let out the breath he didn't know he'd been holding, tore off his jacket, and pulled his damp shirt away from his chest.

Good Lord, he was too old for shenanigans like this. He looked down at his balled-up jacket leaning off the chair. Peg's red paisley oven mitt poked out of one of the inside pockets; his idiot flag. He tore it out of the pocket. "You're lucky you got this far," he muttered. The pot holder was to muffle the sound of the gunshot. He'd thought of that when he thought he might have a chance of getting away with this.

Now . . . now he figured that the finest police force in the world was going to catch up with him, no matter how carefully he covered his tracks. Between the descriptions Kelleher would give of the "bald, tall senior cop" and the question of who had reason to want Curtis dead, well . . . all roads would lead to his modest house in Bayside.

But that didn't matter now.

Brendan's life was over, and Sully's life had started to eclipse even before his son's death.

He'd had a good run, and he would go out doing the right thing.

For the hell of it, he slid the oven mitt onto his left hand and opened the door with it. There were two beds in the room; only one was occupied.

The man in the bed seemed smaller than Sully had expected from his photos, thin and spindly. He was either asleep or drugged out. There was a monitor behind him that showed blood pressure, pulse, and whatnot. But there was no breathing tube, no lifeline that could be yanked.

Curtis would recover, just fine. Three good cops were dead, and this guy was in a cushy bed, getting the good drugs to ease the pain.

"Wake up, you son of a bitch."

When Curtis didn't respond, Sully smacked his feet. Still, no sign of consciousness.

It would be better if he was awake. Then he could see what was happening to him. Feel the sting of fear, the hot metal of the round.

Curtis's shoulder was bandaged from where they'd removed the shredded bullet. Sully stepped closer, found a spot that he figured would be tender, and gave a shove.

"Aaah . . ." Curtis moaned and turned his head to one side, but his eyes didn't open.

"Okay, fine. Sleep through it, for all I care. But for the record, I want you to know that I'm here to help you pay for what you did. My name is James Sullivan, and you killed my son Brendan. Brendan Sullivan. He was a cop. You killed two other fine young men, too. Their names were Sean Walters and Kevin Puchinko."

Sully took the gun from its holster. Fuck the oven mitt. He didn't care who heard the explosion of the shot.

"All three of those young men will be missed," Sully told the sleeping monster. "They will be missed, and you?" He pressed the barrel of the gun to Curtis's forehead. "People will applaud your death."

Chapter 40

Oh, dear God, please let me be wrong.

Bernie repeated the prayer that had run through her head all the way here as she hurried through the halls of the hospital. She had never been to Queens General, and the two different wings connected in odd ways.

Still, she knew that Peyton Curtis was on the third floor. It was one of the bits of information Keesh had gotten from his friend in the Queens DA's Office. Curtis was on the third floor, but in what wing?

She was going to have to ask.

On the third floor, she stopped at the first nurse's station she could find, but it was unoccupied. She stopped a passing woman in pink scrubs and asked if she knew.

"Peyton Curtis?" Bernie asked breathlessly. "He's a prisoner, in police custody."

"I'm sorry, I'm just a volunteer here, but even if I knew, I couldn't tell you. We're not supposed to give out any personal information, you know."

"Oh, I'm here on business." Bernie fished in the pocket of her coat for her wallet.

"What, you're going to bribe me?" The woman's painted-on eyebrows shot up.

"No, no, I just wanted to show you my ID. I work for the district attorney's office. I'm here to interview the suspect."

"Oh." The woman peered at Bernie's card. "You changed your hair since then."

"Yes, yes, I did. But I need to find Mr. Curtis right away. Do you know his room number?"

The volunteer looked over her shoulder cautiously. "Who knows numbers?" She gestured with her head. "He's at the very end of that hall. Last room on the left. You'll know it from the adorable young cop waiting outside. But you didn't hear it from me."

"Of course. Thank you." Bernie took off running down the hall.

"No running," the woman called after her. "You'll hurt yourself!"

There was no cop standing guard, just a chair with a jacket strewn over it. Bernie pushed open the door frantically and froze, her wildest nightmare realized.

The man with his back to her was her father . . . her father pressing a gun to the patient's forehead.

"Dad, no!" Bernie rushed forward, her arms stretched out in front of her as if she could reach out and stop the terrible scene from unfolding.

"Jesus H. Christ, Bernadette! What are you doing here?"

"I figured it out, Dad." She came up behind him, then swung around and put her hands on his forearms and tugged at the straight line of muscle and bone leading to the sickening steel weapon.

God, he was strong . . . but she had to shift . . . his . . . aim.

"Stop it!" Sully's face hardened as he held tough. "Just get the hell out of my way! You won't win, Bernie. Get the hell out of here before you become an accessory to murder."

"Grrr!" She growled in frustration and banged her body into his.

Although her weight had no impact on his stance, it angered him enough to lower the gun and turn to her.

"You know better than to mess with a man with a loaded gun. I said get out." His face was beet red, and the malice glittering in his eyes chilled her to the bone.

"I'm not leaving," she said steadily. A pulse drummed in her ears, but she ignored the fear.

He didn't shoot yet. He's not aiming at him now.

This is progress.

"Darlin', you need to get out of here or you're going to have an image in your mind that will haunt you the rest of your life."

"I'm not leaving, and you are not shooting this man. I won't let you."

"Oh, please. You're the daughter, Bernie. The liberal, litigating daughter who thinks everyone deserves an equal chance. You're wrong."

"Okay, okay, then let's talk about it. Put your gun away before someone comes in here. Talk to me." She tried to force her way between him and the bed, but he kept pushing her away. "Talk to me, Dad. Because you can take words back, but if you fire that gun, you're going to destroy everything you've worked for. Your reputation. Your family. Our family."

He stared straight ahead at the sleeping man's face. "You don't get it. I wish you hadn't walked in here, but nothing you can say will change the truth." He went up to the monitor behind the bed and pressed a few buttons until it was off. "Go, Bernie. Get out of here," Sully said, raising the gun to Curtis's head.

Fear was a fist, squeezing tight in Bernie's chest. She had no doubt her father would kill this man, and then . . . then they would both be guilty of murder and there would be nothing separating them from the most barbaric animals, from rats who killed and consumed their own young.

She left her father's side and went behind the bed, slipping into the narrow space between the headboard and wall.

"Okay, Dad. Go ahead and shoot, and with any luck your bullet will go right through him into me." She braced herself on the headboard. "If it doesn't, then promise you'll finish me off with another shot, because I'll be as good as dead. You will, too."

The muscles in Sully's face tensed as his extended hands began to tremble. "Get out of there." His voice was a low, ominous grumble. "Move out of the way."

She shook her head, emotion balling up in her throat.

It was horrifying to defy her father, even more terrifying to wonder if this man who had once resembled her father was going to pull the trigger.

"Go!" Sweat glistened on his brow. "Get the hell out of here."

She stared into his troubled eyes, looking for a hint of a break in the storm, some connection to be made . . . but he was so far away. Miles away. "I'll leave with you when you put the gun down," she said, trying to keep her voice calm.

His fingers moved toward the trigger. Such a slight movement, with huge impact.

"Please don't shoot us!" she begged, bracing against the headboard in dread of the explosion of gunfire.

"I'll kill myself first," he said bitterly.

She opened her eyes to see him turning the gun on himself, aiming at his chest.

"Daddy, no!" The last word escaped as a whimper from her throat as she lunged forward to stop him, but was caught by the headboard.

He stared at the barrel of the gun . . .

Then dropped it to his side.

"Dad . . ." She burst into tears, awash with relief as he holstered the gun and then stood there swaying, lifeless and drained.

She rushed around the bed and hugged him hard. "Thank you. Thank you. Thank you," she whispered, her face mashed against his shirt.

She felt him sag under her fingertips, heard the air leak from his lungs, but he didn't say a word. And as she guided him toward the door, she noticed that his arms hung limp at his sides. He wasn't hugging her back.

When she lifted her chin, his face was expressionless. The menace had drained from his eyes, along with all signs of life. The act of putting one foot in front of the other seemed to require all the strength he could muster.

He was a zombie, but still alive.

She was wiping her wet cheeks with the back of her hand when a moan came from the bed.

"Angel . . ."

Chapter 41

"Angel..." He was calling, but wasn't sure if he was making a sound in the real world.

He had heard the man's voice. Growling bear of a man. The bear had a gun on him, pointed right in his face. Peyton knew the unmistakable feel of a cold barrel on his forehead.

Peyton would have been frightened if sleep wasn't tugging him down into a sea of calm.

Then there was a woman, young, he could tell from her voice. An angry girl, yelling at him to stop.

The bear growled back, but she kept up her cries.

When Peyton finally was able to push his eyes open to stare through the haze of narrow slits, he saw her pushing and pulling on the bear, tugging like crazy. But the big man stood there like an old tree, solid in the ground.

And damned if that wasn't a gun in Peyton's face.

He let his eyes close and dropped back under the surface of sleep, waiting under the ice for the explosion to shatter everything. Waiting for the world to go black. Fizzle black, then burn out to nothing.

But the explosion didn't come.

He saw the girl swing around him again, her thick hair like a veil. Or a big, thick halo.

He thought maybe she was his angel of death, fighting with

big ol' St. Peter at the Pearly Gates. The angels were fighting, rocking his bed, voices booming.

Thundering angels ... that was what Mama said when thunder rumbled from the sky. The angels were fighting. She wanted him to go through the Pearly Gates to heaven, and St. Peter kept saying no. She lifted her wings wide. Trying to cover his sins? His angel.

His angel.

What happened to Angel?

Remembering was like squeezing water from a stone, but at last he found her in his mind, a round dumpling of a woman with chocolate eyes and cheeks that were always pink. His angel. She said her name was Angela, but he called her Angel. She believed in him. She was the only one who understood and tried to help him.

She gave him the walking stick. A walking stick with a faux ivory rat carved on the handle.

What happened to his walking stick?

He needed it to help him stand up and get out of this cold swamp. "Angel ..." His throat was dry and rough as bare pavement. "Angel, help me. Help me get my walking stick. I need my cane."

"He's asking for help." The angel's voice was clear as a bell.

Peyton summoned his strength to drag his lids up just a notch. And there she was, standing beside his bed, this time without the tall bear of a man. Her hair framed her face like a veil. Jesus's mother.

"Help me." *Pull me up for air. Pull me out of this black hole. Get me my walking stick.*

There was so much to say, but his weak body couldn't push the words out, and he couldn't see whether or not she was really his angel or just some white girl staring at him.

"I'll try to help you," she said in a thick voice. "I'm an attorney and ... maybe I can help. I'll do my best."

PART III

PART III

Chapter 42

Lunch with Bernie was supposed to be a sort of farewell for Keesh. It was his last day with the Manhattan DA's Office, and Wing Wong was his favorite place in the neighborhood. And though he'd anticipated needing to prop Bernie up a bit, he'd never expected to hear a tale of attempted murder.

Keesh stared at Bernie over a plate of roast duck. "Sully went to the hospital to kill him?"

She nodded, then took a drink of water. "I don't know how I figured it out, but I did, and I got there just in time. But even so, it was tense. I . . . for a few seconds there, I thought Dad might shoot me if I didn't get out of his way. He was so convinced that getting rid of Peyton Curtis was the right thing to do."

"Holy shit." Keesh reached across the table and squeezed her wrist. "This is scary stuff, Bernie. As if you haven't been through the wringer in the past two weeks."

She nodded, looking down at his hand on hers. "Dad's still furious. He's barely speaking to me."

"After you saved him from life in prison?"

"He doesn't see it that way."

"Of course he doesn't. He believes in the rules of the street. But his brand of street justice is just the sort of thing that undermines the criminal justice system. We work hundreds of hours every year to make sure . . ."

She touched a finger to her chin, a signal he recognized. Disinterest.

"I'm preaching to the choir."

She nodded.

"Sorry, but this is scary shit. Your own father had a gun drawn."

"He's a cop. I've seen that gun a thousand times." She nabbed a dim sum with her chopsticks. "I've just never been staring down the barrel."

"Does anyone else know?"

"The cop who was standing guard might have figured out that something was off, but he's a rookie. And what's the worst that could be charged? Sully impersonated an officer so that we could visit a suspect in a hospital?"

"Somehow, that doesn't reflect the horrifying reality of the situation." He forked two slices of roast duck onto his plate and spooned on some plum sauce. "Do you think he told your mother?"

She sighed. "I don't know. Sully's not doing a whole lot of talking these days." She dipped a dumpling in mustard. "And there's one other person who knows. Peyton Curtis woke up while we were there. He was dazed, but talking. He asked for help."

Keesh rolled his eyes. "Was this while there was a gun pressed to his head?"

She swallowed. "No, after that."

"Well, he's probably already forgotten the encounter. You said he was medicated, right?"

"But he was coming out of it when we left, and he was very clear. He called me an angel and asked for my help."

"That's creepy." Keesh could tell Bernie had some kind of agenda here.

"There was something so pathetic about it. It made me want to help him."

"Bernie." Keesh cocked his head. "We think he killed your brother."

Her whiskey-colored eyes flared. "He probably did. But if he's found guilty on the three counts of murder, the prosecutor will go for the death penalty. We know that."

He nodded. "And . . . ?"

"And I know for a fact that Brendan wouldn't have wanted that. We talked about capital punishment one night at dinner. He said it was wrong. He even crossed Dad on it." She screwed up her mouth, as if something had gone sour. "Wouldn't it be awful if Brendan's killer was executed?"

He nodded. "If it comes to that, you could probably speak against the death penalty for Peyton Curtis."

"While the rest of my family is lined up on the other side of the courtroom to demand justice?" She closed her eyes. "My family is going to disown me."

"For voicing your opinion?"

"For helping Peyton Curtis. I've already been in touch with his attorney. Do you know Laurence Saunders?"

"The name doesn't ring a bell."

"Well, he didn't sound happy to hear from me. Even though I'm volunteering my services."

"Okay. Now you've lost me."

"I'm going to volunteer my time to work with Curtis's defense team. Not on the actual trial. I know I need to stay out of that. But I'm thinking that I can compile information and testimony to be used in the sentencing phase."

The idea was unorthodox and edgy; this was not Bernie's style. "That sounds like a disaster waiting to happen."

"I know, but I can't help myself. After everything that's happened these past two weeks, the shootings and my job, this is the first thing that feels right. It's like I've finally found my place in this big terrible situation. I think I know where I fit into the puzzle now."

"As Curtis's attorney?"

"As the person who saves his life. There's a difference."

He put his chopsticks down as the ramifications of Bernie's decision set in. "I don't like it, but you know I'm thinking of it from a selfish point of view. I don't want you working for the other side. What will that do to us?"

"Our relationship is stronger than a court case," she said flatly.

"Do you really want to put it to that kind of test?" He hated talking about "relationships," probing and poking as if the tenuous bond were an organism with a life of its own. In his experience, you had to run with what was working for you, and since the day they'd met in law school, Bernie worked for Keesh.

"Can I ask you something?" she asked. A ridiculous question, as there was no stopping Bernie when she was on a roll. "What happened to that nice Armenian girl you started dating?"

He wasn't quite sure how to admit failure. "She's still a nice Armenian girl."

"Keesh, don't toy with me. I'm in a vulnerable state."

"We're taking a break."

"A break? After what? Two dates? Three?"

"How am I supposed to pursue a relationship with all this going on? I can't just leave you in the dust to go ice-skating or grab a movie."

"You're taking a break because you miss me." She grinned, tapping his chest. "That's it. Every time you're with her, you think of me."

It was true, and he was secretly thrilled that she was onto him. "When you and I split up, it wasn't because we didn't want to see each other," he pointed out. "It was all the other forces at play."

She was shaking her head, the restaurant lights striking a reddish sheen on her hair. "We should get back together."

Yes, immediately, he wanted to say. He could imagine sweeping back her hair to run his lips down her neck. That pinstriped blouse would be unbuttoned to reveal a wispy bra and the tiny gold St. Bernadette medal that tended to fall in the generous crease of her cleavage.

That was his genuine response. The more intellectual Keesh could not let go of the obstacles between them.

"Now is not the best time." It killed him to keep her at arm's length, but they both knew the reasons. "Your life is like an episode of *Law and Order.*"

"You miss me." She leaned across the small table, teasing him with those whiskey eyes. "Admit it."

Her face was inches away, so close he could feel the air her lashes stirred when she blinked. "I like you, Bernie, but—"

"Don't ruin it with an argument, Keesh. We both know what we're up against, but I say we have more going for us than against us. Forget the families. They don't have to deal with dating in the age of Facebook and HIV. There's something special between us, something you don't find on this planet too often. Life is short, so let's hold on and let the planet spin us around. Why don't you come to my place after work tonight? I'll make you dinner."

He winced, hating to be the heavy. In some ways, he'd never really broken ties with Bernie. But if she was serious about working with Peyton Curtis, now would not be a good time for the two of them to hook up.

"Okay, I'll bring in takeout. Chinese or Italian?" She smacked her head. "We're having Chinese now. Italian it is."

Why did he feel warmed by the smile that lit her face? Bernie was under his skin; had been for a long time. "It's not for lack of desire, believe me. But can I point out the professional implications of the two of us hooking up with me working for the Queens District Attorney's Office and you now working to defend a suspected cop killer we're prosecuting? Something is wrong with that picture."

"You're right. So we'll keep it a secret." She looked around at the other diners. "No one will know. You're starting in Queens next week, and I can't spill the truth at the office because I don't have an office anymore."

He snorted. "You are too much." He leaned across the table so that he could whisper. "And I've missed you, too."

Chapter 43

The law offices of Myers and Arndorffer were contained on the floor of an old downtown warehouse that had been converted to office space. Apparently the architect who had been let loose on this particular floor had favored cavernous space and canvas umbrellas, as the floor stretched back dizzily, punctuated only by a series of canvas drops that reminded Bernie of tents in the desert.

As Bernie sat waiting under one canvas creation that marked the reception area, she tried to remember the details of the conversation that had brought her here. Not the odd moment when she'd told Peyton Curtis she would try to help him. She wasn't even sure if he would remember that. It was Brendan's comments about capital punishment that drove her to step out of her comfort zone, piss off her family, and cross this defense attorney who didn't want to deal with her.

It was something he'd said at dinner. What had they been talking about? She remembered that it was the day he'd shared the story about the two little girls who'd been removed from their home. Somehow, the death penalty had come up . . . and what had Brendan said?

You can't kill a killer. Or, *when you kill a killer, you become an animal, too.* Something like that. He had said it calmly, secure in his belief. And he'd said it right to their father's face.

The canvas awning overhead twisted into a peak at its center; a white vortex sucking her into snowy nothingness when she tipped her face up. Creepy in a bland oatmeal sort of way. She stared up, wondering if anyone felt comfortable in this space.

"Miss Sullivan." The African-American man with large, black-framed glasses startled her. He shoved a hand in her space. "Laurence Saunders."

She rose and shook his hand. "Bernie Sullivan. Thanks for seeing me."

Saunders rolled back on his heels and tossed his head back. "You didn't give me much choice. I got five minutes—that's it," he said, leading her back to a small conference table under a canvas that reminded Bernie of a folded napkin.

She sat on the edge of the wooden chair and got right to the point. "I've been thinking long and hard about how I can fit into Peyton Curtis's defense. I want to compile evidence and testimony that we can use in the sentencing portion of the trial, if need be. Marvin Green has already announced the prosecution's intention to ask for the death penalty for these crimes. I'm here to help you get Peyton Curtis off with a life sentence."

"I'm confused, Miss Sullivan."

"Call me Bernie."

"Okay, Bernie." Saunders lifted his chin, as if he needed a new perspective on the situation. "What are you here for, exactly?"

"To help you with the penalty phase—"

"I heard all that. I just can't fathom how the Manhattan District Attorney's Office could send a green attorney over to me and expect me to buy a story of defection."

"The Manhattan DA has nothing to do with this."

"Then you're spying for the Queens DA?"

"Listen, Laurence, I—"

"Mr. Saunders, okay." He flicked two fingers between the two of them. "We are not friends."

"Mr. Saunders, neither district attorneys' offices know I'm speaking with you. I'm on a leave of absence from the Manhattan DA. I'd like to work for you strictly as a volunteer. I'm a hard worker, and the price is right."

He pursed his lips, staring at her. "Everyone knows I'm tapped out. I'm one of the few black attorneys doing pro bono work in this city. I need help, all right. But I don't think it's going to come from the sister of one of the men my client is accused of killing."

"I know, that must seem weird." Bernie raked the side of her hair back with one hand.

"Weird doesn't begin to describe it. Try bizarre. Outrageous. Ludicrous."

"Mr. Saunders, my brother Brendan was not an advocate of capital punishment, and neither am I." The image of Peyton Curtis with a gun to his head flashed in her mind. She could tell Saunders that she had saved his client's life once and had a vested interest, but she restrained herself. She had to protect her father, and Saunders probably wouldn't believe her, anyway. "I can help you. I can help your client."

"And how are you planning to do that?"

"I'm not expecting to be a part of the defense team, but I would like to sit in when you interview Curtis and other character witnesses. I would gather their testimony, things that put a positive spin on your client's character and circumstances. The testimony I gather will help in the sentencing hearing."

"And you're going to sit in on interviews and depositions."

"That's right."

"Thanks, but no thanks." He rose. "Excuse me if I don't walk you to the door. I've had enough theater of the absurd." He walked away.

"But . . . wait. I'm offering you free help."

He paused. "Miss Sullivan, did you ever hear mention in law school of an ancient device called attorney-client privilege?"

"I . . . well, of course." She blinked. "It protects the communications between a client and his attorney from disclosure to the court."

"So you were paying attention. Think about it. Attorneys don't bring an audience when they consult with their client. Of course you can't 'sit in' on interviews." He rolled his eyes. "If you'll excuse me . . ."

He walked off, leaving her standing beneath the floating napkin tent. She reached up and pinged the canvas, then headed off in a funk.

As soon as the kitchen door squeaked open, Bernie sensed the heavy air in the house.

"Hey, how's it going?" She tried a light tone, but the question fell flat in the kitchen full of women.

"Oh, Bernie, love, close the door tight." Her mother sounded like a wounded hen as she briefly looked up from rinsing dishes at the sink. "I feel a draft."

Sarah sat in her new spot in the corner chair, peeling potatoes. *My old job,* Bernie thought.

"Did they fix your furnace yet?" Bernie asked. Sarah and the girls had moved into the back bedrooms when their furnace conked out.

"Please." Sarah shook her head. "The part that finally came to fix the old one still didn't get it working. I'm meeting the contractor at the house tomorrow so they can install a brand-new furnace."

"You're lucky your pipes didn't burst," Mary Kate said. "Conner had the idea of using space heaters. At least it's keeping the house from freezing."

"I'll be glad when it's all working again." Sarah put the last skinned potato in the pot. "Brendan used to take care of that stuff, and now I know why. These contractors hear a woman on the phone and they think I'm an idiot."

"I hope you flexed your muscles for them," Bernie said, peeking into the living room for her father. She had expected

267 THE DAUGHTER SHE USED TO BE

to see him in his Barcalounger with the television on low, but the room was empty, the television off. "Where's Dad?"

"Down at the Spinnytop, probably head in the soup," Peg said.

"Dad?" Bernie had seen her father with a beer in his hand nearly every day of his life, but she'd never seen him drunk.

Peg nodded toward the back room. "I don't think he wanted the granddaughters to see him that way."

"Ma, none of us wants to see him like that." There was a clang of pots as Mary Kate fished around in a cabinet. "He put Sully's Cup up for sale. He met with one of those Realtors who specializes in commercial properties."

Sarah dumped the mound of potato skins into the trash. "I wish he hadn't done that."

"Hence the morose cloud hanging over this house," Bernie said. She herself had mixed feelings about the future of Sully's Cup, but Sully was going to be lost without it.

Still, Sully seemed to see it as the source of his downhill slide, which had begun the day of the shooting and accelerated when she'd stopped him from shooting Peyton Curtis that day in the hospital room.

He'll never forgive me.

That was a tough burden to bear, but she would gladly shoulder it if she thought he could begin to forgive himself. He still believed it was his "cop" coffee shop that had lured the shooter in. Sully saw himself as the cause of the tragedy, and he couldn't move past that.

Killing Curtis would have provided a sort of closure for Sully, who saw it as his only chance to end the evil he'd unleashed. And she'd taken that away from him.

Of course, this was the analysis she and Keesh had come up with last Friday when he'd stopped over after work and stayed the night. Keesh was the only person who knew about the hospital episode, and though his judgment was sound, the explanation they'd come up with was pure conjecture.

No one really knew the multifaceted bloom of Sully's suffering, and he wasn't talking.

Bernie took a Diet Pepsi from the fridge and sat down at the table. "Maybe it's good that he's not here, because he's not going to want to hear what I have to say."

"What have you done now?" Mary Kate asked in that disapproving, older-sister voice that made Bernie cringe.

"It's worse than you can imagine." Bernie let her eyes trace the familiar path through her mother's kitchen that always calmed her, starting at the statue of the Virgin Mary facing east on the windowsill over the sink, to the teapot-shaped clock over the cabinets, then to the simple wood crucifix over the dining room doorway, and finally landing on the wreath of baby blue flowers on the wall over the table. This room, this home, had always brought her comfort, but today the walls seemed like a hollow façade. There was dust on the clock and she noticed that the satin flowers of the wreath had faded to gray. Suddenly, her heart ached for the simpler days of her childhood.

"Bernie?" Sarah broke the silence. She added water to the potatoes and set them up on the stove. "What's up with you?"

"I'm getting into an area that's going to make Dad mad at me. And you guys probably won't be so happy about it, either." She told them about her meeting with Curtis's attorney. "He rejected me, but I can't let it go. Even if I have to resign from my job and start some sort of nonprofit organization, a campaign to end capital punishment, or something like that, this is something I need to do."

"Working for the enemy," Mary Kate said. "At least, that's how Dad will see it."

"But I'm really working for our brother's memory. Don't you remember that night when he talked about the death penalty? Do you remember, Sarah?"

"I really don't." Sarah's eyes were the blue of a sea churning before a storm. "I don't think I was in on that conversation, but it makes sense. He had a gentle heart. Such a softy for kids.

A real people person. I could see him defending life." She folded her arms over her chest, drifting off in thought.

Well, at least Sarah wouldn't hate her. Bernie took a swig of diet soda, wondering if Sully would be back for dinner. Maybe this would be her last supper here for a while.

"So what's troubling you most about this, Bernadette?" Peg asked, her hands busy forming biscuits on a tray. "Is it the disapproval of this family, or are you not sure of what's right?"

"I know what's right, Ma. Brendan knew it was wrong to take another man's life, even in the most heinous cases. Think about it. He wouldn't want Curtis to be killed. He can't speak for himself, but I'm here, and I can defend his beliefs. I have to do it."

"Then you have to go for it and stop worrying about what other people will think. And I say good luck to you." Peg wiped her hands on her apron and turned to face Bernie. "Our Brendan is dead, and there's no bringing him back. I say we find the killer, lock him up, and throw away the key. That's good enough for me."

"Same," Mary Kate said. "I don't believe in execution, either, but I just don't want this guy to get off because he's crazy or had an underprivileged childhood or some lame excuse like that."

"Nobody's looking for that to happen," Bernie said.

"Good." MK shredded a carrot into the salad. "So I guess we'll let you stay in the family then."

"Yeah, thanks." Bernie took a sip of soda, thinking that Sully wasn't going to be quite so generous.

Chapter 44

Sarah sat on the edge of the paper-covered examining table, her bare legs crossed. She had told the nurse she didn't need an exam, but the woman had insisted that she change into the drafty gown.

"Doctor Newbury will want to examine you," the nurse had insisted with wide eyes, as if there would be a terrible punishment if they defied the doctor.

Which Sarah was about to do. "I don't want to be examined," she told the doctor. "I don't want anything that will compare this in any way to my girls, to the babies I had with you. I know I'm pregnant, and I need to terminate the pregnancy."

Dr. Patricia Newbury didn't register shock or disapproval as she gazed up at Sarah. For the first time Sarah noticed that Newbury's short cloud of blond hair had streaks of gray running through it, and she wondered if her OB-GYN was too old now to have any more babies. What a blessing.

The doctor closed Sarah's chart and rose so that she could look Sarah in the eye. "You don't think you can handle a new baby on your own."

"I know I can't."

"That's understandable. You've been through a lot, Sarah."

"And I've got more torture to come. The prospect of harming a living thing disturbs me, but I can't think of any other way."

"You're an educated woman," Dr. Newbury said. "Scientists tell us that the fetus has no awareness and no pain sensation until after the fifth month of pregnancy. If that has any bearing on your decision . . ."

"I'm just trying to look forward, to the future, in a realistic way, and a baby . . . I wouldn't have a minute for Grace and Maisey, and they need me now."

Dr. Newbury nodded, her gray eyes soaking it all in.

"So I just want the pill you give to people that causes the . . . the medical abortion. I read online that you can take it up to the seventh week, and by my calculations I'm right around the fifth week. Or sixth. Somewhere around there."

"Seven weeks is the range we're comfortable with giving a medical abortion." Newbury stepped back to lean against the counter. She looked to the ceiling and sunk her hands into the pockets of her white coat. "But I'd like to do an exam. Your chart says you're on the Pill."

"But barely." Sarah looked down at her hands, her index finger worrying the loose cuticle on her thumb. She'd been tearing at her cuticles the past two weeks, but if that was her nastiest vice, she figured she'd survive. "I wasn't so good about taking a pill every day. And when the last month's packet was done, I couldn't make it to the pharmacy. I kept trying to, but . . . Anyway, I figured I'd take a month off and start again. I thought the hormones would stay in my system."

"Sometimes they do."

"Except for the unlucky few." Sarah tugged hard on the loose strip of cuticle, pulling until she felt pain. There. That made her feel better somehow. It made the psychological pain recede somewhat.

"There's the possibility that the fetus isn't viable," the doctor said. "Usually that's not the news people want, but in your case, I suspect it might help alleviate some guilt."

The doctor was right, but Sarah did not want this to feel like a real pregnancy. She didn't want an exam. "Can't I just get the medicine and go?"

"Sarah, it's not that simple. I'm concerned about your health, physical and emotional. Some women feel relief after their abortion. Others report feeling sad or overwrought for days or weeks afterward. If you choose to terminate, we'll need to address any emotional fallout, too."

"So I'll go for therapy. I just lost my husband. I wouldn't mind talking to someone once a week. An hour on a couch would be heaven right now."

"Therapy sounds like a good idea for the long term. But the abortion isn't something you can work out over time. If your calculations are right, we have two more weeks for a medical abortion. Surgical, you can go up to twelve weeks. That would give you another month to think about it."

"I don't want to think. I want it to be over."

"Sarah." Dr. Newbury moved closer and took Sarah's hands in hers, surprising Sarah. Her hands were surprisingly soft against Sarah's dry cuticles. "I have no qualms about terminating your pregnancy if you're absolutely sure. It's your choice. But this is such a difficult time for you. I'm sure you're feeling . . . fragile at best. You owe it to yourself to take a few more days to think about it. Meet with a therapist."

When the woman's sincere gray eyes met hers, Sarah felt the corner of her lips curl in that screwed-up way she had of holding back tears.

This time it didn't work. Hot tears filled her eyes, running down her cheeks. "I'm such a mess."

The doctor released her hands and reached for a tissue box. "You seem to have your priorities in the right place, to take care of your girls. But I want to make sure you take care of Sarah, too. You have a lot of work ahead of you. I can give you a list of psychologists who take your insurance."

Sarah pressed a wad of tissues to her eyes. "Okay."

"And since you're here, I'm going to be the pain-in-the-ass doctor and insist that you let me examine you."

Sarah laughed, then sniffed.

"I knew you would say that."

"Okay?" The doctor glanced to a cart beside the examining table. "Janice has you set up for a transvaginal ultrasound. How about I do that right now? It doesn't take long. I'm sure you remember the vaginal wand."

Sarah took a deep breath, then nodded in resignation. "Okay."

Dr. Newbury's practiced, capable hands were reassuring, despite the usual discomfort of having someone work down there. Slathered with gel, the wand moved inside while Sarah stared off in the distance and tried to imagine herself anywhere but here. She was a speck inside a small crater on the ceiling tile. She was hovering over the roof of this cheesy flat-roofed building, ascending among the angel hair clouds in the cerulean sky.

A rapid clicking sound brought Sarah back to the here and now. She turned her head to Dr. Newbury, who was facing the monitor. "There it is." With her left hand she reached for the mouse and moved a cursor on the monitor to a small, peanut-shaped object. "That's the fetus. The sound you're hearing is the fetal heartbeat."

The pulse was quick, like the flutter of butterfly wings.

"So fast?" Sarah asked.

"That's normal. I'm just going to take some quick measurements. The CRL. We measure crown to rump. Do you remember any of this from your last pregnancy?"

"Not really." It had been almost five years since Maisey's birth, and Brendan had been with her for every step of the pregnancy and birth, never missing an appointment. He had focused on details, and she had focused on his joy.

"At this stage, the fetus is called a fetal pole." It looked like a knobby pole with a tail. "The head is right here." The doctor marked it with the cursor.

It didn't look like much. Not even as elaborate as the paramecium cells you viewed under a microscope in school.

But the sound . . . the quick little flutter of the tiny butterfly inside her . . . it tapped a tiny message.

I'm alive. I'm alive. I'm alive.

If you choose.

Chapter 45

It was almost noon and Bernie was still in a robe at her laptop. Her second cup of coffee had grown cold, but from her online research she was starting to feel better about her choices.

If she chose to fight capital punishment as a general issue, she wouldn't be alone. Groups like the American Civil Liberties Union were entrenched in a long-standing campaign to abolish the death penalty in each of the fifty states. The arguments and blogs on their website were clear and to the point. She knew they would support Peyton Curtis's right to live.

But the ACLU . . . Dad would be horrified.

Her cell started jingling, and she picked it up. Keesh.

"This is really weird to be the new kid," he said. "They want me to go on a bus tour of Queens with all the new hires."

"Well, don't get too cozy, because we're moving to Canada."

"What's that?"

"Canada has abolished the death penalty. I say we pack our stuff and head north."

"Too cold. Any warmer options?"

"Australia?"

"They have seasons, but we'd never get snow at Christmas."

"Well, most of the European nations are good. Then you have China. Very disturbing. The Chinese execute prisoners by the hundreds."

"Sounds like you're getting into it."

"It's like writing a research paper. That love-hate thing."

"The HR person is back. Gotta go."

"Enjoy your tour. Wave if you pass my place."

Bernie stretched and went to the window of her bedroom, which was cracked open a few inches to take the edge off the dry heat. She had chosen this ground floor apartment with intentions of hanging out in the backyard, tanning and reading and throwing parties for friends. But it had never happened. As landlord, her father had put a charcoal grill on the patio, but she didn't like to cook, and the weather rarely beckoned one to a Queens backyard. Summers were too hot, winters too cold, and in between, the yard was either a mud pit or a bed of leaves.

Face it, you're not the domestic type. Her sister Mary Kate would have gotten out there and planted. She'd have flowers popping up in rows in front of sculptured bushes. But Bernie preferred to spend her weekends sleeping in, going for a run, or hanging out with her friends. Not in the backyard.

When the phone rang again, she assumed it was Keesh. Instead, it was a 212 number she didn't recognize; Manhattan.

"Hello?"

"Bernie Sullivan, what did you do to my client?"

"Excuse me? Who is this?"

"Laurence Saunders. Tell me why my client keeps calling you an angel. Or is Angel a nickname of yours?"

The hospital . . . Curtis must have been more lucid than she had realized. "You could say it's a nickname."

"You are not making my job easy. Peyton Curtis was finally discharged from the hospital, and the first two minutes I get with him at Rikers, he's asking about you, saying he wants you to handle his case."

"Really?" Bernie was up on her feet, pacing.

"It's totally fucked. Since when does a DA defend a triple murder suspect?"

"Oh." Reality hit. "You're right. But I do want to help on the case."

"I don't need this. My first big-profile case, and the client's asking for some Nancy Drew from the DA's office."

"I told you, I want to help, Mr. Saunders. And if it makes Peyton Curtis feel better having me there, that would help, right?"

"This is crazy," Saunders said, though he no longer sounded totally convinced. "Listen, are you willing to resign your position with the DA's office? Cut your affiliations there?"

"Absolutely."

"And you can't just sit in on meetings like we're all getting pedicures together. I need to protect my client's privacy."

"Right. So you could make me an official part of the defense team. Not that I expect to sit at the table or anything."

"I should hope not." He let out a bellowing sigh. "What's minimum wage in New York State these days?"

Her pulse quickened. A door was opening here. "I don't know, but I'll find out."

"Do that. And listen up. I'm going to give you an address, and I want you to meet me there tomorrow."

"Rikers Island?" she asked.

"No. I'm done with Curtis for now. Got some preliminary information from him. Tomorrow we're going to try and get some more background information to fill out the story. Meet me at this address, tomorrow at two."

She copied down the address he gave her, which was an apartment in nearby Flushing. "Who will we be interviewing?"

"Yvonne Curtis, Peyton's mother. I asked her to come to us but she's afraid to leave her apartment right now. She's had some trouble with vandalism and break-ins. She sounds scared, and I don't blame her. Maybe she'll feel better having a woman there."

"Okay, Mr. Saunders. I'll be there."

"That makes me sound so old. Just call me Laurence. And make sure the DA gets your resignation in writing. I don't want any judge looking at me with crossed eyes."

Although the Blair Housing Project was a short walk from Main Street Flushing, Bernie felt as if she were stepping into a foreign land as she crossed the tarred lot that skirted the building complex, barren but for a few bony gray trees and a small playground that cried out for some wood chips and renovation. Aside from two Asian men walking on the distant street, everyone she passed was black, which made Bernie very conscious that she was the minority here, walking in her flannel coat with her leather briefcase-sized satchel slung over her shoulder. She bypassed the broken elevator and opened the door to the staircase, on alert from the voices of women and teenagers that peppered her climb.

Yvonne Curtis's door wasn't difficult to find; it had been painted over with gray splotches of paint to cover the graffiti. Bernie knocked, and the door was cracked open.

"Who is it?" called a female voice.

"Bernadette Sullivan. I work with Laurence Saunders."

There was the scraping of bolts and chains, then the door opened to a short, round-faced woman with smooth brown skin and ample proportions. "Laurence Saunders is already here. Who are you?"

"She's helping me," Saunders called from inside. "Come on in, Bernadette."

Yvonne Curtis opened the door and leaned on it, scrutinizing Bernie as she entered.

"Thanks. You're Yvonne Curtis?" Bernie said, trying to break the ice a little.

"Mmm-hmm." Mrs. Curtis kept her lips pursed, her hands

on the door. Saunders had thought Mrs. Curtis would feel more comfortable with another woman present, but his plan wasn't quite working. *She thinks I'm some Yuppie white woman,* Bernie thought. *And she's not far from the truth.*

The apartment was tidy and clean. A home, Bernie thought as she passed a wall with studio shots of a baby boy on her way to the living room, where Saunders sat on a blue microfiber love seat.

"We already started," Yvonne Curtis told Bernie.

"I got here early." Saunders looked up, his eyes unreadable through the glare of his thick glasses. "Have a seat. I'm recording our conversation, but you can take over with the notes."

He handed her a yellow legal pad and she hit the ground running.

"So where were we?" Saunders asked, pointing to the notes he'd just handed over. "Peyton's medical issues."

"Like I said, he was always small, but he was healthy and all. Then they beat him up when he was nine. Boys on the playground whopped him good, damaged his head. That's why he limps that way. My Peyton's got so many health problems now. Part of his face is paralyzed, and he gets seizures, too."

Bernie thought of Gracie, now nine, being attacked by other kids on the playground and beaten within an inch of her life . . . then quickly tried to snap the heinous image from her mind. Certainly a trauma like that would affect the course of a person's life.

"What you looking at me with those squinty eyes, judging me." Yvonne's fists were on her hips as she glared at Bernie. "You think I didn't do enough as his mother? You think I didn't protect my baby?"

"I was just thinking how hard it is for any parent to protect a child." Bernie held the woman's gaze, determined not to back down. "Especially a son." Married men joked about losing sleep over protecting their daughters, but weren't their sons the real worries? Men had to deal with the aggression of other males, as well as the challenge to prove their manhood over and over again. And then society insisted on defining men by their career choices, while women seemed able to play many roles.

Yvonne had turned away, but Bernie was thinking of Brendan, who hadn't chosen to be a cop originally. He'd done landscaping, but it wasn't considered to be a real profession. No insurance coverage, and you couldn't pay the bills in the winter months . . .

Laurence Saunders's voice brought her back to the conversation.

"How about family history. You say Peyton didn't have any brothers?"

"No, sir. Just his two sisters, Janine and Gwen." Yvonne perched on the far end of the sofa where Bernie was sitting. "Half sisters, if you want the real truth. Their father came along after Peyton's daddy took off when he was a baby, Never heard from him again, but I had Peyton. He was my first, my baby."

"Are those Peyton's baby pictures on the wall?" Bernie asked.

"No, that's Baby Wills, Gwen's son. He stays here with his mother sometimes."

"He's a cute kid," Bernie said, trying to find common ground.

Yvonne Curtis sucked a tooth and looked over at Saunders. "My Gwen has two children. Her daughter, Kiandra, is twelve, and Wills is still a baby."

"I thought Peyton mentioned a brother." Saunders screwed up his mouth, pressing two fingers to one temple. "Darnell . . . does that ring a bell?"

"He's my stepson, but I took him in and tried to raise him like my own but it never did work out. His father, he couldn't stay off the booze, and Darnell got into drugs, too. He's trouble, that one. Darnell Tarpley's his name. I wish I threw him out a long time ago. It's hard to come back from the damage a man like that can do."

"Does Darnell live here now?"

"No, sir, he's in Attica, serving twenty years for murder. He's got eighteen to go, and I hope they keep him longer."

"How did Peyton get along with Darnell?" Bernie asked.

Yvonne seemed annoyed by the question, but she answered. "He was under Darnell's thumb. He couldn't help it. Darnell is just that way. A real street thug."

Bernie wrote quickly, hoping that she would understand her own scribbles later. Some of the information had been in the news reports, but the mention of the stepbrother was new.

"It sounds like Darnell was a bad influence. Do you think he influenced Peyton's behavior?"

"Darnell's the reason my Peyton got sent upstate to prison in the first place. Darnell set Peyton up to do this armed robbery, said if Peyton pulled it off he'd have enough money so he'd never have to work another day in his life. Instead, Peyton got five years up at Lakeview Shock."

"That's right. I have that in my notes," Laurence said. "Peyton wasn't out of prison long before the incident happened. Do you think he had trouble adjusting to life outside?"

"He never had a chance." Yvonne's voice hitched, her tight demeanor melting with emotion. "The cops picked him up soon as he stepped off the bus." She paused, staring down at the floor to compose herself. "He didn't even make it home that first night. The second night, we got rousted by a bunch of commando cops. Warrant squad, looking for somebody. Wrong address." She shook her head.

"Yeah, those warrant squads don't care who they wake up," Laurence said sympathetically.

"Next day, he was gone when I left for work. I come home and find him hurt, his shoulder bleeding." She sniffed and two tears trailed down her face.

"I know this is hard." Laurence took his large glasses off and wiped them with a cloth from his pocket. Bernie suspected that he was just giving Peyton's mother a chance to calm herself.

"I didn't know that he was the Coffee Shop Killer. I didn't know," she wailed. "My baby's not a monster. He's not the devil's spawn, like they're saying."

Laurence shot Bernie an awkward look while Yvonne sobbed into a tissue. She sensed that his sympathy was genuine, but most attorneys did not have the time or patience to counsel family members of the accused.

"He was such a good boy," Yvonne said, sniffing. "He was my baby once. My little Peyton."

The photos of the laughing baby boy on the wall caught Bernie's eye again, and in her mind she saw Yvonne jostling him on her lap.

She saw Yvonne cradling Baby Peyton, a single mother, scared and hopeful. When you waded past the details, Yvonne Curtis was simply a mother who loved her son.

Leaving the legal pad on the sofa, Bernie went to Yvonne Curtis and pressed her palm between the older woman's shoulder blades. Mrs. Curtis's sobs went on, but she didn't flinch or object as Bernie gently rubbed her back.

If only a mother's love could straighten the path of her child. If only.

The next day, as Bernie sat beside Laurence Saunders in a hired Lincoln Town Car headed north toward Sing Sing Correctional Facility, Saunders spared her a compliment.

"You did okay with Mrs. Curtis yesterday. I like that you know how to go with your gut. But don't expect too much from Peyton Curtis." Saunders took a stapled report from his briefcase and handed it across the backseat of the car, which was fairly hovering in a sea of automobiles on the West Side Highway.

"What's this?" Bernie asked, trying to swallow back her nervousness. It was her first visit to a prison, her first meeting with Curtis in an official capacity, and the road that loomed ahead was riddled with hazards. What if Curtis recognized her from that day in the hospital? What if the awake and aware Curtis was a seething, spitting monster?

"You are looking at Peyton Curtis's psychiatric evaluation." Laurence pulled out his laptop, presumably to work while they were stuck in traffic. "Check it out. He's not crazy, as you probably suspected. But he does suffer from amnesia."

"Really." She tried to keep the disbelief from her voice. She had always thought amnesia was rare and overly dramatized in movies.

"Certainly, he's had post-traumatic amnesia. That time when he got hurt in the schoolyard, back when he was nine? His memory of that event is hazy. And he's drawing a big blank on the day of the coffeehouse shootings, which the doc says may be dissociative amnesia. That's the inability to re-member details of a stressful or traumatic event."

So he didn't remember . . . at least she wouldn't have to worry about the hospital incident. She skimmed the doctor's report, noting that post-traumatic amnesia was usually due to a blow to the head. It made sense in that context. As a prose-cutor, she had seen people injured in car accidents who often had no recall of the incident.

As the Town Car picked up speed, she allowed herself a deep, calming breath.

"Another thing." Saunders spoke as his fingers pecked at the keyboard. "Don't expect to get any answers on why he did it."

"I didn't—"

"You can deny it all you want, but I've been down this road. Victims and their families want to know why. It's under-standable, but half the time the reasons are insane. The other times, it's about money or drugs or sex. I'm just saying, it never makes sense. Not really."

Although she nodded in agreement, she held on to the hope that things would be different in the case of Peyton Curtis. She would find some answers—maybe not the definitive reason— but she would assemble a puzzle spotted with missing pieces, something to point to and shake her head over and cast aside after the truth had been digested.

The prison was isolated by a strip of deserted land, an oasis along the Hudson. Bernie shadowed Saunders's moves and tried to follow the barked instructions of prison guards who didn't understand that this was her first time.

Countless steel bars rolled open and shut behind them before they arrived at the small meeting room where Peyton Curtis was waiting. He was a small man, hardly intimidating in his orange jumpsuit. He sat in a short wooden chair, one arm cradled in a navy cloth sling, the other dangling in his lap. His head hung to one side in a dejected manner, but when the door rattled open and he lifted his chin, Bernie realized that it was the partial paralysis that gave him that frowning expression.

Laurence entered the room first, his bigger-than-life presence making the space shrink even smaller.

Curtis nodded, slack-jawed. Then he looked around Laurence, to where Bernie stood with the guard. His jaw dropped, eyes popping. "It's you!"

Bernie felt her face grow warm. "That's right. My name's Bernadette Sullivan, and—"

"You're the angel from my dreams."

And you're supposed to have amnesia, Bernie thought as her mouth went dry. She decided no answer was appropriate here. As she and Laurence sat on tiny furniture that looked as if it had been scavenged from a kindergarten classroom, Saunders made quick introductions.

The little chairs made her glad she had worn a long, loose dress. Laurence took the chair directly across from Peyton

Curtis. He leaned toward him and gestured with two fingers toward his own eyes.

"Eyes on me," Laurence said. "It's not polite to stare. Bernadette is here to help us round out your portrait for the judge, jury, and the general public, too," Laurence explained. "We need to teach people what it was like to walk a day in Peyton Curtis's shoes before any of this happened. Lot of folks out there think you're a monster, Peyton. Have you read the newspapers they got in here?"

Peyton shook his head.

"Do you know how to read?"

"Of course I can read." Peyton looked at Bernie, then seemed to remember and turned away. "I went to school, didn't I? Got a scholarship from a Catholic school in Flushing."

"So why haven't you read the newspapers to see what they're saying about you? What your mama's going through?" Laurence asked. "Aren't you curious?"

Peyton's eyes dropped to the floor. "What's the sense in reading about the world out there? In here you learn that things on the outside don't matter. It's a different world in here."

"Anyone messing with you?"

"Nah. I keep to myself and people leave me alone. Someone comes to help with my arm, for physical therapy. He's helping me with the other arm, too, says I can get some of my strength back."

"Good. Good. You get strong, and we'll work on keeping you alive man," said Saunders.

"That's what angels do." Peyton's lopsided grin sent a chill quivering up Bernie's back, though she wasn't sure why.

The trip to Sing Sing became a daily routine for Bernie and Laurence Saunders, who seemed to think that Peyton's references to "his angel" were intended to be pickup lines. Why does he call me that? Bernie wondered. Had he seen her as an angel in a drug-induced hallucination back in the hospital room? It made her wonder if Peyton Curtis believed in God. He had mentioned attending Catholic school; that tidbit of information would curl Sully's toes.

If she ignored the occasional unsettling angel references, the interview process was interesting, sometimes sad when Curtis relayed the difficulties he had faced as a child and as an adult. Curtis's recollection ended when he was on a bus headed south from Lakeview Shock, the prison where he'd spent five years; at least his amnesia would save Bernie from the details of the chilling shooting.

But the pattern of abuse that Saunders was fishing for always broke down when it came to questions about Darnell Tarpley, the stepbrother who had been involved in the cruel playground assault that had left Peyton permanently injured.

"Why the hell won't you talk about Darnell?" Laurence asked in a fit of temper one time when Peyton shut down.

"I got nothing to say about him, that's all."

"Listen, Peyton." Laurence rubbed his face, his big glasses rising to reflect the cold fluorescent lights. "I'm here to help you, but I am not a mind reader. I'm only as good as the information you give me."

"What's the sense in talking about something I don't even remember?" With some effort, Peyton dragged his stiff right hand across his body and rubbed his other arm. "What's the sense in that?"

"You could tell me the parts you remember," Saunders suggested, but Peyton refused.

After more than a week of interviews, Bernie had pages of notes, but no real clue as to what Peyton Curtis was about . . . or why he had unraveled. This dilemma would have made great dinner table conversation at the house, but she had been keeping away, knowing that Dad did not approve of her mission.

Outside her bedroom window, night had fallen and the backyard seemed dense and dark, more like a jungle than a small parcel of yard in Queens. She called home and breathed a sigh of relief when her mother answered.

"Ma, how's it going?"

"Oh, thank the saints! I've been so worried, Bernadette. The house is a tomb without you."

"I think you've got a few grandchildren who can make some noise."

"But we miss you. Though Conner's been coming around and he's such a big help. He drove me out to Long Island on Saturday. Costco. You know how I hate that drive on the Grand Central."

"He's a good kid. I'm glad he's coming around more."

"But you're not one for the small talk. Something the matter?"

Bernie sighed. "I'm just discouraged. Now that I've resigned from the DA's office, I realize I've only trained on one track. I don't know what I'm doing here. I must have slept through half of law school."

She held back her other issues: the downer of checking into a maximum-security prison every day, the sickening karma of working with the man who had killed her brother. She was trying to sew a quilt from the torn shreds of a life, a difficult task made even more onerous by Curtis's memory blanks.

"I'm sure you're doing a fine job with the legal things, love. But if it's worrying you, I'll say a few prayers to your namesake, St. Bernadette. Remember the movie? She faced persecution over and over again. First from the bishop, then Sister Vauzous?"

Although it wasn't Bernie's favorite movie, it made her smile to hear her mother recount it with such joy. "I remember, Ma."

"You have the strength of a Bernadette," Peg said. "She was always concerned about staying true to the Immaculate Conception, no matter what. And you're the same, so determined to stay true to the right thing. I always knew you were special, that you were destined to do great things."

"Too bad Dad doesn't agree with you."

"No, he doesn't. But that doesn't mean you can't come around and argue with him a little. I'm afraid he's losing the gift of gab."

"Maybe I'll stop by," Bernie said, thinking that was a lie.

"He's a hard man, your father," Peg said. "Hard on himself, too, but he'll come around. Someday, he'll see that you did the right thing."

Chapter 46

"Are you ever going to talk to me again?" Bernadette cocked her head to the side, a move she'd had since she was looking up at Sully from her bouncy chair.

Talk? Chat her up so that she could feel better about being a bleeding heart? No, thank you. Sully reached for his beer and swirled the can, just to let her know he was awake but ignoring her.

"Dad . . . I'm sorry." She leaned forward, elbows on her knees, then straightened. "I'm sorry you're in pain. But you're not alone. We're all hurting."

Amen to that. There was plenty of suffering in this world, and Sully had seen his fair share. Bodies mangled by the fall from a ninth-story window or the grinding weight of a bus tire. The cataclysm at the World Trade Center. People had thought the world was ending; he'd been wondering, too. Yeah, he'd been to the dark side and back again.

But looking back on it now, he had to say that the worst of it involved children; it always seemed wrong to see a young life end. Such a devastating loss to a parent, and now he knew that firsthand. That feeling like someone peeled your insides out, just shucked your guts. It hung on like a parasite, so that when the mind got distracted on occasion by something more positive, that pain dragged you right back down into despair.

Bernadette went on. "I'm sorry you're hurting, but I'm not sorry I stopped you that day at the hospital." Her voice was a low hiss, probably designed to keep her mother from hearing. Neither of them had told Peg, but she had good instincts. She might not know the details, but Peg had some kind of inkling. That was just the way she operated. God bless her, she put up with a lot.

"Okay, so you're mad at me now," Bernie said, slipping into a sulk. "I get it. But you know, someday you'll thank me. Someday you'll . . . you'll get it through your thick skull that I saved your life so that you can be here to see your grand-children have children of their own. I did it to keep you out of prison."

He kept his eyes on the television; he would have loved to keep stonewalling, but he couldn't resist goading her. "What do you know about prison?"

"You want to talk prison? I've spent the last two weeks vis-iting at Sing Sing, and I don't think you want to make it your next home. The river views would be great, but they never let you near a window, and you wouldn't look so good in an or-ange jumpsuit. And Mom would have to learn how to make fruitcake so she could bake a chisel inside. That's what I've learned about prisons, and no, I don't see you liking it there."

"Aren't you facetious." Full of piss and vinegar.

She'd always been a handful, more defiant than the others, and her spirit had earned her a special place in his heart.

Sometimes when she cocked her head and looked up at him through her bangs, just the way she was doing now, he saw the little girl who had followed him around the house. His shadow. The older kids tried to look after her, but damned if defiant little Bernie didn't seek him out and mimic his every move. When she was a toddler he would take her to the gro-cery store with him to get her out of everyone else's hair. She used to ride in that little seat in front and say the names of items she knew. Bread. Noodooles. Meelk. One day he caught himself putting a box of Lipton's into the cart, about to recite his old mantra when she said it for him. "Tea bags for old bags," she chirped, as if that were the name of the product.

And as if that wasn't enough to endear her to him, Peg had caught her heading off to the bathroom one day, claiming, "I gotta go drain my dragon."

Sully had laughed for ten minutes when Peg had told him the story. So many years ago . . . probably twenty-five or so. He had disciplined all his kids, but he'd been careful not to break their spirits. His Bernadette, she had spunk. He'd encouraged her, but now her stubbornness was biting him in the ass.

"Dad, you know I don't mean to be disrespectful," she said. "But I'm not backing down on this one. I'm working to save Peyton Curtis from the death penalty, and nothing you can say will stop me."

"So why should I say anything?" Still, he kept his eyes on the talking heads on TV.

"Because I'm your daughter and you want to let me know that you support me no matter what. That we can agree to disagree and you'll still love me."

"Hmph." What could you do when your kids went off track . . . so far off that you could barely recognize them as your own anymore?

Did Charles Manson's mother still love him?

How about Hitler's parents, with their son becoming bigshot head of the Third Reich? There had to be a breaking point. A line your children crossed that put them on the side of the enemy.

The bad choice.

The wrong choice.

His baby Bernadette had crossed that line when she teamed up with the likes of Peyton Curtis. A monster, that one. A sick, depraved animal.

"Dad . . . come on. You're never at a loss for conversation when your cop buddies are here."

"They don't work for the enemy."

"I'm not defending him. I'm fighting to restore civilization. Punishment with dignity."

"Yeah?" He smacked his beer can down on the end table. "And where's the dignity for your brother? For Kevin and Sean? Peyton Curtis walked into my shop and killed my son in cold blood, along with two other innocent cops. Guys with families, children. He almost took out your friend Indigo, too. That sick monster crushed families. He destroyed my business, which is nothing compared to the damage in here." He pointed a finger to his chest. "Thanks to your client, I got nothing but pain."

"Dad, there's nothing that—"

"Don't argue with me, 'cause I'm telling you, I'm this close to losing it." He pointed toward the door. "You better go."

She rose, sighing. "Dad, I—"

"Just go. Out of my sight. And don't be coming around here anymore. You're not part of this family anymore." He swatted her away. "I can't see you, because you're gone. You're not my daughter anymore."

Chapter 47

"I can't believe your doctor didn't prescribe physical therapy for you before this." Austin Pryzwansky pressed hard into Peyton's wound, rubbing beeswax into the scar.

The prison infirmary didn't smell so good, but the beeswax did. Like flowers or sweet tea. With his cheek pressed to the examining table, Peyton closed his eyes and tried to make the most of it.

"You could have restored use of that right arm years ago if you'd gotten the right therapy. Your uneven gait could have probably been addressed, too." Austin pushed into the muscle, then paused. "Or did you even see a doctor?"

"The prison doctor, upstate. Before that, I didn't have money for any of that."

Austin shifted to the other side of the table and started massaging the ointment into Peyton's right arm. "And no one on the medical staff mentioned how atrophied muscles can be revitalized?"

"You mean how I can get my arms and legs to move again?"

"Something like that."

Peyton snorted into the table. "You don't have experts and therapists and such in prisons. They got some old guy who sits in the infirmary, takes temperatures and calls an ambulance if you're dying."

"Well, you're lucky you got me working on you now."

Peyton knew it was true, and it was because of his lawyer, who freaked when they pushed Peyton out of the hospital. "I'm gonna make sure they take care of you," Larry had told him. "They don't want me complaining that you were denied medical care."

So Austin P. came every other day, and it was helping. The wounded arm wasn't so stiff anymore, and his right arm was getting stronger, his range increasing. He could lift it up now, almost up to his shoulder.

Peyton had been doubtful at first, but it turned out Austin P. knew his shit.

Even though Peyton took a bullet a few weeks ago, he felt good, better than he had in years.

"Okay." Austin P. clapped, then wiped his hands on a towel. "Spa time is over. Let's do some of the exercises I taught you."

As they worked, using fat rubber bands for tension, Austin talked about how the weather was changing, warming up. He'd gone hiking with some friends over the weekend. He said he didn't know how much longer that they'd pay him to come here.

"But you're a great patient. I don't get a lot of patients who make this much progress in two or three weeks," Austin said. "You just keep doing all the exercises I showed you, and you'll be amazed at what your body will do for you. That right arm, too. Keep working those muscles. Use them or lose them."

"Okay, man."

Austin P. was ah-ight, but Peyton didn't have much to complain about at Sing Sing. He got his three square meals a day, and the other inmates left him alone. Both his arms were working again, and now that the guards saw he was no bother, they stopped calling him a cop killer. One of the guards, a big guy with a belly, talked to Peyton sometimes. Bruner got pissed off by guards who abused prisoners. "My chief responsibility is your care and custody," he'd told Peyton. Bruner was ah-ight, too.

The infirmary door rattled open, and the guard waved Peyton out into the next chamber. Sing Sing was all bars and steel doors locking behind you, in front of you, and around you.

As the guards escorted him back to his cell, going from one locked hallway to another, Peyton wondered if the lawyers would be coming today. That was the best part of his day, seeing his angel.

Peyton had thought he had dreamed her up, but the first time he saw her walk in with Laurence he knew she'd been real all along. He remembered her spreading her wings to save him from destruction. Saint Peter was there, and he had a gun aimed at Peyton's head. That was the judgment at the Pearly Gates, and Saint Peter was mad at Peyton. He was growling and shaking and shit. Peyton would have been scared if he hadn't been so drugged out.

Good thing his angel was there.

Peyton's angel had saved him from death.

Or was that the other angel, back at Lakeview? She had given him a mouse or something. Or a walking stick with a mouse on it. That's right. A faux scrimshaw mouse on the handle. Or was it a rat?

What happened to that stick? It had that rat carved in the handle, and it fit his hand just right. That stick was cool.

He couldn't remember where that damn stick went. Some things were fuzzy around the time of the hospital. He remembered the bus ride back from Lakeview Shock, and next thing he was in the hospital with nurses and doctors all around him. Then his angel fighting back Saint Peter.

That lawyer, Laurence the lawyer, he had told Peyton to think about it. "Think long and hard and see what you can come up with," Laurence had said. Laurence was always pressing him to remember Darnell. He wanted to know details, what it was like to have Darnell living in the same apartment. Laurence knew Darnell was there that day on the playground when Peyton got hurt.

Peyton said he didn't remember, but he did. He just knew he'd get killed if he talked about it.

That was a heavy memory. Like a stone, it weighed on his chest, pressing so hard sometimes he couldn't breathe.

Sometimes little strips of memory hit him and he could see parts of it, like a chunk of a torn photograph. Other times there was the pain, the laughter, the taste of dirt and the grit of pavement under his cheek.

That time he woke up in a hospital, too. All kinds of tubes were shoved into him, plastic down his dry throat. Back then the doctors thought he was good to go when he could follow their fingers with his eyes and walk across the room. Mama kept asking them when he was going to get better, but no one answered.

Then, back home in his room, he woke up suffocating every morning. His cries were muffled by a pillow, and he couldn't push it off, but he could pound the person holding it.

"Don't tell." Darnell's face loomed before him, his nose flat and piglike, with beady black eyes. "You tell anyone about the playground, and I'll kill you. Next time I'll make sure it's done. I'll rip your eyes out and feed them to the pigeons, and they'll peck out the insides and swallow the white part whole."

Peyton didn't tell.

Maybe because he woke up smothering every morning, with Darnell's snarling voice by his ear.

"Don't tell. Don't tell, or I'll kill you."

An hour later, Darnell's voice still slid near his ear, a slender dagger whispering under the collar: "Don't tell."

"Did you think about your brother Darnell, like I asked?" Laurence was wearing a suit the color of pea soup, and Peyton kept wondering why anyone would want to wear something so disgusting. "Got anything you want to tell us?"

I'll kill you...

Peyton shook his head, thinking of pea soup with chunks of pink ham hocks floating around in it.

"How about the days after you got back home to New York City? Any memories come back to you about that time? What happened after you stepped off the bus?"

"I remember the bus. It was a long trip back to New York and I was sweating it out, coming back to the city. What was the sense of that, coming back to a place that only did you harm?"

"But your mother is here. She was willing to take you back."

"Nah. That's no way for a man to live." Peyton saw himself sitting on that bus, rocketing through the darkness with just two headlights for guidance. "They kick you out of prison with the clothes on your back and two pairs of socks. But I had one possession. A walking stick. It had a white handle shaped like a rat. Yes, it was a rat and that stick, I used it to get around because of my limp. I needed it." That rat fit so nice in his hand. And ... and there were rats down in the subway. He had watched them galloping along the lane beyond the track. He'd been in the subway when the man stole his cane.

That was what happened to it. Damn.

Some white man came along and ripped the cane from his hand. Took it away and broke it in half.

Peyton rubbed his jaw, staring off at the bars of the door beyond the lawyers as the memory began to take shape.

"Peyton?" Laurence leaned so far forward he nearly fell out of the wooden chair. "What's up? You're a million miles away."

"He took it from me."

"Who took what?" Saunders prodded.

"That skell cop grabbed my walking stick. He stole it from me and ruined it. Broke it in half." He could see the cop, but what was his name? "A cop...I can see him now. Scrawny guy, with iron-gray eyes."

"Did you get his name?"

"He was the one who arrested me." It was an Italian name. Peyton could still hear one of the other cops giving the cop a hard time, called him "Ant-nee." "His name was Marino, I think. Anthony Marino."

Something shifted in the room, as if a wind had blown in. Peyton looked up at the lawyers. What was the sense of him coughing all this shit up? Nobody gave a shit about a gimp black man getting off the bus from an upstate prison.

"You're remembering the cops who pulled you into the precinct. You weren't actually arrested, but they took you into custody because you matched the profile of a serial rapist. Well . . ." Laurence flicked at the air with his hand. "The cops wanted to think you matched the profile. That's something we can expand down the road. Points in our favor."

Sometimes, Laurence just liked to talk in circles. "Are we done with this?" Peyton asked, unnerved by the conversation. Marino had hurt him. He wasn't sure of the details, exactly, but he knew not to go there.

"I'd like to know more about this so-called detainment. This cop, Marino. What was he like?"

No, Peyton didn't want to go there. He turned away from Laurence and let himself steal a look at her. He wasn't sup-posed to stare at his angel; Saunders had warned him that if he did anything that pissed her off, she'd be out of there. But she was shifting in her seat, crossing her legs, and he figured he could get away sliding his eyes that way. One brown boot twitched in the air.

Nice boots. They were suede, the really soft kind that thrills your hand when you touch it. So soft you could rest your face on that boot and just fall asleep.

"I'm over here, man," Laurence prodded, rising from his chair and taking a step toward Peyton. "Tell me about this cop. This Marino."

"I told you, he stole my walking stick, the only thing I had to my name." Peyton could see it rolling awkwardly on the dirty tiles of the subway platform. "He stole it, and broke it in half."

Something clattered in the corridor behind Laurence. Light gushed in through the barred door, a river of light blocked by the lawyer's square bulk.

Peyton's eyes flared, his pulse skipping uncomfortably in his throat at the sight. He gasped as the man stood over him, his bulk silhouetted by the light behind him.

And suddenly it was him standing over him, his eyes gleaming malice as he reared back, the sharp broken stick gripped in his hands.

"No!" Peyton's hands flew up to his face. He meant to duck, but the motion made him slip from the chair. Landing on his knees, he hunkered down, waiting for the crushing impact.

"What the—"

"Oh, my God," the angel spoke in the distance.

But their voices were far from Peyton, who huddled in a tight mass, waiting for the pain. "Don't kill me!"

"Who?" The lawyer's voice was calm. "Who is going to kill you?"

His hands trembled on his head as Peyton searched the face on the hulking man who stood poised, ready to strike. They were on the playground, people gathered around and it was . . .

"Marino! Marino's beating me." His whole body was shaking now, enmeshed in the horrible memory. "Marino's got my walking stick whittled down sharp, and he's stabbing me with it. Got me in the shoulder." He gasped as phantom pain penetrated that tender spot.

He choked on a sob as he heard the voice.

Don't tell, or I'll kill you.

Chapter 48

"Hot damn!" Laurence snapped his fingers as the heavy door of Sing Sing Prison closed behind them. "Took us awhile, but I believe we finally got something worthwhile from Peyton Curtis."

"You're kidding me." It was hard to breathe around the dense weight that had fallen on Bernie's chest when Curtis first mentioned her brother-in-law's name. She had hoped Laurence would dismiss the Marino story as some sort of wild hallucination, but she couldn't be so lucky. "The accusation has holes in it," she said as they walked through the cordoned-off area to their hired car.

"Like what?"

"Like the fact that the wound in Curtis's shoulder was caused by a bullet. Specifically a bullet from Indigo Hilson's gun."

He turned toward the parking lot. "There's that."

"And think of the chronology. Marino and his partner brought Peyton in the first night he arrived back in New York. That was a Sunday night, Monday morning. Yvonne Curtis didn't notice anything amiss until days later—Wednesday afternoon. In fact, she and Peyton were rousted by that warrant squad Tuesday night, and no one was aware that Peyton was injured then. He didn't get hurt until some time Wednesday."

Laurence growled, rubbing his chin. "Yeah. Maybe Marino came back and got him with the stick Wednesday?"

Bernie shook her head. "A stick with a bullet on the tip? Come on, Laurence. You can't argue with hard evidence."

"You're right. And I appreciate your recall of the facts. Bonus points on your timeline, Bernadette. But something happened between our client and Marino. There's no doubt in my mind about that." He pointed to the black car, waiting beside a taxi line by the curb. "Or didn't you find Curtis's story convincing?"

Bernie considered the question as she got into the car. "His story was bone-chilling. Absolutely horrifying. And he was utterly convincing." She pulled the door shut. "But, still . . ."

"Still, what? You're not a believer?"

"The details don't match up. I'm beginning to wonder if the psychiatric evaluation missed something. Maybe there's more going on here than amnesia."

"Like . . . ?"

"Schizophrenia? Borderline personality disorder?"

"And this is based on, what? Your experience in Psych 101?"

"Don't be that way, Laurence. I'm sorry if it disappoints you, but Curtis's story is flawed. And I wouldn't be surprised if it morphs into something else on the stand."

"Oh, I don't know that we'll ever put Peyton Curtis on the stand," he said, moving a finger over the screen of his iPad.

"Then how can you make the story count?"

"I'm getting it out right now."

"Oh, God." She blew out a sigh. "Doesn't that violate attorney-client privilege?"

"The information I'm going to release doesn't incriminate our client in any way. Watch and learn. We'll shake the bushes, see what comes hopping out." He held the phone to his ear and spoke to his assistant. "Asia, see what kind of media contacts you can round up in the next two hours. I need to do a press conference on the Curtis case. No, it doesn't have to be a lot of reporters. Just a few key media people."

As he went over a few other details with Asia, Bernie sank down into the seat and tried to conşider what this would mean for Tony . . . and for Mary Kate. There would probably be an investigation, and if Tony had assaulted Peyton Curtis, he would be punished. If the assault was true, Tony deserved whatever punishment the courts threw at him.

She just didn't like the inconsistencies. And if Curtis's memory was incorrect, if Tony Marino's name was cleared, who was responsible for the stress and fear the complaint would arouse?

"Asia's running with it. I'm going to share some of this alarming news with a few reporters before the end of the day. With any luck, we'll make it to the evening news."

"Laurence." Bernie pressed fingers to her temple, hoping to massage away a blossoming headache. "There's something you should know about Tony Marino."

One eyebrow arched over his thick glasses. "Say what?"

"The cop, Anthony Marino? He's my brother-in-law."

"What the—" He let out a snort. "Bernadette, are you related to every officer in the NYPD?"

"Seems that way."

"This makes things messy." Laurence tapped his phone against his thigh, as if he could shake out an answer.

"To complicate things further, I think I was working intake when Tony brought Peyton Curtis in. I don't remember all the details, but Tony wanted the arrest to stick so much, he came into the DA's office to lobby for it. Curtis had refused to give his name, so he was just listed as a John Doe. The DA who caught the case was willing to arraign Curtis, but then the fingerprint results came back, fast. They identified Curtis, who had refused to give us his name. He had just been released from that upstate prison, so he was cleared and released."

"Mmm. Did Curtis look beat-up to you?"

"I never saw him. Neither did Keesh, the ADA on his case. He wouldn't have laid eyes on him until arraignment."

Laurence leaned back in the seat and let out a sigh. "And I had to go and hire an attorney from the DA's office. I knew you were trouble the minute I laid eyes on you."

"Sorry. But it does help to fill out the facts even more, right?"

"Yes, but it makes it just about impossible for me to keep you on my staff. You know I have to pursue this, and chances are it won't look good for Marino."

"I know."

"Damn. And I was just getting used to having you as my shadow."

"Thanks. I guess."

"This is all too close for comfort. I'll accept your resignation when we get back to the office."

Bernie nodded, sharing his disappointment and wondering how she'd managed to lose two jobs in less than a month.

Chapter 49

"Would you like a toothbrush?" Mary Kate asked, sliding open the deep drawer of her desk.

"Sure." Standing under the door frame of the examining room, Craig Schiavone seemed taller than she remembered.

"How about a blue brush . . . and mint floss?"

"Perfect. Thanks, MK."

He had called her MK. She didn't think he had remembered her nickname.

"You've made this dreaded process relatively painless."

"Thanks, I guess." She laughed, enjoying the moment. "But you're not alone. Somehow, the dentist's office is not on the top of most people's fun list."

He left the corridor and swung 'round to peer through the pass-through. "I could make an appointment for six months, but that's too far to plan ahead."

"True." From this close his deep blue eyes reminded her of the morning glories that climbed her back fence, that vibrant color you wanted to capture though it was impossible to hold. "We can send you a reminder card."

"Okay. In the meantime, I'd love to get together someday if you've got the time. Maybe for coffee or brunch?"

He was asking her out. A real date!

"I'd like that. It would be great to have a chance to really catch up. To see what you've been up to these past few years."

"You'll get to hear about all the headaches of starting up a sports accessory company." He was scrolling through the calendar on his phone. "Great stuff. It's not too late to back out now."

"I'm a good listener," she said with confidence that surprised her. Where had this self-assurance come from? She'd always considered herself to be a competent mom, but when it came to dating, Tony was the one with all the pizzazz.

They agreed on a date and time, and then he lingered, chatting until the next customer came in.

"I'll let you get to work." He held up a hand. "Take care, MK. See you soon."

"Take care," she called after him. It was no problem waiting for old Mr. Finnegan to hobble into the examining room. When he was settled, she was so energized she just about skipped back to her desk.

She had a real date. She didn't know what would come of it, but it felt good to know someone was interested.

The outside door opened and Mary Kate looked up curiously. She wasn't expecting another patient yet.

"Bernie?" Her sister was wired up so tight, Mary Kate left her desk and went into the waiting room. "What are you doing here? Dental emergency?"

Bernie gave her that pained smile; Bernie so rarely let loose with an unconditional, wholehearted grin. "I need to talk to you, MK."

"Is it Dad?" Mary Kate felt a stab of fear. "I know he's been in such a funk these past few weeks."

"He's hurting, I know." Bernie slipped off her coat and tossed it onto a chair. "But I'm here to talk about you."

"Oh. Okay. Have a seat."

Bernie sat, while Mary Kate lingered over the coffee table, straightening magazines and fanning them out decoratively.

"I've been avoiding the house," Bernie admitted. "So I haven't seen you lately. If you don't mind me asking, how are things going between you and Tony?"

MK shoved a wrinkled copy of *People* magazine under the stack. "He moved in with his mother. You remember Gina? She lives in one of those marble Italianate row houses off Horace Harding. That house has been in their family for fifty years. I hear it's kind of run-down now, but it's a free roof over his head. I met with this lady who does mediation. It's like a cheap divorce lawyer, when it's not contested or anything. Tony and I both have to meet with her to divide things up and make financial arrangements for the kids. But it looks like it's going to happen."

"And you're okay with that?"

"Honestly? I'm relieved. I've got a good life, Bernie. Good kids. A nice house. Tony was the one person bringing me down. He wasn't into it anymore. It's better, now that I've accepted it."

"You're doing great. I'm so proud of you. It's got to be tough sometimes."

Mary Kate waved her off. "I got a thick skin. I was worried about the kids at first, but they don't seem fazed when we talk about divorce. In fact, when Erin was home from college she told me it was about time I wised up to her dad. You know, I sort of feel sorry for him now . . . but not enough to let him move back home."

Bernie reached over and squeezed Mary Kate's wrist. "I'm so happy things are working out for you. Really. I guess you know I was never a huge fan of Tony's."

"Yeah, and you weren't alone. He's one of those guys, either you love him or you hate him."

"Oh, yeah." Bernie withdrew her hand and stared down at the display of magazines. "That's the real reason I came tonight. I . . . legally, I'm forbidden to talk about what my client told me. But..." She winced. "I really can't... but I have to."

"Don't get yourself in trouble on account of me," Mary Kate said. "And really, the less I hear about that Peyton Curtis, the better. It's all really painful for me."

"I understand." Bernie bit her lower lip.

Such a bad habit for oral hygiene. Mary Kate wanted to give her a free sample of lip balm and ask her to stop.

"It's going to be in the news tomorrow," Bernie said. "He is."

"Curtis? He's always in the news."

Bernie shook her head and pointed at MK.

"He..." She looked over her shoulder. "Dr. Parsons?"

"No... Tony." Her voice was low.

"In the papers and everything?" Generally, Tony sucked up publicity. "And it's bad?"

"It's not good, and I don't even know when it's going to break. Maybe the word is out already on tonight's evening news. Maybe it won't break until tomorrow."

Mary Kate's spirits sank. She didn't wish Tony any ill. "Will he lose his job? That'd kill him."

"I don't think it's that extreme, but it doesn't cast a positive light."

Mary Kate took a breath and held it. "If he can keep his job, he'll recover." She looked over at her sister and gave her a shove. "You had me really worried. But now you've got me all curious. What happened?"

Bernie groaned, raking her hair back with one hand. "No, no! I can't divulge!"

"Just give me a hint." A sudden pang tore through Mary Kate's chest. "It's not about a woman, is it?"

Bernie waved off the question. "No, nothing like that."

Thank God. She was getting over Tony, but she didn't want the kids to suffer humiliation over their father's antics. "There has to be some part of it that's legal for you to tell me."

"I wonder . . ." Bernie pressed a finger to her lips. "I could tell you what happened when I was with the DA's office. Okay, let me just tell you what I knew before I met with Peyton Curtis as a client. Tony picked up a guy one night. He fit the profile of that serial rapist in the Manhattan subways? Anyway, Keesh was the DA doing intake that night. He told them to release Curtis. There wasn't really much of a case, but Tony persisted. He thought there was a gold shield in it for him if he nabbed the rapist. Before Curtis could even be arraigned, we got word back that he had just been released from a prison upstate. There was no way he could have committed those rapes."

"Okay." Mary Kate ran her hand over the edge of the coffee table. "So Tony arrested this Curtis, but then let him go."

"Right. But Curtis was pissed. Understandably. He steps off the bus from prison, then gets arrested for no good reason."

"I can imagine that wasn't so good." Mary Kate had never seen her husband in action as a cop, but she imagined that he wasn't so nice to the people he considered to be the "criminal element," as he put it. "Pardon my French, but Tony can be a real prick when he's on a power trip."

Bernie nodded. "From what Curtis says, it was not pleasant. Somewhere in the process of transport or arrest, Tony started bragging about Dad's shop. Curtis thought it belonged to Marino's father, but he understood enough to know it mattered to Tony. That morning, when he went into the precinct, he was looking to shoot Tony. It was a simple act of revenge. When finding Tony proved more difficult than he could handle, he turned, saw Sully's Cup, and decided that a shoot-out in Dad's coffee shop would be the next best thing."

"Oh, my God. You're telling me Tony was the instigator? He got this Curtis guy so mad that he started shooting cops?"

"Looks that way right now."

"That's sickening."

"Whether or not it's true, the story is going to break tonight or tomorrow. I just didn't want you to get broadsided."

Mary Kate nodded. "That's the kind of thing that makes me lose sleep at night. You and I find it haunting. Tony? It won't bother him. As long as he can keep his job and spin things his way, it won't bother him at all. He'll sleep like a baby."

Chapter 50

"You know, everyone deals with grief in different ways," Mary Kate said as she slowed to stop at a light. "Some people say I'm heartless because I keep pushing on. But I know myself. I can't let sadness stop me, because if I stop, I'm afraid I'll never get going again."

"I try to escape through work, too," Bernie said. "I think most New Yorkers are workaholics. Maybe that's Dad's issue. He's retired from the job, and without Sully's Cup he's got nowhere to go."

Bernie couldn't remember the last time she rode in a car with her older sister, but they were both heading over to their parents' and Mary Kate had wheels. So here she was in the passenger seat of a modest but clean Chevy Aveo, discussing how they were going to get their dad out of his depression.

"Dad would pop a vein if he knew we were talking about him this way." Mary Kate turned onto their parents' block and cruised slowly, looking for a place to park on the street.

"Oh, I know. He's always got to be the parent."

"Sarah's here," Mary Kate said as they passed her car. "And I think that's Conner's car up by the service road. What's going on? Is someone throwing a surprise party we didn't know about?"

"Just another night at the Sullivans'." As they got out of the car, Bernie wondered what it was about Mary Kate that had changed. She seemed lighter, not so critical. It had been fun driving with her. She reached into the back for the box of cookies. MK had agreed to stop at Marietta's Bakery so that Bernie could bring a peace offering.

"Or a bribe," Mary Kate had said with a sanguine smile.

"Wish me luck," she said as they approached the house, its golden windows a contrast to the purple night. "Dad promised to throw me out if I ever stepped foot inside again."

"Stick with me and you'll be fine. There's safety in numbers." Mary Kate led the way up the driveway. "Though I might have fallen from Dad's good graces, too, if he's heard that my husband is being indicted."

"Let's hope it's not that bad." Bernie's last words were nearly blotted out by the sounds of a party: half a dozen conversations, footsteps, a tinkling piano, and laughing voices.

"Sounds like a party." Mary Kate stepped into the kitchen to find Sarah handing two little girls juice boxes from the fridge.

"Come on in, join the show."

Bernie slid the cookies onto the table and gave Sarah a quick hug. "What's going on?"

"Hey, stranger. Some of Maisey's classmates are here, rehearsing a number for the end-of-year show. Your mom's all over the piano accompaniment."

"Of course she is," Bernie said, exchanging an amused look with Mary Kate. "Ma's still annoyed that none of us sing in the church choir."

The living room was thick with warm air, chipmunk voices, and children. Peg sat at the piano practicing chords, and wonder of wonders, Sully stood tall at the center of the room, directing the dozen or so little girls to take their places in two lines in front of the couch.

Resurrection was in the air.

"Dad, where'd you find all these kids?" Mary Kate teased.

He looked up and winked. "Hello, ladies. You're just in

time to hear them rehearse their song for the Spring Show. But wait, did you hear the good news?"

Mary Kate winced at Bernie.

"Apparently not," Bernie said.

Sully flung his arms wide. "The family's getting bigger. I've got another grandchild on the way!"

Bernie and her sister looked down the line of little girls, wondering ... Their eyes landed on the end of the line, where Conner was hitching Maisey up behind him for a piggyback ride.

Conner's jaw dropped as he caught wind of their conversation. "Don't look at me."

"It's Sarah!" Sully announced.

"That's right." She stepped into the living room, wiping her hands on a dish towel. "I'm pregnant."

"Congratulations!" Mary Kate swept her sister-in-law into her arms and patted her back as the news penetrated Bernie's consciousness.

Another baby, without Brendan. He had wanted a third; he'd never made a secret of that desire. Bernie wasn't sure which weighed on her more heavily, the sadness of Sarah doing this on her own or the loveliness of having another touch of Brendan on earth.

After that, Sully called the group of little girls to order and they formed two crooked lines, clinging to each other and scratching and sipping from juice boxes. Peg showed them their notes on the piano, and Sully acted as conductor as they sang "Do-Re-Mi" from *The Sound of Music*. The song was sweet and flawed, but Sully savored it all like a true maestro leading the choir.

Halfway through the song, Sarah sank into the upholstered chair that had been pushed off to the side, and Bernie joined her, leaning on the rolled flared arm.

The song ended with a flourish, and everyone clapped, including the little girls.

"Don't forget to bow!" Peg got up from the piano to praise them, as MK engaged Sully.

"Hey, Mommy." Bernie rubbed Sarah's shoulder. "You okay?"

Sarah wrinkled her nose. "Morning sickness. That's what gave me up. I've been spending lots of time sitting on the edge of the tub. I think Sully and Peg were ready to send me to bed, thinking I had the flu."

"Bernie, did you hear the other news?" MK called across the room.

Bernie turned toward her older sister.

"Dad is going back to work. He's opening up Sully's Cup tomorrow morning."

"Really?" Bernie couldn't believe how much could change in a day.

"I called the Realtor and took the shop off the market today," Sully said. "When I heard Sarah's good news, it just gave me a boost. Life's too short to sit around in a funk. I won't be able to get Padama and some of the others back right away, but I know how to brew a cup, and I'll have enough staff to get by for now."

"It's a good move, Dad." Mary Kate nodded up at him. In her pretty turquoise sweater, she looked poised, but younger. Younger and more confident. She'd married so young. Bernie wasn't sure, but she suspected that MK had quit college to get married because she was pregnant with Erin. Married at twenty. She'd been married and responsible during the fun years.

Suddenly the noise of the giddy girls and the warm air spiraled too close around her. "I'm going to step outside a minute."

"I'll go with," Sarah said.

Outside, the night air was cool but a soft whisper, no longer the menacing shriek of winter.

Pulling her wool blazer closer, Sarah buttoned it, then tugged on the hem. "Anne Klein. I've got all these gorgeous work clothes, and suddenly I have nowhere to wear them. Pretty soon I won't have the body for them, either."

"You'll get it back. You look great after having two." Bernie still couldn't believe that God or fate or whatever was rotating the planet had left Sarah pregnant with Brendan gone. "So you're really going to have your hands full with three."

"You know what they say: Three's the charm!" Sarah's brows shot up and her eyes went wide.

And then suddenly those eyes shone with tears. "I'm scared, Bernie."

"Oh, honey . . ." Bernie slid one arm around Sarah's shoulders. "You've got a right to be scared. And angry. And thrilled and ecstatic, all at once."

"It's worse than you think. When I first found out, I didn't know how I would cope. I still don't. But I went to the doctor with every intention of ending the pregnancy. I just wanted out." She sniffed. "I hope you don't think I'm a terrible person."

"Never. You're my hero." Bernie put her arms around Sarah, her own eyes misting over.

No, she wouldn't judge Sarah. Bernie had always been a defender of *Roe v. Wade,* but the idea of aborting Brendan's last child, the final genetic trace of him, was a knife in her heart. As she hugged Sarah, she felt her St. Bernadette medal shifting under her clothes, the chain pulling against her neck as if to remind her of the saint's promise.

Healing, not hurting.

"I'm a mess." Sarah sniffed.

"You're allowed to be a mess right now," Bernie said. "At least for a few minutes, until you have to face your daughters and ten other shrieking girls again."

They leaned against the porch railing, folding their arms against the cooling night. There were no stars to be seen in the overcast sky, and Bernie's eyes were drawn instead to the small brick- and vinyl-sided two-story houses that ran up and down the street. As a kid she had always created scenarios of what went on behind the lit windows and neat façades of these homes. She had imagined kids studying under the light of a desk lamp, moms who baked cookies, and dads who had the house under control, the evil held back from the front doorstep. All these years, she had thought she was imagining magical families who inhabited the homes up and down the block, but in truth, that scenario described her own family.

At least it had been the Sullivans until recently.

Sarah leaned back, sucking in a deep breath between her teeth. "I hope you're good with a screwdriver. I've got a crib to reassemble."

"I'll help you. I'll take the girls for overnights, cook and clean for you. I'll be a night nanny for the baby. It doesn't look like I'll be having any of my own, so I might as well get the mother thing out of my system."

"The mothering instinct is a strong one," Sarah said. "I learned that when I heard this baby's heartbeat in the doctor's office. Don't count yourself out yet."

Bernie tried to imagine herself living with Keesh in the house across the street, the one with the little fake balcony over the front porch. There'd been a FOR SALE sign on the lawn forever, and renters were living there. Would she make spaghetti for dinner? Would Keesh figure out how to mow the lawn? The scenario was hard to picture.

Her future was like the sky: opaque and gray as an old strand of pearls.

Chapter 51

What the . . . ?

Peyton rolled to the edge of his cot. He needed to get a drink, get up and get a drink, man. But his body just hooked onto the bar at the edge, his arm flopping down to the floor. Useless.

He did all the exercises. He went through all those sessions with Austin P. And just when his arms and legs were finally starting to move and get strong, they broke all over again.

Curtis's body had imploded. His muscles ached and his head . . . his head was swollen so big it was filling up his cell. The sounds from the other inmates in the cell block scratched and poked at his head, like ice picks dragged across his skull.

And the earth below him kept rocking and tilting, shifting back and forth beneath his cot. Like it was going to vomit him and the bed up through the concrete roof of the prison.

In the frenzy of twists and turns, he was hot and cold and hot and cold. He shivered through tongues of fire. What the fuck? *What the fuck!* Mama had taught him not to curse, but she couldn't hear him now. No one could hear him even though he was yelling, shrieking through time and space.

The face of a guard loomed before him, as if Curtis had fallen into a fishbowl and the world around him was warped. Bruner's nose was huge. His whole face was enormous.

"Curtis. What's wrong?"

Peyton could only stare with unblinking eyes.

"Come on, man. We got to get you to the infirmary." The guard's voice shot past him and ricocheted around the four walls of the cell. Curtis watched it bounce like a little black ball. A peppercorn. A hockey puck.

Why is Bruner playing hockey in my cell?

Hockey was not his sport, and Peyton would have to be careful or he'd be hit by a hockey stick.

He wished he had a stick. His walking stick, with the smooth white handle. Faux scrimshaw, carved into a rat. That rat used to fit into his hand so nicely. A perfect fit.

But he couldn't move his hand.

My hand!

It was tied down, with a needle taped into it.

No needles! I don't do drugs!

He tried to rip the needle out, but his other hand was strapped in, too.

Buckle your seat belt. This bed is ready for takeoff.

His fingers curled around the metal rails as the bed lifted, spun, and then rocketed through space so fast that the stars that surrounded him like Christmas lights became lines of light against the blackness of the universe.

The cool, quiet universe. Here you could float around forever and never meet another person, good or evil. He liked the nothingness. The dark, empty sea of space was peaceful.

This was where people went to die, and Peyton was okay with that. In the end, he made it to a place where he'd be left alone.

When he opened his eyes, his cell had grown larger and brighter, and the smells were sharper and cleaner.

A hospital.

Maybe he didn't die.

But he was still on the edge, one foot in deep space and the other in this bizarre world of pain. Blistering hot skin and icy cold chills. His head was still swollen and he thought that his brain must be infected, a huge, swelling canker sore that would explode and spray pus through the rest of his body.

He faded in and out, hot and cold. Night and day. Time didn't matter, but the restless ache in his head told him to get up. Get up and out.

Where? Back to deep space?

"Get your ass out of bed and out of this hospital!" He opened his eyes to see Darnell hovering over his bed like a cartoon genie. Darnell floating in a thought bubble.

Peyton would have laughed if he wasn't so pissed off to have Darnell like a bug up his ass. "I can't move. Can't you see I'm dying?"

"You always got something wrong with you." Darnell's flared tooth showed when he smiled; his grin was always mocking.

"Go! Get out of here!" Peyton rasped.

But Darnell settled down behind his head, a thorny ache in the back of his neck, and much as Peyton tossed his head on the pillow he couldn't shake Darnell out.

He went off again, this time to a restless gray place of dust, ashes of dead bodies that the hospital burned in their incinerator. Every time he tried to breathe, the dust swirled up into his nostrils.

Ash Wednesday. No . . . soon it would be Palm Sunday. And they burned all the palms to use the ashes for next year. He had fallen into the ashes from the burning palms. He coughed, and gray ash blew into his mouth.

"Oh, Lord! Just take me!" he cried. Anything would be better than this. Besides, he wanted to get to the gates of judgment because his angel would be waiting there for him. Saint Bernadette was her name.

"Did you hear that?" a woman asked from far away.

"Yeah, he's been talking."

"Making any sense?"

"Not really."

The voices echoed, as if coming through a tunnel.

"It sounds like hallucinations, probably from the fever. His temp's still high."

"I'm turning the television on. It helps pass the time . . . time . . . time . . ."

He tried to get back to deep space, but now there was a new noise: the tinny voices. These voices chipped away at his head. Relentless. Big. Fake.

"News at eleven . . ."

"Our top story . . ."

"Coffee Shop Killer . . ."

"That's him," one of the distant voices said. "Let's see what they say."

Peyton forced his eyes open and tried to focus through the glare of light. Two figures, nurses or aides, stood beside his bed, but they were both looking up at the television screen.

"Laurence Saunders, the attorney for Peyton Curtis, says his client may have been tortured and assaulted by police officers just days before the shooting in Sully's Cup that killed three officers and injured a fourth. And in a bizarre twist, Saunders alleged that the cop leading the assault was Officer Anthony Marino, son-in-law of James 'Sully' Sullivan, the coffee shop owner."

Marino.

Hatred flared in his chest at the shot of the man, the photo taken from his police ID. That twitchy smile . . . those icy blue eyes.

"It gets complicated, Chase. We actually have photos arranged in a family tree to show you. Retired NYPD cop Sully is the family patriarch. Marino is married to Sully's daughter Mary Kate. Sully's son Brendan was killed in the shooting. And Sully's daughter Bernadette resigned from the district attorney's office to assist with the suspected killer's defense."

Bernadette.

He gasped under the mask at the sight of her. They had her tangled up with all the others on the screen.

Bernadette . . . his angel.

And . . . and St. Peter! The man who wanted to shoot him. He was there, too. Owner of the coffee shop, they said.

He closed his eyes as one of the aides washed his leg down with a cool sponge. It cooled the burning inside, the fires of hell. Maybe St. Peter had already turned him away, sent him straight to hell.

Or St. Sully.

He owned the shop. Bernadette's father.

It couldn't be. That was part of his nightmare.

But reality was leaking through now, penetrating in uncomfortable ways.

Peyton moaned as they rolled him to his side, fiery shards of glass sticking in all his joints.

His angel . . .

She had deceived him. Her wide wings weren't spread to protect him.

A thumping sound grew louder, and he saw her mighty wings stirring the gray ash. Thumping, beating, ropy muscles pumping. Her wings were hideous weapons.

Her wings were beating against him, knocking him from the sky, and suddenly, he was falling.

Chapter 52

This was cool.

Keesh had stayed the night, and Bernie actually had milk for coffee and fresh bagels in the house. She schlepped around the kitchen in her robe, preparing a little tray of coffee and toasted bagels for them. While the coffee was still brewing, she opened her laptop and went online to check the weather. If the sunshine streaming in through the living room window was going to hold, maybe they could do something outside.

It was a Sunday, so neither of them had to get out of bed and rush off to work. Her online calendar reminded her that it was Palm Sunday. Well, she should go to Mass, but she could work that out later.

As she clicked her way to the weather, a headline about Peyton Curtis caught her eye. She clicked on the story, wondering if it was more of the same dreck that had been circulating since the story broke about Tony's alleged torture of Peyton.

When the Marino story broke, half their family had been dragged in somehow. She had been shocked to see her own face pop up online as the questionable lawyer who had left the district attorney's office to join Curtis's defense team. Someone had cropped her image from a photograph taken at Brendan's funeral, and so she had appeared in newspapers, on TV, and online in her dark clothing with sunglasses shielding her eyes. Those idiots had used the same photo to extract images of Mary Kate and Sully, so the three of them, in their dark clothes and glasses, made their family resemble some sort of Irish mob family.

She braced for more muckraking but found only an image of Peyton, the photo that showed the lines of his broad forehead and the slight droop of the right side of his mouth. And those sad eyes, always the sad eyes that spoke of persecution.

The news brief said that Peyton Curtis had been moved from Sing Sing Prison to a Westchester County hospital due to a debilitating high fever. A prison official revealed that Curtis was suffering from a Group A strep infection so severe that it could not be treated in the prison infirmary. Doctors had diagnosed Curtis with streptococcal toxic shock, which could cause fever, rash, severe pain, dizziness, confusion, and even death. Currently Curtis was under guard, listed in critical condition.

Wow. The news piece was vague about Curtis's chances of recovery.

She mulled it over as she poured two mugs of coffee and brought the tray into the bedroom. "Rise and shine! I got coffee and some strange news."

Keesh made a growling sound that was kind of sexy, then sat up. He propped up some pillows and scooted back so that he was leaning against the headboard. "Coffee first."

"We can multitask." She placed the tray on the nightstand beside him and handed him a mug. "I just read online that Curtis got moved to the hospital," she said, then shared the details of the article.

"A strep infection. Like a strep throat?" Keesh held a hot mug in both hands as he considered. The sight of him barechested in her bed, with the comforter pulled up to his navel, made Bernie feel sort of like she'd won the lottery. "It can kill you, if it goes untreated."

She sat beside him on the bed, pushing against his knees. "I looked it up on Web MD, and it sounds serious. What if it kills Curtis?"

"Well, it could." He took a sip of coffee. "Honestly, I have mixed feelings about that. Maybe that would be for the best." When she started to object he raised a hand. "I know you've been working hard to save his life, but you've been trying to save him from the executioner. The inhumanity of man against man. I get that. And I think it's going to make a huge impression on Brendan's kids when they learn what you did."

"I hope so. For a while there I couldn't step foot in my parents' house. It was like I was the criminal."

"You took a stand against your father, and I know it wasn't easy." He reached forward, moved her hair aside, and toyed with the gold chain around her neck. It tickled a little as the St. Bernadette medal lifted from between her breasts.

"But now . . ." He leaned forward to kiss the side of her neck. "It might be better if this infection, or whatever it is, just takes Curtis away. It would end pain and misery for so many people." He turned down the collar of her robe and trailed his lips lower to the sensitive nook on her shoulder.

Bernie sighed. "Are you trying to get me off topic? Because it's working."

"Good. But at this point it's out of our hands, right? If Curtis's case goes to trial, we'll be spectators at three manslaughter trials, and you know it's a costly, clunky process. The wheels of justice are slow and squeaky. In need of oil and bearings."

"I've seen that firsthand."

"And with your brother being one of the victims, it's going to be exceedingly painful."

She bunched the hem of her robe in her hands. "I know that."

"I'm just saying, I wouldn't be upset if the hand of God intervened and took this criminal case off the dockets."

He put his mug down and slid his arms around her waist. "So. Why don't you let me offer some serious distraction?"

Coming from Keesh, it seems like an exceedingly romantic question.

She covered his hands with hers, then fell back across the mattress. "Distraction, please."

Chapter 53

"Wake up, bro. Wake up and get your ass out of that bed."

"Shut up, Darnell." His eyes still closed, Peyton twisted and tried to turn over, but the binding on his right wrist yanked tight. Darnell was always waking him up, telling him he was a lazy-ass mo-fo. Darnell didn't care that he was sick in the hospital with a fever that fried his brain and made every muscle in his body ache.

Peyton hated it when Darnell came to visit, scolding him like an old woman. "You ain't my mama," Peyton said.

"Get up and get going. You got a plan? 'Cause now you see it's more than Marino that's trying to fry your ass. Your angel is in thick with him. Related to him. They family. And you, thinking she was gon' save your ass."

Damned if Darnell wasn't right about that.

She had lied to him, pretending to be his angel when all the time she was in deep with Marino. She was probably in with old St. Peter, too, though she had stopped him from shooting Peyton. Why'd she do that? Peyton couldn't figure it.

"What are you, Einstein or something? Don't think about these things too much," Darnell told him. "You know what you gotta do."

Darnell was right on that. Peyton knew what to do, and

now that he was waking up he realized he was better. Not cured, but definitely better. His shoulder and chest were still sore, but he wasn't burning hot anymore.

Shifting in the bed, Peyton let his eyes open a slit. Nobody in the room. He tried to sit up a little and realized that only one of his cuffs was fastened, so he had the use of one hand. Some aid or nurse must have screwed up.

With his free hand he unfastened the right side and tried to figure a way out of here. He couldn't just walk out, 'cause there was a prison guard right outside the door.

He wondered if the doctors knew that his fever had broken. Probably. They'd be shipping him back to prison soon. He had to make a move before that.

But how?

Something quick and quiet. Quick and quiet. He looked around the room for possibilities till his eyes lit on a metal stand holding a plastic bag of fluid going into his arm.

A heavy metal stand.

Checking the door, he got up on his knees in bed and gave it a try. A gut-buster. But if he unhooked the bag of liquid, the top part of the post separated from the rest.

Nice.

He slid it under the sheet, keeping the top within reach. The metal was cold against his bare leg, but it was good to know it was there.

He was ready.

"You awake?" The man in navy scrubs came in wheeling a cart. "I'm Bert, your night nurse."

The image was hazy because Peyton's eyes were barely cracked open.

"Open your mouth, please. I need your temperature."

Peyton let his jaw drop so Bert could shove the stick in. Otherwise he kept still while the man held onto his wrist and the cuff squeezed his arm for blood pressure and whatnot.

But as soon as Bert went back to the cart to record all that stuff, Peyton came alive.

His fingers closed over the metal bar in his bed and his muscles tensed.

One quick hit on the head; that was what Darnell told him to do.

Bert looked down at the cart, humming something as he let out a breath.

Now.

Peyton sprang up like a ninja, the bar in his hands. In one move he lunged, dropped to his knees at the edge of the bed, and swung that bar like A-Rod going for a home run.

The metal hit the night nurse's head with a thud. Bert crumpled forward, down to the floor.

Thanks for going down quiet, Bert.

Peyton shoved the bar onto the bed. He tore back the tape on his arm and lifted out the needle. Thank the Lord he was done with the torture here.

He climbed off the bed and started working the dark blue scrubs off the man. The pants weren't so hard to peel off, but it wasn't easy to get a shirt over a man's head when he couldn't lift his arms. The scrubs were a little baggy for Peyton, but the white Air Jordans were a good fit. "What, you shooting hoops during break?" Peyton asked Bert.

Curtis wished for a hat or hood or something to hide his face. His hands trembled as he reached for the cart and headed out the door. He kept a dead expression as he pushed it past the cop outside his room.

Would the guard notice that a white man had walked in and a black brother was walking out?

With measured steps, Curtis moved down the hall, trying to keep his strides even to cover up the limp. When he looked in the reflective glass on the other side of the hall, he saw the prison guard with his head down, reading a magazine. The guard didn't even notice.

Curtis punched the button to open the double doors at the end of the hall. They opened, easy as one, two, three. Biting the side of his cheek to keep from grinning, he pushed his cart into the next corridor and followed the buzzing white fluorescent lights to freedom.

Chapter 54

Everywhere Bernie turned, the alarm was sounding: suspected cop killer on the loose.

Indigo, Elijah, and their girls had moved in with Indigo's mother, Tiana. The accommodations were tight, sleeping bags and a shower schedule for the one bathroom. "But we're not taking any chances," Indigo had told Bernie. "I started wearing my nine millimeter when I leave the house. The physical therapists don't want to see it, but it makes me feel better to have some line of defense."

The media had reported that cops were on a citywide alert. At roll call sergeants warned their personnel to be on the lookout. Cops in the five bureaus and all departments in the tristate area memorized the pedigree information for Peyton Curtis.

At the coffee shop, Sully was ready.

"That's not a myth you know, about criminals returning to the scene of the crime," Sully told Bernie and Keesh, who had met her there Tuesday morning on his way home from a night shift.

"Arsonists return a lot," Sully went on. "I think to check out their handiwork. Serial killers are known for it, too. They derive some sick pleasure out of reliving the crime."

Perched on a stool, Bernie let her eyes skim the line of customers at the kidney-shaped counter. Personally, she felt more uncomfortable about what had transpired here than the prospect of Peyton Curtis returning. "Wouldn't it be kind of stupid for him to return here?" she asked.

"You're giving him a lot of credit," Keesh said. "Criminals aren't as intelligent as people tend to think."

"Well, if he does come back, this time, *this time* I'll be here, loaded for bear," Sully said, patting the bulk under his shirt at his waistband.

"What about you?" Keesh said to Bernie. "I'm worried about him coming after you. You're one of the few women he had any dealings with while he was locked up."

Bernie shook her head. "I don't think so. Laurence called me with the same concern, but I don't see why Curtis would target me. From everything he told us, it was Marino he hated. That's where the police should be looking. Midtown South, where Tony works, or wherever he's living these days."

"But what would you do?" Keesh pressed her. "What if you opened your door to find Curtis there?"

"Keesh . . . he doesn't have my address. My phone isn't even listed in the directory."

"You need to be careful, darlin'." Sully put his hand on her shoulder. "You can't be too careful with a psycho like this."

Bernie didn't see Curtis as a psycho or a sociopath. In all the interviews, he had not seemed devious. Borderline, maybe, but what did any of them really know about his mental state? When Sully was called over to the counter, Bernie cast a disapproving scowl on Keesh. "See what you did? You've got my father riled now. He's going to lock me up in my old bedroom and take away the key. I'll be like Rapunzel, unfurling my hair out the window so you can climb in and visit."

"Sounds kind of hot," Keesh said with a grin. "But this is serious biz, Bernie. Why don't you pack a bag and come stay with me awhile?" He put a hand on her knee. "Come home with me now."

"Keesh . . ." She cocked her head to the side, flicking her eyes over to make sure her dad wasn't listening in. "Honey, I'd like nothing more than to share your bed for the next few weeks. But may I point out that you're not even going to be home nights this week? You've got the night shift in the Complaint Room all week, right?"

He groaned. "Right."

"You'll be sleeping all day and I'll just disturb you if I'm there. I want to use this time to clean my apartment, clear out my closets. I'm going to run every day, look for a job. I might even paint. And I've got Chuck and Candy right upstairs if I need anything. I'll be fine."

"You could stay with your parents," he suggested.

"One word: *Rapunzel*."

"Stay with Sarah?"

"I don't want to freak her out. You're overreacting. And if you don't cool it, you're going to have my father in a tizzy."

Keesh looked over at Sully, who was showing the new guy how to ring up a gift card. "Men like Sully don't do tizzies. They put their daughter's boyfriend under a white light and sweat confessions out of him." He squinted. "How'd I do? Do you think he likes me?"

She slid off the stool. "Sure. You guys will be fishing together in no time."

"Sully fishes?"

Bernie laughed, shaking her head.

As they left, she glanced back at the cops talking over coffee. An older couple sat reading the paper, a mom fed her toddler son Cheerios, and two men were engaged in a game of checkers. Bernie smiled, warmed by the sight. There was healing going on here. It was good that her father had reopened Sully's Cup.

Chapter 55

It was late Thursday morning when Sully tucked the bag of twenties into an empty canister in the storeroom and returned to the front of the shop. He had decided not to make bank deposits during shop hours anymore. That was his commitment to himself and his staff when he reopened the shop. He was going to be here during business hours, every day.

It was the least he could do, if the shop had his name on it. If something went down again, he would damn well be in the thick of it.

He returned to his usual spot behind the till and the servers, the nook with bags of coffee beans decoratively lined up on shelves. With his bum back, leaning beat sitting, and from here, he could see it all.

Two undercovers sat at the deuce by the restaurant. There were three uniforms, one online and the other two standing by the bar. They faced inside the shop, keeping watch on the other customers as they talked casually. About a dozen regular customers were in the shop, some settled in, others were just here to grab and go.

They had come back. The cops, the workers, even the retired people in the neighborhood who had made a stop at Sully's Cup part of their routine, had returned for their daily cup. That made Sully's heart swell. It felt good to know that you mattered, that you were doing something that mattered to people.

They were good people, his fellow New Yorkers. People always bitched and moaned about how harsh and uncaring they were, but those were people who didn't understand the heartbeat of New York. Yeah, this city had a pulse, a quick one at that. But anyone who could step lively, take care of business, and have a sense of humor would be just fine here.

Over at the machines, a new kid was foaming milk for lattes. Mike Willis was Sully's first male employee, and so far, it had been almost a week now, he seemed to be keeping up with the gals. Mike was a student at Queens College, but Sully liked the fact that he was six-two and African-American. Let the media get ahold of that. Calling his family racist. Deplorable.

But besides that, Sully figured that Mike's appearance might be a good robbery deterrent.

He shifted and scratched the back of his head. Of course, the racist comment had been directed at Tony, and Sully couldn't vouch for his son-in-law. Not a hundred percent. Truth be told, he was glad Mary Kate was making a move away from Tony Marino. A certain amount of ambition was a good thing in a young cop. But Tony was older now, and his unfulfilled ambitions had soured into a sick lust for the gold shield. Add to that the fact that Tony didn't always give everybody a fair shake. It might not have been corruption, per se, but it wasn't a quality Sully liked to see in a cop.

How far had Tony gone with Curtis? Sully didn't know. And though nobody was a fan of Internal Affairs, Sully believed that a cop who was doing the wrong thing needed to be weeded out. No question about that.

On a few occasions Sully had taken him aside to discuss the issue of integrity, but Tony didn't want to hear it. No, sir, Tony thought he had it all figured out.

Until now, of course. Through MK, Sully had heard that Tony was not happy to be the subject of an internal investigation. And now that Curtis had slipped away from the hospital, Tony actually had the gall to ask for police protection—a grown man with a licensed weapon and the brotherhood of NYPD backing him up. What a pansy.

Only a few pastries remained in the glass case, and Sully was eyeing one of the almond croissants. He had a weakness for those things. If no one snatched the last ones up by noon, he'd indulge in one as a part of his lunch.

A flicker of movement beyond the shop window caught his attention, and Sully glanced up from the pastry case to see someone standing at the glass, staring in.

African-American, male, wearing a hood despite the sunny day.

Don't go jumping to conclusions, he told himself. *We'll have no racial profiling here.*

Sully didn't move as he studied the face, comparing it to the face engraved in his mind from news photos, etched in his memory like the Shroud of Turin. Broad forehead. Mouth drooped on right side. Same nose.

Point for point, it was a perfect match.

It was Curtis, returned to the scene of the crime.

Sully's ears buzzed with adrenaline as his hand went to his belt for his piece. The gun was out of its holster and pointed in a second, but he couldn't shoot—too many innocent bystanders. The plate glass alone could take out the people sitting by the window, not to mention stray bullets flying out to Union Street.

Some woman in the coffee shop screamed, but Sully didn't have time to calm nerves.

Curtis had jerked back from the window, obviously seeing the gun.

Sully gauged the distance around the kidney-shaped counter. Too far. Ignoring his bad back, he sucked in his abs and vaulted over the counter. By the time he was out the door, Curtis was scurrying away, scuttling down the sidewalk like a wounded rat.

The bastard! He'd had the balls to return to the scene . . .

back for more? Well, this time, Sully was here to give him a taste of his own medicine. Take him down, once and for all.

Down the street Sully barreled, giving chase. For a man with a limp Curtis could move quickly, though he still had an odd gait.

He's running faster because of the goddamned therapy he got in prison, Sully thought as his heart thundered in his chest. Yeah, he'd read all about the special treatment that lawyer had gotten Curtis in prison. Everything but a fucking manicure.

Curtis ran down Union and turned right on Roosevelt, heading into the center of the congestion.

Their progress was hindered by people on the sidewalk, vendors with hand trucks, women pushing strollers, but Sully had the advantage. Once people spotted the gun in his hand, they got out of the way.

Sully was almost on him when Curtis knocked over a woman with a kid and disappeared down the subway stairs. Bastard. Sully leaped around the fallen boy, who seemed upset but okay, and dropped onto the staircase.

The sudden shadows were blinding, but Sully's legs hammered on the steps, relentless.

He wasn't letting this fish get away.

"Police!" Sully shouted to the transit worker in the booth as he jumped the turnstile. "NYPD! Call for backup!"

By the time Sully barreled down the last short flight, Curtis was a good twenty yards ahead of him, tearing off toward the end of the platform.

The fifty-yard dash. His lungs burning, Sully launched himself after the younger man. Adrenaline tingled through his blood, keeping his legs pumping, his mouth dry.

Ahead of him, Curtis was approaching the tiled wall at the end of the platform, a dead end, but he wasn't slowing. What the hell?

As Sully closed in on him, he realized Curtis's plan. He was reaching around the wall there, feeling for the ladder to bring him down onto the tracks.

A suicide mission.

"Stop! Police!" Sully raised his gun, his feet pounding to a halt. "Hold it there or I'll shoot!"

The man turned back from the wall and stared, like a deer caught in the headlights. His hood had fallen away, and Curtis's features were unmistakable now.

This was the guy.

Panting, Sully took aim and fired.

The gun's report echoed through the underground passage as Curtis went down . . . down onto the tracks.

Sully raced ahead, but before he got close he saw Curtis up and running along the tracks toward the tunnel.

Damn! He'd missed.

But Curtis was flirting with disaster, running near the third rail. One misstep and he risked making contact with the high-voltage current, a jolt that would kill him instantly.

Sully lifted his gun to fire again, but the rush of air and the rising sun of light in the tunnel told him a train was coming.

He couldn't chance shooting into an approaching train. He also couldn't risk chasing Curtis down the tracks himself. Sully wanted this guy, but he wanted to live, too.

With any luck, the approaching train would crush the monster.

The blast of the train's horn indicated that the driver had seen something on the tracks.

Sully lowered his gun as light showered the tunnel. Thirty seconds later the train barreled into the station, whistle blowing.

The noise of the rattling subway cars nearly drowned out the warning from the platform.

"Police, don't move!" the shout came from behind Sully.

He froze, leaving his gun dangling at his side.

"I'm a police officer, retired NYPD," Sully shouted. "James Sullivan. ID is in my right, rear pocket."

The uniforms behind him were in charge now. Sully would

follow their instructions to the word. They might even call in some backup and search the subway tunnel.

But they wouldn't find anything.

Damn! You couldn't step it up, old man? Run a little faster? Use the long legs that the good Lord gave you?

But what was done was done.

Curtis had returned to the scene of the crime, and Sully had let him slip away.

Chapter 56

*M*aybe I'll forget about law and order and just paint houses. Bernie found great satisfaction in running a roller over her bedroom wall and leaving a trail of warm Toasted Mocha where once there was only boring white. When she was finished, her bedroom would be a cozy sanctuary.

Yesterday she had covered the bathroom walls with Orange Crush, a bright color that made her want to throw a wild Cinco de Mayo party with fruit floating in a bowl of punch.

It was a beautiful April day, sunshine with just a touch of a spring breeze; perfect weather to throw the windows open and paint. Bernie had just finished using the roller on two walls when the phone rang. The caller ID said Sarah. She dropped the roller in the pan and used her clean hand to pick up her cell phone.

"Sarah, hi. I'm painting my apartment."

"Oh, Bernie, I'm sorry to bother you but I need your help."

"Sure. You okay?"

"They say everything's fine. I'm at the hospital. I had some severe cramping and my OB-GYN thought it was premature contractions." Sarah's voice sounded calm, at least. "The doctors say I should be fine, but they want me to rest here for the next few hours. Can you pick up Gracie from school?"

"I'm on it." Bernie was already tapping the lid on the paint can shut. "What about Maisey? You want me to pick her up, too?"

"Peg already got her. But she can't leave to get Grace because she's got Maisey there, and she's dealing with Sully's back pain and a houseful of cops."

"What?" Bernie held the phone to her ear with her shoulder while she rinsed her hands at the sink. "What happened?"

As Bernie hurried through the apartment, grabbing keys and her wallet, Sarah explained that Peyton Curtis had appeared at Sully's Cup around noon that day. "Thank God, there was no shooting. He didn't seem to have a gun. Apparently Sully chased him to the subway, but Curtis jumped onto the tracks and got away."

"Oh, my God! Dad thought Curtis might come back. He was right!" Bernie pulled a denim jacket over her sloppy painting clothes, stepped onto the front porch, and locked the door behind her.

"Fortunately, your father is fine. Just some back fatigue, Peg says."

"And why are the cops at the house?"

"For moral support, I guess. Everyone loves to hear a good cop story."

"I know how that goes," Bernie said as she strode down the street at double-time. "Listen, I'm on my way to the bus stop now. I'll call you and check in once I've got Grace. She'll probably want to talk to you."

As soon as Bernie met Grace on the steps of St. Pete's, the nine-year-old's face drained of color.

"What's wrong? Where's my mom?"

Bernie explained what had happened, but Grace's concern only amplified.

"She's in the hospital?" Her face went pink and her eyes filled with tears.

"Oh, honey, she's fine." Bernie hugged her niece and guided her to the side of the staircase where pale pink cherry blossoms lined the skinny branches. "Hold on and I'll get her on the phone so you can talk to her yourself."

Gracie's tears ran freely, sliding down her cheeks and splashing onto her shirt as her mother tried to console her on the phone. A few minutes later, Grace handed Bernie the phone, quivering. "She wants to talk to you."

"Bernie? I was afraid of this. She's still traumatized after Brendan, and now the doctors are saying they want to keep me overnight."

"Why don't we come visit you there?" Bernie suggested.

Grace nodded eagerly.

"That would be so perfect. But you'll have to take a bus or cab."

"The bus is an easy shot," Bernie said.

"If you can get here, you can take my car home," Sarah offered.

"Wheels! That definitely makes it worth it. See you soon."

Bernie and Grace spent two hours at the hospital. They went downstairs to get Sarah some fruit, ice cream, and magazines to hold her over for the night. While Grace hung out with her mom, Bernie went down to the courtyard to check in with Peg.

"It's a bit loud here. We've got a houseful of cops," Peg said. "I got Maisey helping me sprinkle cheese on my lasagna. Good job, lovey. But I think the chicken is ready to come out."

"But Dad's okay, right?"

"A little back pain, but nothing that Advil won't cure. But what a story he has to tell! He really scared that guy away today. I don't think he'll ever come back."

"Let's hope the police catch him before he gets a chance," Bernie said. To hear her mother recount the story, you'd think she was talking about a schoolyard bully who got a warning.

She told Peg that Sarah would be hospitalized overnight, and Peg was happy to keep Maisey. "You and Gracie can come, too. We've got room," Peg said.

"Grace and I are going to have a girls' night at my place.

You've already got your hands full there." Besides, Bernie sensed that Grace wouldn't be so comfortable in a houseful of raucous cops right now.

By the time they found Sarah's car in the parking lot, Grace had grown comfortable with the situation and was looking forward to a school night spent at Aunt Bernie's.

"So should we get pizza for dinner, or Chinese food?" Bernie asked as she pulled out of the hospital parking lot. "I've got numbers programmed in there for Lucky Chinese and Gino's Pizza. Do you know how to use the directory?"

"I know how to use it. I wish Mom would let me have my own phone." Grace was fingering Bernie's cell phone.

Bernie smiled. The kid was nine. "Maybe next year. So what do you think? Pizza?"

Grace pursed her lips, considering. "How about pasta with capers? And pickles on the side."

"Mmm. That sounds oddly delicious. Can we put some red sauce on the pasta, too?"

"You can put it on yours."

"Okay, then. But you'll have to guide me through this. I am not the cook your mother is."

"Trust me," Grace said, nine going on nineteen. "I got it all under control."

They stopped at the grocery store, then headed back to Bernie's apartment.

"What do you think of my Orange Crush bathroom?" Bernie asked, showing off her paint job.

Grace folded her arms, looking the walls up and down. "I like it," she said decisively.

While Grace tended the pasta, Bernie shifted some of the furniture in the bedroom. She moved the ladder to the windows and rehung the shades and sheers on the finished walls. "The paint is dry, but it still smells kind of cheesy in here," she called to Grace. "Maybe we'll sleep in the living room tonight."

"That would be fun," Grace called back. "I'll use the sleeping bag."

Bernie descended the ladder, admiring the rich mocha color. She left the windows open for now, and went in to watch the pasta and caper chef at work.

After dinner Bernie did the dishes while Grace worked on her homework. By eight o'clock, they had changed into pajamas. Grace used one of Bernie's oversized T-shirts as a nightgown, and she brushed with the pink toothbrush they'd purchased at the grocery store.

Snuggled together on the couch, they watched reruns of *Seventh Heaven,* one of Grace's favorite shows. In the episode, Ruthie and her brother Simon were mad at each other, and their dad, the reverend, pointed out that anger made a person weaker.

"I wish my family had seven kids like the Camdens," Grace said.

"Well, you have another brother or sister on the way."

"That's still just three. And I don't have an older brother like Matt." Grace yawned. "You have lots of brothers and sisters. You're lucky."

"I am."

"Is Grandpa still mad at you?" Grace asked as she nestled into the pillow.

"He wasn't really mad. Or maybe he was, in his own way." Bernie thought of her father at age sixty-nine, running down into the subway, chasing a killer. "My dad is a protector. I guess all dads know they have to protect their kids. When your father was killed, my dad felt like he'd failed him, and that's got to be a terrible feeling to let your son down in a huge way."

"How come Grandpa said you weren't his daughter anymore?"

Bernie sighed. "Your grandpa is trying hard to take care of everyone, but he and I don't agree on the best way to do that anymore." She shook her head. "Does that make any sense at all? Because I'm getting confused."

Grace brushed blond wisps from her eyes, reminding Bernie of herself. "You're still his daughter. You're just not the daughter you used to be."

"That's it." Bernie nodded. "Wow, you're better at this than I am."

"Because I watch too much TV."

Bernie laughed. "Have you learned everything you know about human nature from television?" she asked.

When Grace didn't answer, she looked down and saw that she had fallen asleep, her angel face peeking out from the fleece blanket. She looked so peaceful.

When the doorbell rang a few minutes later, Bernie's first thought was that she didn't want to disturb Grace. Her second thought: Who the hell was at her door when it was pushing nine o'clock at night?

Moving gently, she extracted herself from Grace and the blanket and hurried to the door. Through the peephole she saw Tony Marino, tired and small in the yellow light of the porch.

She pulled open the door so that he wouldn't press the bell again.

Through the glass storm door his eyes were bloodshot, his hair thinner and grayer than she remembered. But then he couldn't have changed that much in just a week. She unlocked the outer door and opened it a few inches.

"Hey, Bernie. Can I come in?"

Bernie glanced back at the sofa, where Grace was nestled under a blanket. "Gracie is asleep on the couch and I don't want to disturb her." Bernie stepped onto the porch, letting the storm door close behind her. "Grace is staying the night while Sarah's in the hospital."

"Oh, Jesus. Is she okay?"

"The doctors are keeping her, just to be safe, but the baby

seems fine." She paused. "Wow, did you know that Sarah is pregnant?"

"I think Conner mentioned it." He scratched his head behind his ear. "Bernie, I need to talk to you about the department charges against me. I'm a wreck. I haven't been able to sleep a wink since this whole thing broke. If all the allegations against me stick, I could lose my job. You gotta help me here."

Bernie blinked, not sure why any of this was her problem. "Tony, I'm sorry you're in a predicament, but really? I've got my hands full here, and I don't know why you think I could help you."

"You're the only one who knows both sides, Bernie. You've been working with Curtis, and you know me, too. You got to know these charges are trumped-up."

"I wasn't there, Tony. I'm not a witness."

"I got a witness. My partner, Minovich, was there the whole time, but do you think they're listening to him? The thing is, you could talk to Saunders and get him to back off. Tell him I didn't hurt his client, not like they're saying. You know me better than that; I might kid around, but I would never put my hands on a perp, not like he's saying."

Bernie pulled her robe closer around her, wishing Tony hadn't come here. It was cold out here, and she didn't have any answers for him. "Look, I can't talk about this now. Call me tomorrow and . . . I can't promise anything. We'll talk, okay? You have my cell number?"

He nodded, his chin burrowed into the collar of his jacket. "You gotta help me, Bernie."

"Tomorrow, okay?" She opened the storm door and stepped inside.

"I'll call you," he said. "What time?"

"After nine. Good night, Tony." She closed the door and locked it, then stood peering through the peephole. As she suspected, he just stood there like a zombie.

Go home, Tony. He was creeping her out.

At last, he shoved his hands into his pockets and turned

away. Ooh, annoyance. Bernie didn't know what she would tell Tony tomorrow, but it was time to call Keesh and wake him up. She grabbed her cell phone and went into the kitchen.

"Hello." His voice was thick with layers of sleep.

"Hello, you gorgeous hunk of man. This is your evening wake-up call."

"Mmm. That's nice. Only it would be better if you were beside me."

"Do you know who this is?"

"Very funny. Really, why don't you come over?"

"I'm busy here." She told him about Sarah's call to take care of Gracie. "If you want, I'll meet you for coffee in the morning after I drop her off at school."

"Yeah, okay. But I still don't like you being there. Why didn't you stay at Sarah's place?"

"Because this is my home. I painted again. Halfway done with the bedroom and it looks great."

"I just don't think you're taking the right precautions."

"Curtis is not coming here," she said, dreading the news. "I know you just woke up, but here's the news update: He made an appearance at Sully's Cup today. Dad chased him down to the subway, but he got away."

"Anyone hurt?"

"No, thank God."

Keesh had a dozen questions, and as Bernie tried to answer them, she could tell he was out of bed now, moving around. Probably getting online for the latest updates.

"See that?" he said. "The guy returned to the scene of the crime. Don't think he won't try it again, either. What if he comes after you, Bernie? What then? Did you ask the police to put a watch on your place?"

"That's a stretch to think he'd come after me. That he could even find me . . ."

"Have your old man call the precinct. They'll do it for him." When she didn't respond, he grunted. "Okay, then I'll call."

"Keesh . . . I am not having the police come by here. That's just the stuff of a drama queen." His concern was sweet, but the last thing she wanted right now was to alarm her father, and once she set off the slightest alarm, he'd be over here, moving Gracie and her to the family house for protection. "You need to get ready for work. Call me in the morning, before you leave the office, okay?"

"I'll call you before I leave for work. I'm not going to let this go."

"Fine. I'll call my father."

"Good. Bye."

As she hung up and went in to check on Gracie, she wished Keesh weren't so stubborn. She could call Dad later . . . or even tomorrow.

Gracie had burrowed into the couch; only the silk of her golden hair was visible. Bernie tossed her phone on the coffee table and went into the bedroom to get a sleeping bag.

The sheers were blowing over the open window. No wonder it was so cold in here. Bernie went over to close the window, but realized something was wrong. The screen was gone. She shielded her eyes from the light in the room and peered out into the darkness. Had it fallen to the ground? She didn't see it on the pavement below the window, but perhaps it had fallen into the bushes.

Well, there was a good reason to call Dad in the morning.

She closed the window and locked it. A chill ran down her spine as she recalled her dream, the nightmare in which the face of her father turned to a bad man staring into her bedroom. Creepy. Thank goodness Gracie was here to keep her company tonight.

The second window still had its screen, so she left it half-open to air out the wet-paint odor.

When she slid open the closet door and looked to the top shelf for the sleeping bag, she sensed something amiss. Hadn't she just straightened out this closet this morning? Now it looked like a tornado had hit.

A blanket had been unfurled in a heap, and the shoes were tumbled. A pair of men's sneakers down below caught her eye, and she followed the line of black-jeaned leg up to see a man's body barely hidden by a blanket.

A man in her closet.

A gasp escaped her throat as the body came alive. The blanket rose, and she was staring into Peyton Curtis's shiny eyes.

"Aaah . . . aaah!" She meant to scream but only a desperate stream of air panted from her throat.

Her hand jerked the door, trying to close it, but he stuck out his foot and jammed it open.

Her heart beat like a wild bat in her chest, telling her to fly, move, get the hell out of there! *Go, get Gracie and escape!*

She let go of the door and turned to run, but he exploded out of the closet and tackled her. She flew back, aware of the smell of sweat and blood, the uneven keel of falling, and then the feel of the hard floor on her bottom and elbows as she landed.

The world spun around her, crazy and off its axis, but she had to set it right. She had to get past him to Gracie. Bracing on her elbows, she steadied herself, opened her eyes, and found herself staring down the shiny barrel of a gun.

The cold metal set her whole body quivering. "Let me go . . . please," she begged. She meant to sound firm and confident, but her voice was a wispy crackle.

"I don't think so." The gun butted closer and she panted. She wanted to look him in the eyes, better to negotiate, but she couldn't tear her gaze from the steel chamber looming before her.

"The police are watching this place," she said. "But if you leave now you have a chance to—"

"Bullshit. The police aren't coming by here, 'cause you're not a *drama queen.*"

Oh, God, oh God! He'd heard her . . . He'd heard and he was pointing the gun at her head and he was going to kill her here in her own bedroom with Gracie sleeping outside!

Tremors rippled through her body again as she anticipated the bullet between her eyes.

Then, suddenly, the gun withdrew from her focus as he stepped back to close the bedroom door.

Get away! the survival voice shouted.

She crab-crawled backward, slipping on the drop cloth until she bumped into the foot of her platform bed.

"Don't move," he growled, right back on her, looming over her with the dizzying pistol. "Stop moving and just chill."

That was impossible, because every cell in her body was quivering in shock. "You have to go . . ." she said in a shaky voice. "You have to go or . . . I'll scream. And the people up-stairs will hear. And they'll call the police."

"What's the sense of that?"

She cowered as he leaned closer and glared into her eyes.

"What's the sense of screaming? I'll just shoot you and the little girl sleeping out there. Shoot you both and be out of here before the police are even in the neighborhood."

The edge in his eyes chilled her even more than the sight of the gun. She let her head drop, desperately trying to think of her next tact as her cell phone began to ring out in the living room, the sound twanging through the short hall.

"My phone." She swallowed. "I need to answer it. People will worry if I don't answer."

She tamped down hope as her eyes lifted to him.

He wiped sweat from his forehead and shook his head. "No. You're staying right here."

Chapter 57

Keesh dropped the steaming microwave dinner onto the kitchen counter and paced away from the food. "Pick up, pick up," he said, focused on the cell phone at his ear. Bernie got mad all the time, but she usually didn't cut him off and refuse to answer his calls. Thank God she didn't play that game . . . until now.

"Answer the fucking phone," he said, but it went to her voice mail. Again.

He looked back at the hot tray of mystery meat tucked into rice that he needed to choke down before he headed off to work. A very unappetizing night, one he would have preferred to spend with Bernie. Even Bernie and the niece would have been okay.

He called her again. No answer.

This was not sitting right with him. Maybe there was a logical explanation, like Bernie took Grace to her parents' house and she'd lost track of her cell.

Still . . . it was a worry.

He opened the contact list on his cell and scrolled down to the S's. He was going out on a limb, but what the hell. He called her parents' number and paced from the counter to the fridge and back.

When Peg Sullivan answered, the din in the background was a huge distraction. Laughter and conversation.

"Hey, Mrs. Sullivan. It's Bernie's friend Keesh. Sounds like you're having a party."

"Not a party, really. Just some of Sully's friends. But Bernie's not here."

"Actually, I'm looking for your husband. I'm sorry to interrupt, but it's important. Could I speak to him?"

"No problem at all. Hold on, Keesh."

After some delay, and the noise of low voices and muffled murmurs, the authoritative voice answered.

"This is Sully."

"Mr. Sullivan, it's Keesh, Bernie's friend."

"Yeah, Keesh, Peg said it was you." Sully didn't sound too glad to hear from him, but at least the noise had died down. He'd probably stepped outside.

Keesh took a breath, wishing he didn't have to work though the racist crap Bernie had told him about. According to Sully, Keesh was the enemy, one of those "Middle Eastern terrorist types," despite the fact that Keesh was born in Ohio.

"I don't mean to be out of line, sir, but I'm worried about your daughter. With that psycho on the loose, I don't think Bernie should be spending the night alone . . . alone in her apartment except for her niece, but she's nine. It doesn't seem safe. Do you think you can talk some sense into her?"

"I've never been able to talk sense into my daughter," Sully groused. "I'll reach out to her. I'll give her a call right now."

"I hope you have better luck getting through to her than I did," Keesh said. "She's not answering my calls. In fact, I was hoping she was there with you, away from her cell phone."

"Nope, we haven't seen her tonight."

"She promised me she'd call you." Keesh rubbed his jaw. Hell, he should just call in sick to work and go over to Bernie's himself. It wouldn't be a lie; working the night shift always made him feel as if he'd just spent a week on a space station. "You know, I could go over there myself."

"I'll take care of it," Sully said in a proprietary voice that said: my daughter, my family business. Clearly, he didn't want a terrorist type like Rashid Kerobyan meddling.

"Okay, then. Thanks, Mr. Sullivan." Keesh hung up, feeling like a first-class pain in the ass. Yeah, Sully was really going to love him now.

Chapter 58

"Is that blood?" she asked as she scrambled up onto the bed.

He yanked open a drawer of the dresser, looking for something to tie her down with. There were scarves in the top drawer. Good enough. "Just get back, against the headboard," he instructed, waving the gun at her.

"But you're bleeding. Are you hurt? I've got some bandages—"

"Nah." He held the gun steady but lifted the other arm, inspecting his sleeve. "It's not my blood."

She shook her head in confusion, and Peyton wanted to laugh. How could she not know?

"Must be Marino's," he said.

Terror flared in her eyes, and her lips clamped shut like she was going to lose it.

"Now why you so surprised? I saw you talking to him out front on your porch," he said. "He's the one that brought me here. Person like Officer Marino was a lot easier to find than some girl who flunked outta the DA's office and pretended to work on my case for a while." He tied her arms loosely to the bedpost. Just tight enough that she couldn't jump onto him and grab the gun.

"I don't believe you," she said. "Tony would never bring you here."

He snorted. "He didn't know it. I was hiding in the back of his car. Sunk down low behind skis and a cooler and shit." Peyton was good at hiding. It probably helped that he'd been invisible for years. People didn't want to have to look at a cripple; they started looking away or looking right through him. Pretty soon, they didn't see him at all. He was just invisible.

"So you hurt Tony?" She was coiled up against the bed frame, her knees to her chest.

"Marino? I killed him."

"You couldn't. He had a gun. Tony always carried a gun."

He turned the pistol in his hand, a nice-looking Luger. "Yeah, he had a gun. It's mine now. But he doesn't need it anymore."

She whimpered, pressing a fist to her mouth. It was almost funny. She was the mousy one now, and for the first time in his life, Peyton was strong. He could use both of his arms, with real power. He'd been able to choke Marino from behind when the cop had gotten into the driver's seat of his car. Choked him with some wire from his own fishing kit in the back of the car. Marino had fought, but Peyton had been stronger. And he knew he had more power than Bernadette now. He could feel it.

He had the power.

"You killed him," she said in a shaky voice. "And now you're going to kill me, too. Why, Peyton? I'm on your side. I tried to help you."

"You're a liar. My defense attorney? You joined up with Saunders and pretended like you were on my side, when your brother was the one who tortured me. You're full of shit."

"Tony wasn't my brother. He was married to my sister. And I'm sorry if he hurt you, Peyton, but that's no reason, *no reason* for you to go on a rampage and kill three people. My brother was one of those cops. And there's no excuse for what you did." She stopped suddenly, as if she'd run out of breath.

"Marino is the reason I did what I did." Fury ballooned in his chest, as dense weight that threatened to ignite. "Marino needed to die. And when I couldn't find him and I turned around and saw that coffee shop, I remembered something he said. That his father owned it. So those three cops I killed, they were random. But hitting Sully's Cup was no accident. A coffee shop owned by a cop, right across from the precinct. Marino was bragging about it. I knew it would get back to him, one way or another. I shot those cops to pay Marino back."

"And you sound like you're proud of it." She wasn't quivering anymore. No, she was staring him down, all tough and mad like she was his mama. "Killing is always wrong. That's why I was trying to keep you alive. I was trying to save your life, Peyton."

She's trying to trick you, Darnell's voice popped in the air. *Don't let her deny the truth. She's a cop's daughter, a spoiled white Catholic girl from a cop family, so deep into the cop shit that when she bleeds, her blood probably runs blue.*

"What you're doing is wrong." Her voice was stern, like a teacher. "I am not the enemy."

"Don't judge me. I'm gon' leave my judgment to St. Peter at the Pearly Gates." The real St. Peter.

"I'm not judging you. I'm just telling you to stop this insanity now."

Hear that? Darnell poked at him. *Now she calling you crazy!*

"That's enough." Rage tasted bitter on his tongue as he put one knee on the bed and got in her face, pressing the pistol to that bone below her throat. "Shut up. Shut up!"

Chapter 59

She froze with the gun to her throat, afraid to even breathe. So the authoritative approach wasn't going to work. Damn. It had been her last hope.

In a fit, he pulled back and wiped the sweat from his brow. He mumbled something indecipherable, then aimed the gun at her again, squinted as if honing in.

She trembled from the outside in, steeling herself.

But he laughed and let the gun drop to his side.

She breathed in relief, realizing she'd gotten a reprieve, even if only for a moment. The profuse sweating and gibberish suggested he was feverish. Not making sense. There would be no reasoning with him now.

She wondered about Gracie.

If he kills me now, will he just go and leave her alone?

Beyond him, a breeze billowed the sheers into puffs, making Bernie recall the dream of the bad guy at her window. After all these years, her nightmare had come true.

Oh, God, dear God. He'd killed Tony. And she'd sent him away. . . .

Acid rose in the back of her throat, and she thought she might lose her dinner. She hugged her knees, trying to ignore the tremors that rocked her body.

He'd killed Tony.

Or maybe he was lying. Maybe Tony was just injured, faking dead behind the wheel of his car. Maybe it was all a lie . . .

Watching Curtis, she dared to sneak one hand to her throat for the gold chain. Lost in some cursing diatribe, he didn't seem to notice.

Clasping the medal, she prayed to St. Bernadette to ask God for a miracle. *Short of that, please spare Gracie.*

"Ah-ight, ah-ight. Enough! I said enough!" With one knee on the bed, he bore down on her and shoved the gun to her head.

The cold circle of the barrel marked the spot between her eyes. *That's the spiritual chakra,* she thought, her thoughts far removed from her quivering body. Maybe a bullet there would send her straight to heaven. Spiritual peace.

"I need to have this over, you hear me?" he growled.

She could feel heat radiating from his damp skin.

"You got a minute to say your prayers, get right with the Lord," he said. "Then you got nothing else to worry about. You'll be outta here."

Her blood thrumming with adrenaline, Bernie twisted slightly, straining against the bindings. She had to get out. How could she get away? He'd tied her loosely, but there was no way she could rip free in an instant.

She stared at the window, desperate for escape. And then, just like in the dream, the sheer curtains blew to the side and her father was standing in the window.

She squinted. Was she hallucinating?

No . . . It was real. She was staring at her father's broad, rough face. He watched, assessing, his eyes marbles of fury.

She bit back relief, not wanting to tip off Curtis.

Besides, if her father took a shot, would she get hit, too? She was not sure whether or not the gun pressed to her forehead was cocked, but she knew she needed to do something.

She needed to do whatever she could to save her own life.

"Please . . ." She tried to make her voice humble, sincere.

"Can you take the gun away, just while I'm saying my prayers? It's . . . it's distracting."

He snorted. "Yeah. I'm not goin' to get in the way of prayer." He lowered the gun.

And Bernie squeezed her eyes shut, bracing. Her pulse raged in her ears, a painful thumping. *Oh, Bernadette, pray for us . . .*

A loud pop filled the air.

And Curtis fell forward, his body crumpling onto the bed like an accordion folding across her lap.

And then . . . then the night was so silent she could hear the traffic moving out on Union Turnpike.

Chapter 60

Ignoring the ache in his back, Sully hooked his arms over the windowsill and hoisted himself up. The window wasn't that high, but it wasn't easy pulling his six-foot frame inside while holding his gun in his hand. Still, he managed, landing on a bunched-up drop cloth. He rose quickly and went to the bed, where the monster's body covered his daughter.

"Darlin', are you okay?"

"I think so." It was the high-pitched, quivering voice of a child . . . his child.

He grabbed Curtis by the shoulder and rolled his body to the side, giving Bernie a chance to slide out from under him.

"But my arms." She yanked against a black and white polka-dotted scarf. "He's got me tied down."

Quickly, Sully used his pocket knife to cut her free. She pushed away from the bed and let out a whimper, like a wounded dog.

"Bernie." He put an arm over her shoulders and she pressed her face to his chest. Better to keep her from eyeing the ghoulish sight.

The gun had fallen from Curtis's hand and skittered across the floor. It was out of reach of the perp, but then Sully knew he got off a good shot and Curtis was still. The bullet hole in the back of his head was small, but it was enough.

"You sure you're okay?" he asked his daughter tenderly. "He didn't hurt you, did he?"

"He was going to shoot me," her voice quavered. "And he said he killed Tony. Do you think it's true, Daddy?"

"Oh, dear God . . ." Sully let out a breath. "We'll find out."

"Grandpa?" Grace called from the bedroom doorway. "Grandpa? Is it okay to come in?"

"Stay right there. We're coming out." He led Bernadette away from the dead man and ushered both girls into the living room. Better to let the crime scene be and keep Grace from having to see the body.

"You did good, Gracie," he said. "Calling me, keeping quiet. You did real good. I'm proud of you, darlin'. I'm proud of both of you." Of course, by the time Gracie had called he'd been on his way, but she had filled him in on the situation, helped him with the logistics. If he had come barreling in the front door, Curtis would have shot and fled.

As he put his gun in his holster, he saw that Grace was patting Bernie's back, trying to console her quivering aunt. Wise for her years, Gracie. Just like her father.

Choking back the ball of emotion and strain in his throat, he put his arms around the two girls. As the whining sirens grew louder and lights flashed over the windows, he hugged them close and thanked the good Lord he could be here to protect them both.

One shot . . . one shot could have changed everything.

Thank God he'd gotten that shot off first.

Epilogue

Easter Sunday, one year later

Sunrise over the Atlantic.

Bernie linked her arm through Keesh's as pink and orange light washed into the purple sky over the ocean.

"Easter sunrise." She shivered against the ocean breeze as the sky around them opened up with light. Beyond the waves that crashed below them and swept back to the sea, a diamond of light winked on the horizon.

One flash of light expanded into a rising sliver on the water, so bright that Bernie had to look away toward the colorful clouds.

"Beautiful." Keesh reached over and rubbed her upper arm; then, as if needing to be closer, he moved behind her and linked his arms around her, making adjustments for her round belly.

She settled against him, her backbone, her strength. "Thanks for getting up at the crack of dawn."

"It's our last day at the beach, and I've never seen the sun rise over the Atlantic." His palm caressed her abdomen. "Besides, we need to get used to losing sleep. In two months we'll have a screaming baby in the house, keeping us up all night with crying and feedings and dirty diapers. What have you gotten me into, woman?"

"I can't wait."

So much had changed since last Easter, when family emotions were so raw that Bernie had not been able to go to the house at all. Mary Kate had been mired in the funeral arrangements for Tony, and Bernie had been steeped in fear and guilt, so traumatized that she wasn't able to return to her apartment. She had stayed away from the family back then, holing up at Keesh's place. And though Keesh was glad to have her close, he had insisted that she get help. "You can't hide from your family forever," he had said. Wise old Keesh. She had thought she was hiding from the world, but he'd been right. She'd had some family issues to work through.

Now a year later, the Sullivans were able to assemble as a family once again, but there had been some major changes.

James had retired from the NYPD and taken a teaching job at a private high school in Queens.

On Christmas Day, Sarah had given birth to Michael Brendan Sullivan, a beautiful healthy boy who had his mother's eyes and his father's mischievous smile.

Bernie and Keesh had gotten a marriage license and done the deed at the Queens Courthouse with Mary Kate as their witness. They wanted to be together no matter what their parents thought, though they need not have worried. After the incident, Keesh's parents, Ara and Salat Kerobyan, had come to recognize Bernie's courage and love for their son. Sully, too, had realized that Keesh was far from a terrorist, even if his first name was Rashid. In fact, Sully was learning a few Armenian words to use with the grandchild who was on the way.

Sully still reigned over the dining room table for protracted conversation after Sunday dinners, but Bernie could no longer participate. The world of cops and criminals no longer made her heart race with excitement.

It had been Grace's idea to have a family reunion of sorts so they could spread Brendan's ashes on the beach. Mary Kate and Sarah had found "Paradise," a palatial beach house that they could rent for Easter week here in North Carolina's Outer Banks. Even Sully left his beloved New York for the twelve-hour drive to the skinny chain of coastal towns. Of course, it was off-season, which translated to cold, but the weather had held enough for them to have a memorial service on the beach for Brendan yesterday.

With Beach Boys' music playing, Sarah had waded in up to her knees and scattered his ashes in the surf. "So that he can surf forever," Grace had said.

Mary Kate had swung her wide in the sand as they'd danced to "I Get Around." Everyone had danced—even Sully, with his bad back. Maisey and Grace had continuously written their dad's name with a stick in the hard-packed sand. Conner had banged out accompaniment on overturned plastic beach pails. Keesh and James had tended hot dogs on a makeshift beach grill. Peg had dispensed hot apple cider from a large Thermos. Brendan would have enjoyed his send-off.

They had gone around the big circle of family, sharing stories about Brendan. No one had cried, but there'd been heartfelt smiles and plenty of laughter.

What a difference a year could make.

Now Bernie had to pull tight to zip Keesh's big jacket over her belly. Nothing of her own fit her these days. When they got back to New York she would brace herself and visit one of those overpriced boutiques for pregnant women.

She had lost her taste for the law, and she would never again be able to sit through a cop story at her parents' dining room table. But she had found Keesh and together they were finding their way to a new life.

Not to mention the tiny new life that would find its way to them in two months. The pregnancy had come along at the right time, just when Bernie had been ready to let go of the guilt and the second-guessing, the doubts and the empty shadows of death. Time to look forward instead of behind her.

With Keesh behind her and a new life inside her, she looked ahead to the swelling light and allowed herself a glimmer of hope. Maybe she could still change the world. Her life had been redefined, but her heart still beat to do the right thing and help people who needed it. People like Peyton Curtis.

This was probably the reason she had never discussed Peyton's death with Sully. Her heart had been broken and yes, she had been hurt by evil in the world. But her broken heart still beat for justice, and as long as it kept pumping in her chest, she would keep trying. She couldn't stop trying.

Please turn the page
for a special conversation with
Rosalind Noonan.

Q: The novel is very New York, but it's not the glitzy Manhattan we tend to see in films. How did you come to know Queens?

A: I lived in Queens for twenty-four years, which is the longest I've ever stayed in one place, so the land of loud-talking and quick-thinking is a big part of my background now. When I moved to Flushing back in the 1980s, I was excited to be in New York City, close to the fast pace of Manhattan. Over the years I learned that the outer boroughs of New York can be as small-town and provincial as any town in America. Many people dig their roots in and patronize the same barber or bakery year after year, generation after generation. My husband grew up in Queens, and our first home together was seven blocks from the house he grew up in. His brother bought a house on the block behind their parents' home, and built a connecting gate in their backyards. That small neighborhood feeling in a big city surprised me.

Another characteristic of many longtime Queens residents that surprised me was the fierce loyalty to their borough and their city. Some of my friends had no aspirations to move to a larger apartment or look for a better job outside the city because they couldn't imagine life beyond their neighborhood. My husband recalls growing up in Bayside, when he and his friends rode bicycles around town within boundaries set by their parents. "We knew not to go beyond Springfield Boulevard on one side, Northern Boulevard on the other." He compares it to those maps used by fifteenth-century explorers, in which sea monsters and devastating cliffs marked the borders of the Atlantic Ocean. If a kid went beyond the borders of Bayside, he was likely to drop off the edge of the world.

The more people I meet from neighborhoods of New York City, the more local loyalties I encounter. One of my friends almost ended his marriage when his wife insisted he move from Queens to Brooklyn. Another friend keeps insisting that

Brooklyn is the new Manhattan, while the rest of us roll our eyes. But whatever the borough, whether you root for the Yankees or the Mets or the Metropolitan Museum of Art, New York is an amazing combination of culture within its divine neighborhoods. As David Dinkins said, New York City is a "gorgeous mosaic," and I am grateful to have been a small stone in the mural for a few years.

Q: How did you research the district attorney's office for the scenes showing Bernie and Keesh at work?

A: My sister Denise is an attorney, and though she works in a different area of the law, it's been interesting hearing her anecdotes from the workplace. Also, a friend in New York City who started his career with the Manhattan District Attorney's Office was very generous with his recollections. Both the Queens and Manhattan DA's offices have excellent websites. Sometimes I marvel at how research time has been enhanced by the Internet.

Q: Much of the novel weaves through the fringes of the law enforcement community. Do you have friends or family who are cops in New York City?

A: My husband, Mike, served in the New York City Police Department for more than twenty years. When we met, I was actually dating another cop—a friend of Mike's, who also happened to have blue eyes. For the first few years of our relationship, Mike teased me by calling me a "blue-eyed cop groupie," which bugged me because I was definitely attracted to people based on who they were and how they acted. Really, when we were first dating, the cop thing was a huge drawback. Imagine your boyfriend working weekends, Thanksgiving, and Christmas. But we worked around the bad schedule, which did get better. And maybe there is something about his blue eyes . . .

Q: *Are any of the stories in the novel lifted from your husband's experiences in the NYPD?*

A: The anecdote about Brendan and his partner intervening to save two children from an abusive parent came directly from Mike's experiences as a cop. It was one of the few cases where he appeared in court, and it gave him a sense of closure to see the case through to its end. Given the circumstances, the removal of these kids to foster care was a good thing, though a hollow victory, given the trauma a kid goes through when he or she is plucked from their home.

Beyond that, Mike's attitude and street language infuse every "cop incident" in the book. I stole from some of the stories Mike would tell at the end of a shift. When you're married to a cop, the "How was your day?" question is a volatile one. He would get home from work and tell me about some of the jobs he handled, often barely believing that people could do such bizarre things: the naked man walking down the center of a busy street wielding a machete . . . the lady who called the police to report that her cat kept pooping in the tub . . . the man who killed his wife but worried that his books would be overdue when the police arrested him while on his way to the library.

Other times, he was still reeling from a tragic circumstance that he couldn't fix. My husband has a helping nature, and it bothered him when he couldn't reach out to help someone. I remember one job that haunted him: a fluke in the weather brought torrents of rain down—something crazy like three inches in an hour—and there was flash-flooding in low-lying areas. Two teens were in a car that got swept into a sudden pond of water. The girl went for help, probably thinking she was a good swimmer. She didn't realize that there were downed power lines in the area, and the water was electrified. Seeing her struggling in the water, her boyfriend left the car and was also electrocuted. That incident hit my husband hard, and I use it as an example of how a police officer has to handle incidents and get the job done even when it's killing him or her inside.

Q: Did you ever consider becoming a police officer?

A: Are you kidding me? When I'm home alone, I'm afraid to open a closed shower curtain for fear that something wicked lurks in the tub. With my imagination, I need to stay out of law enforcement. But it's great to have a direct connection through my husband.

THE DAUGHTER
SHE USED TO BE

Rosalind Noonan

ABOUT THIS GUIDE

The suggested questions are included to enhance
your group's reading of Rosalind Noonan's
The Daughter She Used to Be.

DISCUSSION QUESTIONS

1. At the beginning of the book, Bernie mentioned how she used to enjoy mashed potatoes, but her taste for them had faded. Do you think it's really potatoes she doesn't like, or is she thinking of something else that has lost luster in her life?

2. Were you surprised that, in a family that valued police work, Bernadette and her sisters did not become cops? What barriers, both inside and outside their family, stood in their way?

3. Do you think Sully was a good father to his children? What would you say was his major flaw as a parent? What was his major strength?

4. What do you think motivated Tony Marino to destroy Peyton Curtis's walking stick?

5. Sometimes children or people with dementia speak without the filtering system that keeps the rest of society from voicing their thoughts. Did you think Granny Mary was lucid when she told Mary Kate that her husband, Tony Marino, should have been killed instead of Brendan?

6. Was Yvonne Curtis wrong to help her son? What would you have done in her position?

7. Was Bernie correct in thinking that her brother Brendan was against the death penalty? How do you think most cops feel about capital punishment?

8. When Bernie took up the cause to defend her brother's suspected killer, she knew her decision would not be

well-received by her family. Who would have been harmed if she'd stepped away from Peyton Curtis's case?

9. Why did Peyton Curtis want to return to prison at the beginning of the novel? If he hadn't walked into Sully's coffee shop that day, what do you think his future would have entailed?

10. Why was it important to Curtis that Bernie know that Tony Marino was responsible for his rampage? Would you say that Peyton Curtis is victim or prey?

11. What is the significance of the final scene occurring on Easter Sunday?

12. Discuss the themes of redemption and transformation as they relate to the novel.

Acknowledgments

Although writing is a solitary profession, it takes a village to publish a book well, and I am grateful to the Kensington community for their work in everything from copyediting to art to subrights. My editor, John Scognamiglio, is a steadfast supporter, long-distance friend, and reliable touchstone for stories.

Tory Groshong and Julia Rayne find mistakes that have slipped through the cracks, and I am grateful for their diligent attention and sharp red pencils.

To the reading groups I have spoken with and those who've invited me into their homes in Oregon, North Carolina, Maryland, and New York, I am eternally grateful. Thank you for keeping the flame burning for authors like me.

My agent, Robin Rue, was the one who found the emotional pulse of this novel. I owe her big-time, but she'll probably settle for a walk on the beach.

Love and best wishes go to the Queens Seidels, who taught my kids how to play street ball and who hosted many a family gathering. You guys are inspiring, but I don't think I gave away any of the "family business."

Thanks to my friends who support me 24/7: Susan, Nancy, Shannon, and Wendy. It's great to know you've got my back.

To my big, colorful, rambunctious family, thanks for talking my books up in your various geographic locations. Please don't look for yourselves in these pages. It's fiction.

My husband, Mike, is the best police expert a writer could hope for. With his twenty-some years with the NYPD, two master's degrees, and a voracious appetite for the *New York Times,* he's got my questions covered. Cop shows and films pay big bucks for a consultant like you; I'm so lucky.